The Third Millennium

A NOVEL

PAUL MEIER

The Third Millennium

A NOVEL

A
JANET
THOMA
BOOK

Thomas Nelson Publishers
Nashville

Published in Nashville, Tennessee, by Thomas Nelson, Inc.,
and distributed in Canada by WORD Communications,
Ltd., Richmond, British Columbia, and in the United
Kingdom by Word (UK), Ltd., Milton Keynes, England.

Library of Congress Cataloging-in-Publication Data

Meier, Paul D.
   The third millennium / by Paul Meier.
     p. cm.
   ISBN 0-8407-7571-7
   1. Millennialism—United States—Fiction. 2. Jewish
families—United States—Fiction. 3. Michael
(Archangel)—Fiction.
I. Title.
PS3563.E3457T48   1993
813'.54—dc20   93-18464
                                           CIP

Printed in the United States of America
16 17 18 - 99 98 97 96

ACKNOWLEDGMENTS

I wish to give special thanks to Robert Wise, a very successful novelist and personal friend, who not only traveled to Israel with me to help complete the political and geographical research for this project but also provided extensive editorial assistance.

I greatly appreciate the historical and sociological research I was able to obtain from a local Conservative Jewish synagogue, as well as from Rabbi Robert Gorelik, of the Adat HaMashiach Temple in Irvine, California, a messianic Jewish synagogue.

I also want to express my appreciation to a now-deceased hero of mine, Jim Irwin, the American astronaut who stepped foot on the moon. My trip to Mount Ararat with a Probe research group to meet Jim Irwin's team in search of Noah's Ark in 1985 and the refusal of the Turkish government to allow us to explore that part of Mount Ararat inspired me to begin the extensive research required for this book.

I have had a rare privilege as a psychiatrist—the privilege to study the spiritual aspects of human beings as well as to study biblical prophecy at Trinity Seminary in Chicago and Dallas Theological Seminary in Dallas. I also had the opportunity to teach at both wonderful institutions while doing research that helped me develop this novel.

The direct or indirect teachings of wise men such as Gleason Archer, John Walvoord, Dwight Pentecost, Robert Lightner, and Charles Dyer were particularly helpful in the development of prophetic themes. Grant Jeffrey's research, books, and telephone assistance are also greatly appreciated, as is the long-distance help I received from Dead Sea Scroll scholars and other scholars who eased my compulsive quest for accuracy and feasibility.

Paul Meier, M.D.
Los Angeles, California

MEMO: To the Archives of the Hosts
of Heaven
RE: The Final Decade of the Second
Millennium
FROM: Michael, Guardian Angel

Issues have been raised about the fate and final years of planet Earth. A desire has been expressed for study of the circumstances that brought about the ultimate shifts in history and society preceding the third millennium A.D. Therefore, I have undertaken to report the major events of the 1990s (as human beings measure what they call time).

Questions will be raised about my capacity to file this report prior to the occurrence of the actual events. Please be aware that the heavenly Father granted me the unusual privilege of leaping into the future to the year 2001 to complete my personal assignment during this last period.

As a personal guardian angel (G.A.), I have for thousands of years been given responsibility for various human beings, generally of Jewish origin. My work through the centuries has given unique insight into the character and problems of the human race. Of course, I have battled with principalities and powers of overwhelming proportions while completing my work. Therefore, I am also eminently qualified to understand the problems of evil and deception that have constantly been at work distorting the human situation.

During the 1990s, my assignment was the family of Dr. Larry Feinberg. The Feinbergs were a nonpracticing Jewish family living by the ocean in Newport Beach, California, United States of America. The area is almost identical in latitude to that of the Holy Land. The story of Larry, Sharon, and their two children,

Ben and Ruth, will explain the upheavals of the last days of travail.

We will begin midpoint in the decade at the point that the family began to recognize that history was shifting like the plates of the earth over the San Andreas Fault. As we shall see, it was an astonishing time!

This period of explosion and fraud, technical discovery and overwhelming chaos, is surely worthy of angelic scrutiny. The entire globe became as a woman in the last throes of labor. From the fall of the Berlin Wall and the collapse of the Soviet Union to the rise of spirit guides, crystals, and white witches and the distribution of condoms in the public schools, each year passed like the crescendo of a hard rock band increasing in volume to ear-splitting proportions!

Consideration of this period begins on what humans call New Year's Day, 1995, and continues to the end of the year 2000. As we look in on the secret world of my special charges, the truth will be evident.

1

New Year's Day, 1995

Howling blizzard winds hurled sleet and snow against the White House. The President of the United States stood silently looking out the Oval Office window, into the darkness. He lingered, waiting to answer the two men who sat in front of his desk as if he enjoyed creating consternation at this secret predawn meeting. Damian Gianardo turned and gawked at his secretary of state. The executive squirmed and looked away.

Gianardo was a tall, distinguished man of commanding presence. Long before the presidency fell into his hands, he acquired the art of walking into any room in a way that immediately demanded everyone's attention. His intimidating black eyes and penetrating stare always produced a disconcerting feeling that he knew what others were thinking. He had an uncanny intuitive capacity to accurately read the intentions and motives of his opponents. Once he grasped the position of another, there were no restraints on Gianardo's pursuit of his own ends.

The president's graying hair was carefully combed over the right side of his head, down across his temple toward his neck. Even hair transplants could not conceal the reminder of the near fatal head injury. His vanity caused him to keep the damaged side of his head toward the window as he spoke.

"Yes, of course, I am completely serious," the president spoke condescendingly. "I want you to implement fully and totally every last directive that I have outlined in my proposal. Got it?" He paused and leaned toward the secretary. "I made the unusual move of calling both of you in so early on New Year's Day because the press and usual observers of my every action wouldn't expect us to be talking this morning." Gianardo crossed his arms and glared at his secretary of state. "There must be absolutely nothing of this conversation in any file or on any tape recording. And timing will be of the utmost importance."

Jacob Rathmarker turned to the secretary of state. "Mr. Clark, I want you to know that in my capacity as vice president I am putting my full support behind the president's objectives. He and I have had full and complete discussions of the matter."

The secretary looked at the outline in his hand and fidgeted nervously. "I have to let someone in," he searched for words, "at least several aides. After all, you are asking me to contact the ten most significant nations in the world. I can't do that entirely by myself. At least a dozen people need to be in on the possible negotiations. You want to change the total alignment of world power. The entire idea is simply mind-boggling."

"You think I'm crazy." Damian Gianardo turned from the window and smiled cynically. "I know what's just run through your mind." The president leaned over the desk and stared fixedly into the eyes of the secretary until the man looked down. "You're thinking that I'm going power crazy." Gianardo enjoyed his uncanny ability to sense the secretary's feelings.

"NO! No." The secretary shook his head defensively. "I wouldn't ever think such a thing of *you*." Clark's instantaneous response was revealingly apologetic. *"Never."*

"You just did." The president winked at Rathmarker. "As easily as I read you," Gianardo continued, "I've foreseen what lies ahead. Mr. Secretary, what seems impossible now will be quite plausible in another year. You will be shocked to see how easily this alliance will fall into place."

The secretary gritted his teeth in frustration. "But you are proposing that ultimately each of these countries would give up its sovereignty to form a confederation with us. If it accepts your idea, each nation would become like one of our states."

"Yes," the president said, slowly picking up a dagger letter opener from the top of his desk. The president's perfectly manicured fingers were long, tapered, and unusually thin. Though they might have been the hands of an artist or a surgeon, the fingers had the disconcerting look of the caricature expected of the undertaker in a horror movie. Damian Gianardo held the sharp weapon between his palms, pushing the tapering point into his hand as if to demonstrate his imperviousness to pain. "You are grasping the implications of what I intend. I spare no expense in meeting my objectives." The president ran his narrow fingertips down the edge of the blade as he laid the letter opener down. "No expense."

"Can you imagine how much power that would consolidate in our hands?" The vice president bore down on the secretary.

"Imagine?" The secretary of state rolled his eyes. "Why . . . ," he fumbled for words, "if this consolidation is accomplished, you would in effect re-create the Roman Empire!"

"Interesting choice of words." Gianardo licked his lips. "Such a possibility had occurred to me."

On the opposite coast, members of a Jewish family were once again preparing for their usual annual observance of New Year's Day. The family of Larry and Sharon Feinberg were irrevocably tied to rituals. In most things they were contemporary to the core, yet vestiges of their Jewish past still demanded a firm grip on the traditions that defined and redefined who they were. Unexpected tension on this fragile linkage was serious business.

New Year's Day had become one such event. Although they seldom observed Passover or Rosh Hashanah, the Feinbergs judiciously guarded their family events on the start of each secular year on the calendar. Sharon expected the entire family to start the year together with bagels and lox, grapefruit, hard boiled eggs served in silver cups, and a side dish of pickled herring. The entire meal had to be consumed before the beginning of the Rose Bowl Parade which everyone watched with at least pretended rapt attention. The annual TV special of the year in review always followed. And then the football games began. A different matter, indeed.

Life with the Feinbergs was supposed to move in well-ordered annual compartments essentially predetermined nearly five decades earlier by the shape of Larry and Sharon's long-displaced rituals of childhood. At least that had once been what was now a fading hope and intention.

"Ruth?" Ben called out. "The football game is about to start. Ruth?"

An endless line of bands and floats paraded across the TV screen until Ben punched the clicker and changed channels to the sports network. "Where in the world is Ruth?" Ben asked his father. "She was here a minute ago."

"I don't know where your sister is." Larry looked mystified. "You know how your mother is about this family stuff on New Year's Day *until* the football games start when she and your sister always get scarce."

"I thought maybe Ruth would watch the game with us since UCLA is playing." Ben's strapping two-hundred-pound frame settled in the chair. He was about the same size as his father, and their hair was an identical dark brown. Ben always looked like the latest page from *Gentleman's Quarterly* even when he dressed casually.

"Maybe Ruth took a stroll down to the ocean." Larry walked to the window.

"We could play chess for a while." Ben pointed to the chess table where their last game was still unfinished. "Maybe Ruth will change her mind and watch."

When Ben was fourteen, Larry had thought it wise to let his son win to boost what the doctor considered a sagging self-esteem. During the last four years, Ben had turned out to be a young master of the computer and reveled in any challenge that demanded strategy. Now that Ben regularly beat Larry, many games were left dangling while Larry searched for a better move before having to throw in the towel. The unfinished game was its own commentary on the subtle tension between the psychiatrist and his son.

"The football widow is leaving now," Sharon called from the hallway. "Jennifer McCoy is meeting me at the movie. I'll be back by the time the game is over."

"You do this every year! Even if she's your best friend, you're blowing it again," Larry grumbled.

"Hey, Mom! Where's Ruth?"

"She went whirling out of here a bit ago." Sharon waved good-bye. "Said that she's meeting Heather and Amy at a movie too. We will all be here for supper."

"You're going to miss watching UCLA stomp Michigan State," Ben chided.

"Please," Sharon shook her head, "we've had enough violence in the last year to last a lifetime. I'm gone." She closed the door behind her and started for the car.

Sharon paused to look at the profusion of flowers around the front walkway, which became a path winding its way down to the ocean. Even in the midst of the mild winter, the flowers lacked nothing in color. The pastel pinks and blues helped Sharon believe that there might still be some peace left in the world. She tried to drink in their colorful reassurance each day before she left the house.

Kind and gentle by disposition, Sharon didn't look forty-seven. She enjoyed teasing Larry that the difference of two years in their ages looked more like twenty. Her glowing olive skin and dark brown eyes added to her natural youthfulness. A little too plump for her own good, Sharon was tall and carried herself confidently. The fussy quality about her elegant clothes betrayed her perfectionistic and controlling tendencies. Sharon always knew where she was going.

From the window, Larry affectionately watched his wife drive away. Their home had become a haven for them against the boiling turmoil of the outside world. Not far from Balboa Island, the family estate backed up to a private beach. Larry could see over to Catalina Island on a clear day. He was fortunate to have been able to get a buy on such a luxurious tract. Larry felt secure in his traditional home contrasting with the more contemporary Mediterranean styles around them. Something about the wood-frame house pleased him. Even though he congratulated himself on being an avant-garde psychiatrist, Larry couldn't suppress a conservatism that more than occasionally popped out. His religious Jewish ancestors had made their indelible mark, which was reflected in the white trim on his gray house. Knowing that he could close the shutters anytime he liked similarly comforted him.

"Kickoff!" Ben called to his father. "Better off watching the game without the women interrupting all the time anyway."

"Strange how Ruth slipped out." Larry turned from the window. "I'll take Michigan State by ten points." He slipped down in his large overstuffed chair.

The TV cameras panned the stadium as the players lined up for the kickoff. "President Gianardo is attending the game today," the announcer's voice boomed across the living room. "Security is incredibly tight, but Gianardo and his wife are in presidential box seats."

"Takes guts for the president to come out in a crowd like that one," Larry noted. "But that man seems to be fearless."

Ben glanced down at the large commemorative magazine on the table. "IN MEMORIAL—1994" was embossed in gold on the cover. He picked up the magazine and began flipping through the pages. Scenes of two caskets pulled by horse-drawn carriages filled the first pages. In the middle were different shots of the White House on fire with the windows blown out. "Gianardo must have seven lives." Ben closed the magazine quickly.

"I still can't believe he survived that terrible head wound when the bomb went off," Larry answered. "The concussion killed the president and vice president instantly. Those other senators died very quickly. How he got out I'll never know."

"He's an amazing man, Dad. Who would have guessed that he was the brains behind that secret agreement the U.S. reached with Israel and the Arabs back in '93 to stop all the hostility? Even though he was the speaker of the House then, he did what the secretary of state couldn't accomplish. He got Israel to make that land deal in order to achieve peace."

"He's certainly cemented relations with the Arabs since then. The emergence of the United Muslim States is an incredible change."

"Yes," Ben agreed, "and with a new capitol in the rebuilt ancient city of Babylon, Arabs are emerging as a world power."

"The seven-year pact Gianardo pulled off protects Israel until the year 2000. I think it was good for everybody," Larry said nonchalantly.

Michigan State kicked off, and the ball bounced on the twenty-yard line. Ben immediately rooted for UCLA while Larry cheered his team. The game would be hard-hitting and close.

Ben reached for a handful of potato chips, but he no longer seemed to be focused on the game. His thoughts abruptly shifted to Cindy Wong. Ben first noticed Cindy at an interstudent council workshop when he was a junior and she was a sophomore. Even though they were from different high schools, Ben had made it a point to find out everything he could about her world. Distance had only intensified his interest.

Ben was drawn to Cindy because she was different. Neither of them was really part of the establishment as Ben saw things. He was Jewish, and she was oriental. The fact that she was both Chinese and blind truly put her in a world by herself. Ben felt an unspoken kinship with her. She was also a displaced person of sorts. Ben thought of his upbringing as being thoroughly American, but he knew that was only marginally true. They were Jews who had come from somewhere else. The Feinbergs could again become outsiders at a moment's notice if the tides of social opinion turned against them. Though Ben had never broached the subject with her, he knew that Cindy would thoroughly understand his feelings and misgivings.

"Hey!" Larry poked his son in the ribs. "You're not even in the game."

"What?" Ben jumped.

"UCLA just scored and you didn't twitch a muscle."

Are you slick or what?" Jimmy Harrison pulled Ruth closer to him as the Ferris wheel made its final turn.

"I love Balboa Island." Ruth looked out over the amusement park and the ocean that surrounded it. "Most fun place in southern California." As the wheel settled toward the ground, she watched people getting off other rides and entering the little amusement shops around the island. "But I think I like you better."

Jimmy laughed. "How did you shake free of your people on New Year's Day without them blowing a gasket?" He could sense that Ruth liked the warm feel of his hand over hers, and his aggressive flirtatiousness flattered her.

"They think I'm at the movies with my college roommates, Heather and Amy. The old man would blow his mind if he knew I was taking a spin with the guy who sold us my car last week."

Jimmy smiled and bit her ear teasingly, but he didn't like the inference. When the Feinbergs wheeled into the used car lot in their big black '95 Mercedes, Jimmy felt the challenge instantly. He watched the family flash their Rolexes around and immediately knew they would pay top dollar. Halfway into the deal the challenge of seducing a little rich girl gripped him. Jimmy had made the possibility of having a relationship with Ruth as much a goal as getting the most money he could out of Dr. Feinberg, who obviously thought of himself as the supreme negotiator. He couldn't believe it had been so easy to pull off seeing Ruth twice in the last week.

Ruth turned her head sideways and kissed Jimmy eagerly. Only the abrupt stop of the Ferris wheel at the bottom ended the overpowering moment. As she walked away from the seat, she swung her hips carelessly and tossed her long hair over her shoulder.

"You're my kind of woman." Jimmy grinned as they walked out into the park. He watched Ruth's eyes light up when he put a heavy emphasis on "woman." Like her mother, Ruth was tall and could easily slide toward the heavy side. While she had her mother's dark brown hair, Ruth had striking blue eyes. Any possible plumpness was poured into a figure that clearly held Jimmy's full attention.

"Just what's your old man's line of work?" Jimmy put his arm around Ruth's waist.

"He's a shrink," Ruth replied. "He thinks he's God when it comes to sizing up people. Can you imagine that we were barely out of your car lot when he told us that you were some kind of character disorder, con man type? He'd really be steamed if he knew that I was cruising this place with you."

Jimmy's smile hardened. The psychiatrist's diagnosis cut through his façade and made him nervous. Moreover, he felt uncomfortable being a twenty-five-year-old uneducated used car salesman. A six-foot-four-inch blond Nordic weight lifter, Jimmy was the master of creating appearances. The thought of conquering Ruth pleased him. "Let's truck over to my car in the lot. I've got a couple of joints hidden under the seat of my Corvette. How about a little grass to loosen us up?"

"Sure." The pitch in Ruth's nervous voice raised.

Instantly, Jimmy knew that Ruth hadn't ever done

marijuana. She might go for it big and get high quick. On the other hand, Ruth might cough and sputter, and nothing would come of the opportunity. "Well, let's give it a try." Jimmy smiled wickedly.

The couple cut across the park, winding their way past popcorn vendors and men selling balloons, and headed for the parking lot. Straight ahead, the ferry was bringing another load of cars across.

"My father's a real pain!" Ruth suddenly blurted out. "He's so self-confident all the time."

"Tell me about it," Jimmy sneered. "I hate my old man. What a big-time jerk."

"What does he do?"

Jimmy froze. That was the one question he hadn't expected, and the answer might blow everything. Jimmy gazed into Ruth's eyes. She had an innocent, all-accepting look that meant she was really on the hook, but Jimmy knew Ruth was Jewish and that might make everything more complicated.

"Come on, honey," Ruth cooed. "There isn't anything you can't share with me."

Jimmy's eyes narrowed. He let "honey" rattle around a moment. No question Ruth was going for him. "He's a Christian minister," Jimmy answered haltingly. "Has a big church in Dallas, Texas. My old man's a big daddy in Big D."

"Seriously?" Ruth asked incredulously.

"Turns you off, doesn't it?"

"No, no." A sly grin crossed Ruth's face. "I've just never been around preacher types."

"I avoid him at all costs," Jimmy said sternly. "The fanatic spent his whole life saving souls at the expense of me and my four brothers. He was so busy making God happy, Mr. Holy couldn't even take in one of our baseball games. Don't worry. Reverend Big Time has taken care of any interest I'll ever have in God or religion. I don't buy anything the old creep is preaching."

Ruth stopped and abruptly kissed Jimmy passionately on the mouth. She reached up and ran her hands

through his hair. She breathed heavily, "I like everything about you. Don't worry about some family hang-
up. My world's not any different."

"Really?" Jimmy felt his blood rushing to his face.
This girl's a keg of dynamite, he thought. At the same
time he felt an unexpected sense of caring.

"Look," Ruth took his hand, "my parents got it all
wrapped for me as well. They've already got some rich
Jewish doctor or lawyer staked out." She paused and
tossed her long hair back. "But a long time ago I figured out that my father lives his life by the book. All I
ever get out of him is what the latest psychiatric jour-
nal party line is. I figure out what he wants to hear, and
I just feed it back." Ruth's eyes snapped with fire. "I'm
sick of being analyzed by him every time something
goes wrong."

She thought a minute. "I'm going to have to go to the
movies to cover my tracks. I think I better not do a joint
today. Next time."

Jimmy smiled. *Date a shrink's daughter, get psychological excuses,* he thought. "Sure. Next time, we'll
make sure that we have plenty of uninterrupted time.
I'll call you at your apartment at the university."

"You bet." Ruth put her arms around his neck. "I
hate to run, but if I don't, I'm going to get into the movies too late. I have to make sure I don't get into problems with the traffic." Ruth started for her own car and
then turned back. "I can't wait for us to be together
again. Just maybe I'm falling in love with you, Jimmy
Harrison." Ruth ran back, kissed him passionately
again, and then ran for her car.

Jimmy stood beside his '89 classic red Corvette and
watched her drive away. *Isn't this wild?* he said to himself. *I believe I'm in the home stretch on this one.*

*He's not at all like my father. Jimmy is so deep and
feeling.* Ruth's thoughts raced as she frantically drove

toward the Fashion Island theater. Jimmy made her feel sexy and alive. Ruth loved the exhilaration. Her face flushed. *Oh, I hope I wasn't too obvious.*

Ruth saw the underground parking entrance to the theater and pulled in. *Amy said the movie was "Marital Fatality,"* she thought as she hurried toward the ticket window.

"Really only twenty minutes are left at most," the girl in the window said.

"I've seen it twice," Ruth lied. "Just wanted to catch the ending again. Couldn't I just slip in?"

"Who cares?" The girl waved her through the door.

"Owe you one." Ruth waved and hurried inside.

In the dark Ruth found it difficult to adjust her eyes. Finally, she saw the familiar outlines of her two roommates' heads, and she slipped in beside them.

"Hey," Amy whispered far too loud, "how was your little man?"

"Awesome! Just beyond words."

The girls giggled and then settled back to watch the final scenes of the terror on the screen. When the lights came on, the interrogation began.

"Tell me everything you did!" Heather insisted. "Did you make out?"

"You are just too clever." Amy rolled her eyes. "I can't believe the way you're able to snow your—," she stopped abruptly. "Oh, my gosh!" Amy was looking over Ruth's head.

"What in the world is going on here?" A voice came from the aisle.

Ruth turned. "Mother!" she choked.

"I want an explanation of what you think you're up to!"

"Mother, what are you doing here?"

"Jennifer and I changed our minds after we saw what was on at the big Newport theater. We just happened to stop here."

"Great movie." Ruth tried to be casual.

"Yes," Sharon said intensely. "It's too bad you didn't see any of it."

"Wh . . . what do you mean?"

"We got here late," Sharon bore down, "but as soon as we could see in the darkness, we saw Amy and Heather were just in front of us. At first I thought you were out getting popcorn. Then I began to worry about why you weren't here. Several times I almost got up to ask the girls, but I decided that maybe I misunderstood you when you left in such a hurry. When I saw you slip in, I knew something was very wrong."

Ruth looked at her roommates out of the corner of her eye. Nothing that she could say could hide their guilty looks.

"Excuse us, girls," Sharon spoke firmly. "My daughter and I need to talk privately." Sharon took Ruth's hand and started for the lobby. They stopped in a dark corner in the hall. "Have you been lying to us again?" Sharon's voice quivered.

"I'm very sorry." Ruth tried to look regretful. "I didn't think I could tell you the truth, though. I met a boy I knew you wouldn't like."

A look of disgust crossed Sharon's face. "I don't like deceptiveness. Who is he?"

"His name is Jimmy Harrison. I knew you might—"

"The guy at the used car lot? Not him!"

"See! I told you that so—"

"Why can't you find someone of your own class? Really!"

"You are saying *exactly* what I knew you would. And you wonder why I didn't level with you about where I was going?"

Sharon shook her head. "I just don't understand. You and your roommates live like royalty at Pepperdine. You even have a maid to clean your apartment each day. We have given you the best. Yet you keep having these . . . these problems with honesty. When you were at home, we knew of at least five times you crawled out the window after twelve at night. Who knows how many times you really left!"

"You going to throw those incidents up in my face again?" Ruth said indignantly.

"Go home." Sharon began walking away. "I'll meet you there."

"Are you going to tell Dad?" Ruth hurried after her. "Really, he doesn't need the stress."

"Since when did you start worrying about your father's feelings?" Sharon turned and headed for the entrance.

☐   ☐   ☐

Sharon Feinberg was generally not overly aggressive, but she tended to hover over her family like a mother hen. She carefully chose her confrontations. On the other hand, Larry fussed constantly over what was psychologically appropriate. In fact, the family cringed every time he cleared his throat and suggested "appropriateness." Still, Larry's personal preoccupation added to Sharon's natural tendency to choose her timing well. Two weeks passed before she told him about the movie incident.

"Such a little thing to deceive us about." Larry's neck reddened as he sank down in his overstuffed chair in front of the TV. "Is there anyone more understanding than I?"

"I really thought you overreacted in suggesting counseling. After all, that's a psychiatrist's answer for everything." Sharon threw her hands up in the air. "But now I must agree. I hope that therapy will put an end to her lying to us."

"The counselor is excellent." Larry sounded defensive. "I've known Dr. Ann Woodbridge for a number of years, and I have total confidence in her ability."

"All this talk about being a Christian counselor bothers me," Sharon said. "I'm not sure I'm comfortable with someone tacking her religion on her profession like an advertisement. What would our Jewish parents think about sending our daughter to a Christian?"

"Dr. Woodbridge makes no bones about her values." Larry frowned. "She's an expert on adolescence and character development. I don't think a strong dose of honesty and integrity will hurt our daughter a bit."

"Maybe this psychologist will try to convert Ruth."

"Sharon," Larry pleaded, "the woman isn't an evangelist. Don't you think I know what I'm doing? She and I have had long talks about professionalism."

"I don't know." Sharon shook her head. "The woman's capacity is the question. Something is wrong. We've had Ruth in the best schools. You'd think that by age twenty-two she'd know the difference between the truth and a lie."

Larry opened his mouth to speak and then stopped. "Perhaps," his voice faded.

"We haven't been particularly religious people." Sharon looked at the marriage plaque on the wall. The parchment was in Hebrew with fancy flourishes around the edges. "I went to the synagogue every week when I was a child. Ruth can probably count on her fingers how many times she's been in one."

Larry shook his head emphatically. "We haven't used religion to create guilt. No apologies there."

"But we haven't particularly encouraged religious values either. The Christian counselor makes sense for that reason."

"Perhaps," Larry bit his lip, "we need to look elsewhere. There are good psychological reasons for her behavior."

"The whole world's crazy," Sharon agonized. "I can't even stand to listen to the news anymore. Everything is scrambled. Maybe the times are to blame."

Sharon walked in front of the Hebrew marriage scroll and ran her hands across the edge of the frame. "My father gave us this memento hoping that our children would see it every day. We haven't done well,

Larry. Did you know that Ben is attracted to a Chinese girl whose parents are Buddhists?"

"Really, Sharon. This is the Los Angeles area. We're living inside the melting pot itself."

"Your parents would be just as upset. They wouldn't want our children to assimilate. It's just hard to accept such wide departures from our heritage."

Larry sat up straight in his chair and stuck his chin out. "We are modern Jews. We can't inhibit the natural expressions and interests of our children."

"Then what are we going to do, Larry?"

"I'll talk to her. I'll try to see if I can bring some insight." He added, "At the appropriate time of course."

Sharon stiffened as he finished the sentence. "Perhaps we might try a different approach this time. Let's bring the boy over here. Maybe if we got him out in the light of the day, Ruth would recognize the truth."

"We'll take the secret forbidden quality away." Larry's eyes lit up. "That will kill it! I love to use paradoxical intention like that—encouraging the forbidden so the patient will rebel by doing what is right instead."

"At least we can ask the sort of questions that will clarify who he is."

Larry nodded eagerly. "That's exactly the idea I had in mind!"

CHAPTER

3

Being the guardian angel of the Feinberg family was no easy matter. Because I knew the importance of their role in the divine plan for the future, I had to carefully oversee details that I might have otherwise ignored. No one would have guessed that I placed the advertisement for Jimmy Harrison's car lot in front of Larry, nor would Sharon ever have an inkling that by a similar ploy she was directed toward the same theater on New Year's Day that her daughter was going to attend.

However, trying to make the drama work out right while Dr. Appropriate and Mrs. Hen arranged the props on the set proved to be as challenging as the problems I once had in getting Sisera to drop into Heber's place for a drink and a little nap in Old Testament times.

Jimmy Harrison was invited for dinner several times. A maid was hired for the evening to serve on the Feinbergs' finest china and best linens. The pizza-and-hamburger kid got the message very quickly.

Even though Larry and Sharon subtly slipped in their questions between the salad and the soup, the bludgeoning was obvious. The more the parents whacked the used car salesman, the more Ruth defended. With the parents' help, a relationship that might have lasted a month was becoming a permanent fixture in their home. In their wildest dreams, they couldn't have foreseen that Jimmy Harrison was a part of God's plan for their lives.

Neither did they realize what an important role Cindy Wong would play in the divine scheme of things.

While Ruth and Jimmy struggled with the Feinbergs' attempts at supervision, Ben went relatively unobserved in his pursuit of Cindy. One of his favorite ploys was to *happen* to show up at the Golden Dragon, the Wongs' family restaurant.

One evening in late May, Ben dropped in.

"Cindy here?" Ben asked the waiter.

"Ah . . . you . . . ah . . . know Miss Cindy?" the Chinese server in a black tuxedo asked.

"Good friends," Ben sounded professionally distant. "Social acquaintances. I would like to speak with her if she is here," he said, knowing completely well Cindy was somewhere in the restaurant.

"One moment, please." The man hurried away.

Ben looked around the elegant restaurant. Although the Golden Dragon was in a fairly common shopping center area in Lake Forest, the interior was lavishly decorated. Large tanks of tropical fish lined the walls. The ceilings were covered with gold-and-red dragons, and the tables were made of thickly lacquered black ebony. Linen napkins added the final touch. Ben picked up the ornate silverware to admire the design.

"Name, please," the waiter interrupted his inspection. Cindy was a few steps behind him.

"Cindy!" Ben stood at once. Her skin was smooth like porcelain china—warm olive colored with a blush of color in her cheeks. Her heart-shaped mouth was perfect.

"Ben?" she answered. "Ben Feinberg?" She offered a dainty hand.

"Just happened to be in the area." Ben smiled but sounded obvious. "Thought a little chow mein would be great. Can you sit down?"

"Sure." Cindy felt for the chair, and the waiter helped her find the edge of the table.

"How are things?" Ben liked everything he saw in Cindy. Even though she was petite, her figure lacked nothing in maturity. Her sightless brown eyes looked completely normal. The only hint of irregularity was in her slightly unfocused look. Jet black hair framed her flawless face.

"School is going quite well. I have been accepted at UCLA next fall."

"Great!" Ben beamed. "Outstanding place!"

"They are going to provide a guide dog, special tutors, everything!"

"Only a very smart girl could pull that off."

Cindy blushed. "I work hard."

"I really admire you, Cindy. You don't let anything get in your way. You never seem to need help."

Cindy's smile froze. "No one will ever need to feel sorry for Cindy Wong. I am quite capable of making my way."

"Oh, exactly," Ben backtracked. "That's what I meant."

"Perhaps I can suggest something for supper." Cindy changed the subject.

"What's your specialty tonight?"

"Ever try Kung Pao Squid? I think you'll find it to be one of our best exotic dishes."

"Only if you eat with me," Ben said slyly.

The smile returned. "Maybe a little hot and sour soup."

"Waiter!" Ben snapped his fingers immediately and waved to the Chinese attendant.

☐   ☐   ☐

As summer approached, Ruth took advantage of her parents' attempts at openness and invited Jimmy over for frequent walks on the family's private beach. The salty mist swept in from the sea over the rocks and up the gentle sloping sandy beach. The waves of the ebbing tide and the tranquil ocean made a swim seem deceptively plausible, but June waters were seldom warm enough.

Ruth stopped and dug her toe into the white sand. "I think I ought to tell you several things," she said slowly. She looked up and watched a sea gull making a lazy, long swoop toward them. A large pelican bobbed up and down on the ocean. "I hope you'll take it OK."

Jimmy realized that his feelings had changed during the past six months. What started as a chase had turned into feelings that he had not known before. "You've decided to push on? Got somebody else in mind?"

"Come on!" Ruth poked him in the chest with her finger. "Silly, you know better. I want to share something with you that is, well, rather sensitive to say."

"Anything is OK as long as I don't have new competition."

Ruth started to walk again. "I've had to face some problems I had before we started hanging out together." She chose her words carefully. "I've needed a counselor to help me get some things straight."

"What do you mean?" Jimmy raised his eyebrows and grimaced. "About us?"

"Got a guilty conscience?" Ruth laughed. "No, I don't talk much about us. I've had to get my act together. The visits have helped a lot."

"So?" Jimmy shrugged. "Why are you telling me?"

"I want you to be happy." Ruth put her arm around Jimmy's shoulder. "I know that your problems with your parents bother you more than you admit. I know that it's hard for you to trust people sometimes."

Jimmy scanned her face. The innocent eagerness he had once seen was still there, but now he realized how much he truly cared for the dark-haired beauty. She was stunning in her black-and-white swimming suit.

Ruth's stylishness reflected taste, savvy, and class. But there was something more powerfully attractive than just her physical appeal. Jimmy saw an inner quality that he had not seen in many women. Her genuineness was the best thing that had ever happened to him. "I *really* do love you." He was surprised at the strength of his feelings.

"I never thought you didn't." Ruth laughed.

But Jimmy knew how far he had come. Only slowly had he come to trust himself with her. Ruth had taught him a great deal in a few months.

"Let's test the waters!" Ruth suddenly pulled away and ran for the ocean. "Dare you to jump in." She kicked her sneakers off and dropped them in the sand. She hopped toward the surf rolling up on the beach and ran into the water.

"You won't last long!" Jimmy called after her. He left his tennis shoes beside hers.

Jimmy watched her. Ruth's virtue had affected him. She had been teaching him a straightforward honesty he hadn't known since childhood. Jimmy had even come to like the feeling.

"Ohhh!" Ruth squealed. "It looks sooo good, but the water feels like it's floating ice cubes."

Jimmy skimmed across the surf as he plunged in up to the top of his ankles. "Good grief!" he gasped. "The current's straight down from Alaska!"

For a few moments they tiptoed around the edge of the sand and the sea before giving up their dance. Ruth splashed the salty water on Jimmy and ran for her shoes with him in full pursuit. He caught up and spun her around.

"You're going to get it!" Jimmy mimicked fierceness and rolled his eyes. Just as abruptly, he kissed her passionately on the mouth.

"Hmmm, you're something else." Ruth gasped for breath. "I've got to sit down." She dropped down on a driftwood log to brush the sand off her feet.

"Thanks for telling about your feelings." Jimmy

helped Ruth back up to her feet. He led her toward the house. "I know that I need to think about my resentment of my dad. I really do try."

"I know," Ruth said simply as they walked up the path toward the house. She stopped at the little gazebo and slipped khaki pants and a loose blouse over her swimsuit. "I know more about you than you think, Jimmy Harrison."

Ruth stepped up on the redwood deck surrounding the back porch. Large pots of geraniums and flowers covered the patio area. She and Jimmy stomped their feet to make sure they didn't track sand into the house. Once inside they made sure no tracks were left across Sharon's immaculate kitchen floor.

Ruth and Jimmy slipped into the den unnoticed because the parents were totally engrossed in watching the news. Jimmy shuffled nervously toward an overstuffed leather chair near the game table covered with onyx chess pieces. Ruth plopped into a plaid colonial chair near the fireplace.

"Oh, come in," Sharon abruptly looked up. "Please sit down," she sounded formal and distant.

"What's happening?" Ruth tried to sound cheery.

"Amazing breakthrough in Israel." Larry pointed to the TV. "They've found that the oil discovery several months ago has turned out to be an extraordinary field. Israel has gone from being an importer to swimming in the crude."

Pictures of elaborate construction work filled the screen. "The new oil money is being used to rebuild the temple of Solomon in a lavish way," Sharon explained. "The cameras are showing the first stages of the new construction that will finish the temple like it was thousands of years ago."

Jimmy's countenance changed. "Really?" He moved to the edge of his seat. "Reconstruction was predicted," he began excitedly and then paused, "in some people's opinion, by the Bible."

Larry looked at Jimmy with a puzzled expression.

"Of course, they're going to kill more animals," Ruth said scornfully.

"As a matter of fact," Sharon answered, "the announcer reported on sacrifices just before you came in. In spite of litigation by animal rights activists and some environmental protection groups, the priests are continuing their work unabated."

"Those people are crazy," Ruth glowered. "They're giving Jews everywhere a bad name."

"The Arabs are certainly getting in on the act." Larry sat back in his chair. "They're protesting louder than anyone. I doubt if they really care that much about the animals being sacrificed, but it's an opportunity to criticize Israel."

"Muslims make me nervous." Jimmy tossed out. "The growth of the United Muslim States ought to worry us. The linkup of Arab countries creates a power bloc of frightening potential. The Bible says . . . ," Jimmy stopped. "I understand the Bible makes references to such a possibility. I'm sure Jewish people everywhere are very sensitive to these issues."

"Absolutely," Larry expressed an unusually genuine interest in Jimmy's opinions. "We have too many strange things happening in the world right now. When too much change occurs, people get a little crazy. They accept ideas they shouldn't and let political leaders easily deceive them. I'm worried by the present political climate."

Jimmy sensed an acceptance that hadn't been there before. Larry was treating him with new respect, and the feeling was exhilarating. "I guess your generation grew up worrying about Russia and the Reds taking over the world. Maybe mine ought to be nervous about the Middle East and the new Arab empire."

"Everything is too interwoven with treaties, computers, banks, economic interest." Larry shook his finger at Jimmy. "Too much like political conditions were just before World War II. Something simple could upset everything! I'm deeply troubled by Gianardo's casual acceptance of assisted suicides and his indifference about euthanasia."

"It's a bad sign." Sharon shook her head. "There's no concern for life."

Larry beckoned Jimmy closer. "The new legislation the president is proposing would essentially allow legal guardians to put severely retarded people and people with physically handicapping conditions to sleep whenever it is convenient. If this bill passes, infants under two years of age with severe disabilities could be terminated with written consent of parents even this year. As a physician, I am very, very alarmed."

"I don't know if this makes sense to you, Jimmy," Sharon's voice was more sincere and personal, "but as Jews, we are deeply committed to life. We fear political intervention in any procedure that would allow the state to kill human beings."

"I hate it!" Larry hit the arm of his chair. "I don't care if public opinion is on Gianardo's side. *All* human life has value. If we don't stand against this trend, the same holocaust that happened in Germany could be repeated here on helpless people and ones with infirmities. It started this way in the Third Reich. First there were abortions on demand, and then one thing led to another."

Ruth shuddered. "This whole conversation gives me the creeps. I know there was a lot of civil rights progress back in the sixties, but Israel isn't very popular right now. Things could get out of hand."

"Not this time!" Jimmy crossed his arms over his chest. "People would rally around the Jews if this nonsense started up. At least I'd be leading the parade!"

The room became very quiet.

Jimmy was startled with the forcefulness of his words. From somewhere deep within him, a stream of conviction had erupted. Values and ideas that had been covered with layers of anger had pushed their way forward. "We must stand above moral compromise," he said quietly.

Larry smiled warmly at Jimmy. "You have encouraged me greatly. Maybe one day we'll need a drum major."

"I know that we don't practice our religion." Sharon looked distressed. "But being Jewish is like having brown eyes. It's always a part of us, noticed or unobserved. We're stuck with who we are no matter which way the political winds blow." Sharon drew her feet up in the chair and wrapped her arms around her legs, drawing into a tight ball. "I can still see my father give the Sabbath toast." She smiled. "He would hold up the glass and say, 'The *chaim,* to life.'"

"We don't know you as well as we should," Larry said. "We need to have these conversations of substance every time you are here. I am very impressed by your moral fiber."

Jimmy retreated back into his chair. "Ah . . . sure . . . sure, any time."

"Jimmy and I will get some Cokes." Ruth stood up and beckoned for Jimmy to follow her. "Let's go to the kitchen." Instead of stopping in the kitchen, Ruth led him out to the patio.

"I can't believe what you said in there." Ruth rolled her eyes. "You certainly knocked them out of their chairs. Did you really mean it?"

"Gosh," Jimmy shrugged his shoulders, "it wasn't that big a deal. But yeah, sure. I meant what I said. My parents did put morality in my head whether I listened to them or not. Even now when I ignore my father's teachings, I know what's right."

Ruth smiled shyly. "I saw every bit of it the first day I met you. You're good in spite of yourself."

Jimmy breathed deeply. The day had vastly exceeded his expectations. He had come to the Feinbergs feeling like a carrier of a social plague invading their antiseptic environment, only to be received as a moral hero. The feeling was better than anything he could remember.

"I saw the truth behind that macho salesman veneer." Ruth kissed him. "The best is yet to be."

Jimmy looked uncharacteristically embarrassed. "I'll try to do my best."

CHAPTER

4

For several minutes, Jimmy looked at the letter in his hand. He could still hear his words ringing in his memory: *I'll try to do my best.* He opened the letter carefully. The handwriting was so familiar that he didn't need to glance at the return address. The letter kept evoking the sentence running through his mind.

Jimmy walked through the small living room with the letter. Unlike many bachelors, he kept a tidy place. On the front wall was a large poster of James Dean in a leather jacket. On the opposite wall was a framed print of Marilyn Monroe, Humphrey Bogart, and James Dean in a deserted restaurant. The melancholy late-night scene fit Jimmy well. A modernistic couch was pushed against the adjacent wall in front of a TV and VCR unit. Piles of tapes were stacked on an end table. His small desk and files were cramped in the remaining space near the bedroom door.

Jimmy sat down on the bed in his small apartment as the July sunlight streamed in the windows. He had said those very words—"I'll try to do my best"—at least fifty times in the last several weeks, and he didn't like the sound anymore. Each word haunted him. It felt like he had said those identical words every day of his childhood.

Dear Son, his mother began as she always did, *your*

*father and I pray for you every day and hope you have
found a church to attend by now.*

"Couldn't she have begun some other way?" he lamented out loud. "Why do they always start there?" He felt himself almost say, "I'll try to do my best," but stopped.

*We know you are making good money these days
and we are proud of you. But the time is short. Your
father just finished another series of teachings on
what the Bible says about the end times. I know
you don't like to hear what he teaches but please listen to the tapes we are sending. Your father's study
of the Bible has convinced us that at any moment
true believers could all be called out of this world.
We know that God has an important plan for your
life, Son. We want to spend eternity with you.*

Jimmy stopped reading and laid the letter on the bed. He walked over to the refrigerator and got a beer. Running his fingers nervously through his hair, Jimmy turned up the volume on the stereo.

They never stop, he thought. *I hate that hokey preaching junk my father keeps grinding out! Why can't they just let me be?*

But the words came back to his mind again: *I'll try to do my best.* Jimmy pulled open the drawer on the night stand and pulled out his savings book. The balance read $12,000. He smiled and shut the drawer. Flopping back on the bed, Jimmy began to read again.

*Of all five children, you were always the dearest to
my heart. Perhaps your father and I cared too
much. Maybe we punished too hard, but you were always so bright, so quick. I wanted to write you something that we've never told you before. Remember
when you were two years old and got so deathly
sick? Of course, you don't remember, but you heard
us tell about the time. I don't think that we ever*

*told you how close you came to dying. The doctor
put you in the hospital because you were so dehy-
drated, but they couldn't get the vomiting to stop.
The nurses believed you wouldn't pull through.*

Jimmy stopped and opened the drawer again. Under
the checkbook and a pile of papers, he found a picture
of his mother and father together. John Harrison was
a tall, handsome man. In the picture he was waving a
cowboy hat. Sally Harrison was holding her husband's
arm and smiling broadly. She looked taller than her
five-foot-seven-inch height. Always in fit condition, she
radiated health. Even though the picture was black and
white, Jimmy could almost see her deep blue eyes and
black hair.

Jimmy brought the picture closer to his eyes. Her
face had a classic profile, and her features were filled
with character. His mother was a striking woman, even
if she looked a bit out of style. The picture caught the
warmth and compassionate glow she always had about
her. Her clothes were simple, but she was elegant in her
unique way.

In the background was their church in Dallas. The
big brick structure had large stained glass windows
and expansive stairs leading up to massive double
wooden doors. The old trees around the front were bent
by years of unyielding plains wind. "With love always,
your parents," was written across the bottom in her
hand.

Once more Jimmy began reading.

*Your father and I came to the hospital late in the
evening. We were terrified that you would die.
Throughout the night, we held you and prayed over
you. We wept, prayed, and paced the floor. You
didn't improve. Around two in the morning, your father picked you up and walked to the window. I can
still see him hold you with outstretched arms. Shaking all over, John told the Lord that if He'd spare*

you, you would be our gift to Him. Your father put you back in that bed and we knelt on the tile. We wanted you to live more than anything in the world. About thirty minutes later, the fever broke. The next morning you stopped vomiting and that afternoon they took you off all the I.V.s that kept fluid in you. We knew God had spared your life for His purposes.

Jimmy's hand trembled as he lowered the letter. He took a big drink from the beer can and reached for a cigarette. He started to light up but dropped the cigarette by the side of the bed. He felt a knot forming in his throat.

Perhaps we should have told you, but we didn't want to coerce you into some life direction that would be of our choosing and not the Lord's. That's the reason your father always preached and pushed you. He knew your life was supposed to be different. I guess we didn't do a very good job, but we believed you were a unique and special child.

Tears began to run down Jimmy's cheeks. He pulled his knees up against his chest and rested his chin in his hands. From deep down in his stomach he felt a churning pushing its way up. His whole body shook, even before the sound came out. Jimmy had no idea how long he cried before the inner wellsprings dried up. His body sagged against the bed.

Finally, he picked up the letter again.

Son, I don't care how you make your living. I want you to know that you are still the most significant child in my life. There is a good in you that nothing can stop or hide. I want you to know that my prayers are still with you every day of your life and they always will be. Don't be afraid to let God have His way. Your loving mother.

Jimmy sighed deeply and picked up the picture again. He stared at the smiling, waving woman, her Sunday coat and hair blowing in the Texas wind. For the first time, he recognized something so obvious that he had completely missed it. Her dark hair, her blue eyes! Yes, they were so much like Ruth's that he hadn't let himself see the resemblance. Something within hadn't wanted him to see, but there was the plain truth. Once again the words came back to him.

"I'll try to do my best," he mumbled. "Oh, yes, I *will* try."

□   □   □

That evening Ruth found Ben on the redwood back porch of their home looking out over the ocean. The large clay pots were filled with blooming flowers. He was leisurely sprawled in a patio recliner. His six-foot-two-inch frame extended far beyond the end of the chair. He was reading a book on computers.

"Bother you a minute?" she asked pensively.

"Got a problem?" he grumbled, turning in the opposite direction. The recliner squeaked beneath his weight.

"Sort of . . ."

"About?" He didn't look up.

"About you and Jimmy."

Ben looked out sourly and shook his head. His brown hair shifted sides.

"I want you to be friends."

He didn't say anything but turned a page.

"Of course, you don't argue, but you don't seem to approve of Jimmy either."

Ben raised an eyebrow but kept looking at the page.

"I don't want Jimmy to feel like an outsider in this family."

"Family?" Ben rolled his eyes. "Things getting that serious?"

"Come on, Ben. You know I care for Jimmy a lot. You

could work harder at overcoming the atmosphere Mom and Dad create."

"Hey, count me out of that battle. If you want to fiddle with the used car man, that's your business."

"See!" Ruth protested. "That attitude is exactly what I mean."

"Don't start putting a bunch of stuff on me." Ben dropped the book onto his chest. "If you want to go with this guy, that's your problem. Frankly, I don't see what you have in common with him, but I'm not pushing the issue."

"And what do you have in common with the little Chinese number you're interested in?" Ruth swung her legs sideways and sat on the edge of her chair.

Ben stiffened. "You quit snooping into my business!"

"Not quite as much fun when two play the game, is it?"

"At least I don't bring her around . . . ," he stopped and then added, "here."

"At least," Ruth repeated him, "I'm honest."

Ben picked up the book and started trying to read again.

"Ben," Ruth pleaded, "I'm not trying to embarrass you, but I know our parents would not really prefer to have an oriental in our family. They would rather that we both marry Jews. You need my help as much as I need yours."

Ben's eyes darted back and forth as if he were reading, but his eyes were focused somewhere else.

"The truth is that we are all outsiders, Ben. That's the really crazy thing that Mom and Dad won't face up to. Jews were the original outsiders. Surely, we can recognize the place that strangers can have in our midst. Haven't we all tried to carve out a place for ourselves?"

Ben looked around their expensive family estate that was in its own way a statement. "Yeah," he said, "I guess you're right. This family seems to be rather preoccupied with being on the inside."

"All I ask is a little help, Ben."

"OK, Ruth, I'll be a good boy and put in a good word for the Corvette man."

"Treat him with respect." Ruth's voice had a sharp edge. "That's all I ask."

"Sure." Ben went back to his book with a decisiveness that signaled an end to the conversation. "Sure." This time his eyes followed the words. After Ruth went back into the house, Ben stopped reading and stared out over the ocean. The sea looked calm enough, but Ben knew that dangerous riptides lurked beneath the surface this time of year.

◻   ◻   ◻

Cindy Wong was also reading later that evening. She was perched on her favorite stool in the kitchen of the Golden Dragon. Large pots and pans hung from the ceiling. Steaming and shimmering kettles of rice and vegetables were cooking on the big stoves. In one corner crates of lettuce and tomatoes were stacked on top of boxes of oranges. On the counter in front of Cindy was a large, thick book.

"What are you reading?" Frank Wong asked in Chinese.

"Last year in my discussion group at the library, this book was recommended. It is called the Bible." Cindy's fingers ran across the raised dots of the Braille.

"Bible?" Across the table, Jessica Wong began stirring herbs into the special sauce she was making. Her face was wrinkled and worn, but her hair was still jet black. It was pulled back in a tight knot behind her head, making her plain face look uncharacteristically severe.

"Christians believe this is a holy book," Cindy explained. Her small voice matched the petite features of her lovely face.

"Indeed." Frank continued to speak in Chinese. His eyes were so narrow that they were barely slits. Most of his hair was gone, and he was slightly humped forward. "We must always respect such things."

"Especially because we are in a country where the majority are Christians," Jessica added in Chinese. When Cindy had come unexpectedly late in their lives, Jessica had been overwhelmed with the new responsibility. And discovering that the tiny baby was blind had sent her into a panic that occasionally surfaced in her oversensitivity to their ethnic origins. "We must offend no one."

"Are the teachings like those of the Buddha?" Frank stared down at the blank page filled with the raised dots.

"The first part is the history of the Jews," Cindy told her parents. "But in the second section is the teaching of Jesus."

"Jesus is like the Buddha?" Frank asked.

"Sort of," Cindy puzzled. "He was a Jew too. I really don't understand a lot of the story."

"Maybe you should talk to a Jew," Jessica observed. "Do you know any?"

Cindy smiled. "As a matter of fact, I do know a Jewish boy. He is one of our best customers."

"Really?" Frank began dicing the water chestnuts.

Cindy's grin widened. "In fact, you've not been too happy about the time I've spent talking with him when he was here. Remember Ben Feinberg?" Cindy bit her lip to keep from being too obvious. Inadvertently, her overprotective parents had provided her the excuse she had been seeking.

"The big boy?" Frank looked at his wife. "The one who eats the Kung Pao Squid every time?"

"Exactly," Cindy nodded.

"For heaven's sake," Jessica threw up her hands, "why didn't you tell us that you were discussing religion?"

"Indeed!" Frank shook his finger at Cindy. "We highly respect such discussions. After all, we can learn from all religions."

"A Jewish boy," Jessica mused. "How interesting."

"Does the Jewish boy understand the Bible?" Frank asked.

"I must have more discussions with him." Cindy tried to cover the widening grin with her hand. "I hope you will not worry if we have more discussion times."

"Of course not." Frank picked up a handful of mushrooms. "We want our daughter to be as well informed as any American."

"Then I will continue my religious meetings," Cindy said with a straight face.

One of the waiters burst through the kitchen door. "A young man ask for Miss Cindy. Very large boy."

"His name?" Frank's voice became stern.

"Something like Fein . . . Feinberger."

"Ah, so," Frank nodded his head to one side in deference, "a fortuitous moment. You must continue the religious talks with the Jewish boy."

"If you insist." Cindy bowed in respect to her father.

Damian Gianardo and Jacob Rathmarker stood side by side in the Oval Office listening to the secretary of state make his report. Occasionally, they looked knowingly at each other.

"In summary," the secretary turned his final page and cleared his throat, "your suggestion of a federation of ten nations has been met with total consternation. The idea of a common market and new trade agreements was welcomed. However, the notion that we have a joint military combining all land and sea forces was met by bewilderment. And when I talked of governmental linkage, they ran."

"Thank you, Mr. Clark," the president smiled condescendingly. "Did you bring it to their attention that we have the nuclear attack capacity to make compliance advantageous?"

"Sir," Secretary Clark pulled at his collar, "such a suggestion would have been seen as coercion or an implied threat. I didn't feel that such a course was helpful."

"Not at this time . . . at least." Rathmarker smiled cunningly. "I trust all discussions have been completely and totally confidential."

"Absolutely. I spoke only with my counterparts at the

top level of government. No one wanted a word of these discussions leaked."

Gianardo turned and walked to the opposite end of the office. He crossed his arms and paced back and forth. "Something is needed. A new political climate is required. Some extraordinary event must happen that will cause each of these nations to realize how much it needs my leadership. The world needs a good shaking."

"I don't understand what you are suggesting," the secretary answered nervously.

The president paced with his right side to the wall. "Obviously, I am changing the political face of our country very quickly. People have learned that my leadership is flawless. On the domestic scene we are successfully creating complete dependence on me. We need a good worldwide disaster to accomplish the same thing abroad."

"A *good* disaster?" The secretary swallowed hard.

"Come now, Clark," Damian Gianardo laughed wickedly. "Be a little imaginative. Surely, we can create a nice little crisis that will demonstrate a demand for my proposed alliance."

□   □   □

Through the summer of 1995, Cindy studied the new Bible. Her quick mind was challenged by a new world that began to unfold before her. As her parents worked in the kitchen of the Golden Dragon, Cindy read selected passages to them. Frank commented sometimes, but mostly he said, "Ah, yes, ah, so." Jessica only listened and nodded.

Cindy tried to ask Ben questions about the imposing book. Most of the time he was far more absorbed with Cindy. Yet her fascination with the Bible had its effect on Ben.

"I really don't know anything about the New Testament part," he confessed on a hot July evening as they sat by the ocean in the middle of Laguna Beach. In front of them, a volleyball game was in progress. Just beyond, teenagers were running into the ocean. "The story of the Jewish people is in the first section of the Bible. I know that much." He shrugged. "We call that part the Torah."

The breeze from the ocean swept Cindy's coal black hair back. "In the new part is the story of Jesus," Cindy spoke softly. "He was a Jew too."

"So they tell me." Ben reached for her hand. "Jews have always had a big problem with Jesus."

"But Jesus was a very good man in this book."

"I guess the difficulty wasn't Jesus as much as His followers." Ben let his fingers slide in between hers.

"The story says that Jesus died for us." Cindy didn't move her hand. "Amazing story."

"I've never read the tale." Ben put both of his hands around Cindy's. "Most of the Christians I've known didn't do much for me so I didn't pay any attention to the book. In fact, the Christians persecuted Jews for centuries." Ben leaned forward. "But you are *another* story!"

"What?" Cindy looked surprised.

"You completely hold my attention." Ben put his arm around Cindy's shoulder and kissed her.

☐   ☐   ☐

"Dr. Woodbridge," Ruth said to her therapist, "I'm really frustrated with my parents. You've helped me accept their love and concern, but they just aren't open to Jimmy."

"I thought you'd made progress," Dr. Woodbridge said. She got up from her mahogany desk and walked to the window. The pastel colors in her office added a sense of harmony and order. Pictures of peaceful farm scenes were on the walls. "Communication seemed to be better a few weeks ago."

"Jimmy broke through their stereotypes of used car salesmen." Ruth looked out the fourth-story window with its expansive view of the ocean. "Now, they're terrified that I might marry a Gentile . . . at least Mother is. She knows I'm that serious about Jimmy. No one cared about our being Jewish until I came home with a man whose last name is Harrison."

"Your parents seem threatened?" Ann Woodbridge chewed on the end of her pencil. "And you feel you can't communicate with them."

"Exactly!" Ruth shook her head in disgust. "We can't get past the log jam in our different perspectives."

"What would you think of getting all of us together?" the psychologist suggested. "We could have a family session dealing with communication."

"Dr. Woodbridge, I think you've done it again! I'd also like to have my brother Ben come. For some reason, he and Jimmy seem to lock horns."

"Anyone else?" Ann Woodbridge laughed. "We could rent the Hollywood Bowl for the gathering."

"There's just so much hostility at home," Ruth said thoughtfully. "Dad and Mom are horrified about Jimmy's father. He is a preacher who specializes in Bible prophecy. I believe my parents would run for the ocean if the Harrisons actually flew in from Texas."

"Isn't Jimmy far more accepting of his own father now?"

"You've taught me how to help him." Ruth smiled. "Yes, Jimmy is even talking of attending a church again. I'd go with him if it would help him make peace with his memories of his father."

"As a Christian," the therapist added, "I understand much of what occurred in Jimmy's family. I know his father's reputation. He's an outstanding preacher."

"Really?" Ruth's mouth dropped. "The way Jimmy talks, I thought his father was a sort of nobody . . . a little on the peculiar side even."

"Quite the contrary. Reverend Harrison may not have given Jimmy all the attention he needed, but the minister is an outstanding authority on the Bible."

"I'm really glad to hear that! You can bet I'll make sure Mom and Dad Feinberg hear those facts."

"I hope your contact with our office staff has made you more comfortable with Christians," Dr. Woodbridge said earnestly. "In this office we are believers, but that doesn't mean we're perfect people any more than Jimmy's father is. We simply believe we have found the truth that will help us live in harmony with what God intended from the beginning."

The counselor pulled out her appointment book and began thumbing through the pages of 1995. "I'm going to take a vacation for several weeks. Our get-together will have to be in late September." Dr. Woodbridge ran her finger over the calendar. "Let's go for September 25 and see if we can get everyone in." The counselor stopped and looked at the page more carefully. "The fine print says that day is Rosh Hashanah. Maybe it's a bad time."

"No, no." Ruth stood up. "My parents never observe the Jewish holidays."

"Then I'll see you again on the day of the Jewish New Year."

☐　☐　☐

Rosh Hashanah was one of the days that held the two worlds together. On the Feast of Trumpets, as it is called in English, the shofar is blown as the ram's horn tells the world that Jehovah Rafah has provided the world another year of existence. My memory is filled with thousands of these exciting celebration days. I was there when Obed taught Jesse up in the hill country of Judah. Unfortunately, I was transferred just about the time that Jesse's boys got to an exciting age, but this high holy day I was going to be right in the center of the action when the trumpet blew.

Angels revel in holy days. Such times help us keep our bearings as we move between time and eternity. We do not measure as humans do; clocks and calculators do not mean anything to creatures who prefer the imperishable.

On the morning of September 25, 1995, Larry and Sharon had a fleeting discussion about dropping by a synagogue on the way to Dr. Woodbridge's office. Their intentions were good, but anxiety about the confrontation at the counselor's was high. As a result, thoughts of the worship service disappeared as the Feinbergs agonized over what lay ahead.

Ben had been irritated for several weeks about being coerced into the gathering. He considered the entire business Ruth's problem. The fact that he was certain Jimmy was a jerk only added to his conviction that there was no good reason for him to go to a meeting about communication.

That morning Jimmy picked up Ruth from her new graduate-level classes at Pepperdine and headed south on Highway 5 in his red Corvette. "Got to hand it to your counselor," he told Ruth. "I didn't believe she could pull off getting all of us in one room."

"Ben won't be pleasant." Ruth pouted. "He's been such a creep lately."

"I thought I was doing well with your parents." Jimmy stared at the cars in front of them. "Then they started suspecting that something serious was going on, and I went back to the bottom of their list. I guess they just don't want someone with my limitations in their family."

Ruth bit her lip and winced. "Expecting a professional person is their hang-up. You make a very good living, and you've been offered a percentage of a new partnership. You don't have to apologize to anyone."

"Don't kid yourself, Ruth. A college education is everything to them. And also I'm not Jewish."

Ruth said little as they drove south through the pack of cars. Traffic was heavy, and the late September weather was still hot and irritating. Jimmy took the 405 to the MacArthur exit toward Newport Beach and the counselor's office. He pulled into the parking lot in front of the five-story building.

Jimmy turned the key off. "Here goes nothing." He hopped out to open the door for Ruth.

Ruth's parents and Ben were already waiting to enter the conference room on the fourth floor. Their casual greetings were stilted and stiff. Once she ushered the group in, Dr. Woodbridge stood to one side, watching how each person took a chair.

Dr. Feinberg was so nervous he forgot that the psychologist would be observing and immediately claimed a space in the center of the room. Six chairs were arranged in a circle in the plain room. Sharon pointed controllingly to two chairs that she felt Jimmy and Ruth should take. Ben straggled into a corner.

"Why don't we put our expectations on the table?" Dr. Woodbridge spoke pleasantly. "Let's explore the agendas that we brought with us today."

"I'll start," Ruth blurted out. "After all, the meeting is somewhat at my instigation. No one thinks that Jimmy is good enough for me."

"Oh, come now!" Larry protested. "We are very liberal-minded people and, I might say, very accepting."

"Absolutely," Sharon objected. "We have friends from all walks of life." Her dark brown suit seemed unusually severe for her.

"I pride myself on openness." Larry shook his head. In contrast to his usual southern California casualness, he wore a tie and sport coat.

"How do you feel about what you just heard?" Dr. Woodbridge asked Jimmy.

"I know you mean well." Jimmy tried to smile. "But you sound like I'm the gardener you invite in for a sandwich every Christmas."

Sharon's jaw tightened and Ben rolled his eyes.

Larry sat upright and stuck his chin out. "If I have any hidden agenda, it's shaped by what I know professionally. The statistics just aren't good. Ruth's dated only one boy in her life. The odds are even worse for a Jewish girl and a Baptist boy making it work."

"And what are the dangers of a girl with a Ph.D.

marrying a used car salesman with a high-school education?" Ruth added. Defiantly, she tossed her hair sideways.

Larry shrugged. "You know as well as I do. That's strike three."

Dr. Woodbridge kept trying to smile. "At least, we're getting it out quickly."

Sharon cleared her throat. "I don't like what I need to say. I don't even like how it makes me feel to speak up, but I can't be honest if I'm not forthright." She scooted to the edge of her chair. "Maybe it's totally self-ish, but I am self-conscious about how my Newport Beach friends will view any future son-in-law who is a used car salesman. After all, we're professional people."

The room became intensely quiet. Jimmy looked down at his feet, and Ruth was obviously pained.

Sharon broke the silence. "Yes, and I feel guilty be-cause I didn't contribute enough of our family back-ground to help Ruth make sure she stayed within our race when she was looking for a spouse."

"I'd like to add a word." Ben pulled himself up to his full height in his chair. "We've always been a close-knit family. We have our little rituals and ways of doing things. It's not easy to bring someone into the inner circle." Ben stopped and smiled unexpectedly at Jimmy. "But I appreciate how it feels to be an outsider. Ethnic differences shouldn't matter if we're as liberal as we profess. All of us need to get over thinking we're better than other people."

"I didn't say that," Sharon bristled.

"In fact, we did." Larry fidgeted in his chair. "It's not flattering, but that's about the sum of what we've said so far."

"I know it doesn't sound like much to your family," Jimmy winced as he spoke, "but I really like selling cars. Sure, it doesn't take much education to be a sales-man, but I'm good at what I do. I have an excellent repu-tation in Laguna Hills. I've done well enough that I've saved $12,000. The boss said that he wants me to manage our new place in Laguna Niguel, and I'll get 10 percent of the profits."

"You sound apologetic," Dr. Woodbridge said thoughtfully, turning to Jimmy. "I sense the conversation is painful for you."

Jimmy smiled weakly. "Can't your Newport friends simply think of me as a businessman? Maybe someday I'll own a chain of car lots."

"Jimmy has been very good for me." Ruth reached out for Jimmy's hand. "He's been the best friend I've ever had."

Ann Woodbridge seemed distracted. Her usually rapt attention faded as if she was hearing something that no one else heard. She turned her head slightly and began looking at the ceiling. The conversation quickly faded.

"Ann?" Larry repeated, "Ann? Are you with us?"

And then it happened. In the twinkling of an eye, Dr. Ann Woodbridge was gone.

6

For a moment no one moved. Larry stared at the ceiling in shock. Sharon's eyes blinked rapidly while she shook her head. Ben started to point, but his hand stopped in midair. Larry reached out for his wife, but Sharon covered her face with her hands.

"Oh, no!" Jimmy was the first to speak. "No! NO!"

Ruth slid to the edge of her chair. "Ann? Ann! Is this a joke?"

Silence once again filled the room.

"She was right there!" Ben pointed at the empty chair.

"This better not be some kind of crazy psychodrama experiment." Larry stood up.

"It's happened," Jimmy gasped. "Just like Dad said it might. He preached about the Rapture."

"I'm losing my mind." Sharon pressed both hands against her face. "I'm going stark raving nuts."

Larry took several steps toward the vacant seat. "She was right there." He reached out to touch the arm of the chair.

"Mom was right," Jimmy moaned. "The time is at hand."

Larry spun on his heels and raced toward the offices. "What's going on?" he called out before he even had the door open. "Where did Dr. Woodbridge go?" He burst into the receptionist's empty office. For a moment he stared at the three desks.

"Where are they?" Ben stopped behind his father. "The women were here when we came in."

Father and son wandered aimlessly through the unoccupied office. The receptionist's headset was lying on the desk next to her phone. On the other desks, pencils and papers were scattered about as if everyone had abruptly left on a coffee break. The faint sound of a radio playing soft music came from one corner. Nothing was amiss or irregular except everyone was gone.

"Larry?" Sharon called weakly from the doorway. "Wh . . . what's hap . . . pening here?"

"I don't understand," Larry muttered. "It doesn't seem logical."

"Dad, there's just nobody in the whole place. This is real crazy!"

"The whole world is turning into scrambled eggs." Larry marched to the window. "We can't all be having the same delusion at the same moment."

"No delusion." Jimmy held to the door jamb and stared at the floor. "My father preached that this would happen someday. The time has come. He must have figured out that Rosh Hashanah was the key to the timing of the Rapture."

"Rosh Hashanah? Stop it." Larry spun around. "Don't add to the confusion. We've got to keep our heads."

"But they've disappeared," Sharon said. "Gone . . . just vanished into thin air."

"There's got to be a rational explanation." Larry looked out over the ocean. "If Ann Woodbridge is playing some sort of trick on us to force communication, I'll kill her. I'll have her license for this."

"Mother tried to tell me." Jimmy slumped against the door. "She tried to warn me. Dad had figured it all out."

"What in the world are you babbling about?" Larry glared at Jimmy.

"My father called what's happened the Rapture. God's people are taken out of the world. They're with Him."

"Now that is goofy!" Ben shook his head in disgust.

"Would you call this rational?" Ruth took hold of Jimmy's arm. "Do you think what's just happened in this building is logical? Do you have a better idea of what's going on, Ben?" Ruth raised her eyebrows defensively.

Ben turned away contemptuously.

"Look out there." Jimmy pointed out the window. "Do you notice something strange? Several cars have driven off the road and been abandoned there on Pacific Coast Highway and Avocado, causing several fender benders."

"If you're in on this with Dr. Woodbridge," Sharon snapped and shook her finger angrily at Jimmy, still denying what she had seen, "I guarantee you'll wish you hadn't pulled this prank on us."

"Mother, stop it." Ruth protested. "Get a grip on yourself."

"I suggest we all go back to our home." Larry walked decisively to the outside door. "This place is getting to us. I need to contact someone who knows Ann to see if we can get some answers for this behavior. We've got three cars here. We can rendezvous at the house. The drive will help us settle down."

Ruth and Jimmy took the stairs and left through a side door. Once they reached the parking lot, they took off in his red Corvette without waiting for the rest of the family to catch up.

"Jimmy?" Ruth grasped his arm. "What were you talking about up there? What's a Rapture?"

"If I'm right, my parents will have disappeared. There won't be anybody at the church." He veered off the street into a driveway of a convenience store with an outside drive-up telephone. Jimmy punched in the set of numbers followed by his credit card number.

"What are you doing?" Ruth pleaded. "What is this Rapture business?"

Jimmy stared into space as the phone rang. A minute later, he hung up. "This is always the busiest time of day at the church in Dallas. No one is there. No one is left. They are all gone."

"Gone where?" Ruth tugged on his sleeve.

"I've got to get to my father's books . . . the tapes Mother was sending me. They will give us the clues."

"Stop it!" Ruth pounded on the dashboard. "You sound like Columbo! Don't play Dick Tracy with me. What clues?"

Jimmy pulled back into the street and drove the two miles to the Feinberg home, too stunned to even consider stopping to help the other people, crying and wandering along the streets. He ran his hands through his hair and then rubbed his forehead. Finally, he answered, "Many Christians believe that the second coming of Jesus will be preceded by a great conflict. An Antichrist will appear and plunge the world into great tribulation and chaos. Surely, you've heard of this idea."

"Sorta." Ruth frowned. "But I wouldn't listen to such nonsense."

"I thought it was ridiculous, too . . . until this afternoon. My father was an expert on this teaching. For some reason, he really believed these terrible things were about to happen soon and even suspected that they could occur on the Jewish New Year. The whole process starts with God removing His true believers so they won't go through the pain and suffering. The Rapture is a name for their sudden disappearance."

Ruth stared at the sky a few moments before letting go of Jimmy's sleeve. She settled back against the door and silently looked straight ahead.

Jimmy pulled his car into the Feinbergs' driveway. Without saying anything more, he went through the back gate and started down the flower-lined path that led to the beach. Ruth watched him disappear behind the little hill at the bottom and then went into the house by herself. Four or five times, she tried to call Jimmy's parents' home, but no one answered. Even after the other family cars pulled in, Jimmy stayed on the beach. Finally, he noticed the sun was setting and started back to the house.

When Jimmy walked in, his eyes were red and his face drawn. Sharon was placing glasses on the bar in the den. She had already drunk a large glass of wine. Dr. Feinberg was hanging up the phone as Jimmy shut the back door.

"That was Abe Staub," he told Sharon. "Dr. Staub at the hospital. My old buddy who still goes to the synagogue."

Jimmy sat down in the wicker chair by the door unnoticed.

"What did he want?" Sharon threw up her hands. "Someone disappear under his nose too?"

"Yes," Larry said, "they're in trouble at the hospital. About a third of the ambulance drivers just vanished. All the doctors and nurses who attend the weekly Christian prayer breakfast have disappeared. A lot of people have gone up like a puff of smoke. Lots of car wrecks . . . even some plane and boat wrecks. Work accidents too! The hospital is desperate for help."

Sharon raised her eyebrows and shook her head wearily. "What in heaven's name is going on? I can't stand any more of this."

Jimmy listened but said nothing.

"I don't know what's coming down," Ben spoke from the hallway. "Maybe someone will have an explanation. In the meantime, I'm willing to try and help. Maybe I can go with you to Hoag Hospital." Ben stood in the doorway. "After all, I'm a pre-med student now, and I'm certified Red Cross as well. Maybe I could help in the emergency room."

"Abe sounded like they would take anyone with a bit of training right now. I'm going to have to go down to the hospital immediately."

"Heavens!" Sharon leaned on the top of the tile-covered wet bar. "I feel like a character in a 'Star Trek' episode. Sounds like aliens have beamed everybody up."

"If this is widespread," Ben reached for the TV remote control, "there's got to be something on the news channel."

Ruth walked in from the kitchen and sat down next to Jimmy. She put her arm around his shoulders.

A newscaster's voice came on before a picture appeared. "Apparently, about 25 percent of the population has simply vanished," the young man spoke rapidly.

A picture of a man frantically talking to a policeman came on the screen. "A Newport oral surgeon is reporting that his wife vanished from their office while they were working."

"I know that guy." Larry pointed at the screen. "He came here from Oklahoma. His office is just behind Dr. Woodbridge's building."

The policeman was jotting down information. "But I thought I was a believer," the doctor kept telling the police officer. Suddenly, the picture on the screen changed. Notre Dame Cathedral in Paris appeared.

"Europe is reporting about 5 percent losses while virtually no one is missing from Muslim, Hindu, or Buddhist nations," the announcer continued. "This factor is forcing an analysis of a possible religious component in the disappearances."

Ruth watched Jimmy's face while he stared blankly at the television as if he knew what was coming before it was said.

A picture of an empty podium with the seal of the President of the United States flashed across the screen. "Please stand by," the broadcaster spoke very soberly. "We have a statement live from the president."

Damian Gianardo walked briskly to the stand. He appeared nervous and edgy. "My fellow Americans, tonight we are facing one of the strangest crises in national history. There is no current explanation for the disappearance of thousands of our citizens. Key military and police personnel are absent without reason. To ensure orderly process and security, I am now declaring a state of emergency. The National Guard and reserve units will patrol our streets until further notice. I am asking all medical personnel to stand by, since we seem to be in a medical crisis created by similar disappearances. Telephone operators will be asked to work additional shifts to compensate for those who have vanished."

"At least we're not the only crazy people out there." Sharon started shaking her head. "The whole world can't be hallucinating." She stopped and looked at her husband. "Can it?"

Gianardo shuffled his papers and seemed confused. "Please do not call the White House at this time. The switchboards are completely jammed. While we have no explanations, we are doing everything humanly possible to solve this mystery. I have directed the FBI and CIA to spare no effort in gathering every possible shred of evidence. We are quite aware that a couple of African nations have lost nearly half of their populations. Data are now being assembled that seem to indicate that Russia and some Eastern European nations have also lost large numbers."

The president stopped. He stared abstractly into space somewhere beyond the camera. Speaking as if the thoughts were forming as he talked, he said, "Worldwide unity is required! The world needs our leadership at this moment as never before. I will immediately dispatch the secretary of state to major foreign capitals."

"This has got to be an invasion from outer space!" Ben blurted out. "There's no other possible explanation. We are getting ready to be invaded from some planet light years away."

Once more the president returned to his prepared text. "I am discounting early hysterical reports that correlate these disappearances with fundamentalist Christian teachings. Obviously, many priests, rabbis, and clergypersons are still here, erasing the claim that religious people have been taken. As you know, I have steadfastly resisted the intolerance of reactionary Christian groups who have worked to deny basic human rights in areas such as abortion, homosexuality, and euthanasia. Now is not the hour to capitulate to these same divisive clichés in explaining this current tragedy. This is not a time to revert to superstition."

Jimmy smiled sadly but still said nothing.

The president jutted his chin out and spoke defiantly. "Go back to work! Let us double our efforts day and night until our nation returns to its normal production standards. You can rely on me and my government to protect your interests and guide you through this difficult time. In the name of human goodness, we will gain the inevitable victory!"

"He's wrong," Jimmy said quietly as the picture faded. "This time the head man is completely deceived."

Ruth squeezed Jimmy's hand and grimaced.

"I was a fool not to listen to my father." He paused and added, "And now I can't even talk to him."

"Maybe we should have gone to the synagogue this morning after all," Sharon said aimlessly. "Some way to start the Jewish New Year."

7

Nothing would ever be the same again. The disappearance of millions of people sent waves of chaos across the world. When Ann Woodbridge could not be located or her disappearance explained, the crisis deepened for the entire Feinberg family.

Larry no longer worried about the "appropriateness" of his comments and conversations. When there was no quick scientific explanation for the phenomenon, his consternation was obvious. The professional exterior crumbled, and he lost the façade that had long been his insulation against anything that made him uncomfortable.

Sharon became very clinging and chattered aimlessly much of the time. Her babbling only made Larry more nervous. She checked out books on Judaism and made several appointments to talk with a rabbi. Nothing gave her much peace of mind. Fortunately, Larry developed a new interest in religious matters and talked with her about her discoveries. In the weeks that followed September 25, Sharon and Larry talked more about what they believed than they had during their entire marriage.

The catastrophe hit hard in Frank Wong's restaurant as well. The Golden Dragon lost many customers and a number of its best employees. Frank and Jessica had no explanation for the disappearances. Consequently, both receded into a comprehensive silence. Most of the time they spoke Chinese and avoided unnecessary conversations with Caucasians. However, Ben considered Cindy's questions about the Bible with new seriousness.

"Amazing numbers of people are converting to evangelical Christianity," Cindy said as Ben consumed Hunan Chicken, the Golden Dragon's special of the day.

"So it seems." Ben ate without looking up.

"I heard one report that also says thousands of people in Eastern Europe and parts of Africa are accepting the ancient faith," Cindy added.

Ben put his chopsticks down and sat back in the black ivory chair. He said, "Apparently, thousands of Orthodox Jews have suddenly embraced the idea that Jesus is the Messiah. Some discovery from a just-released portion of the Dead Sea Scrolls has convinced them. The Essenes, who wrote the Dead Sea Scrolls, had eight copies of the book of Daniel, a book that predicts some of the things that seem to be happening right now. They thought these things would happen in their era."

Cindy swallowed hard. "We've got to recognize that something incredible is going on."

"The Jewish converts have also come to another conclusion," Ben stated. "They expect there will soon be another worldwide persecution of Jews that will be worse than Hitler's holocaust."

"Oh, Ben!" Cindy stiffened. "Those words are too horrible to be said out loud. Don't say such a thing."

Ben looked up at the elegant ceiling. The long figure of a dragon wound its way across the top of the dining room. "We once thought smog was the worst thing in the air. Now a little pollution seems innocuous." Ben began eating silently again.

Ruth struggled in her own way, but the tension was different. She was caught between her parents' discomfort about Jimmy's new convictions and her boy-friend's growing faith. The Feinbergs were polite enough to Jimmy, but they were also bothered by his firm sense of what had occurred.

In late October of 1995, Jimmy took Ruth's car to Dallas, Texas, and returned with his father's books and cassette tapes. The rental trailer provided ample space to bring back quite a haul.

Jimmy dropped the first box of books on his living room floor beneath the picture of Jimmy Dean. He flipped on his stereo and opened the curtains on the large front picture window. "Been gone too long." He felt how dry the bonsai tree on the ledge was.

"Do you really understand this stuff?" Ruth looked at one of the titles as she helped Jimmy unpack the books.

"It's been a long time." He carried an armful of books to a bookshelf on the bedroom wall. "But I read part of a book in a motel on the way back. Much of my father's teaching is coming back to me."

Jimmy's apartment wasn't large, so the piles of boxes made it even more crowded to get around. Books were stacked on the stereo speakers, and the kitchen counter was lined with cassette tapes.

"I don't know." Ruth shook her head as she thumbed through the index. "Antichrist, beasts, strange numbers, hmmm. I can't decide how I feel about these ideas."

"Take it a step at a time," Jimmy called from the kitchen. "Remember, Christians have been working on this problem for two thousand years. You can't expect to get everything in a day."

Ruth sat down on the bed. "This paragraph says that a world leader will appear who will deceive everyone. He will become a great enemy and persecutor of Jews. That's frightening talk! How do I know this author's not just another nut?"

"Look at the copyright." Jimmy walked in and sat down on the bed next to her.

"It's 1965."

"OK." Jimmy opened the book to the first chapter. "Thirty years ago, what did this man predict would happen?"

Ruth skimmed down the page. At the bottom she began to read more carefully. Her finger moved slower and slower down the next page. "My gosh!" Ruth looked at Jimmy in wide-eyed astonishment. "The author has perfectly described our experience in September!"

"If he was right about the Rapture, isn't it logical to believe his description of the Antichrist might be on the right track too? You can see that we do have a point of reference from these books."

"Amazing. Simply amazing."

"I'm going to work night and day to see if I can really find what my father discovered. I believe all the clues to figure out what is coming next are in this pile of tapes and books."

Ruth slid up against the headboard of the bed. She pulled a pillow behind her head. "I think I'll read some while you finish opening the boxes."

"Ohhh," Jimmy drawled in teasing tones. "Surely, an honor student from Pepperdine can't be interested in such biblical nonsense."

The national security adviser's eyes flashed with anger as he talked with his top-ranking staff member. "Any second now we will have to walk into his office and talk with the president. We don't have the answers we promised him. Do you understand the seriousness of our plight?"

"He's a harsh man," the staffer looked grim. "But we've been unable to find anything but religious answers."

"God help us if you bring that up!" Any further comments were ended when the president's chief of staff opened the door to the Oval Office and motioned for the two men to enter.

"Good morning, gentlemen." Damian Gianardo stood and offered his hand. "Excuse me for a lack of pleasantries. We must get right to business. We are facing an increasing financial crisis across the world. I must quiet public fears. Time is running out. Please give me your report explaining the disappearance of millions of people."

"Sir," the national security chief smiled but spoke haltingly, "we really don't have a written report."

"A verbal explanation is sufficient for now," the president answered sourly. "I promised the world an answer before the end of 1995. A quick synopsis will do."

"The problem is . . . ," the security chief stopped and turned to his assistant. "You tell him, George."

"Mr. President, we have found no rational explanation. We have been unable—"

"You've what?" Gianardo's neck began turning red. "I promised the world that *I* would have an answer. You had best not make me appear to be a fool." His black eyes narrowed and glared as if he could burn holes through the assistant's face.

"The only explanations are religious," the staffer blurted out. The national security chief covered his face.

"Religious!" the president shouted. "You expect me to come out on the day before Christmas and make a religious pronouncement about this disaster? Financial markets are collapsing everywhere, and you want me to offer superstition to reassure the masses?"

"It's all we have." The assistant held up his empty hands.

Damian Gianardo turned slowly to his national security head, looking so fierce that the man was forced to look down. "I would suggest two things. First, you fire this incompetent fool before sunset. Second, you have a plausible answer for me before December 31 or prepare yourself for new employment immediately thereafter. Good day, gentlemen." The president turned back to a letter on his desk and continued reading without looking up as the two bewildered men scurried from the office.

1995 ended without the promised explanation about the unusual disappearances that President Damian Gianardo said would be immediately forthcoming back in September. No one—not the FBI, the CIA, the National Geographic Society, or MIT—could unravel the deepening mystery. Uncertainty toned down the New Year's Eve celebrations that welcomed 1996.

The Feinbergs' holiday rituals were somber. Heaviness hung over their house like the Los Angeles smog.

"I don't think that I'll go to a movie this year," Sharon said as she dropped down in her favorite plaid-covered chair in front of the large screen TV. She wore jeans rather than her expensive slacks.

"Really!" Larry looked up from his chess game with Ben.

"Rose Bowl will be on in a while." Sharon sounded unusually detached. "I'll just tough it out."

"The games won't be that great this year," Ben said sourly. He moved his knight into position to checkmate his father. He, too, wore old jeans rather than the usual expensive pleated slacks. "All the good players and coaches are gone. Check," he said mechanically.

"Life is rather gray in a post-Rapture world." Ruth threw a log on the fire and closed the metal screen on the large fireplace.

"I really don't like that phrase." Larry frowned at the chess board. "Then again, what I like and don't like doesn't buy much these days. I guess I might as well get used to the term."

Jimmy turned a page in the book he was reading. He

watched the exchange between father and daughter without comment.

"Jimmy, you've really studied this Rapture idea lately," Ben observed. "You truly believe that's what's happened?" Any hint of competitiveness in his voice was gone.

Jimmy nodded his head but didn't speak. He turned uneasily in the leather chair.

Larry crossed his arms over his chest. "You win again, Ben," he said disgustedly. "I've lost my touch everywhere. Even atheism went out of style this year."

"You've certainly changed your tune." Sharon rolled her eyes. "Aren't you the same man who insisted that religion was the universal neurosis of humankind? How often did I hear you preach that God was a projection of our childhood father-images?"

"I guess the problems of some of my patients confused me." Larry pushed his king over on the board. "I was just too arrogant for my own good. Confusing God with an earthly father doesn't prove at all that there is no God."

Ruth's mouth dropped. She ran her hands through her long hair. "I didn't believe that I would ever hear those words from the mouth of my father, Dr. Larry Feinberg."

"I guess we've all been seriously affected by what happened in September. Your mother and I have had lots of conversations about religion recently. I think it's time for me to be more open."

"What's changed your mind, Dad?" Ruth probed.

"I guess I started paying attention to some of the implications of my medical education. There has to be a Designer behind anything as complex as the human body. We have at least thirty trillion cells—each of which has thousands of components. The odds are against a body simply happening, just evolving from the mud."

Ruth shook her head and stood up. "I've got to go in

the kitchen and get a glass of Coke. I can't believe my ears. Never have I heard such talk from my dad."

Ben pushed Jimmy. "You've decided that Jesus is for real, haven't you? You think He's the Messiah?"

Jimmy nodded and didn't look up from his book.

"You really believe in this Rapture idea, don't you?" Ben asked again.

"I'll help my daughter," Sharon stood up. "I think we all need a cold drink. I'm taking orders. Anyone want some potato chips?"

"Religious talk makes this family very nervous," Ben chided his mother.

"I'll pop some popcorn," Sharon added. "Maybe the game will be interesting after all."

"Not much danger of that," Larry groused. "The talent's gone. I can't believe that UCLA came in last in the PAC-10."

Jimmy closed his book. "The whole world is in such a state of turmoil and confusion that it's hard to get interested in a diversion."

"Jews certainly aren't in style anymore," Ben said as he began repositioning the chessmen on the board. "We have good reason to be sober."

"I can't believe that the Israeli Knesset voted to expel all the Palestinians with less than one-eighth Jewish blood from the small province in the Jerusalem area that was created by that secret treaty back in 1993. The government completely sold out to those right-wing leaders like Yuval Neerman of the Tehiya Party and Reha Van Zeevi of the Moledet Party."

"International reaction has certainly been violent," Ben sighed. "I try to avoid talking politics at school. Other students eat me alive."

"It will get worse," Jimmy said wearily. "Everything is in place."

"What do you mean?" Larry frowned again.

"Israel's been using its tremendous new income from the recently discovered oil strikes to rebuild the temple exactly like it was centuries ago. When it's completed, the next piece of the puzzle will be in place."

"I don't understand the significance of a new temple," Ben acknowledged, "but I understand the implications of the way that Gianardo has sided with the Arabs. He recently expressed regret over signing the seven-year treaty of unconditional support for Israel, even though he is part Jewish and Vice President Rathmarker is totally Jewish. Did you see that picture in the paper last week of him standing with the leaders of the United Muslim States?"

Larry stood up and walked to the windows overlooking the ocean. "The winds are blowing the wrong way. The Muslims have really rallied around their new capital of Babylon. Their fundamentalist clergy predict a future conversion of the world either by persuasion or by a holy war."

Ben smirked. "All we need now is for Israel and the Arabs to start throwing A-bombs around. They could finish off our problem of a shrinking population."

Sharon and Ruth came back into the den and set the colas on the coffee table. "I'll have some popcorn ready in just a second," Sharon interrupted the conversation. "Let's switch to the news channel before the game starts. Maybe we should catch up on what's been going on."

"On New Year's Day?" Ben laughed. "My, but we are edgy."

Sharon snatched the TV remote control from the coffee table and flipped the channel.

The announcer's voice boomed. "Happy New Year to everyone out there. As we begin another year, the top story is fear. Current polls demonstrate that recent unprecedented events have left their mark on every person on the globe. In America the fear of failure, abandonment, and death haunts us hourly. The still unexplained disappearance of multitudes has only heightened the tension."

Cameras panned vacant streets, empty desks, and

unkempt lawns. "Fear has increased extramarital sexual activity. Both homosexual and heterosexual activity has dramatically accelerated across the entire globe. Consequently, the spread of AIDS has also risen. We are now in danger of losing entire populations, especially in Third World countries."

Larry reached for a cola and turned to his wife. "Is this your idea of a little holiday cheer?"

"Oh, dear!" Sharon chewed on her fingernail. "I didn't expect such a depressing report."

A different picture filled the screen. People were crowding and pushing their way forward in a bank lobby. "The sudden loss of population has played havoc with the U.S. economy," the announcer continued. "Hoarding money was common during this past fall. The result sent a tidal wave across foreign markets, causing economic depression and collapse. With the greatest nuclear arsenal in the world, America is still rapidly going bankrupt." Scenes of Wall Street appeared. People were frantically running up and down stairs. "Stock prices fell, sending the prices of gold and silver skyrocketing. Because of the catastrophic decline in the Dole Index, President Gianardo will make a special live address this evening. He is expected to make major changes in the economy to stave off bankruptcy and loss of political leadership around the world. We will bring you that address."

"I think I've heard enough." Larry clicked to a football game. "Rough days are ahead. You might as well get ready. We are looking at tough times in 1996."

"Indeed!" Jimmy answered. "What is before us will exceed our wildest dreams . . . and nightmares."

8

Sharon found it hard to pay attention to the football game, so she began to read a novel. Shortly after halftime, Jimmy started reading his book again. Ruth munched on potato chips and curled Jimmy's hair around her fingers. Only Larry and Ben really followed the lackluster Rose Bowl game.

Ben was the first to notice that a car had pulled into the driveway. "Look's like Jennifer McCoy."

Sharon put her book down. "I told her I wasn't going to the movies this year. I'm sure I called her." Sharon hurried down the hall to the front door.

"Hi!" Jennifer hugged her best friend. "I know we called our annual movie off, but I wasn't sure that you really meant no." Jennifer sailed into the living room.

Next to Sharon's five-foot-eight-inch height, Jennifer looked very small. While Sharon tended toward the plump side, Jennifer was thin and slight. "Sorry to barge in," Jennifer chattered in her usual energetic way, "but I just couldn't wait to call." Her movements were quick like those of a little bird flitting from one branch to the next. Sharon had always admired her friend's boundless energy.

"What a surprise." Sharon followed Jennifer across the living room. "No, I had planned to be with the family this year."

"I thought maybe you might change your mind. Anyway I had something very important to tell you."

"Please sit down and tell me what's happening." The TV in the den was barely audible.

Jennifer's countenance abruptly changed. "I hope you won't end our friendship," she stammered. Her short brown hair bobbed from side to side.

"Oh, come on! We've been best friends for over fifteen years."

"Last night . . . ," Jennifer carefully chose her words, "Joe and I went to a New Year's Eve party at Jane McGill's . . . a religious New Year's Eve party. Well . . . a Christian New Year's Eve party." She rolled her bright blue eyes.

"Really?" Sharon furrowed her forehead. "I don't understand the difference."

"With all this Rapture talk, Joe and I wanted to know everything we could about what's going on. You know my parents disappeared." Jennifer's eyes became watery. "I believe we have started to unravel the mystery. The speaker explained that Jesus of Nazareth was really the Messiah and why He is coming back again. The Rapture was tied to His return. Our discussion was simply awesome."

"Jennifer," Sharon frowned, "where are you going with this?"

"When the meeting was over, Joe and I knew we could trust Jesus to be our Lord and Savior. We made a decision to ask Him into our lives."

Sharon's mouth dropped, and she shook her head in disbelief.

"Our children are very upset." Jennifer's eyes pleaded for understanding. "I hoped you would be positive . . . accepting . . . still friends."

Sharon's chest heaved as she sighed deeply. "My goodness! We do have a most unusual New Year's Day at the Feinbergs." Sharon suddenly stood up. "Thank you for coming over, but I must see about the family now."

"Please," Jennifer reached for Sharon's hand, "you're turning me off without even understanding what's happened to us."

"Perhaps I could call you tonight. Maybe after the president's address."

Jennifer followed her best friend to the door. "Sharon! Say something about my decision!"

"I'm stunned." Sharon opened the door. "Obviously overwhelmed. Please, I need time to sort this business out. I'll just have to call you tonight."

Jennifer looked in dismay at her friend as Sharon shut the door in her face.

Long after the sound of Jennifer's car was gone, Sharon leaned against the front door and stared into the vacant hallway. As the rest of the family watched the bowl game, Sharon stayed by herself. Her world had become a lonely, empty place; the solitude seemed strangely appropriate for this New Year's Day.

The game was in the final minutes when Sharon returned to the family room with a plate of sandwiches. Ruth and Jimmy were still reading.

"Who's winning?" Sharon asked.

Ben blinked in surprise. "I guess I lost track. I'm not sure."

Sharon put the sandwiches on the table. Larry and Ben each reached for one, but Ruth and Jimmy remained oblivious as they continued reading.

"I've just had the most amazing conversation," Sharon finally said. "Jennifer tells me that she and Joe have become Christians. Accepted Jesus and the whole bit!"

Larry's jaw slightly dropped and he froze in place. "You're kidding."

"*Now* my best friend believes in the Rapture." Sharon's smile was clearly artificial. "Seems the world is moving in that direction these days."

Jimmy smiled broadly but said nothing.

"Come on," Ben said. "Jimmy, I know that you've got a lot to say on this subject."

"I don't think now is the right time," Jimmy said timidly. "I'm not interested in pushing my convictions on anyone."

"I know you're trying to be sensitive to us," Ben declared as he reached for another sandwich, "but I'm beginning to think we're the people with a problem. No one has come up with a better explanation for the disappearance of these evaporated people than you have. What if we're missing the boat? It's a really scary thought."

Larry and Sharon stared at each other.

No one answered Ben's question. The winds suddenly picked up, and the family could hear the waves pounding the rocks along the beach. Each listened to the unexpected gale that had come in from the sea. The rumbling was foreboding.

Little was said through the rest of the afternoon. After the game ended, Ruth and Jimmy walked down to the gazebo and watched the boiling sea. As night fell a rainstorm blew in, sending them scurrying back to the house. Once again they returned to their reading. Sharon had disappeared, and the father-and-son chess game was back on. An unusual quietness prevailed throughout the house. The unprecedented presidential address was scheduled to begin immediately after the Orange Bowl. By then the entire family had reassembled around the TV. The afternoon sandwiches were still piled high, and the popcorn bowl had been refilled.

"Should be on in just a minute." Larry swirled his vodka and tonic and drank in large gulps.

Sharon sipped on a Bloody Mary, staring silently at the screen.

"And now, the president of the United States," the announcer said. The emblem of office appeared on the screen as the camera zoomed backward from the podium. Damian Gianardo stepped to the stand and began speaking at once.

"My fellow Americans, we start this new year of 1996

with grave problems confronting us. I am taking the unusual step of speaking on New Year's Day because I am proposing a new, dramatic path to recovery. I want you to sleep well tonight, knowing your president is about to turn our deficits into assets."

Larry laughed. "If Gianardo can turn the current financial collapse around, he'll be the financial Houdini of the second millennium A.D."

"The loss of all those people certainly tore a hole in the economy," Jimmy said thoughtfully.

"Congress has just completed an emergency session that I called two days ago." The president stared into the camera. "All foreign assets have been frozen. We will hold hundreds of billions of dollars in assets for a period of six months. The nations that vote to become states of the U.S. will receive their assets back while the obstinate will lose their holdings."

"What?" Larry came out of his chair. "They can't do such a thing. Every principle of international law is being violated!"

"During the past week, Vice President Jacob Rathmarker and I have also flown secretly to the major capitals of the world with leaders of Congress accompanying us. In secret negotiations, I proposed the creation of a new Roman Empire, resulting in a new world order. Though there was some initial resistance, my explanation of the mutual benefits brought some degree of compliance." Gianardo stopped and smiled wickedly at the screen. "Particularly if they wanted their money back."

"Madness!" Larry pounded his chair. "The world wouldn't stand for such blackmail!"

"As I conclude my address, world leaders will begin explaining the new system to their countries. For example, Japan needs our massive nuclear arsenal and military to protect its interests. Of course, we are the reigning military force in the world. The Japanese want the same representation in Congress as our fifty states. In turn, Japan will be divided into ten new provinces, like our own states. Japanese citizens may keep individual savings and holdings. However, as of today, they will be taxed on their earnings for the past year."

"My gosh!" Ben's eyes widened. "In one stroke, the president has eliminated the national debt. Overnight we will be the strongest financial nation that ever existed. Think what free trade in sixty states will do!"

"The Italians have asked for interesting concessions." The president smiled broadly. "Italy will be divided into five states with Rome becoming the European capital of the United States. When the transition is completed, we will change our national name to the New Roman Empire."

"Can he be serious?" Sharon pushed her drink away and tried to clear her head. "I can't believe my ears."

"My family originally emigrated from Italy." Gianardo continued to smile. "Of course, I've overcome the confusion of my Catholic heritage, but I will find considerable satisfaction in presiding over a Roman-based political system. In addition, our close traditional ties with Great Britain will make an easy transition as we create five new states there. Ultimately, the European Economic Community will see the wisdom of joining us, once they realize the power and prosperity of our new seventy-state union. We will retain the American flag with seventy stars and thirteen stripes.

"Israel and the United Muslim States have some apprehension, fearing we might annex them," the president admitted condescendingly. "Negotiations are under way even now with Babylon, the capital of the Muslim world. Naturally, free trade in oil and similar goods would benefit us greatly while we help the Muslims restore their ancient Babylonian Empire. Once again I have single-handedly re-created history, linking a New Babylonian Empire with a Neo-Roman American government in a confederation of cooperation."

Ben pulled at his father's sleeve. "We could be on easy street overnight. Dad, we've got something to celebrate."

"Regrettably, Israel has not understood its opportunity," the president frowned. "Because I helped negotiate the 1993 peace treaty with Israel, we will honor the terms until the year 2000. However, failure to come into compliance with the New World Order can only further isolate the Israelis."

"We're Jews." Larry glared at his son. "This far-flung scheme of Gianardo's could backfire on *us*. Don't be so jubilant."

"An international computerized banking system will be located in Rome for our central banking system. While the dollar remains current, I propose an exciting breakthrough. Cash will soon no longer be needed across the empire. Credit cards will offer speedy business transactions. You will receive a universal social security number along with our fellow citizens in Japan, Italy, and Great Britain. Laser technology will etch the invisible number on the bones in your right hand. The number can also be placed on the forehead if there is a problem with the hand. The method is painless. You wave at a cash register, and the computer will deduct the purchase from your bank account. A completely fair line of credit will be established based on your record of the past three years. A new chapter in economic history is being written."

Larry shook his head. "Universal identification means the possibility of total surveillance. I don't like any of it."

Gianardo was obviously ecstatic. "As a concession to the United Muslim States, we will be using the ancient Babylonian system for numbering names. Common denominations by 6 will be employed since 6 is the number for humanity. For example, the letter *A* would be equal to 6; *B* equals 12; *C* equals 18; and so forth. Using this system produces a numerical equivalent for my full name of 666. Since I am founding the system, I am asking that all social security numbers be preceded by 666 despite the silly superstitions surrounding that number."

"Jews in the death camps were numbered," Larry said as he sank down into his chair.

President Gianardo shook his fist in the air. "Let us affirm the power of humanity; 666 is a triple way of asserting the capacities of a human race set free from old religious superstitions.

"Now I need your endorsement." The president put his manuscript down, folded his hands, and looked straight into the camera. "Do you want an end to our national debt? I am offering an annual surplus. We have the potential to systematically reduce taxes, but I need your approval since Congress has taken an unusual step of calling for an immediate plebiscite by unique means. Those supporting me can register their vote by dialing 1-900-666-6666. Opponents can call 1-900-777-7777. Phones are ready for your immediate response." Numbers flashed across the screen.

Larry folded his arms over his chest. "No country has the right to freeze another nation's assets. Congress buckled out of fear and intimidation. If this man can pull this coup off, there's nothing that he can't get away with."

Jimmy spoke firmly. "There is no hope if you put your faith in the government or the cleverness of men. The end of all things is at hand."

"What do you suggest?" Ben said.

"I'd begin by listening to what your friends the McCoys have to tell you."

An hour after the presidential address, Sharon called Jennifer. The phone rang only once before Jennifer answered. "I'm afraid you caught me off guard this afternoon," Sharon began.

"Oh, I'm so very, very glad you called. Joe and I talked about you all evening."

"Everywhere I turn," Sharon apologized, "I'm hit in the face with so much change that I guess I don't absorb surprises very well anymore. Your announcement was . . . well . . . very unexpected."

"Joe and I have so much we want to share with you. We're not trying to be pushy, but we've found out some incredible facts that you and Larry just have to hear."

"We'd like to get together. Larry wants to know what's happening in your lives."

"Wonderful!" Jennifer sounded relieved. "Since we started studying the Bible today, a whole new world has opened. Along with what we heard last night, we're beginning to make sense out of the craziness going on."

"I'm glad somebody is! That presidential address was another sample of major distraction."

"Sharon, that is *exactly* why we've got to talk immediately. Joe and I were stunned tonight. Did you know that over nineteen hundred years ago the book of Revelation predicted that a world ruler would survive a mortal head wound and the numerical value of his name would add up to 666?"

"What?" Sharon nearly dropped the receiver. "It said 666?" Her voice trailed away.

"Joe spilled coffee everywhere when Gianardo announced that number this evening. But that's just the start."

"There's more?" Sharon leaned against the wall and then slid down to the floor.

"This world dictator will ride on a white horse, implying that the world will see him as a hero, winning battles without bloodshed. Do you know what the president has named Air Force One?"

"No."

"Look at the morning paper. Gianardo has dubbed his private jet *The White Horse*."

"Good grief!" Sharon stared at the floor as she brought her knees up to her chest.

"At the New Year's Eve party we heard something else that we had a hard time accepting until this evening. Prophecy says that first three nations and then seven more nations will join this world ruler before a great war starts, probably between Russia and Israel. Worldwide famines and environmental disasters will occur, then a terrible battle will eventually follow at a place in Israel called Megiddo, or Armageddon. Tonight the President of the United States put that scenario into motion."

Sharon didn't answer for several moments. "You've got to be making this up."

"The teacher at the party taught us that this despot would come from a 'little horn,' a Hebrew expression implying a young country. Do you know of any other nation that came out of the original Roman Empire that is young but ours?"

"Jennifer, I've never heard any of what you are telling me in my entire life."

"I hadn't either." Jennifer laughed nervously. "But here's the clincher. According to the book of Daniel, exactly 1,290 days before the Messiah returns to earth to establish His kingdom, the world ruler will stop Israeli sacrifices. Then 1,260 days before Jesus returns, the world ruler will enter the rebuilt temple of Solomon and declare himself to be sort of a god. Then he will immediately start a worldwide holocaust against both Christians and Jews."

"No one could do such a thing!" Sharon protested.

"Think not?" Jennifer answered cynically. "The whole world is lining up behind Gianardo. Look how Congress has turned over like a bunch of puppy dogs. This man can do anything he wants."

Larry's words just an hour earlier came back to Sharon. *If this man can pull this coup off, there's nothing that he can't get away with.* Sharon cleared her throat. "Yes, we must talk immediately. I can see why the party affected you like it did."

"Tomorrow?" Jennifer pushed. "OK?"

"We're booked for the next two days. How about three nights from now?"

"I don't see why not. And invite your whole family . . . Ruth's boyfriend . . . Everyone needs to hear."

☐　☐　☐

The next morning Larry and Sharon knew the news report would clarify the scope of the president's power. Sharon quietly set the box of whole grain cereal next to Larry's favorite coffee mug.

"You're OK?" Larry asked his predictable first question of the day.

"Yes, thank you," Sharon answered as she had each morning for the past twenty-five years. "Coffee?"

"Please," Larry automatically answered while turning on the TV. They sat together at the breakfast bar watching the news.

"The 'morning after' polls indicate that 88 percent of the American public are strongly behind the president's plan for world realignment." The announcer spoke in clipped tones. "Most world leaders report a similar firm backing of the plan in their countries."

As the TV cameras zoomed from nation to nation, there were only small, sporadic protests and demonstrations. The world had simply acquiesced to Gianardo's demands. Fear of America's enormous nuclear and economic powers brought about the effect Gianardo hoped for.

"Never!" Larry shook his head. "Never would I have believed that people would quietly accept what we heard last night. I see no hope for us."

During the next two days, little was said about the fast-moving events breaking in the news. Politicians scurried and parliaments voted. The New Roman Empire was becoming a reality with the speed of a fax machine. An impending sense of doom made it difficult for the Feinbergs to make small talk, and emotional uncertainty made anything else too ponderous to discuss.

The following morning Larry and Sharon once again began their morning rituals.

"You're OK?" Larry remarked perfunctorily.

"Yes, thank you," Sharon answered mechanically. "Coffee?" Sharon held the coffee pot over Larry's personal mug.

"Please," he answered while turning the TV to the usual news channel. Another day began in the never-varying manner of the Feinbergs.

"The presidential press secretary has just released the following information," the announcer read from a script in front of him. "Seven additional European nations have petitioned for membership in the New Roman Empire. Germany, France, Greece, Spain, Portugal, Croatia, and Switzerland are seeking inclusion on the same basis that Japan, Italy, and Great Britain entered. National identities will be preserved while nations become states. English will be the primary language, and each nation will embrace the 666 financial system."

The color left Larry's face. He pushed his coffee mug away.

"The former government of the United States will have control of the newly structured Senate," the announcer continued. "Future presidents must arise from within the geographic boundaries of the former U.S. Previous oil agreements that President Gianardo negotiated with the United Muslim States will guarantee abundant oil supplies for the new international alignment."

"Not a shot was fired," Larry turned to Sharon. "Not a bomb was dropped, and the world was quietly taken by storm. Silently, they marched off to the trains waiting to make the journey to the death camps."

Sharon took his hand. "Our house appears to be built on top of the San Andreas Fault."

"Yes. We seem to be sliding toward an abyss with no rescue in sight. I wonder what our ancestors said at the moment when they stood on the edge."

"I think they would have prayed, Larry."

"Unfortunately, they were better at it than we are. What time are the McCoys coming?"

"About 7:30. The kids will be here as well."

"We must listen well tonight."

The two families gathered in the Feinbergs' living room. In contrast to the cozy warmth of the den, the large room was quite formal. Expensive antiques were interspersed with classic furniture with carved arms and legs. A large oil painting of a castle on the Rhine River was the prominent wall hanging. The McCoys sat down on an expansive silk brocade-covered couch.

For the first hour Joe and Jennifer talked without interruption about their newfound conviction that Jesus of Nazareth was the Messiah. Then they handed out a printed sheet listing the prophecies fulfilled in the first coming of the Messiah. On the back was a list of Scriptures yet to be fulfilled.

"You can see that many of these yet-to-be-completed prophecies are being fulfilled right before our eyes." Joe pointed to key verses describing the Antichrist. "The Bible is the only information we have that can make sense out of what we're watching on our own televisions."

"We believe the next major event will happen this summer on July 25," Jennifer continued. "If the next phase begins on this day, there will be no question that we are racing toward the Great Tribulation at breakneck speed."

"You are exactly right," Jimmy broke in. "My reading clarifies that July 25 will be the ninth of Av, the next Jewish holiday."

"Jewish holiday?" Larry frowned. "I've never heard of a summer holiday."

"The Feast of Tisha Be-Av," Jimmy confirmed.

"Never heard of it," Larry sounded condescending.

"I have!" Sharon corrected her husband. "I'd forgotten about Tisha Be-Av, but my father kept the day. Solomon's temple was burned by the Babylonians on Av 9 in 587 B.C."

"Really?" Larry's eyes widened.

"Few days in Jewish history have been as significant as this one," Jimmy continued. "My father was big on the meaning of this holiday."

Joe slid to the edge of his chair. "Centuries before the temple fell, the twelve spies sneaked into Canaan and returned in terror on Av 9. Their faithlessness caused another forty years of wandering in the wilderness."

Jimmy smiled knowingly. "Titus and the Roman legion destroyed the second temple in A.D. 70 on Av 9. A year later the Romans plowed Jerusalem under on the same day."

"I've been reading Jimmy's books," Ruth joined in. "Because Reverend Harrison underlined so much, it's easy for me to get the high points. Simeon Bar Kochba led the last Jewish uprising against Rome, and his army was destroyed on Av 9, 135. Here, Dad, look for yourself." Ruth handed a book to her father.

Larry turned uncomfortably in his chair. "Are you sure that your information is correct?" he mumbled.

Jimmy opened his Bible on the table. "We've barely scratched the surface. On July 18, 1290, England expelled all its Jews on this same day. France expelled all its Jews in 1306 on Av 9, and later Spain repeated the same injustice on Av 9. Anyone want to guess what year that was?"

"It was 1492," Ben immediately answered.

"Exactly," Jimmy confirmed. "The year Columbus left Spain, the Spanish Empire expelled eight hundred thousand Jews by August 2. Anyone want to guess what day August 2 coincides with on the Jewish calendar?"

Larry shook his head. "Av 9."

Jennifer continued, "Our Bible teacher taught us that World War I and Russia's renewed killing of Jews began on August 9, 1914. Want to guess what day that was?"

"I don't need to," Sharon answered. "My great-grandparents were driven from their village in eastern Russia on Av 9."

"And Hitler and his henchmen made their final plans to kill Jews worldwide on Av 9, 1942," Jimmy added.

"Do you have any idea of the mathematical chances of such a thing occurring?" Joe asked. "Numbers are my world, since I am an accountant. I'd guess that the odds are about 1 in 265 to the eighth power. Literally 1 chance in 863 zillion . . . 863 with 15 zeros after it!"

"Feels like the twilight zone, doesn't it?" Ruth added.

Larry breathed deeply and rubbed his temples. "The whole business is scary, but then everything else in the world is rather terrifying right now."

"Larry . . . Sharon." Jennifer held her hands out. "When we put all the numbers together, the first thing we thought of was your family. Jews haven't fared very well on Av 9. We love you and want to make sure that nothing bad happens this year. We are ready to protect your family from any form of anti-Semitism."

"This page mentions a war with Israel," Larry gestured feebly. "Russia, it says. This book speculates it may happen on the ninth of Av of 1996, which would fall on July 25 this year."

Jimmy opened his Bible to Ezekiel, chapters 38 and 39. "The description of the fall of Russia sounds like a great explosion of fire and brimstone. We know Israel has atomic capacity. We can't discount the possibility."

"We don't know what's ahead," Jennifer pleaded, "but we are your friends. We want you to do everything possible to get ready. You need to study this matter thoroughly in the days ahead. If we're wrong, then write us off as kooks. But if we're not, this is the most important issue in your lives."

"Ben, you're a college math expert." Jimmy pulled a piece of paper out of his Bible and unfolded it on the table. "We worked out these numbers in our Bible study last night. Israel was in captivity in Egypt for 430 years before the Exodus. Turn to Ezekiel 4:4–6 and note what God had the prophet do. He lay on his side for 430 days to signify that Israel would be in another exile for that length of time because of her sins. Jeremiah predicted seventy of those years would be in Babylon from 606 to 536 B.C. Right?"

"I don't get the point." Ben shrugged.

"Watch this!" Jimmy wrote Nisan 1, 536 B.C., on the paper. "That's the date the Jews should have returned from the Babylonian exile when Cyrus released them. Unfortunately, most didn't come back, and that displeased God. Because of their lack of repentance, their punishment was multiplied sevenfold, as Moses had warned it would be in the Torah in Leviticus 26. Sounds strange until you add it to Nisan 1, 536 B.C."

Jimmy wrote out the answer. "I'm going to translate this into the modern calendar." He held the paper. "Anybody recognize the significance of this date?"

"May 14, 1948," Larry sputtered.

"The date modern Israel was born!" Sharon's mouth dropped.

"Precisely," Jimmy said.

"Can you understand why we made our decision for Jesus?" Joe asked quietly.

"I pride myself on being a scientist," Larry answered. "I have to take facts seriously. It's all coming so quickly. I just don't know. I feel like I've been hit by an avalanche. I just can't put it all together this fast. I guess I need some time to think the whole matter through."

"Of course," Joe answered. "Why not study all of the predictions that were fulfilled in the coming of Jesus? They will give you a sense of perspective."

"We want you to know that we are with you no matter what," Jennifer added.

"Thank you." Larry stood. "I'm sure we'll give this entire matter our undivided attention."

Ben offered his hand to Jimmy. "You've been studying a lot more than the *Blue Book* on used cars lately. A lot more."

"There's much more at stake," Jimmy answered. "Money's one thing. Eternity is another."

For years I had studiously observed the Feinberg family. Angels cannot read human minds, but we are very perceptive about what is in people's eyes, the door to the soul. Having practiced for centuries, we can detect the subtlest changes of thought and motivation. Near the end of the twentieth century, many Americans registered duplicity in their faces. Mouths said one thing while eyes conveyed another.

The Feinbergs began to recover facial coordination when they started saying what they meant. Once the family began to suspect they might have lost their souls somewhere along the way, they began to make progress. Naturally, one would expect congruency from Larry, the psychiatrist, but his problem was not confused emotions. The issue was the state of Larry's soul.

Angels are inevitably entertained with human consternation when people begin to discover the obvious. The Feinbergs were no less amusing. Joe and Jennifer McCoy came to their home on a weekly basis, and Jimmy began feeling the freedom to talk openly about his discoveries. Larry seemed to think he was making unparalleled breakthroughs as he synthesized what had been undisguised forever. From an angelic perspective, things were moving right along.

However, Larry and Sharon had an unspoken tentativeness about final conclusions, pending the coming of Av 9. The Feast of Tisha Be-Av was to arrive on Thursday, July 25. Should Av 9 prove to be a turning point for the world, the Feinbergs knew the day would be the pivotal event in their lives.

That day the bedside alarm went off with irritating electronic precision. Trying to find the off switch without opening his eyes, Larry finally picked up the clock. Once he looked, he knew he couldn't go back to sleep again. The block letters pulsated like the timer on a bomb, THUR.—JULY 25.

"The day," he said as he stared at the ceiling. Sharon reached for his hand.

After showering and dressing, Larry hurried down to the kitchen. Whole grain cereal was already sitting next to his favorite mug.

"You're OK?" Larry routinely asked.

"No," Sharon broke the two-decades-old pattern. "I'm not."

Larry looked at her really for the first time that day. "I love you," he said. They sat down together as he turned the TV on. The coffee pot remained on the stove.

The black screen exploded with color. Soldiers on horseback were riding over rough terrain.

"Last night's report of large-scale movements of Russian troops on horseback now makes sense," the reporter said. "Continuing economic troubles apparently have some bearing on this unusual approach of horse brigades for combat. At this hour Russian troops are in control of the mountains of Lebanon and are bearing down on the state of Israel."

"It's happening!" Larry leaned toward the television.

Columns of troops lumbered down a dusty road. "Libya and Iran have dropped paratroopers on Israel," the reporter continued. "Ethiopian soldiers are reported moving toward Jerusalem at this hour."

An anchorman appeared on the screen. "The State Department is now releasing its assessment of this attack. New hard-liner Russian President Ivan Smirkoff apparently concluded that the current anti-Israeli sentiment would permit a quick strike. Using allies in Iran, Libya, and Ethiopia, Russia evidently had designs on Israel's new oil and gold discoveries. However, world leaders are now expressing their shock. The report of the sudden and unexpected invasion is rocking capitals around the world. The responses point to a serious miscalculation on the part of the invaders. We switch you now to a live statement by President Gianardo, who went to Spain two days ago for unexplained consultations with European leaders."

"Spain!" Sharon gasped. "Oh, no!"

"Fits exactly what Jimmy said." Larry's eyes widened. "He said that Ezekiel predicted that the people of Tarshish or Spain would be surprised."

"And five-sixths of the Russian army will disappear in fire!" Sharon put both hands to her cheeks. "We have already studied what the reporters are going to tell us."

The camera cut away to President Damian Gianardo surrounded by European leaders. "From Barcelona, Spain, a live statement from the President of the New Roman Empire."

"We are outraged at the outbreak of war." Gianardo jutted his chin out as he spoke defiantly. He stood before microphones in a large ballroom of a castle. "We are asking all parties to cease before Israel responds with its quite sophisticated nuclear capacities. While Russia still has some nuclear armaments, we do not want to have an unnecessary exchange from the New Roman Empire." Behind the president, large paintings adorned the wood-paneled walls. "We must honor our treaty with Israel if help is requested. However, at this time, Israel seems quite confident of standing alone. If necessary, we are ready to join with the Israelis in this unprecedented violation of their territorial rights. I will keep you informed as developments progress."

"Get that paper . . . that prophecy sheet . . . the one Joe gave us." Larry shook his head in disbelief. "I'll find a Bible. Hurry."

Sharon grabbed the list of Scriptures and ran back to the kitchen just as Larry found a Bible at the bottom of the bookcase. She pulled her silk bathrobe more tightly around her. Immediately, he looked for the index.

"Chapters 38 and 39 in Ezekiel are supposed to say something about the Russians," Sharon read from the Scripture list. "Look at verse 13 in chapter 38."

Larry read slowly. "Says the people in Tarshish will be surprised all right."

"That's Spain?" Sharon read over his shoulder. Sunlight streamed in on her face, making it look washed out. "Right?"

"The Bible says that Israel will take seven months to bury all the dead Russian soldiers." Larry thumbed the pages. "Let's try this part from the prophet Joel."

Sharon put her finger on the page and started reading, "I will remove far from you the northern army, and will drive him away into a barren and desolate land, with his face toward the eastern sea and his back toward the western sea . . ."

"That description would fit the Dead Sea and the Mediterranean Sea perfectly," Larry interjected.

"His stench will come up, and his foul odor will rise, because he has done monstrous things," Sharon kept reading.

"All Israel would have to do," said Larry as he looked up at the ceiling, "would be to nuke them and leave their radioactive bodies to decay, then this twenty-six-hundred-year-old prophecy will be fulfilled."

"And who's the father of that weapon?" Sharon slowly sank down in a kitchen chair. "A Jew! Albert Einstein! Larry, everything fits."

"We heard every bit of today's headlines last night. Today is the ninth of Av, right on schedule."

"What can we do?" Sharon clutched her husband's arm. "We must do something."

Larry searched Sharon's face, his eyes darting back and forth. "I really don't know how . . . but I think we need to pray."

"You start," Sharon pleaded. "I'll just repeat silently whatever you say."

Larry lowered his head into his hands and closed his eyes. *"Shama Yisrael,"* he recited the words he had heard at the synagogue as a boy, *"Adonai eloheunu Adonai echad.* God of our fathers Abraham, Isaac, and Jacob, please hear us today. Whoever You are, I believe in You. Forgive my arrogance in ignoring You. Please forgive my stupidity in failing to recognize You. I must believe that You intervene in history and that You are sovereign over all things. Whoever You are, please make Yourself known to us."

"Yes," Sharon said softly.

"If Jesus is the Messiah, please show us what to believe. Even if I don't like the truth, I want to see it before my eyes. Help us to know how to help our fellow Jews in Israel. Please help us find our way out of this confusion. Amen." Larry blinked his eyes but didn't move.

"Do you think He heard us?"

"We shall see," Larry sounded weary. "We shall see."

"Why don't you call the office and tell them you will be late?" Sharon suggested. "I think we ought to wake up the kids and talk to them."

"Definitely." After making the phone call, Larry summoned their children to the kitchen. Both slipped on terry cloth bathrobes but stood with bare feet. Ben and Ruth watched the TV in amazement as Larry and Sharon read the passages from Ezekiel and Joel.

"It all fits," Sharon kept saying.

"Just like Jimmy said." Ben stared sleepy-eyed at the CNN report of troops riding out of the Lebanon Mountains toward Israel. "The Russians must be in such bad financial shape that they've gone back to World War I tactics."

"And the Bible really predicted this," Ruth said. She reached for the book and read the passage again.

"Jimmy's been right about everything," Ben told his sister. "I have to give him his due."

"Look up the Isaiah part," Sharon told Ruth. "We need to study everything on this sheet again. Start with verse 3."

Ruth quickly ran down the index to find the right place. Her fingers thumbed through the pages until she found the fifty-third chapter. She started reading, "He is despised and rejected by men, a man of sorrows and acquainted with grief. And we hid, as it were, our faces from Him; He was despised, and we did not esteem Him. Surely He has borne our griefs and carried our sorrows; yet we esteemed Him stricken, smitten by God, and afflicted. But He was wounded for our transgressions, He was bruised for our iniquities; the chastisement for our peace was upon Him, and by His stripes we are healed. All we like sheep have gone astray; we have turned, every one, to his own way; and the LORD has laid on Him the iniquity of us all."

"Isaiah must have been talking about Jesus." Ben asked, "Is it really possible?"

Larry answered, "Yes, children. We must take this possibility very seriously. This morning your mother and I prayed. I've never done anything like that in my adult life . . . not since my Bar Mitzvah. I want both of you to know that I am asking the Holy One of Israel to guide us . . . all of us . . . into the truth. We have to be more open than we've ever been in our lives."

Sharon added, "Sometimes I've treated Jimmy like a second-class citizen, but for a long time I've had the feeling that he was more important to us than we could ever have guessed. Now we must listen to everything he can tell us."

Ruth looked down at the Bible and nodded.

"Our world was once so routine and predictable."

Ben looked out the window toward the ocean. "Things fit together like an equation and could be anticipated. Now ... ," his voice trailed off, "now nothing fits. I feel like an exile in my own land."

"You've become a Jew again," Larry said poignantly. "In the past the Feinbergs were just another American family chasing the carrot that society dangled in front of their faces. These strange events have made us wander with our father Abraham. We, too, are being called into a strange place of which we know not."

Sharon's eyes filled with tears. "Larry, my father talked like that. You have touched my heart deeply."

"Honey, I'm just struggling. I used to think I was one of the smartest men in the U.S. Now I know that I don't know anything!"

"Never have I been as proud of you nor have you ever been as much a sage as this morning." Sharon kissed her husband's cheek.

"Dad?" Ben bit his lip. "I'm going to pray like you did. I'm going to ask God to show me what is real and true."

"Do you want us to pray with you, Son?" Sharon asked pensively.

"No," Ben withdrew. "I think this is something that I must do by myself. The whole business is too personal."

"But we're all in this together." Larry stood up. "Whatever you need we'll do our best to provide. Well, I must go to the office. I know that each of us has many things to do today. Of course, we want to keep up with what's happening in Israel, but I think we know the end of the story."

"I will call you when Israel drops nuclear bombs on them," Ben said resolutely. "Amazing! Yesterday we had no idea what was going on. Now we are waiting with certainty for an explosion."

"In a couple of years we've seen what people prayed centuries for." Ruth stared at the TV. "Only heaven knows what's next!"

□   □   □

The hot July sun beat down as Ben rushed toward the UCLA library with the latest paper under his arm. Cindy was sitting outside on the front steps with her new German shepherd guide dog, Sam, at her feet. Eucalyptus trees swayed in the light breeze. Students walked lazily across the campus.

"Hope you haven't been waiting long." Ben dropped down beside her. "I got held up on the freeway."

Sam sat up. "Par for the course." Cindy reached out for Ben's hand.

"I'm really impressed with your German shepherd. Beautiful dog." Sam looked up casually at Ben but didn't move.

"Very obedient. People don't frighten him at all."

"Well, Cindy, I know Sam will be of tremendous help in going to class.

"I want you to hear what's in the paper." Ben spread out the *Los Angeles Times* before them. "The headlines read 'Russians Vanish in Fireball.' Listen to what the atomic explosion did. Only about a sixth of the Russian army is left after the bomb went off. Many of the survivors rushed toward the Dead Sea, and others ran into the Mediterranean."

"And the earthquake?" Cindy asked. "The big one caused by the explosion?"

"The paper says that the mountains in northern Lebanon shook so badly that the earth cracked open and many Russians were swallowed. They are finished."

"Ben, we've been studying the Scriptures that Joe McCoy gave you. Everything is just as the Bible said it would be. We can't ignore the implications."

"I know. I know." Ben closed the paper. "For the first time in my life I've asked God to show me the truth. I don't want to accept what the McCoys have been telling us, but the handwriting sure seems to be on the wall."

"I've been trying to tell my parents." Cindy patted her

dog on the head. "They listen, but they are more terrified than anything else. Nothing in their background prepares them to understand. Half the time the news report terrifies them, and the Bible lessons I give them leave Mom and Dad in complete consternation the other half. I feel that nothing is like it was."

"Certainly not for the Russians." Ben rolled his eyes. "And not for any of my family either. No one has said it out loud yet, but I think we're all ready to throw in the towel. How can we ignore the meaning of the total defeat of Russia?"

"Ben." Cindy looked toward the sky. Her sightless eyes seemed to be trying to find something she couldn't quite perceive. "I've been trying to pray like the Bible says. I have been ending what I ask in Jesus' name. Very interesting result."

"In what way?"

"I have the strangest sense that Someone is there, that I'm being heard. I think it's working."

"I thought the issue is what we believe. Having the right ideas . . . beliefs."

"Maybe it's much more," Cindy pondered. "What if this whole business is about making contact?"

"That's a new wrinkle."

"Here's another one for you." Cindy smiled mischievously. "I've been having these unusual intuitions. Hunches if you like."

"And? And?"

"I think the issue is even bigger than you've thought. I think that God has something very important for you to do in the days ahead."

Ben jerked. "You've got to be kidding."

Cindy's smile faded, and she became very serious. "I can't tell you why, but I feel a strong inner sense of guidance. You have a special task that God wants you to do."

Ben stared. "Cindy, this is getting way too far-out for me."

"Well, at least think about it. OK?"

Ben stood up. "Can I walk you back to the dormitory? I've got to get to my next class."

"I need to stay here and study for the next hour. I'm going back inside in a few minutes. See you at lunch?"

"Yeah, sure." Ben backed down the stairs. "Lunch at the usual place." He waved and then realized it looked a little foolish to wave at a blind girl. "Lunch," he called one last time, heading for the parking lot.

Their conversation made him nervous. He had expected the fall of the Russians to be confounding, but Cindy's suggestion was far more disconcerting.

"Take her seriously." The voice came from behind him.

Ben spun around and found a very large man standing behind him. His face looked ancient but did not have any wrinkles. The man's eyes looked young, yet they had such intensity Ben found it difficult to look directly at the man's face for more than a few moments. The wisdom of the ages was in his stare. The big man was an odd blend of antiquity and the present moment.

"Who are you?" Ben recoiled.

"Michael," he said. "I am your friend, Ben."

"I don't know you." Ben retreated further toward the street.

"But I know you. I have known you since the day you were born. Do not be afraid. I bring you good tidings."

"What?" Ben squinted. "What are you talking about?"

The man abruptly reached out and squeezed Ben's hand firmly. He stared deeply into his eyes. "You asked for guidance. Do not be afraid to receive it."

Ben pulled away from the all-revealing stare. Impulsively, he started running down the sidewalk. When he looked back, the man was gone.

Cindy was still sitting on the library steps when Ben came running back. She listened to the approaching footsteps. Her guide dog looked intensely up the sidewalk and barked. "Ben? Ben, that's you? Back so soon?"

"Cindy," he panted, "I just had the living daylights scared out of me. A big guy ... a strange man appeared out of nowhere. And then he was gone. Disappeared."

"What are you talking about?"

"The guy said he'd known me all my life. I swear I've never seen him before. Maybe I really am going nuts."

Cindy tilted her head and turned her ear toward him. "You're serious. This man really did frighten you."

"He called himself Michael."

"Michael? I know a Michael. Did he have an unusually deep bass voice?"

"Why, yes. Exactly."

"Talk sort of strange?"

"Yes, yes. You've seen him?"

Cindy laughed. "Not hardly. But I have met Michael on a number of occasions. I always thought he was a student. Sort of shows up at very opportune moments."

"Listen, Cindy. This guy is big. Strange. Terrifying."

"Come now, Ben. I've always found him to be extremely considerate."

"You know anything about him?" Ben sounded skeptical.

"Actually nothing. When I've tried to ask questions, he changes the subject. Certainly, he's been no problem. Really, Michael has a knack for appearing when I really need help."

"It was almost like the Rapture experience." Ben ran his hands through his hair. "One minute he was there; the next he was gone. I think I'm getting an overload. Too much happening for me to absorb." Ben looked around the steps and bushes. "I'll see you at noon." He kept glancing over his shoulder as he backed away. "See you at lunch."

"Ben ... ," Cindy called after him, but he kept trotting toward his car.

11

Through the rest of the summer, the headlines were filled with stories of the cataclysmic results of the defeat of the Russians. Their radioactive bodies and the consequent contamination completely fulfilled the predictions of Scripture. Momentarily dumbfounded, most of the world population went on their way without any awareness of the significance of the event. Such was not the case in the Feinberg household.

As the first weeks of September slipped past, I knew that it was time for me to act decisively. The hour had come for direct contact with Ben and Cindy. My assignment was clear. Once again human beings needed an annunciation to prepare for a critical task in the eternal plan. As always, I chose a day dear to the heart of the Father.

I watched Ben walk toward Cindy's dormitory. Cindy was sitting on a bench in front of the dorm with Sam lying at her feet. The German shepherd perked up his ears when he heard the leaves crunch beneath Ben's feet. "Hey, I'm here," Ben called out.

"My hero cometh." Cindy beamed. "Big day for you!"

"Huh?" Ben puzzled. "I don't think I have any examinations today."

"Come on," Cindy chided. "You're not paying attention to the calendar. A girl down the hall is Jewish. She said today's Yom Kippur, the Day of Atonement. Your big day for repentance."

"September 23! I forgot all about it!"

"Naughty boy," Cindy teased. "Now you will have to make double confession."

"Wow!" Ben slapped his forehead. "All the strange things started happening a year ago on Rosh Hashanah. I should have paid more attention to the calendar! Interventions seem to come on Jewish holidays."

"Yom Kippur is a time for getting right with God?"

"Something like that, Cindy. Unfortunately, we didn't pay much attention to our traditions."

Like an actor hearing his cue from backstage, I slipped into the scene from behind the veil of time as only an angel can do. "There are times and seasons appointed for all things," I spoke from behind Ben. Sam barked.

"What?" Cindy turned her head. Sam looked nonchalantly toward the sound.

"You!" Ben jerked.

"These days are your special times," I said.

"Michael?" Cindy asked. "Is that you?" Sam wagged his tail.

"Where did you come from?" Ben stared. "You weren't there a moment ago."

"You are very important people." I stood beside them. "I am honored to be a comrade." Cindy reached for my hand. Her grip was gentle but firm.

Ben was shaking slightly. "Look! We haven't done anything to you. What do you want with us?"

"The issue is what I can do *for* you." I kept smiling. "You are part of a great plan, and I will help you execute your part."

"Why do you keep coming and going?" Cindy asked.

"I have special work to do."

"Who do you work for?" Ben held up his hands defensively. "You're an extraterrestrial? A spaceman?"

"I come from the center of reality itself, but I know

your world exceedingly well, Ben. I have been watching your people from the beginning."

"My people?"

"Are you Jewish?" Cindy asked.

"No. But I do work for a Jewish carpenter." With that I stepped back into eternity and disappeared from their view.

Cindy's fingers around my hand collapsed upon themselves. "He's gone!" Cindy exclaimed before Ben could react.

"My gosh!" Ben choked.

"Where did he go?" Cindy groped around her.

"Right before my eyes! Boom!" Ben stared at the empty sidewalk.

"Ben, we're not crazy. This isn't a hallucination. Michael *was here!*"

"Let me sit down." Ben started walking backward. "Anywhere. Just sit down . . . for a few minutes." He dropped down on the bench. "I must get myself together."

"He wasn't some outer space movie character," Cindy reassured Ben. "When Michael talked, I felt great peace. He said very good things to us."

"I guess so."

"Ben, we were Buddhist before our family came here, but I've been reading my Bible. I know enough to understand what it means to say a 'Jewish carpenter' is Michael's boss."

"What are you driving at?"

"In the Bible there is another person named Michael. I don't know if this guy is the same one or what . . . but I do know that the Michael in the Bible was an angel."

"An angel!" Ben sputtered.

"Well," Cindy held up her hands and shrugged her shoulders, "it makes a lot more sense than spaceman talk."

"An . . . an angel?"

"I read one place in the Bible where it said that many

people had entertained angels unaware." Cindy sounded defensive. "Why not?"

"Listen!" Ben took her hand. "I'm not putting anything down these days. It's just such a mind-boggling idea . . . as if everything else in this past year has been normal."

"Working for a Jewish carpenter?" Cindy beamed. "He had to mean Jesus. The whole thing fits together."

Ben ran his fingers through his hair. "Maybe we're both getting caught up in a psychotic mass hysteria sweeping the country after all of the strange experiences. Maybe—"

"Stop it," Cindy said firmly. "I'm not crazy, Ben, and neither are you. Maybe my blindness is an asset. I have to depend on far more than my eyes to make sense out of things. I know that we have been talking to a real person regardless of how he comes and goes. Let's be scientific about this encounter. If Michael is for real, he'll be back. If he is an angel, Michael wants the best for us."

"How in the world can we set up an experiment with an angel?"

"Doesn't Michael seem to show up around Jewish holidays?"

Ben rubbed his chin and bit his lip. "Seems so," he said reluctantly.

"When's the next special day? Come on, Ben. You're the Jew."

"I think," Ben said slowly, "yes, it's the Feast of Tabernacles! I would have to check, but it's probably coming in a week or less."

"Let's have a date that night!" Cindy's consternation turned to enthusiasm. "If we're on to something, we ought to be able to make contact with Michael then!"

"If I told my father about this, he'd think I'd gone nuts! For heaven's sake, don't let anyone know."

"It's our secret." Cindy reached over and hugged Ben.

As a matter of fact, the Feast of Tabernacles fell on Saturday, September 28, five days later. During the week, Ben stewed like a character in an Edgar Allan Poe short story. The words *Jewish carpenter* rolled around in his head with disconcerting frequency. Ben's few developing religious convictions were shaken further. I could not wait for the big evening. I had not had this much fun since I watched John the Baptist's father try to get his voice back.

Ben did not think taking Cindy to a Chinese restaurant was quite the appropriate thing to suggest. They ended up eating at a little corner pizza place two blocks down from the young woman's dormitory, and talking. Ben had not yet realized that conversation with Cindy was the most natural thing in his world.

The corner hangout was a popular UCLA landmark. The walls were adorned with pictures of football triumphs from the past. They laughed, kidded, and joked through a large pizza and endless refills of colas. As the evening passed, other collegians came and went. A couple of students sat in booths studying as if the endless noise and chatter did not exist.

"I guess our little experiment failed," Cindy finally said. "But the evening has still been the best of my life."

Many times that evening, Ben had looked carefully at her. He did not turn from her sightless eyes in the self-conscious way he usually did. Ben's gaze swept across Cindy's lovely olive colored skin and beautifully contoured face.

"You're the most beautiful girl I've ever seen in my life."

Cindy's cheeks turned pink, and she lowered her head.

"I've never known anyone like you." Ben's voice was

filled with emotion. "I don't want to ever be away from you, Cindy."

"We . . . ah . . . better go." Cindy's voice became softer and lower.

"Don't retreat from me." Ben took her hand. "Don't hide from me."

"Please," Cindy's voice cracked, "don't toy with me. I am a very lonely person, Ben. I've learned to accept the fact, but I can't live with false expectations. It would be too painful."

"Oh, Cindy!" Ben took her hand in both of his. "I only want to fill your life with happiness. I would never mislead or use you."

Cindy nodded her head as a tear ran down her cheek.

"You make me very happy." Ben leaned over and kissed her tenderly on her hand. "You can trust me."

"May . . . maybe we should go," Cindy sniffed.

"Yeah," Ben said. "I'm starting to sound like someone on 'As the World Turns.'"

Laughing, they walked out of the restaurant arm in arm. Sam trotted along beside Cindy. Obviously, their preoccupation with each other had pushed thoughts of me completely out of the picture. The timing was perfect for reentry. I watched them walk back to the dorm. Ben stopped behind a tree near the door to the dorm and kissed Cindy forcefully.

"You turned out to be my angel tonight, Ben." Cindy ran her hand down the side of his face.

"You really got shortchanged!" He kissed her again.

This time, I decided that I would at least give a hint before I appeared. I chose a spot about ten feet away to begin walking into time and toward them. Sam immediately picked up the sound and barked.

"Someone there?" Cindy called out.

"*Shalom*," I answered.

"It's you!" Ben gasped.

"*Shalom Alecheim*," I responded.

"You did come!" Cindy clapped her hands. "I was right! You are an angel!"

"No." Ben shook his head. "I refuse to believe my own eyes."

"I want you to meet a friend of mine someday." I sounded sincere and serious. "You will enjoy Thomas. He had a problem similar to yours."

"Why are you here?" Cindy was nearly dancing with glee.

"This is a hoax!" Ben was predictably defensive. "You're a fraternity prank. I know it!"

"My Master has a wonderful sense of humor, but I assure you that my reasons for following you are very serious. In fact, it has been my total preoccupation since the day you were conceived."

"Then you ought to know everything about us," Ben said critically. "You should be able to answer questions that no one can know anything about."

"Sure," I answered smugly. "Want to try me?"

"What was my favorite toy as a child?" Ben crossed his arms over his chest.

"You expect me to say a football," I said. "You worked hard at convincing everyone you were going to be an athlete because you knew that would please your father. However, your favorite toy was the stuffed bear you secretly slept with until you were well into grade school."

Ben turned white and his mouth fell open. His arms dropped listless at his sides.

"Good question but not too tough. Cindy, got a really difficult request for me?"

Cindy thought a moment. She was obviously enjoying what was terrifying Ben. "I once had a family keepsake locket that I lost. It was my mother's, and she was very upset when I couldn't find her treasure. It's been years ago, but I would like to have it back. Do you know where it is?"

"Your parents had just started the Golden Dragon, and you helped them put napkins in the holders. You were quite small. Remember?"

Cindy nodded enthusiastically.

"You reached out to find more napkins in the storage cabinet but could not touch anything. When you stretched forward, the necklace fell down inside the cabinet and through a crack in the bottom. If you will move the cabinet, the treasure will be on the floor underneath."

"Wonderful! Wonderful!" Cindy clapped.

"Can you . . . can you read our minds?" Ben's eyes were filled with fear.

"I am your best friend, Ben. You do not have to worry. No, I cannot read your mind. Angels do not do that sort of thing, but we can affect the way you see things. You might say that we influence you for the best. We nudge you in the right direction."

"Please help us." Cindy reached for my hand. "We want to believe the right things. We just can't sort it all out. If you work for a Jewish carpenter, then you must know the truth about who Jesus was."

"Was?" I smiled. "Try 'is.' Ready to find out, Ben?" I watched his eyes. He could only nod.

"His Hebrew name is Yeshua. That's what we all call Him in heaven. Angels know that He always existed. The fullness of God was pleased to dwell bodily in Him. When He died on the cross, He had both of you in mind. He has a most special plan for your lives and has sent me to help you find your place in that destiny."

"This is why you have appeared to us?" Ben asked weakly.

"I have important secrets that I cannot yet fully disclose, but the hour is coming. You will not see me again until Passover of 1997, but I will be guiding you toward the time."

"What are we to do now?" Cindy reached out for my hand.

I clasped Cindy's warm palm tenderly. "Keep yourselves pure. Love each other profoundly but chastely. In the days ahead you will need great moral strength."

"Hard time coming?" Ben asked meekly.

"Pasch, 1997, will be a terrible day for the descendants of Abraham. Cindy, your life will be spent well, and Ben, you shall see the glory of the Lord revealed. Learn now what the love of Yeshua offers, for His love will be your salvation."

I held up my hand in a blessing and then was gone.

Ben and Cindy began to weep. They held each other and swayed back and forth as the darkness of the night settled over them. Periodically, they said something, but most of the time, they huddled together in silence.

Finally, Ben said, "I think I want to pray. I've never really done that . . . I mean in a personal way."

"Me too. You say the words and I'll follow."

"Jesus . . . Yeshua, we're still very confused, but we must place our faith in You. We want to believe the right things and get ready for whatever is ahead. Thank You for sending Michael to warn us. I know I've done a lot of selfish things, and I need Your help. Please forgive me where I've messed up in the past . . . today . . . in the future. Thank You for remembering us on Your cross. We now offer You our lives."

After a long silence, Cindy said, "Amen. Thank You, Yeshua."

12

New Year's Day, 1997

Whator angel couldn't resist a quiet walk
along the beach on a winter morning in southern California? The salty mist sweeps in from the sea, and the
pale blue sky's reflection bounces off the tides gently
rolling up the sandy shore. The tranquil ocean deceptively makes a swim seem plausible even for this time
of the year, but the chilly nip in the air restores perspective. The towering palm trees seem to stand aloof,
drinking in the promise of the day and the year ahead.

The winds rolled off the ocean toward the Feinbergs'
home. There was no need for a fire in the den fireplace
with the sunny, seventy-two-degree weather, but Larry
felt the flames in their large stone fireplace were a necessary part of the holidays.

"Great to have Jimmy and Cindy with us today,"
Larry said casually as he stoked the fire.

"Jimmy's gotten to be a real old-timer at these annual
family gatherings," Ben chided. "He's got the day's routine down pat."

"We'll have to break Cindy in," Jimmy acknowledged.
We're so glad you're here, Cindy."

"Thank you, Mrs. Feinberg."

"Just call me Sharon. After all, anyone who goes around with my son talking to angels shouldn't be on a formal basis with us."

"If anyone but you had come up with that story, Ben," Jimmy grinned, "I would have bet money the whole thing was a hoax. But when skeptics like you start seeing angels, I know the heavens are about to split open."

"Hey, don't put any stuff on me," Ben rolled his eyes. "You started us down this road with all that prophecy talk you got from your father's books."

"What can I say?" Jimmy laughed. "The more I studied, the more it all came into focus. Just look at all the world history we've watched unfold sitting here staring at your TV. The New Roman Empire, the Russian-Israeli one-day war, the events of Av 9 . . . all were predicted centuries ago."

"I have to admit it," Ben acknowledged. "I came kicking and screaming. The Bible predictions just seemed impossible to swallow."

"Oh, I understand!" Jimmy raised his eyebrows. "Bible prophecy can be very confusing, but once a few pieces fall into place, we can really begin to see where the future is going. We have to remember the different ways in which the Bible calculates time. One thousand human years are but as a day to the Lord. Sometimes a day in the Bible can mean a twenty-four-hour period. Sometimes it is a 360-day prophetic year or even a one-thousand-year period of time. The main thing is to believe that our heavenly Father truly communicates with us and that the Bible is His inspired Word."

"Yes," Larry said softly, "that's what's important. We must believe that God wants to speak to us."

"I've got a hunch we may discover that we've never had a year like the one that's ahead of us," Ben added soberly. "Our guardian angel Michael gave us a stiff warning."

"Wait a minute," Jimmy frowned. "You didn't mention any problems before."

"Perhaps the whole experience was so overwhelming that I've only given it to you in bits and pieces, Jimmy. Yes, on Passover, 1997, Michael said a terrible day would occur in the history of the descendants of Abraham."

The expression on Jimmy's face went flat. "My Bible study group has been studying *exactly* this same possibility. I can't believe what you're telling me. It really fits."

"Fits?" Larry puzzled. "I take everything seriously these days. What fits?"

"What we believe the Bible says," Jimmy spoke deliberately, "is to expect on Passover of this year a repeat performance of what Antiochus Epiphanes did in 168 B.C."

"That's what started the Maccabean rebellion!" Sharon exclaimed. "The temple was defiled and the holy place desecrated."

Jimmy nodded his head and began to speak forcefully. "As bizarre as it may sound, we are convinced that President Damian Gianardo will stop sacrifices somehow on Purim, March 23. Thirty days later, Gianardo will go to Jerusalem, enter the newly constructed temple on Passover, April 22, and declare that he be worshiped as world emperor. He will try to make himself into the god of this world. A worldwide persecution of both Jews and Christians will follow."

Silence fell over the room.

"We could all be killed," Larry finally spoke. "We must take very seriously what both Ben and Jimmy believe they have heard."

"This all makes Gianardo's special presidential address today even more significant. I can hardly wait to hear what he has to say," Ben added.

"I think we ought to turn on the channel right now," Ruth walked toward the TV. "I usually hate this part of the day, but I think I'll pay very close attention this year." She pushed the on button.

"I think we ought to call the McCoys to come over for the president's speech," Larry told Sharon. "They've been such an important part of this journey. They need to be in on anything we can find out."

"Great idea. I'll call them in the few minutes we have left." Sharon reached for the phone.

"If we're right," Jimmy said, "we'll never have another family gathering like today's until Jesus returns."

Larry listened carefully. "What does all of this prophecy mean for us, Jimmy?"

"I believe this will be the year that the Great Tribulation begins. I think that staggering events will begin on Passover."

"I have so much to learn," Dr. Feinberg mumbled. "And so little time left."

☐   ☐   ☐

"Thanks for calling us," Joe McCoy said as he sat next to Jennifer. "We were watching the news when you called. It showed horrible scenes of the famine in Russia. Takes a day's pay there to buy a loaf of bread."

"Well, we still have plenty of chips and colas." Ruth came in with a tray piled high.

"Last year was really wild," Jennifer noted. "Makes listening to the president all the more foreboding."

The group became silent as the image of Damian Gianardo filled the screen. Standing behind the podium with the great seal of office, he began speaking immediately.

"My fellow citizens of the New Roman Empire, I have only a few brief remarks because the state of the country is in such excellent condition. Most of you will find it difficult to realize that one short year ago, we were on the verge of collapse. Today we are enjoying unparalleled prosperity.

"This year will prove to be another time of continued growth of the gross national product. My new welfare system has provided housing and government jobs for anyone who is unemployed or homeless. The many unclaimed houses and buildings left by their vanished owners have been turned into property for the homeless. Previously, the incurably mentally ill accounted for over a third of the homeless, but today we can provide homes for these destitute citizens. The reclamation of these properties has opened new ways to help our people. Because of my benevolent concern, this segment of the population is receiving care today.

"I believe the law allowing me to sign a bill into law *before* it goes through needless committees and is stalled in congressional debate is another leap forward. Of course, Congress can still pass laws, but the members must now have a 75 percent majority to override my veto power or to veto my bills. Your president is personally the guarantor of a system of government that will respond to your every need. As long as I have your total support, you will reap unlimited benefits.

"Let us now turn to the global scene. We are realizing the fulfillment of a dream that has eluded the world throughout this century. I have personally brought about a New World Order. We are at peace with all nations, even though they have turmoil among themselves. Today no nation would dare violate a treaty with us. We have the nuclear superiority for instant response. No one—from Alexander the Great down to the dictators of this century—has enjoyed the power that I now have to affect the world . . . for good, of course.

"Let me be frank. Israel has taken serious advantage of our nonaggression treaty and must be chastened or else new problems will be created for the New World Order.

"Because Vice President Rathmarker is Jewish, and I am part Jewish, there can be no possibility of anti-Semitism in our position. Unfortunately, Israel's wealth has resulted in distorted thinking and ungrateful response to the benevolence I have shown in the past. Israel is insisting on trade terms that are completely unacceptable and certainly not favorable to us.

The New Roman Empire *cannot* allow any group to carve out a better position than we hold. Our superiority must be affirmed and embraced by the world.

"The Israelis are attempting to rebuild their stockpile of nuclear weapons. In the past, other presidents assisted in the acquisition of this weaponry. Now I see clearly that a small nation with neutron bombs can resist the great powers. This capacity must be stopped. The time has come to demand compliance or act accordingly.

"In addition, I am constantly receiving complaints about Israel's outrageous sacrifices. Such barbarism gives us pause and puts the meaning of the country's nuclear capacity into perspective. With all animal lovers, I am incensed. These practices must stop in 1997, or I will be forced to stop them myself!

"Now I must address a serious problem at home. One particular political group continues to create difficulties. Evangelical Christians have always affected the common way of life far out of proportion to their numbers. In the past their value systems were assumed to be of benefit. However, in the last decade their intentions have become clear. This faith is definitely not in the best interest of the New Roman Empire.

"The issue has come to a head with the sect's refusal to comply with our credit-card-in-the-right-hand plan expediting commerce. Their strange superstitions about the number 666 continue to create noncompliance, resulting in such problems as slowing shopping lines, flawing our credit processing systems, and spreading dissatisfaction and dissension. Therefore, by the new authority given me, I have signed my own bill into law today. Businesses can now discriminate against evangelical Christians who refuse to obey social laws and rules for national order. Businesses can refuse to hire or promote anyone who is identified with this faith. Christians without lasered identification can be demoted or fired without compensation for refusal to comply. Persons who cannot pass the checkout test at grocery stores can be refused the right of purchase. Evangelical Christians will line up with the state or suffer the consequences.

"In closing, I have the firmest confidence that our greatest days are before us. There is nothing that cannot be done through human efforts. We are invincible!"

Once again silence settled across the room. No one knew what to say or wanted to comment. Issues were so ponderous that words failed.

"I don't think we need to hear more," Larry reached for the automatic tuner. "Let's turn it off and talk."

"Really!" Ben sat up on his knees. "I'm ready to forget the football games. We've got pressing issues to consider."

"Jimmy," Larry smiled affectionately, "I've really come to respect your opinions. I want to know what you think. You've spent an enormous amount of time studying what the Bible says."

Jimmy picked up a large leather binder and unzipped it. Inside were a Bible, a notebook, and lots of loose pages. "I guess my father's teachings rubbed off on me more than I realized. I didn't think I was paying much attention as a kid, but I absorbed a great deal. It was easy for me to follow his line of thought since he heavily underlined in his books. I could really make up for a lot of lost time quickly."

"You have a fine mind." Sharon was equally warm. "I marvel at how you have put everything together."

Jimmy blushed. "Thank you," he answered softly. He spread out his notes on the floor. "Actually, I have my Bible with me all the time now, so it's not difficult to talk about the meaning of what we're seeing."

"Tell us what you've learned," Larry suggested. "Put things into perspective."

"Remember a prophetic day is 360 days."

"And a *day* can also mean a literal day or 1,000 years," Ruth added.

"Exactly," Jimmy affirmed. "This Antichrist will trample the Jews for 1,260 literal days before the Messiah comes, defeats him, and restores sacrifices. The Feast of Trumpets on September 29, 2000, is just three years and nine months from now, which means the Antichrist will desecrate the temple on Passover *this* year. That's three and one-half years before the Second Coming!"

"Good heavens!" Sharon exclaimed. "Jimmy, you're a genius."

"Feast of Trumpets fits," Jimmy sighed. "I believe that day is a very probable time for Jesus to return, defeat the armies gathered at Armageddon, and restore the sacrificial system in the temple. Here's the big point. Jesus would probably start the sacrificial worship again a few days after His return since the Battle of Armageddon will probably last a few days and Jesus will send angels around the world to give individuals one last chance to trust Jesus as their Messiah and Savior."

"There's strong evidence to believe that the Antichrist will actually stop the sacrifices 30 days before Passover, on the Feast of Purim coming on March 23, 1997. Daniel hints that something very significant will occur 1,290 days before the defeat of the Antichrist and that there will be a transition period of 45 days after his defeat until the Millennium officially begins. The start of Christ's kingdom is 1,335 days after that mystery event on Purim."

"Incredible!" Sharon shook her head. "Absolutely incredible!"

Jimmy pulled a pencil from his leather case and began writing. "From Passover, 1997, to the Feast of Trumpets, 2000, there are exactly 1,257 days. The war of Armageddon will probably take 3 or 4 days, which would take us to October 3, 2000, which is exactly 1,260 days from the time when the Great Tribulation began and 1,290 days from the Feast of Purim when sacrifices ceased. It all fits perfectly."

"Astonishing," Ben muttered.

"Here's another mindblower." Jimmy began scribbling quickly. "From the end of the Feast of Purim, 1997, to the beginning of the seventeenth of Heshvan—which is the date that God saved Noah's family—are 1,335 days. On this day in Heshvan, the Balfour Declaration was signed on November 2, 1917, declaring a Jewish national homeland. Just as Noah and as the nation of Israel had a new beginning on Heshvan 17, so will we . . . the third millennium, with Yeshua as ruler, on Heshvan 17, 2000."

"I had no idea the Bible could tell us such things," Larry said. "To think of the years that we wasted when we could have been learning these essential truths . . ."

Joe pointed to a page in his Bible. "Hosea, in chapter 6, suggests there will be a two-day period between the former and the latter Reigns of the Messiah. During these two days, Jews across the world will suffer persecution and great problems, but on the third day, the Messiah will return and heal their wounds. How do you put this together, Jimmy?"

"I equate the former Reign with the beginning of Jesus' ministry. Actually, our current calendar is several years off, and the true date of the beginning of His public ministry is A.D. 28. If I add two thousand Jewish prophetic 360-day years to that date, guess where I come out?"

"My hunch is," Ben answered first, "you're just about on the Feast of Trumpets, A.D. 2000."

"Exactly." Jimmy thumped the pages of his Bible. "If the 'two days' in Hosea 6 are two one-thousand-year periods, then the Antichrist would start persecuting Jews on Passover, 1997, which is almost 1,260 days earlier. Suddenly, all the prophecies fit together."

They all looked around the room at each other, mulling over the implications of what Jimmy had just said.

"What Jimmy has just explained," Joe added, "fits what I've been studying at our church and is what we heard the night of the New Year's Eve party when we

committed our lives to Jesus. We *must* anticipate that
this Passover will be the start of a terrible persecution."

Ben inched toward Jimmy. "Michael gave us this exact warning."

"I was trained to be a scientist." Larry sat back in his
chair. "Probably lots of passages have various interpre-
tations. I think we need real evidence that our conclusions are correct."

"Definitely," Jimmy said. "Everything is conjecture
until we see Gianardo enter the temple and demand
worship. But once that happens, we'll know that the
1,260-day countdown is on. If that occurs this year,
we'll know where we are in the Great Tribulation."

"I don't need to hear more," Larry concluded. "Tomorrow I'm taking a big hunk of our savings out of the
bank and putting it into gold bars and cash. I think it's
important that we hide some of our reserves and put
other cash in a safety deposit box under a false name."

"Maybe we ought to get false driver's licenses," Ben
threw in. "I know a place in Las Vegas where you can
get new ID's for fifty bucks each. I want one with a
name that doesn't sound so Jewish. Ben Jones would
do just fine this year."

"Will we ever see the people who were raptured
again?" Ruth asked.

"Oh, yes!" Jennifer was enthusiastic. "We learned in
our Bible study that they will return with Jesus."

"Will you know your parents?" Ruth asked Jimmy.

"Absolutely," Jimmy reassured her. "I'll know them
because the Bible says we will know each other as we
were known."

"What an incredible promise!" Ruth hugged Jimmy.

Events moved quickly that winter. Ruth continued in
graduate school at Pepperdine pending the outcome of
the approaching Passover, April 22. She had not yet
found either the courage or the boldness to let anyone
know about her faith. Ruth simply avoided revealing
that she was not lasered and kept a low profile. Most

stores were strict about it, but a few sold things for cash—at higher prices.

Jimmy's situation was easier because his boss had no interest in his religious and political ideas. Jimmy plodded away at the car lot in Laguna Niguel selling everything in sight. Now that he owned 10 percent of the business, his efforts were rewarded well. His savings fund was growing steadily.

Valentine's Day was too significant for the young lovers not to do something romantic. Ben asked Ruth and Jimmy to join Cindy and him at the five-star Five Crowns Restaurant in Corona Del Mar for an elegant dinner. The valet service parked the car, and the couples walked into the Tudor-style restaurant.

"What a place!" Jimmy looked around at the stucco-covered walls and the exposed thick, rough boards. Large beams went across the ceiling. English coats of arms decorated the walls, and hunting trumpets accented the melancholy atmosphere the dark-stained wood created. "Really makes me feel like the king of England to eat in here."

A hostess dressed in garb of English days of old led them across the plank floors to a table next to an antique fireplace. Overhead, a candle-style chandelier lit the table.

The waitress came quickly to take their orders and before long the gourmet meal was served.

"Their prime rib is the best on the coast," Ben talked between bites.

"Oh, I like the walnuts in their special house salad." Cindy squeezed Ben's hand. "You do such nice things for me."

"I don't think we'll be able to come to places like this much longer." Ruth twirled the fettucini around her fork. "I just pray we can all stick together."

"Sure." Jimmy reached over and hugged her. "I'll take care of us no matter what happens."

Cindy ran her sensitive fingers over the fine linen

tablecloth. "We know that God is going to take care of us," she said quietly. "No matter what . . ."

"Things have completely changed." Ben passed the thick-sliced homemade bread around again. "In the past I wouldn't have given much consideration to anything more serious than my next want. Now, we're caught up in a great adventure. I know bad stuff's out there, but I feel alive and part of something very exhilarating. Sure, we have some very formidable enemies, but we're on the side that's ultimately going to win, although the Bible says that vast numbers of believers will die during the Great Tribulation."

"We have Michael watching over us." Cindy cut into her petite filet. The waitress hovered, pouring water and iced tea.

"Our lives used to be flat and overindulged." Ben looked at his sister as he spoke. "We were spoiled rich kids, but that's behind us. I wouldn't go back to the old ways for anything."

"Me too!" Jimmy nodded. "I just didn't realize how important my father's ministry was. He was in the real battle every day of his life."

"And I know how special you are." Ruth took Jimmy's hand. "I don't care if my brother and Cindy are here. You are the best thing in my life and I want everyone to know it. I love you, Jimmy Harrison, and I want to be your wife."

"We ought to come to this restaurant more often," Jimmy told Ben in mock astonishment.

"I don't know how much time we have left together." Ruth's voice was low and intense. "Who knows what tomorrow will bring? We have to make the most of every second."

"Yes," Jimmy said soberly. "I'm afraid you're right. Our great adventure is going to be filled with drastic uncertainties."

"I think we need to take advantage of this very moment," Ruth insisted. "I have the perfect idea for finishing the evening. What better time to get married than Valentine's Day?"

Jimmy started to laugh, but something in Ruth's decisiveness checked him. "You're not kidding."

"No, I'm not. Jimmy, I want to marry you tonight."

Ben and Cindy almost stopped breathing.

"To . . . tonight?" Jimmy stuttered.

"Why not? We love each other and that's all that matters."

"But I thought you'd want a big wedding . . . the white dress . . . the walk down the aisle." Jimmy kept blinking his eyes.

"In a short while we may be dying," Ruth's voice became almost a whisper. "I don't want to face that moment alone. More important, I want us to be together through every step of the way into eternity. What's an expensive wedding with all the fancy flourishes compared to what's happening to us? I say let's go for it tonight!"

"But . . . how?" Jimmy was uncharacteristically befuddled. "Where?"

"Mexico!" Cindy and Ruth said at the same time.

"Sure!" Ben clapped his hands. "Mexico is only an hour and a half from here. For a couple of bucks anything's possible. We could leave right now and have you married before midnight."

"Midnight?" Jimmy swallowed hard and then beamed. "Why not?"

"Let's go!" Ruth stood up. "I'm ready to become Mrs. Jimmy Harrison on Valentine's Day."

I watched the happy foursome speed down Interstate 5 toward Tijuana. Hovering over the car, I made sure nothing marred the trip. A few mental nudges on my part sent Jimmy down the most expeditious side streets, winding up in front of one of Tijuana's less-famous Chapels of Bliss. Before midnight, the four-some were back across the border in San Diego.

Of course, I could listen to both sides of the conversation when Ruth called to break the news to her parents. Sharon shed the predictable tears, and Larry went into his psychiatric father role, dispensing immediate advice. I could easily perceive the loss that both parents felt in not being able to give their daughter the wedding of *their* dreams. In the end, they said the right words and clearly recognized how the times had changed all plans.

The two couples listened to music and said little as they sped north from Tijuana to San Diego. Jimmy and Ruth sat in the back seat cuddled together.

"Incredible. What a night!" Ben thumped the steering wheel. "Hey, there's the exit to your place." Ben turned off Interstate 5 at the Crown Valley exit. "Jimmy, you're the only person in the world I would drive to another country so he could marry my sister. Glad to have you in the Feinberg tribe."

"Well, you can drop me and the missus off at the apartment," Jimmy teased as Ben sped up the winding road. "Think we'll spend the evening home alone."

Ruth giggled and snuggled next to her new husband.

"Don't call me till after one in the afternoon," Jimmy chuckled.

"Sure thing, bro-in-law." Ben wheeled into the driveway. "By the way, congratulations again."

Ben returned to the freeway and headed for Cindy's dorm. "What do you think is ahead for us?"

Cindy felt the window on the door as if rubbing a magic looking glass. "I don't know." She seemed to be peering out into the black night. "The angel said . . . ," she stopped.

"I guess we can't get married." Ben was clearly pained. "I don't understand it. Michael seemed to be clear that we were to maintain a certain proper distance."

"Perhaps we are to develop a perfect love for each

other." Cindy turned toward Ben. "Maybe in heaven . . ."

"I don't want to wait for heaven," Ben groaned. "I want now. I envy Jimmy tonight. Cindy, you'd be enough heaven for me."

"We must trust God to know best." Cindy leaned against Ben. "You have something very important to do in the days ahead, and we must not do anything that could spoil your purpose."

By the time Ben had kissed Cindy good night and gone back to his room, it was three o'clock. In spite of near exhaustion and the late hour, he lay on his bed praying. "What is it You want from me?" he finally cried out. "I don't understand." With that last gasp of frustration, Ben fell into a deep sleep.

Standing in the corner, I listened intensely to both his silent and spoken prayers. "You will know soon enough," I said to myself. "Soon enough."

"Can you believe a month has passed since Jimmy and Ruth got married?" Sharon turned out the light on the nightstand. "I wish we could have given them a proper wedding." She threw back the large downy comforter on their king-size bed. The massive mahogany four-poster bed was covered by a spacious canopy that matched the Victorian furniture.

"Who knows what's proper anymore?" Larry laid down the book on prophecy that Jimmy had given him to read. He got up from his comfortable Queen Anne armchair and began turning down his side of the bed.

"They seem to be deliriously happy." Sharon propped herself up with a pillow. "I have to admit getting married was the right thing for them to do."

"I hope so." Larry pushed himself up on his elbows. "All the strange things that have happened sort of made a shambles of my marriage counseling theories. If they're happy, that's all that counts."

"Do you know what day it is?" Sharon suddenly smiled.

"Sure." Larry frowned. "March 22."

"Not the date, ninny. What holiday started at sundown tonight?"

"What are you talking about, woman?"

"Purim! Tonight and tomorrow are the Feast of Purim."

"Good grief, so it is!"

"My parents always had a little party for us when I was a child." Sharon leaned forward and smiled. "I'd dress up like good Queen Esther who saved all the Jews from evil Haman. Someone dressed up like King Xerxes who fell in love with Esther and made her queen. What great fun!"

"We did that once," Larry reminisced. "I dressed up like Mordecai. I always liked the part in the story where Haman was hanged in the noose he had prepared for Mordecai. Seventy-five thousand Jews were saved in one day along with kindly Mordecai. What a great story!"

"Makes today very special." Sharon slid down next to Larry. "We really need to start remembering these special events in the history of our people. I'm sorry we haven't done a better job teaching our children about their traditions."

"Yes," Larry agreed. "I think that—"

The phone rang.

"Who in the world could be calling us at nearly eleven at night? Really!" Sharon barked. "Let me get the phone."

"Sharon!" the voice at the other end was nearly breathless. "Get your TV on! You won't believe it!"

"Joe?" Sharon pulled the receiver back. "Joe McCoy?"

"Sharon, it's 9:00 A.M. in Jerusalem! TV crews have been out on the Mount of Olives getting the whole thing on film. Call Jimmy and Ruth! Call Ben! Everyone must watch!"

"TV?" Sharon questioned. "Turn the TV on now?"

"CNN!" The phone clicked off.

Larry had already reached for the automatic tuner. "News channel." He punched the button. "I know. It's all starting again."

"President Gianardo and Vice President Jacob Rathmarker arrived here yesterday for meetings scheduled to begin at eight o'clock this morning," the announcer spoke as the picture came into focus. "We have no idea what their response is to this amazing sight. However, since they are here in Jerusalem, we will be able to get a statement shortly."

The cameras covered a panoramic view of the top of the Mount of Olives. Clouds boiled and swirled as if a great storm was coming, but there did not appear to be any wind or rain. In fact, a great calm appeared to have settled over the area because the trees were not moving. When the cameras zoomed in, two figures seemed to be emerging from the clouds. The images came and went from sight.

"For the past forty-five minutes," the announcer talked in hushed tones, "we have been observing this phenomenon. The clouds began to gather forty-five minutes ago, but there was no radar evidence of a storm. However, the verbal reports from the area were filled with concern and consternation. Our crews were first dispatched to Mount Scopus to observe the sky." The announcer stopped. "Look! There they are again!"

The two figures were much closer to the ground.

"What is going on?" Larry sat up in bed. "Must be a stunt making it look like people are flying."

"Larry!" Sharon pointed. "They look ancient! Look at those white beards . . . the long wooden staffs!"

"The two figures appear to be descending," the announcer began again. "Perhaps I might be more accurate to say materializing. They just seem to be coming out of nowhere. Fortunately, we have this event on tape since nothing like it has ever been filmed. However, the experience seems like what many New Agers have been describing in astral projection and similar phenomena."

"Are they landing?" Sharon puzzled.

"Looks more like they are just stepping out of another dimension into our world."

"We are going to try to get closer," the announcer's

voice returned. "A CNN correspondent has volunteered to make contact. At this moment he is arriving by car at the point that has often been recognized as the traditional site of the ascension of Jesus. Of course, no one took this place as having serious archaeological significance . . . until now. Our cameras are going to try to zoom in to pick up the correspondent's remote mike."

"The brilliance of radiant light makes it very difficult to walk forward." The man's voice boomed as the screen turned white. "Frankly, I am as terrified as if I were walking into the sun, but there is no heat."

Two shapes began to appear on the screen, looking more like photograph negatives. They raised their arms and the long staffs they held. Suddenly, a babble of sound rumbled over the TV.

"We don't have time to get a translation," the announcer explained. "However, I clearly recognize Hebrew."

The intonation changed. Another language came forth.

"Russian!" Another announcer came on, "I can tell they are speaking Russian."

Several times the language changed as the figures became clearer and the dazzling light receded. The two men had shimmering white hair and beards. Their robes were wondrously white. Each man looked as if he carried overwhelming personal authority.

"They are speaking Chinese now," the CNN correspondent explained. "I think I can get a bit closer."

At that moment, the larger of the two men pointed his finger directly at the camera. His dark-set black eyes looked as if they could pierce steel. "Hear me!" he said in perfect English. "We have come that you might hear the final witness of the Holy One of Israel. Listen well, lest your own words become testimony against you. The hour of accounting is at hand!"

"Please excuse me," the correspondent inched forward holding his microphone at arm's length as if it might protect him from the apparitions. "Who ... who might we ... ah ... be ... ah ... talking with?"

"Moses!" the huge man roared, and his voice sounded as if it might shake the mountain. "I have come with my heavenly colleague. Behold, Elijah the Tishbite!"

The correspondent fell backward, and the two figures moved past him down the hill.

While Elijah and Moses walked down the Mount of Olives, Larry called Ruth and Jimmy. Sharon got Ben on the other line. After the children were alerted, Larry and Sharon turned back to the TV.

"As best we can tell," the announcer talked rapidly as the cameras followed the two prophets down the hillside, "the two strangers are walking down toward the Kidron Valley as if going toward the ancient walls of the city. Because this event is being carried instantaneously around the world, we are able to register public response as we broadcast. New Age psychics are homing in for readings. We are told now that Gianardo and the Israeli prime minister have been watching for some time. They have left the Knesset and are on their way here at this very moment."

"Look at them!" Larry pointed at the TV. "I can't believe my eyes. Do you truly think we are watching the real Moses and Elijah?"

"They're almost gliding down the hillside." Sharon got out of bed and pulled a chair up close to the television.

The camera switched to the highway that ran in front of the Old City wall. Behind the stone walls loomed the Dome of the Rock Mosque, beside the rebuilt temple of Solomon. Truckloads of soldiers began rolling down the highway and stopping at the bottom. Young men with automatic weapons leaped out and took up positions behind rocks, but the two prophets continued to walk with clear determination toward the convoy.

"Precautionary measures are now being taken before Gianardo and the Israeli prime minister arrive," the announcer continued. "No one appears to know what to do. Amazingly, Gianardo seems to be less apprehensive than his advisers. Sources with the presidential party are telling our reporters that the president seems to be almost fascinated with what is occurring. Apparently, there is a television in the presidential limousine, and CNN is being observed even as I speak."

The television lost the two men as they moved through a grove of trees but picked up a caravan of limousines that pulled up behind the parked military trucks blocking the highway. Almost before the cars stopped, Secret Service agents in plain clothes were forming a protective corridor in front of the cars. Israeli agents carrying Uzis joined them. Suddenly, the ancient travelers came out of the trees onto the highway.

"The figures calling themselves Moses and Elijah have just appeared from behind the Church of All Nations." Another announcer picked up the commentary. "The traditional site of the Garden of Gethsemane is at the bottom of the Kidron Valley. The two men are now walking up toward the presidential caravan. We are going to switch to reporters who have been traveling with the president."

TV cameras caught President Gianardo pushing past his bodyguards who tried to restrain him. He walked toward the approaching figures. The prime minister of Israel appeared to be crouching behind him.

"President Gianardo seems to be seeking a confrontation," the news reporter's voice boomed. "He seems to have some insight into what is happening. The Israeli prime minister is deeply disturbed that such an event is happening on the Feast of Purim. He, too, appears to have some understanding but considerably more apprehension. We have now turned special long-range microphones toward the point where an encounter will occur. We believe that we will be able to pick up whatever is said."

The troops stood up and pointed their weapons at the

two holy men while Secret Service personnel scurried forward with pistols drawn. Moses and Elijah held up their hands as if they could repel anything fired at them, but their pace did not slacken.

An agent with a bullhorn jumped in front of Gianardo. "Who are you?" the amplification echoed off the hillside. "Identify yourselves or we will shoot!"

Moses roared with laughter and tossed his long white hair back. "Can you threaten Adonai?" His laughter rumbled.

"We will take you into custody immediately," the agent insisted.

The prophets kept walking.

The Israeli prime minister seized the bullhorn. "Why have you come?" his voice trembled. "Why on this day?"

"If Ahab did not intimidate me," Elijah responded, "do you think you will give me pause?"

As if hit by a blow, the prime minister dropped the bullhorn to the ground and staggered backward. Gianardo walked past him. "Would you toy with our power?" he sneered. "I understand much more about the supernatural than Ahab would have dreamed of knowing. Don't try and frighten us with innuendos. Tell us clearly. Who do you claim to be?"

"Your ears have not deceived you." Moses thumped his staff on the ground. "Your faithlessness will be your demise."

"Demise?" The president snapped his fingers. "I can blow you back to wherever you came from before lightning can flash."

"Your arrogance has no boundaries," Moses solemnly retorted. "Your blindness will condemn you to eternal darkness."

"Prove it!" Gianardo snapped.

The Israeli prime minister peered from behind Gianardo. "I . . . I . . . I really w . . . want to know."

"Fool!" Gianardo snapped. "Don't indulge these people."

"That you may know," Moses leaned on his staff, "my signs will not be of the earth as they were with Pharaoh, but I shall answer you in the terms of your day. Let your computer experts give you the answer."

"Y . . . yes, say something." The prime minister clasped his hands together and started bowing at the waist.

"You already have my book of Genesis in Hebrew in your systems at the Israel Institute of Technology. Instruct them to remove every twenty-sixth Hebrew letter. You will find that the result will spell the sacred name of God, E-L-O-H-I-M. They will find that the word T-O-R-A-H is repeated at fifty-letter intervals."

"Really?" the prime minister blinked. "You're serious?"

"Have them look at my description of the burial sites of Abraham and Sarah, and you will also find the words A-D-A-M and E-V-E there in similar fashion. Let this be a sign! No human could have developed such a system over four thousand years ago. God is God and Moses is Moses!"

Immediately, several aides rushed to the cars. The television announcer interjected, "As best we can tell, Gianardo is now huddling with the prime minister. He seems irritated by the timid response from the Israeli. Gianardo doesn't seem to be confounded by these astonishing figures. We are attempting to get comment on the religious significance of this day because it seems to be a component in these discussions. Look! The Israeli aides are now reporting. The prime minister is pulling away from the president. He's bowing up and down in formal diplomatic posture. Let's see if we can pick him up."

"No question about it. The computers confirm your assertions." The prime minister spoke respectfully. "Why? Why are you here on this day that has such ominous meaning in our history?"

"Do you not know?" Elijah's voice thundered. "Do you not suspect? As happened twenty-five hundred years ago, Haman formed a noose for Mordecai, so does Gianardo draw one for you!"

"Idiot!" Gianardo pushed the prime minister aside. "Don't listen to these apparitions. They are creatures of the lie. Let me deal with them."

"Hear the word of the Lord!" Elijah threw open his arms. "As was true of Haman of old, so shall it be true of you. Within 1,290 days, both of you will surely hang from the rope of your own making!"

"No!" the Israeli gasped.

"Hear us, O world," Moses commanded, "we have come to make the final announcement that Yeshua, whom you crucified, has ascended to the place of all authority and is the Messiah. His return is imminent."

"Good heavens!" the prime minister choked.

Moses turned toward the cameras as if sensing they were trained on him. He began speaking again in low earnest tones that tugged at the heart. "This moment has been chosen because the entire world now has the capacity to hear as if with one ear. Many of you will believe and be saved from the consequences coming on the evil people of this world. Even though you may face death and persecution, you must not yield. The great battle is at hand. Stand with the Lord's people regardless. We will soon give you three signs by which you will know."

"Behold!" Elijah pointed at the sky. "The breaking of the Fourth Seal! A pale horse called Death will ride the skies on Pesach. Passover, Tuesday, April 22, will begin the great unleashing. By Tammuz 17, July 22, one and one-half billion people will have been slain. War, starvation, pestilence, and illness will wipe out one-fourth of the population of the globe. The hard-hearted and the unrepentant will fall because of their own obstinacy. Let him who has ears hear!"

"Another sign!" Moses pointed directly at the president. "A terrible night will sweep across your globe. This Beast will strike and slay one million of God's people who now stand in the Evil Empire. Those Jews who have now come to see the truth about the Messiah will be the major target of this evil war. Behold the terror in your midst!" Moses took a quick, bold step toward Gianardo.

The president covered his face with his arms as the Israeli prime minister fell backward. The TV cameras picked up their terrified faces.

Moses shouted, "From Passover until the Fast of Tammuz, seventy thousand believers will be slain. Their blood will cry up to the sky." The television cameras drew back.

"Larry!" Sharon grabbed her husband. "Do you understand? He could be talking about us! This is the puzzle of terror that Ben and Jimmy were trying to figure out."

Larry put his arm around his wife's shoulder. "Only God can save us," he muttered. "We must get the family together as quickly as we can."

Sharon reached for a pencil. "I've got to write this down."

"Better yet," Larry reached for a tape, "we must catch every word." Immediately they began recording the predictions.

Elijah pointed his staff toward the ocean. "On the seventeenth of Tammuz, July 4, 1776, the Holy One brought forth a new nation that would be greatly used as His instrument in restoring our people. Always a haven for Jews, this country was the primary defender and guarantor when Israel was reborn on May 14, 1948. Once again the gift becomes the curse. You, O America, will be the source of death and calamity!"

Moses roared, "These truths are not hidden to those who seek in faith! You will see that those who have perished will become your intercessors. The martyrs will stand in white robes before the sovereign Lord, crying out for their blood to be avenged. On the day when the Great Tribulation ends at the Battle of Armageddon, it shall be done."

To the consternation of the president's party as well

as the TV cameramen, Moses and Elijah marched forward through the array of men and trucks. The crowds parted before them as if the people were a human sea of water. The camera scurried to line up with the route the two were taking.

"I can't believe my ears." Larry held his head in his hands. "The woes are about to come down."

"But there is so much encouragement here for us," Sharon reassured him. "Just think how hopeless we would be if Jimmy had never come into our lives."

"Maybe we're getting some sense of Ben's place in what's about to start. Oh, God, please help us!"

"He will," Sharon comforted her husband. "I know He will."

"No one has any commentary whatsoever," the TV announcer said soberly. "We have no precedent by which to gauge this message. We are too stunned to even know whether we've been hit with a colossal hoax, an apparition created by spirit guides, or the final truth of history."

"Hoax!" Larry exploded. "He'll eat those words!"

"They're stopping." Sharon leaned forward. "Moses and Elijah are halting before the Western Wall, the wailing wall just on the other side of the new temple."

The two prophets sat down in chairs that Jews had left out for their prayers earlier in the day. Around them, men in yarmulkes and prayer talliths fell with their faces toward the enormous stone wall. Generally, most people backed away in fear. The television cameras switched to pictures of the presidential limousines speeding away from the Kidron Valley. Helicopters appeared buzzing overhead, beginning to circle over the Western Wall. Gianardo's announcement that he had persuaded the Israeli Knesset to outlaw all animal sacrifices as of March 23, 1997, went largely unnoticed because attention was on the two strange ancient ones who descended from the sky in full view of the world's TV cameras.

14

The whole scene left Larry too disturbed to even think about sleep. He slipped on a sweat suit and went down to the kitchen to prepare a pot of coffee. Suddenly, the doorbell rang. To his surprise, he found Joe and Jennifer McCoy outside. They had barely begun to talk when Jimmy and Ruth drove up. About five minutes later, Ben showed up with Cindy.

"Looks like Jimmy was incredibly accurate." Larry turned the volume down on the large screen TV in the den. "I don't have any idea what's next tonight, but I think I see the outline of the future rather clearly."

"I'm worried for them." Ruth pointed at the two prophets on the screen, sitting calmly as more helicopters filled the sky. "A marksman in one of those choppers couldn't miss!"

"I think they can take care of themselves," Jimmy answered. "Next month will be the critical time," he added. "Now we know that on Passover the 1,260-day Great Tribulation will start."

Sharon held up a faded, wrinkled paperback. "Lots of the 1970s and 1980s prophecy books I found talked about a seven-year tribulation. You're sure about a three-and-a-half-year time of 1,260 days?"

"My dad had a solution to your question. He believed that 2 Thessalonians 2:7–8 taught that the Rapture

would occur prior to the Antichrist's being revealed.
True Christians were to be spared the worldwide persecution. Revelation 3:10 is an example of this point. I
think the Rapture could probably have occurred at a
number of different times in the past without contra-
dicting definite prophecies. The real point is that the
return of the Messiah will come seven prophetic years
after the wicked world ruler signs a false peace pact
with Israel. He will return 1,290 days after sacrifices
stop and after 1,260 days of terrible tribulation have
passed starting when the temple is desecrated. There
is clearly a seven-year countdown prior to Yeshua's descending back on the Mount of Olives to destroy the
Antichrist, but the Bible doesn't say that the seven-year
clock starts with the Rapture."

"That's exactly our conclusion," Joe added. "Daniel
9:27 is very specific that the seven-year time slot is tied
to signing the secret peace treaty, which was signed in
November, 1993 by many world rulers, including Gianardo, who was only speaker of the House of Represen-
tatives at the time. No one could have known then that
he would turn out to be the Antichrist."

"No one can be dogmatic," Jimmy affirmed, "until
after that single event when he desecrates the temple.
Maybe Daniel's 2,200 days were actually 2,300 or 2,400.
Our problem is that everything adds up right now. In
fact, the evidence is so clear that I believe we've got no
time to lose. The sacrifices ceased today."

"We must finalize our survival plans," Larry confirmed. "Those fake ID's are no longer a novel suggestion. Fortunately, I already have a number of gold bars
hidden here in the house. I already obtained false passports as well."

"I'm not sure I'll make it," Cindy fretted. "I think
Michael hinted that I might not survive."

"Don't talk like that," Ben sounded angry, but his face
looked pained. "You're going to survive. We're going to
fight this thing through to the bitter end regardless. After all . . . ," his voice became almost inaudible, "you

are the best friend I have. You're the most important person in my life."

"But if something should happen to me," Cindy turned to Jimmy, "I will come back with Jesus in 2000. Right? Like your parents?"

"Yes," Jimmy was quite confident, "everyone will return with a new and resurrected body."

"The worst would be like a short separation," Cindy reassured Ben.

Ben ran his hand through his hair and looked disturbed. "I don't know, but I'll protect you regardless."

"Sure!" Jimmy agreed. "My parents taught me that we ought to pray as if everything depended on God while working as if everything depended on us."

"Let's do it. It's time for us to make concrete plans on how to escape and survive." Larry stood up as he spoke. "I think the first logical step is to make sure that we know everything possible about what lies ahead. We can act intelligently only if we are fully informed. I have been studying this matter constantly since I've had my own change of heart and mind. I believe that I've found the only place in the whole world that will be safe. God has ordained a divinely protected area like the old cities of refuge where none of us will become martyrs." He walked over to his desk.

"Really?" Jimmy was amazed. "As hard as I have studied Scripture, I haven't come up with such an area."

Larry pulled a map out of a drawer in his desk and unfolded it on the coffee table. "There is an ancient and almost totally abandoned city in the cliffs that are about four thousand feet above sea level in the mountains of ancient Edom." He put his finger on the map. "The place is called Bozrah. About eighty miles southeast of Jerusalem and approximately twenty-five miles northeast of the ancient city of Petra, the location is in Jordan."

"How did you come up with this conclusion?" Jimmy puzzled.

Larry opened his Bible that was also on the table. "Look at chapter 12 in Revelation. The passage talks about a woman with a garland of twelve stars on her head. She is obviously the nation of Israel. After she gives birth to the Messiah, which is the first coming of Jesus, the red dragon, or Satan, tries to kill the child. That happened right after the birth of Jesus, but God intervened and saved the child. Verse 6 tells us that before the Messiah rules the world, Israel will again flee to the desert where God will protect her for 1,260 days, preserving Israel from the Antichrist and Satan himself." Larry turned back to the Old Testament. "I have studied Isaiah 63 and the book of Obadiah, verses 15 through 21, and discovered that God is going to protect Jews in two cities—Bozrah and Petra."

"Larry," Sharon asked, "can you be sure that you are correct?"

"Micah 2:12–13 confirms my discoveries. Micah makes an amazing play on words in saying that the Messiah will gather the surviving remnant of Israel like a shepherd gathers his flock. The Hebrew word here for 'flock' is *bozrah*. In these passages we have a picture of Jews fleeing from Israel into a desert area when the Antichrist desecrates the temple. There's even a description of escape on 'two wings of a great eagle,' which will probably be some old American transport plane since the eagle is the old symbol of our country. Moses and Elijah will protect everyone for the 1,260 days of struggle before the Messiah returns on the Feast of Trumpets in 2000 and wipes out the opposition. I think that three days later, He will go to Bozrah for His chosen ones and return with them, going through the east gate right into the temple area to start the one-thousand-year millennial kingdom."

"Makes total sense," Joe McCoy agreed. "I think you need to get packing before Passover comes."

"Exactly!" Larry thumped the table. "I need to sell my psychiatric practice, and Jimmy can close out his interest in the car business. You might say that we are in a position to sell at fire sale prices. When we sell the houses, we'll hide the money in suitcases."

Jimmy added, "After we fly to Tel Aviv, we can stock up on camping equipment, canned goods, and survival gear."

"I've already purchased some medical books on mountain medicine."

"There's another reason we need to leave," Sharon spoke up. "You've always been a very compassionate person, Larry. You'll try to help your patients, but if you witness to your new faith, we'll be dead. They'll come and get us. But in Bozrah, there will be Jews fleeing the persecution. They'll be like survivors of Hitler's death camps and will need psychiatric care too."

"OK, family!" Larry shook both fists in the air. "We're on our way."

"I can't go," Ben said soberly. "I think I understand why the angel appeared to us in such an unusual way. Michael knew we'd leave without an early intervention on his part. Cindy and I have a task that we must do right here. No, I have an important job to do in California."

"Oh, my!" Sharon covered her mouth with her hand. The room became very quiet.

"No matter what happens, we won't be apart more than three and one-half years," Ben tried to smile.

Larry turned to Jimmy and Ruth. "And you?" His face was drawn and his eyes deeply troubled.

"Ruth is Jewish and I am married to her. Seems appropriate for us to go."

"Joe? Jennifer?" Larry probed.

"We can't," Joe sighed. "We've already discussed some similar possibilities, but our kids bought Gianardo's philosophy hook, line, and sinker. They hate our Christian faith. Even if it costs us our lives, we must witness to them to the end. We have to do everything we can to pull them back from the abyss."

"I understand." Tears welled up in Sharon's eyes.

"We must pray." Larry hung his head. "We must pray

for each other as we start this journey that will separate us. The battle has already begun for us."

Ben put his arm around Cindy. "We enter a battle we can't win to gain a crown we won't lose. God will be the difference."

The families joined hands and bowed their heads.

CHAPTER

15

Tragedy can spring forth as quickly and unexpectedly as the winds of a summer thunderstorm that tear limbs from trees and smash flowers to the ground. No earthquake or tornado leaves behind devastation like that of human anger and injustice. I watched in horror when the Babylonian hordes tore Judea apart, and I wept in grief as the Romans burned the temple to the ground. Only an angel who has watched the centuries flow past can fully understand how rapidly circumstances trap the unsuspecting and leave the innocent abandoned to the rampaging torrents of unexpected evil.

World events began to move at breakneck speed. Keeping all the pieces together was nearly impossible as the Feinbergs' world started flying apart. Ruth dropped out of her graduate classes in psychology at Pepperdine and quietly faded from her circle of acquaintances. Because of the rapid turnover in the used car sales business, Jimmy's boss was not completely surprised when he quit. Any questions about Jimmy's intentions ended when he agreed to sell his 10 percent of the business back to the boss for 5 percent value. Ben and Cindy stayed in school while they made their own arrangements. Once Ben received his inheritance money, he began systematically hiding the funds for the future. Cindy continued teaching her bewildered parents about the faith of the Bible. The Wongs listened in consternation.

The Feinbergs' premium oceanfront property moved easily and quickly. Larry gave his reason for selling the psychiatric practice as retirement, and no other questions were asked. Once the funds were in place, the family left for Israel on Tuesday, April 15, one week before Passover. Twelve hours later they landed at Ben Gurion International Airport and were soon moving through customs procedures.

"You said their name is Eisenberg?" Sharon asked Larry as they stood in line to clear Israeli passport control.

"Sam and Angie," Larry said quietly. "Jewish believers. Jimmy's father knew them when they were going to Dallas Theological Seminary. They've been coming and going as tourists for some time so no one would detect that they are actually Christian missionaries."

"They know why we're here?" Sharon inched toward the booth where the customs official was checking documents.

"Jimmy was able to get a message to them. We had to code our intentions, but they got the drift I'm sure. They'll meet us after we clear customs."

"I hope they don't think we're crazy." Sharon rolled her eyes as she handed her passport through the window.

Jimmy and Ruth followed behind them. Just on the other side of the luggage check, the family found the Eisenbergs. Sam was a tall, strong middle-aged man while Angie was small with striking blue eyes. Larry didn't speak to them until they were outside. "You got our message?" he said. "Made sense?"

"Of course." Sam nodded pleasantly. "We weren't surprised." The sun had turned his naturally olive-colored skin a deep tan. Ruggedly handsome, he looked like any other sabra, native-born Israeli, walking down the street.

Angie was plainly dressed, like most of the people standing around them. "We understood easily. We've been storing supplies in the area for some time. We've been expecting you."

"What?" Larry looked shocked. "I don't understand. How could you know about Bozrah? About us?"

"It's a long story," Sam explained hurriedly, "but the insight started in Dallas where we once had a successful dry cleaning business. When some of our Jewish friends became believers, we were intrigued and started attending Dallas Theological Seminary. We pretended that we were believers in Yeshua. After the Rapture, we were convinced that the Bible passages on prophecy were true. During our studies, we found out about what was ahead at Bozrah and Petra. But there's another chapter we'll tell you about later."

"You've known all along!" Jimmy set his bags on the sidewalk. "Of course! You were able to read between the lines and understand our intention."

"How are you getting through the border check points?" Ruth asked.

Sam put his arm around Angie's waist and grinned. "We've got a couple of old school buses and a van with tourist signs plastered all over them. I think the border guards have decided that our specialty is dropping Holy Land pilgrims at the historic sites around Petra. They don't even give us a second look now."

"You're a genius!" Jimmy laughed.

"No," Sam said soberly, "God has just protected us well. We've been able to get in a number of shortwave radios and a satellite dish with some battery-operated TV sets and a generator. I think you will be satisfied with the arrangements."

"God has certainly led us to you." Larry shook Sam's hand again. "Now I know that we will be able to make the right connections. We thought that we were the only people in the world who had figured out the divine puzzle about Bozrah."

"We even have Arab Christians with us," Sam continued. "They make contact with the Arab villages in the area. Places like Rashadiya, Dana, Wadi Musa, and Taiyba have Muslim populations. Recent events have made many of them hostile, but in our area Arab and Jewish Christians live together out of their common love for Yeshua."

"Ben will be relieved to know that we can make contact by shortwave," Sharon said thoughtfully.

"We must change your money into gold and Jordanian currency." Sam pointed to a bank down the street. "We'll need some Israeli money for incidentals. After we get the exchange completed, we'll take in some biblical sights along the way to Jerusalem where we have some very special people you will want to meet."

"Pretty scary!" Jimmy raised his eyebrows. "But what an adventure. Let's go!"

The Eisenbergs pulled their van up to the sidewalk, and the new arrivals piled their gear in the back. Jimmy even had a small box of books to complete his studies. As the van wound its way toward Jerusalem, Sam and Angie stopped at significant historic sites. A great sense of awe settled over the group as they stood before the places they had studied in the preceding months. Finally, the old van climbed up the steep hillside toward Jerusalem. Tall green pines bordered the twisting highway. Here and there the burned-out hulks of tanks or troop carriers remained as silent monuments to the battles that had secured the survival of the nation. Suddenly, new high-rise apartments loomed on the tops of the hills. The ancient and the new blended together in the same ocher-colored stones.

"This is our place . . . our land." Larry reached for Sharon's hand. "I had no idea that I would be so deeply touched."

"How proud my father would have been . . . ," Sharon choked. "He would have given anything to have come here."

The van rolled around the final turn and into the city

limits. Jimmy leaned out the window to drink in the intoxicating aroma of the city.

"For the first time I realize that I've never really been at home anywhere," Larry said with astonishment. "I've been waiting for this city to appear all of my life. I am home."

The van turned down Ben Yehudah Street, cutting through traffic, and headed for the walls of the ancient city. Sam found a parking area close to the Damascus Gate and led the party into the Old City. "Stick close," he called back to them. "We're going to take a shortcut through some alleyways, and we need to move quickly and stay concealed as much as possible."

The group walked through dim, narrow streets cramped between high stone buildings for several blocks and then burst through an arched opening.

"The Western Wall!" Jimmy pointed at the huge stones rising up before them.

Sam guided the group along the edge of the building that ran down to the huge wall. Barricades had been erected several hundred feet away, running parallel to the great wall. Troops were poised with guns pointed at the two men sitting calmly at the base of the former boundary to Solomon's temple.

"The troops are terrified of Moses and Elijah," Sam talked rapidly as they walked. "They haven't figured out that all who come in peace will be welcomed with peace. You're about to have the experience of two lifetimes." Sam guided his group forward.

Moses stood and beckoned them to approach. He was a massive man, towering over everyone. A luminous aura surrounded his pure white hair and penetrating eyes. "We have been expecting you." He motioned that they should stand before him.

Larry and Sharon huddled together more in reverent terror than curiosity. Jimmy shuffled forward, holding Ruth's hand.

"Have no fear," Elijah spoke forcefully as he stood up.

"Each of us is part of the heavenly plan. We welcome you as our brothers and sisters."

Larry carefully edged his way forward, clutching Sharon to his side.

"We are going to protect you," Moses' deep bass voice rumbled as he spoke. "We will stand guard over the entrance to Bozrah and Petra for 1,260 days."

"Do not be dismayed when you hear that we have died in these very streets," Elijah explained. "Exactly thirty days later the Messiah will return. During the three days we lie here, the world will rejoice, but you must not mourn. Our deaths will be painless and then resurrection will follow. We will ascend just as Yeshua did nearly two thousand years ago. The world's jubilation will turn to mourning while your trials become pure joy."

"But you must not leave the cities of protection during this time," Moses warned, "unless you are prepared to become martyrs. Half of all believers left in the world will yield up their lives during the Great Tribulation that will be fought everywhere. Within the boundaries of Petra and Bozrah, angels will stand guard at the door.

"Hear me!" Moses held his hand high above his head. "Study Psalm 139! The world has greatly underestimated the unending love and faithfulness of our heavenly Father. His justice endures. He esteems you beyond any measure of your comprehension. As He leads us, so the Father guides your steps."

"Let us bless you." Elijah held his arms upward as he spoke.

Timidly, the Feinbergs, Jimmy and Ruth, and the Eisenbergs knelt before the spiritual giants. Elijah prayed, "Lord Yeshua, open the eyes of their hearts that they may see the spiritual realm."

The six travelers looked up and gasped as they saw hundreds of thousands of angels surrounding the area while other angels raced across the sky in chariots of fire. Frozen in a trance, no one could speak. As they stared, the sight slowly dissolved.

"Go in peace," Moses blessed the group. "Remember what you have seen. As we have the power to open eyes, we can close them as well. Journey with confidence. The times are in His hands."

Sam tugged at Larry's arm and the group began backing away. Only after they had cleared the barriers did they realize that no one had noticed them. Not one soldier asked for identification. The guards were oblivious to the group.

"They can't see us!" Jimmy whispered to Ruth. "God has blinded the eyes of these nonbelievers."

Rather than return to the alleys, Sam led the party through the main gate and out to the street where they found the van. They pulled back on the highway that edged along the walls of the Old City and down the Kidron Valley. At the bottom of the hill, the van started the incline up the Mount of Olives, rounded the top of the hill, and traveled toward Bethany and the Tomb of Lazarus.

No one said anything for a long time. Finally, Larry spoke. "You've done this before? You talked to them earlier?"

"Once." Sam said. "They told us to bring you here when you arrived. We knew you were coming even before your message got here."

"Staggering," Larry mumbled. "Simply staggering. So that's how you knew."

Sharon began to weep. "Why us? We aren't special. We haven't even been good Jews. Why should we be granted such an experience?"

"Grace is like that," Angie answered. "All of us are more special to God than we realize. There is no other answer . . . except His love."

The van lumbered on toward the wilderness and the Dead Sea. The trees and shrubs disappeared as the air became drier and the ground more barren. Most of the remaining eighty miles to Bozrah were spent in silence.

Jimmy kept looking out the window with his forehead on the glass. Finally, he said, "We can't see them, but we sure know that the angels are with us."

"Even the desert blooms," Larry answered, "and the empty places are filled with new life for surely He makes wind and fire to be His messengers."

CHAPTER

16

The president's black limousine pulled away from the Knesset Building and edged toward the broad boulevard that ran from the modern section of Jerusalem to the ancient city. Armed motorcycle troops of the New Roman Empire completely surrounded the car. Only a few people walked down the streets. Jacob Rathmarker rode in a limo behind the president.

"Mr. President," the new aide in a pin-striped suit sounded edgy, "many Jews will hate you for taking this action on the Day of Passover as much as they will resent the invasion itself. We might have waited at least a day longer . . ."

"Absolutely not!" Gianardo snapped. "There's a principle at stake. The world must recognize my absolute power!"

A phone inside the limousine rang. The aide immediately answered. "Yes . . . I understand . . . it's done. Very good." He hung up. "The nuclear facilities have all been secured, Mr. President. Our troops are also poised to take control of the remaining centers where our intelligence indicates atomic capacity might exist. The job is virtually complete."

"Excellent! Any response from the Israeli army?"

"Evidently, they have accepted the order of the prime minister and have not resisted us."

"Did you see his face?" The president laughed coarsely. "The prime minister's eyes nearly bulged out of his head. He shook like a frightened puppy when I told him they would capitulate or we would nuke the nation off the globe."

"What could he say?" the aide said stiffly. "Their limited nuclear reserves were no match for what was hovering over their heads in our planes. He did the intelligent thing. But on Passover?"

"The world must never forget April 22, 1997!" The president looked out the window at the vacant streets and the closed shops. "The issue is power. Rare power. I'm going to do something that will stamp my authority on this society and convince the world that we are not to be toyed with." The president pushed a button in the armrest and the sliding glass window behind the driver opened. "Straight to the Temple Mount." He pushed the button and the window slid shut.

"I don't understand," the aide fumbled.

"Of course. I didn't tell you. Now you will understand why we came on a high holiday. We're going out to their new temple. I've already arranged for live TV coverage."

"But . . . but . . . isn't that where those two strange apparitions have settled in? Those two men who keep making pronouncements? Gives me the creeps."

"Yes, we're going to stop that little charade in one fell swoop as well."

"Charade?"

"Sure. You didn't believe that hocus-pocus nonsense was real? Did you?"

"Well . . . I did see the initial television tapes. You seemed somewhat shaken at the time."

"Nonsense! Just didn't expect the road show. Took me a while to put it all together. I'm sure the Israeli prime minister was behind it. Probably created trick TV tapes, simulated clouds, and holographic images. Those two clowns sitting down there by the Western Wall are only a Jewish attempt to use ancient prophecy to manipulate both Jews and Christians. Today they've been telling Jews to flee to Bozrah."

"Really?" the aide looked incredulous. "What's at Bozrah?"

"Absolutely nothing but tourist ruins and some obscure Arab villages. They've got every Messianic Jew in Israel and every evangelical in our country running around like chickens with their heads cut off. The Israeli Hasidic Jews are equally panicked. Now I'm going to demonstrate to every stratum of opinion that I am the absolute power in this world. We'll show them what frauds those two impostors are. Moses, my foot!"

"What do you have in mind?" the aide asked cautiously.

"I insisted on a news conference in front of the temple, and the prime minister grudgingly said he would be there."

"I see," the aide frowned.

"I could care less about him. It's the TV coverage I want. I intend to extend my control even over the religious community. It's all a matter of principle, my boy."

The aide smiled but sat back stiffly. Nothing more was said as the motorcade wound its way up toward the Old City. Limited traffic made travel easy. Eventually, the Nablus Road stopped before the Damascus Gate in the ancient stronghold. The driver turned left and drove along the wall until he came to St. Stephen's Gate. The motorcade inched its way through the massive stone gate and down the Old City as the back streets became increasingly narrow. Finally, the entourage stopped next to the Monastery of the Flagellation.

"Passover observance helped with security," the aide mused. "The unexpected drop-in has made matters very simple."

"I think of everything," Gianardo said smugly as the aide opened the door for him. The vice-president's limo pulled up behind them.

When the president and his soldiers reached the

Temple Mount, the area was already packed with Israeli security officers and reporters. Cabinet leaders
surrounded the prime minister. Cameras were set up
in front of the new temple. Gianardo walked quickly
through the crowd but did not stop at the entry to the
temple. "Follow me," he demanded.

"You can't go in!" A cohenim priest rushed forward.

"Try and stop me!" Gianardo and Rathmarker
walked in and beckoned for the crowd to follow them.
The horrified priest watched the reporters trample by.

"Enough!" The Israeli prime minister tugged at Gianardo's arm. "Please, we have had enough humiliation
for one day."

Rathmarker pushed him aside and marched up to
the large elegant hanging curtains in front of the Holy
of Holies. The TV cameramen scurried in every direction to record the details. "Set the microphone right
here." Rathmarker pointed in front of his feet.

"The prime minister of Israel has a statement first."
Rathmarker stepped back and pointed at the microphone.

The bent gray-haired man shuffled forward and began reading from a piece of crumpled paper. "The New
Roman Empire called the Knesset into session this
morning and demanded that control of all nuclear capacity be turned over to the empire. Failure to comply
would bring immediate attack upon our country. We
had no choice but to comply and have now done so. Mr.
Gianardo has also demanded that we recognize him as
the supreme ruling power in the world. Failure to do so
would invite disaster. The president of the New Roman
Empire obviously does have supreme authority." The
old man shuffled away.

Rathmarker stepped to the microphone. "Thank you,
Mr. Prime Minister. We are gathered at this place as a
matter of principle. Clearly, the New Roman Empire is
uniting the globe in order to create a more just and
decent world. We are the last hope for a peaceful order.
The empire will insist on nonaggression even at the

price of going to war in order to stop killing. However, global order demands recognition of our authority at every level. History records that religion has been a constant source of strife and conflict. Therefore, we are going to personally put an end to further discord."

Rathmarker whirled around and jerked a section of the huge curtains open, letting outside light flood into the holy place. The priest screamed and the Israeli prime minister dropped to his knees, but Rathmarker marched into the center of the sacred chamber, knocking aside a golden plate of incense that sat on top of the ancient ark of the covenant. Calmly, the vice president returned to the microphone.

"No longer will Damian Gianardo be known as President. As of this moment, his title shall be World Emperor, and I will be Prime Minister. Our authority extends over matters of state *and* religion. As it is treason to resist the secular office, so shall it be sedition to oppose our religious authority. We will not allow anyone in the religious community to stand in the way of a completely peaceful world. Those two impostors by the Western Wall will submit to our rule or face the same penalty." Rathmarker stopped and glared at the Israeli prime minister. "No longer will religious charlatanism be tolerated in any form!"

An ominous quiet fell over the crowd. No one moved. Even some of the TV reporters let their cameras slide to the ground. People stared in terrified awe. Gianardo's twisted smile had a sinister leer of total self-satisfaction. He drank in the moment of stillness with complete fulfillment.

Rathmarker declared, "Today, I will be placing a life-size statue of Emperor Gianardo in the center of the Holy of Holies so no one forgets where ultimate control and authority lie. It's all a matter of principle!"

A reporter held up his hand. "Mr. Vice President?"

"Prime Minister!" Rathmarker barked.

"Yes, sir. Mr. Prime Minister, what if the Israelis resist your control of their religion?"

"I expect some resistance here as well as in America. We have foreseen the possibility. After our troops secure the nuclear sites, they will systematically execute all citizens in Israel who refuse to worship the emperor or attempt in any way to block these actions. In addition, a special task force is now being created throughout the empire to deal with religious disobedience in similar fashion. As is true of all forms of national betrayal, noncompliance must be a capital offense. We will be dispatching troops to take the Bozrah-Petra area under our control to demonstrate that no sanctuaries escape our surveillance. Nothing will stop the establishment of a complete world order of tranquility and harmony. It is a matter of principle!"

"I am completely overwhelmed." Ben turned to Cindy. "We are sitting here in your parents' living room watching everything that we have studied for months unfold on the TV screen. I actually saw the president and vice president walk into the Holy of Holies and declare emperor worship. Did you hear what Rathmarker said? Opposition to their religious ideas will be sedition. They think they are going to be able to attack Bozrah!"

Cindy's sightless eyes were focused somewhere just above the TV set. "He won't get far if he tries to invade God's desert asylum. Jimmy has been right about everything. Now we know that the days ahead are truly numbered."

"I almost wish I didn't know. If the Tribulation is anything like we've studied, I cringe in fear. I don't know if we can stand up to the days before us."

I had been standing behind the couch watching the television, waiting for the right moment to give Ben his instructions. The time had come. Once more I stepped through the time barrier and stood behind the couple.

Sam looked and barked.

"Someone's here!" Cindy jumped.

"Be not afraid," I said softly.

Ben leaped up from the couch. "Michael! You're here!"

"Yes," I said as I walked in front of them. "The moment has arrived for me to give your complete instructions. Events are moving quickly. The next three years will seem like both an eternity and a flash of time. Some days will feel totally unbearable, but in retrospect they will be a blur. I want you to know beyond any doubt that you can and will survive. Long ago you were chosen for these assignments because we knew that your family had the capacity and the ability to endure during these last times."

"My family?"

"The Feinbergs are of the tribe of Levi. Even though you have largely ignored your heritage, you come from the priestly lineage. You carry a godly capacity to stand before the heavenly Father on behalf of others. Once again your family will fulfill their call."

"We're not prepared for such a thing . . ."

"To the contrary! Who has a better analytic mind than you, Ben? You're the family chess master. Your ability to strategize will serve your survival needs quite well."

"But my parents?"

"The Holy Spirit will be drawing multitudes of Jews to Bozrah. Many will need medical attention, but far more will be so traumatized by the catastrophes unfolding around them that their emotional care will be paramount. The members of your family are extremely well equipped for the work. The hand of God will protect the area, and no one will be able to hurt them."

Cindy slowly raised her hand. "You said 'survive.' Sounds like Ben's going to be a general in a war. That's scary."

"Sit down, children. Listen well."

Ben picked up a pencil and a pad.

"Gianardo has committed the ancient sin of Babel, thinking he can stand tall enough to shoot an arrow into the heart of God. Even as we speak, secret security squads are being organized. Nothing is left to restrain this man's arrogance."

"What can we possibly do?" Cindy shook her head. "A blind oriental girl and a Messianic Jew aren't going to make much difference."

"To the contrary, Cindy. You are going to become our counterintelligence operation. In some instances, you will automatically know what to do. At other times, I will direct you to the people you are to contact. You will be bringing hope and insight during these final days. The first point of contact will be with your fellow students at UCLA where you will continue your studies."

"Amazing," Ben sighed. "I'm going from pre-med to mid-Trib! I know that we will be in grave danger but what an adventure!"

"We know you have a heart for the task. Ben, you are one of the 144,000 chosen ones mentioned in the book of Revelation. No one can harm you in any way."

"Please tell us everything you can," Cindy pleaded. "We'll need all the insight you have for us."

"First, I want you, Ben, to move your operation to a more secluded place. I will lead you to an obscure house in the country that will become your center of ministry. Next, you need to share all of this information with the McCoys. They will assist you in your outreach. The four of you will form the core of our activities."

"I can't wait to share your instruction with my parents. We have shortwave contact."

"You must be very cautious, Ben. As soon as Gianardo's secret police are fully functional, they will have the capacity to monitor radio contact. Be cautious what you transmit.

"Although you have been raised in a world of television violence, no one is prepared for what is ahead. All sense of proportion will be lost. People will kill indiscriminately with the ease of swatting flies. They will not hesitate to slaughter anyone who does not have the 666 mark or who negates the so-called world emperor's authority. Treachery will abound and life will be cheap. Do you understand?"

"We will be taking the message of Yeshua into this world," Cindy answered. "Like secret ambassadors?"

"Exactly. You will be surprised to discover how many people will want to hear. You will be equally astonished at how quickly and with total callousness others will betray."

"We will be in constant danger?" Ben laid the pad aside.

"You will not, Ben, because none of the 144,000 will be harmed. But Cindy is volunteering to risk her life with no guarantees of safety. Are you willing, Cindy?"

"Yes, I am!" Cindy replied emphatically but also with some fear. Ben had tears in his eyes at the thought of Cindy's being less protected than he was.

Michael continued, "Let us begin with the first message I want transmitted immediately to your father. You must do so before the radio detection systems are operational. Tell him that there are a million people between Bozrah and Petra. As long as they stay within the protected boundaries of these cities, absolutely nothing can harm them. Should they step outside God's prescribed spiritual fence, little can save them. Jordanian and Syrian troops will soon be directed toward the area. Egyptian and Saudi Arabian troops will go up from the south and the east. Tell your father to pay no attention to these armies, for intervention is impossible. Nevertheless, they should begin building a hospital for the many people who will be coming in from the outside.

"Ben, tomorrow you are to call into the dean's office and report that you are sick. We want to quietly prepare the way for you to ease out of UCLA. I am going to direct you to a house located near Lancaster. Ultimately, that place will become your home and center of ministry."

"What can we expect next?" Cindy reached for Ben's hand.

"The pale horse of the Apocalypse has already begun to ride, my children. The angel of death has been unleashed on the world. War, famine, plagues, and wild animals will be used as vehicles of judgment. The alarm is being sounded, and none will be able to say that they were not warned. You will see great consternation everywhere. Fear not. The Lord Yeshua is with you to the very end of the age. I always stand in the shadows."

Across the city, the McCoys sat glued to their television. As the last words of the emperor's speech faded, Joe turned the set off. "Now, children, do you see the truth? This is exactly what your mother and I have been telling you would happen."

"Great guess, Dad," Joe, Jr., shrugged. "But I had a hunch that religion was the next thing that Gianardo would go for. After all, he's already picked up most of the chips."

Jennifer shook her hands at the ceiling. "Children! This is a life-and-death matter. Don't you understand what's ahead?"

"Sure," Joe, Jr., said forcefully. "I'd shelf all that religion talk you've been into with the Feinbergs. You could get all of us into a lot of trouble."

"Please, Mom," fifteen-year-old Erica begged, "get rid of those Bibles. One of my friends might see them and think that Joe and I approve of what you're doing."

"Children," their father begged with tears in his eyes, "you've got to change your minds. We're not only trying to avoid trouble. Our eternal destiny is at stake. Don't you understand?"

"Let's not get back into this fanaticism thing again," Joe, Jr., said insolently. "Please drop it before we end up in another family fight."

17

Larry Feinberg urged his horse forward. The desert air was hot and dry. Sam Eisenberg rode quietly at his side. The animals carefully picked their way through the piles of rock. Overhead, the overpowering cliffs were so high that they shut the sun out.

"I thought you'd like to take a closer look at Petra," Sam said. "We really didn't get a good look when you first came to Bozrah. Fascinating place."

"Great idea, Sam. We had to take a break anyway, waiting for that lumber to arrive for the hospital. How much longer are we going to be able to get such large supplies?"

Sam shook his head. "Too many people coming in. We've been able to get around the blockades that the empire's soldiers imposed on the main highway. One of these days they'll find our side roads. Before long, people will be able to take only what they can carry. One day soon Gianardo will unleash his threatened attack on us."

"There's the El Khazneh! The great Treasury of the past." Larry pointed at a huge crevice ahead of them and kicked his horse.

"The Arabs call the entry the Siq. The canyon walls are three hundred feet high at the entry."

Sparks flew as the horse hooves struck the flint

rocks. The two men stopped in front of the massive thirteen-story building carved out of the cliff. Light slipped through from the top, highlighting the red columns and carvings on the overwhelming structure.

"The Nabataeans ruled the desert and controlled the trade routes from El Khazneh." Sam pointed up to the statues that adorned the top level of the building. "At one time, they must have kept a fortune locked inside."

"And you think the apostle Paul stayed here?"

"Many scholars believe the hidden desert years after Paul's conversion were spent in this very place. Maybe he even watched the workmen carve this incredible monument to the power of the Nabataean kings."

Suddenly, the ground began to shake. The horses shied and shook nervously. An ominous rumbling sound arose from the ground. Rocks began to bounce from cliffs.

"Earthquake!" Sam yelled. "Quick, get inside the Treasury."

The horse spun and resisted the hard kicks. When a boulder landed five feet from Larry, his horse bolted forward, nearly hurling him backward out of the saddle. Both men raced between the red stone columns into the black interior of the edifice. They dismounted and tried to quiet the nervous horses, but the shaking floor sent them sprawling. The panicky horses darted toward the back of the huge chamber.

"We'll be killed," Larry gasped. "The building can't stand the strain."

Rocks pelted the earth like hail. Sickening grinding sounds and dust filled the air. After about a minute, the tremor stopped. Both men lay completely still, covering their heads with their arms. The terrified horses beat the ground with their hooves.

"Is it over?" Larry ventured.

"Look's like it." Sam staggered to his feet.

"In all my years in southern California, I never experienced one like that! Only God saved us."

"Let's get out of this building before an aftershock

hits." Sam slowly and cautiously tried to get his horse's reins. "We need to leave this canyon as quickly as possible."

"Immediately." Larry led his horse out. "But I don't think we need to worry. If there ever was a test of God's promise to protect us, we just went through it. There's no other explanation for that mountain of rock not falling on our heads."

"Look up." Sam pointed to the rim of the canyon. "The sky is filled with smoke and airplanes."

"There's an attack going on somewhere." Larry shielded his eyes. "I've got a feeling that we just survived another of God's signs to the world."

"Let's get back to Bozrah as quickly as possible and see what the radio can tell us. By the time we get there, the evening news ought to have some word about what we've lived through."

When the two men rode into Bozrah, the sun was sinking in the sky. Multitudes of people were wandering around the streets and the tent city that had sprung up. After an Arab believer helped with their horses, they went to Larry's house where the transmitter was kept.

Angie saw them coming and ran out to her husband. "Thank God, you're not hurt. We thought the town would fall down around us, but not one building seems to be damaged. We were terrified!"

Sam hugged his wife. "Let's see what Larry can find on the radio. Something big went down today."

Larry flipped the switch of the electric generator and turned on the radio. "I'll try the international station." Larry finally tuned the radio. Other residents of the community crowded around.

For a moment, only static came out. Then an English-speaking voice broke. "Seismographic equipment indicates an epicenter fifty miles north of the obscure and ancient area of Bozrah. The Richter scale has measured a frightening 8. Early reports indicate that as many as five thousand soldiers of the New Roman

Empire patrolling the roads were killed by the tremor. Reports are vague because reconnaissance in the area has not been possible. Equally strange are the radar jamming and confusion occurring in the same locale. For some strange and unexplained reason, jets were flying to attack a target in the same area. Many of these planes crashed into each other. No one is sure of the actual losses since a news blackout has been imposed."

"The Lord *has* saved us. Ben's report and warning were exactly right. Those planes and troops were aimed at us, but we were completely protected."

☐   ☐   ☐

"Terrible earthquake in Israel earlier today." A girl in Cindy's psychology class leaned over. "Just saw the television news. Lots of casualties among our troops. I'm worried."

"I hadn't heard the report," Cindy said calmly.

"My brother's in the army," the girl continued. "I don't know what in the world we're doing over there anyway. Why can't we leave that little country alone?"

"Israel is strategic in the plan of God."

"What?" The girl blinked. "I don't understand."

"Things are going to get much worse." Cindy smiled. "I hope your brother gets out of Israel before the really big disaster hits."

"Hits?" The girl pushed her closer. "What are you suggesting?"

"These unexpected events are a warning to us. If we heed them, we will be spared the pain that lies ahead."

"Where are you getting this stuff?"

"The Bible predicted exactly what's happening today over two thousand years ago. I simply study the Bible."

"Seriously?"

"Quite."

"Look," the girl whispered softly, "this subject could get us both in a lot of trouble . . . but I'm really worried about my brother. Would you tell me more?"

"I would count it an honor. My name is Cindy. What's yours?"

"Deborah. Deborah Whitaker."

"You've probably noticed that I'm blind. This is my guide dog, Sam." Sam perked up his ears.

"Well . . . yeah."

"No problem." Cindy grinned. "But if you'll wait after class and lead me to a place to talk, I would love to tell you *exactly* what's going to happen."

☐ ☐ ☐

Many miles to the south of the UCLA campus, Erica McCoy was sitting in a classroom in Newport Union Harbor High School. Students were piling into their chairs, completely ignoring the teacher who was trying to call the room to order. Mary Higbie, Erica's arch rival, sat next to her. Erica kept talking to a boy beside her in order to ignore Mary.

"Please!" The teacher rapped on her desk. "We have a special speaker. We need your unqualified attention for an important announcement."

The students continued talking as if nothing had been said. Erica flipped a paper wad at a boy several rows over.

"Stop it!" The teacher slammed a book on her desk. The boom echoed across the room. "What do I have to do to get your attention. Kill someone?"

Students jeered and applauded the suggestion but quieted down.

"We have a representative of the office of education. Now listen carefully to what he's got to say. Please welcome Mr. Robert Schultz."

A tall, lean man walked to the center of the room with an indifferent swagger. His voice was cold and hard. "I'm here to talk about abuse. As you know, the system takes all forms of abuse very seriously. Anyone who reports sexual, physical, or emotional abuse will receive immediate care and protection. We simply will not allow parents to take advantage of their children."

"Yippee!" A youth in the back row yelled. "Can you come out and work my old man over? He's been short on my allowance lately."

The class roared.

Schultz walked down the row until he stood in front of the youth. Suddenly, he lifted him completely out of the chair. "You have something to report?"

The astonished student's mouth dropped as he silently shook his head no.

"If you have nothing intelligent to say, don't interrupt." Schultz let the student drop back into the chair. His notebook went flying off the desk. "We're not out here playing with the kiddies." Schultz continued walking through the desks. "Abuse is serious business, and we take it seriously. Get it?"

The room was completely silent.

"Today we have identified a new form of abuse . . . religious abuse. Understand?"

No one spoke.

"The leader of our country is now the supreme authority on all religious matters. Noncompliance can be very deadly business. We are not going to allow rampant misrepresentation of religious truth to be disseminated through our society. Should your parents fail to comply, they could be putting you into jeopardy. Such action would constitute abuse."

"I don't understand." Erica held up her hand. "Please give me an example."

"If your parents try to force religious ideas on you that are not approved by Emperor Gianardo," Schultz spoke slowly, "or teach you that any power exceeds that of our leader, you are being put in an abusive situation."

"Do Christian ideas count?" Erica asked hesitantly.

"If they are used to avoid obedience to rules such as the 666 marking law. However, we are increasingly suspect of Bibles. Let us know if they push Bible beliefs on you."

Erica smiled back pleasantly, but her eyes were fixed wide open. As the man continued talking, Erica began making violent scribbling marks on the notebook on her desk. She didn't even realize that he had finished and sat down until Mary spoke in her ear.

"Didn't you say your parents are always putting fanatical stuff on you?"

Erica looked in horror at the smug grin on Mary's face. "Sure," Erica fumbled. "You know we all complain about our parents at home, but I didn't mean anything like this guy was describing."

"You said they were always studying the Bible," Mary bore down.

"Yes, but they read lots of porno too," Erica lied. "Just broad readers."

Mary smirked and looked the other way.

18

Ben closed the venetian blinds over the living room picture window before going to the back bedroom. He turned on only the small light on the wall. In the dim light, he carefully took the picture off the wall and set it on the floor. He pulled the old transmitter out of the hole in the wall and hooked up the wires. While he waited a few moments for the set to warm up, he slightly opened a blind over the small back door window in the kitchen so that he could see any movement outside. The radio cracked and hummed as the gauges moved back and forth. He glanced at his watch and saw that it was 2:00 A.M.

"Calling the Woman in the Desert, calling the Woman in the Desert," he spoke softly in the microphone.

"We're here." The answer sounded very distant and faint.

"Dad, that's you?"

"Hard to hear you, Son. Lots of electronic interference in the air since the atomic bombs went off."

"You're OK?" Ben talked low but with great intensity.

"Tired," Larry answered. "In the two months since the earthquake that caught us at Petra, we've nearly worked ourselves to death, but the hospital's coming along just fine. And you?"

"Been wild, Dad. But we're doing very well. The ministry is booming. Cindy brought a girl named Deborah Whitaker to the Lord, and in turn she brought her whole family. We've got over fifty people in our group now. We'll be moving the whole operation very soon to our new location. Can't tell you over the air where it is, but all looks good."

"Excellent, Son. We're praying for you every hour."

"People flocking into Bozrah?"

"Yes. Since the war broke out, people have been terrified. We've got everything here from Jews who were atheists to Hasidim who are now praising Yeshua just to be alive."

Static suddenly boomed with a deafening roar. Ben yanked the headset off and waited until the noise faded out again.

" Ben . . . Ben . . . you still there?" Slowly, Larry's voice became clear again.

"Yes, yes," Ben answered. "I'm back on."

"Radiation will be an increasing problem," Larry explained.

"Dad, that's why I'm calling tonight. We're not sure what's really happened. Gianardo has imposed a news blackout, and no one knows what's hit the United States or from where. We're afraid that a nuclear device may have gone off somewhere in the north LA area. We have no way to tell if fallout is occurring. At the very least a big bomb hit up there."

"We've pieced together reports coming out of Jerusalem, Amman, and some of Europe. Apparently, the United Muslim States, China, remnants of Russia, and the Ukraine revolted against the New Roman Empire. The Star Wars Strategic Defense System destroyed a high percentage of the missiles in the air, but a few must have slipped through. The U.S. has shot back many missiles and blasted these countries. No one is sure what damage has been done to the atmosphere, but it must be extensive. People are terrified of what may be ahead. Famine and disease are sure to follow."

"Got any idea of how many were killed?" Ben asked.

"Early estimates are that as many as half a billion people have perished or will die from the effects of the attack."

"Good grief!" Ben gasped. "No wonder Gianardo doesn't want anyone to know what's going on! What should we do?"

"I wish some of those old Geiger counters were still around, Son. Then again, you might not want to know. Watch the water supply. Food will soon be scarce. I guess it all depends on how bad the States were actually hit."

"Perhaps Michael can give us some clarification when he next appears. July 22 is just a few days away, and that's the Fast of Tammuz. I know he'll show then."

"Any word for us about Joe and Jennifer McCoy?"

"They're doing great! Really got a ministry going to parents of kids who are rejecting Jesus. We meet together several times a week. You and Mom would be very proud of what the McCoys have accomplished. How's everyone there?"

"You wouldn't recognize your mother. I bet she's lost twenty pounds out here in this desert heat. She's really helping with many of the children who have been injured. Jimmy and Ruth are doing a great job at the hospital."

Out of the corner of his eye, Ben saw a figure go past the back window. He jerked the headset off and listened intently. Somewhere out on the street, he heard a car door shut. Ben glanced at his watch again . . . 2:15 A.M. . . . no one should be out there.

"Got to run, Dad. Call back soon."

Without further explanation, Ben hit the toggle switch and shoved the transmitter back into the wall. He pushed the wires on top along with the microphone. Ben leaped from the chair and turned the light out.

In the darkness he put the picture back on the wall

and walked to the living room. Carefully, he looked out behind the large blinds covering the picture window. Across the street, three men were standing and talking. One man pointed to the house and waved his arm. A fourth man abruptly ran out of the bushes next door and darted behind a large tree in front of the house.

"Police!" Ben choked. "I've got to get out of here." He ran for the back door.

Just as he stepped into the kitchen he heard a stick break outside. Instantly, Ben dropped to his knees, huddled against the refrigerator next to the door, and listened intently.

"Now!" A bullhorn blasted from the front of the house. "Hit 'em!"

The back door crashed against the refrigerator as two large men broke in. The black figures flew past Ben into the living room. Glass exploded, sounding like the large picture window was smashed. Ben could hear the front door also breaking open.

"Move and you're dead!" A man shouted in the living room.

Ben realized that he had only seconds before lights would go on and they'd backtrack into the kitchen. He scampered through the open back door on his hands and knees and rolled down the steps. For a moment he scanned the backyard. Apparently, all the police were in the house. He crawled through the grass like a wounded dog heading for the nearest cover. At the back fence, Ben edged his way through the bushes and disappeared into the foliage.

Men continued to shout from the front of the house. Ben could hear doors slamming and more glass breaking. His heart was beating so fast that he felt weak and dizzy. Sweat was running down his neck, and his shirt was damp. He pushed himself backward toward the fence. To his amazement, he felt the boards give. The old wood panels were dangling by a few loose nails. Ben easily knocked them out and wiggled his way into the next yard.

Once he was on his feet he ran straight toward what looked like a gate. Something hit his knees, and he went sprawling into the grass with a metal table landing on top of him. The crash echoed across the yard like a truck hitting a tree. Dogs started barking inside the house.

"Oh, no!" The edges of a wrought iron coffee table ground into his chest. "Got to get out of here." He felt the sting of pain and a trickle of blood run down his shin. Ben hobbled to the gate as a light came on in a back bedroom.

Ben shook the gate hard, but it was locked. Without hesitation he went up the side and over the top. As he hit the ground, he knew a good hunk of his shirt was left on the top spike. A searchlight flashed on in the backyard behind him. He tore out for the street.

Only after running several blocks in the pitch-black night did Ben stop. Nearly exhausted, he fell behind a tree in a vacant lot. The air smelled hot, dingy, and smoky. His leg stung and his back was badly scratched. But at least there were no sounds of cars or men following him. An ominous silence hung over the area.

"Well," he said to himself, "we've got one more transmitter stashed. They haven't got us yet . . . but only *one* more left."

□   □   □

The next morning Ben met with the leaders of his college students' group at the McCoys' home. Jennifer passed out colas as the conversation unfolded. Ben described the details of the chase.

"How did they know you were in the house that we rented for radio transmission?" Isaiah Murphy asked.

"I don't know." Ben pondered the question. "I was sure no one was following me, and I waited until very late at night. I didn't really have the radio on that long . . ."

"They can get a fix quick if they're prepared," Joe McCoy countered.

"I remember looking at my watch. Seems like about fifteen minutes had passed."

"Plenty of time," Joe confirmed.

"We can bet they're on to us now," someone added.

"What do you think, George?" Ben asked a tall, lanky student. "Your father's a retired police officer. Could he give us any insight?"

George Abrams ran his hands through his thick black hair. "My dad doesn't say much these days. I think he's terrified. They went to church when he was a boy, and he knows a lot about Bible teaching, even though he never followed it. He's confused and just doesn't want me to get into trouble."

"I don't think we ought to contact our parents," Mary Chandler added. "We could end up putting people in jeopardy without any intention to do so. Matters are just too serious."

"I agree," Cindy added, "no one knows what the truth is anymore. The news is managed, and the secret police have surveillance equipment that we can't even begin to understand or detect."

"For those very reasons, I think we need to move out to Lancaster at once," Joe insisted. "We can watch what goes on in a small town much easier. The police have all the advantages in the metropolis. Once we're out on the edge of things, we can stay concealed."

"We must carefully cover our tracks," George added. "I don't think we ought to let the parents who meet with the McCoys know where we are. If we keep our two fronts of ministry separate, we'll have an additional safety factor."

"I agree," Joe beckoned for Jennifer to come in from the kitchen. "I think from this point on we need to have only one contact person between the two groups. We just can't take any chances."

"Why not me?" Cindy volunteered. "Since my parents live in the area, I'm a natural link. No one could be suspicious of my coming down here to visit the restaurant."

"I don't know," Ben hesitated. "I don't like the exposure."

"But *you* sure don't need to be wandering around down here," George confronted Ben. "A quick computer check of your family background would reveal that they left with passports for Israel. They'd nail you in a minute."

"In addition, you may have accidentally left some clues back at our meeting house," George reasoned.

"I suppose so," Ben waffled. "I'm just nervous about Cindy being pursued. Only my two very good eyes and the grace of God saved me the other night! I know Michael promised that no one could hurt me, but I'm still human. I get scared sometimes."

"We'll take good care of Cindy," Joe assured Ben. "Let's join hands and commit the plan to the Lord." Joe reached out for Isaiah and another student next to him. "We need to pray for protection for us, our families, and all of our contacts."

The group began praying for each other. Eventually, the prayers ended, and they prepared to leave into the summer night. Some left by the back door while others waited a while before going down the front driveway so they would not appear to have been meeting. After everyone else was gone, Ben, Cindy, and Sam left.

"Drive carefully," Jennifer called after them. "Your lives are precious."

Ben and Cindy talked all the way back to the campus about packing and planning for the relocation. Finally, they pulled in front of Cindy's dorm. Sam sat up in the back seat.

"The work is really going well." Ben smiled. "I'm amazed at how many students you have been able to reach. People seem to be especially attracted to your honesty."

"Perhaps my blindness is an asset. I'm easy to trust."

"Maybe so. I've also been amazed at the response

from the people Michael sent me to contact. The results have been equally exciting. I can't say that I miss the college scene much."

"I worry that the university will try to track you down."

"No, I'm just a person who dropped out of school for medical reasons." Ben opened the car door for Cindy. "I think my tracks are well covered. I don't see how they could possibly locate me unless I let myself get caught like I nearly did last night."

"Don't let that ever happen again!" Cindy mockingly scolded. "You're better at getting me around than my dog. You'd be hard to replace!"

They kissed each other good night, and Ben hurried back to his apartment.

□   □   □

I waited until the next morning to talk with Ben. I knew the attack caused him to lose track of time. Without a sound I slipped through the wall of time into his apartment. After turning on Ben's automatic coffee maker, I sat down in a bedroom chair waiting for him to wake up. Shortly, he stirred and reached for the clock.

"Good morning, Ben."

The alarm clock hit the floor. Ben sat straight up in bed. "Who is it?" he shouted.

"I thought you'd recognize my voice by now."

"Don't you ever knock?" Ben looked disgusted. "You scared me silly."

"I apologize. I just wanted to get the day started right for you. Important day, you know."

Ben frowned and reached down to pick up the alarm clock. "Why?"

"It is July 22, 1997. The Fast of Tammuz."

"Already?" Ben blinked. "How did it get here so fast?" He got out of bed and put his pants on. "Let me get a shirt. No telling what's next."

"Actually, nothing you can see today, Ben. Pour yourself a cup of coffee and I will explain."

"Coffee?" Ben stared uncomprehending at the coffee steaming in the kitchen.

"Today a new phase of the Tribulation begins. The Lord Jesus will break the Fifth Seal that John writes about in the Revelation. Seventy thousand saints have died so far during the persecutions and have been kept under the heavenly altar. Today their cries to be avenged will be heard, and the next period of woes begins."

"So, we start again." Ben drank a sip of coffee and sat down at the kitchen table. "The police got very close the other night, Michael. I was really terrified."

"Yes, I know. Perhaps I should clarify some things about your situation. There is no place in the world that is completely protected except the Bozrah-Petra area. Even there, people are still subject to the normal bodily processes like heart attacks, strokes, or injuries. You are living in a genuine war zone.

"You must start now to get ready for what is ahead, and I want you to let your parents know about the next catastrophe. You must also understand what the atomic exchange has done to the world."

"We really *did* get hit?"

"Indeed. Skin diseases will multiply like a plague. You must wash your body often and carefully. Wear long-sleeved clothing and a hat. Expect problems. Crops will fail and food will be in short supply. Animals will go on savage rampages. Wild dogs will roam the streets. Take no chances."

"No kidding!"

"The nuclear explosions have produced large amounts of nitrogen oxides, which are quickly depleting the ozone layer. Great amounts of dirt are beginning to settle into the atmosphere as well. In addition, nuclear fireballs have set many fires around the world. Hundreds of tons of smoke and soot have been released from the burning cities. The nuclear winter is coming that will drop temperatures by an average of thirty degrees in northern Europe, Russia, Canada, and the northern United States. Spring crops will be destroyed next year, and the rains will spread radiation that impedes photosynthesis."

Ben took another long drink of coffee. "What will the results look like when it hits people . . . us?"

"People will feel nauseated and tired, and many will vomit. They will feel better for a while, but they will be developing fewer and fewer white blood cells, antibodies, and platelets. Infections will be hard to fight, and many people will lose their hair. Others will suffer severe weight loss and struggle with internal bleeding. Skin lesions and cancers will be quite common. The degree of injury will depend on how long people are exposed to concentrated radiation."

"And these effects will increase as the days go by?"

"Unfortunately."

Ben set the cup down and looked out the window. "It's going to be a long summer. And what can we expect at the end of the period?"

"In about a month . . . on Tuesday, August 12 . . . Av 9 comes down again. At sunrise in Jerusalem, the Sixth Seal will be broken, and the most violent upheaval the world has ever known will shake the very foundations of creation."

"And I am to tell my parents everything you have said?"

"Yes. They must be prepared for the bad condition people seeking refuge will be in. You must be in a safe location when the earthquakes come, for I tell you nothing of this magnitude has ever befallen the globe."

"I'll get to the transmitter as soon as I can. By the way, Michael, any help you can give me along the way will be appreciated. Something simple would do fine . . . like a warning that the bad guys are coming."

"Fear not, Ben. Great is your reward in heaven."

19

It was now the summer of 1997 and the hot August sun blazed down on Ben's car pulling away from the hamburger stand on the edge of the little town of Lancaster. The aroma of relish and onions filled the car. As he drove down Highway 14, Ben described the scenery to Cindy. "Everything's burned up. The grass is brown and even the weeds are dried up."

"Typical summer scene in southern California." Cindy wiped the perspiration from her forehead. "But it seems much hotter now."

"The dust of death is everywhere." Ben sped up as he left the reduced speed zone behind. "Earth's atmosphere has been severely damaged. I've never seen so many dead animals by the roadside."

"Maybe being blind isn't all bad."

"But I wish you could see my little farmhouse. The place is great." Ben slowed down to turn off the highway. "Everything is just like Michael said it would be. I really got a deal. I was able to lease it for almost nothing because of the economic chaos. Perfect for our ministry."

"Can you see the house yet?"

The car bounced on the ruts on the dirt road, sending clouds of dust across the field. "Just straight ahead.

Looks like at least a dozen cars are already there. The gang is helping put the place together."

Ben pulled under a small carport and helped Cindy out. Sam jumped out behind her. Ben picked up the sacks in one arm and then guided Cindy along the side of the house and up the few steps onto the porch of the old farmhouse. "It's sort of faded," he confided, "but it's still white and is over sixty years old. Was built well by some Okies who came out during the depression years. There's a huge oak tree on the other side of the house."

"Welcome home!" Joe McCoy swung the screen door open. "We almost have your things in order."

"Great!" Ben waved at the students working around the house.

Deborah Whitaker stuck her head out of the kitchen. "Place looks like you've already lived here, Ben. The sink is a national disaster area, and the cockroaches are holding their national drag race finals behind the refrigerator. Only a man could cultivate such a climate."

"Now, now, Debbie." George came down the stairs from the second floor. "Don't be a female chauvinist piglet. Ben, we got your bed put together by the window. You can see completely up and down the highway. No one will sneak up on you from that perch."

"Wow! What a job you've done! Cindy and I brought you some hamburgers. Let's stop for lunch."

George bounded over the stair rail and hit the nearest chair before anyone could take a step. "Don't have to say food but once to a growing boy." He sprawled his lanky legs out on the bare wooden floor.

I"'m fixing a pitcher of lemonade," Jennifer McCoy added from the kitchen. "I'll call the kids who are working out back."

The small living room was soon filled with college students reaching for hamburgers, fries, and lemonade. They prayed, laughed, teased, and devoured the food.

"We've got the transmitter wired up." Mary Chandler told Ben. "I think we've found a good place to keep it protected when the big quake comes."

Mary pointed upstairs. "We've got all the electronic equipment inside a metal box, and it's surrounded with foam rubber padding. If the house falls in, the equipment will make it."

"What a job you've done!" Ben beamed. "How can I ever thank you?"

"Thank us?" the group echoed.

"How can we ever thank *you?*" Deborah answered. "You and Cindy have brought life itself to us. Without you, we would all be hopelessly entangled in the lies and the destruction devouring the world. You have been our lifeline to eternal survival."

"We are just grateful that God chose to use us." Ben reached out for Cindy's hand. "The truth is that anyone who really desires to be righteous or find the true God will find the way even if an angel has to be dispatched. We owe a great debt to our friend Michael. Actually, we found you because Michael directed us."

George pointed to several students. "We Jews came to the Lord through your witness, Ben. No matter what lies ahead we will live and die with the supreme satisfaction that we found what our ancestors prayed to be. God has surely fulfilled our deepest longings and greatest hopes."

"And we've become great friends," Ben added. "I've found a friendship among you that I've never known before." He stopped and the room became very quiet.

Cindy squeezed his hand. "Why don't we try the radio out?" She broke the awkward silence. "Let's call Bozrah."

"Terrific idea." Mary stood up. "We can show you our handiwork. Let's go upstairs." The group fell in behind her and piled up the steps. Mary led them to a sparsely furnished room with only a table and chair in one corner. At the bottom of one wall was a large metal grate covering the heating duct. "Watch this!" Mary dropped to one knee and pulled the cover off. She slid a metal box out of the wall. "Rather clever, I'd say." She opened the top and lifted the transmitter out. "We're ready to talk to the world."

"We've made a new hookup." George put a small speaker on the table and plugged in the wires. "You won't have to use a headset and we can hear."

"Excellent." Ben carefully fine-tuned the dials. "Calling the Woman in the Desert," he repeated several times. Static crackled over the speaker and humming filled the room. "Come in, Woman in the Desert."

"Hello . . . hello . . . ," the voice sounded low, far away but familiar.

"Jimmy? Jimmy? Is that you?"

"Hey, Ben." Static broke in. "It's me. The old used car salesman."

The group cheered. "You've got an audience here," Ben explained. "The whole gang of believers are with me."

"Can't sell you any cars today," Jimmy's voice crackled. "But I've got a couple of low mileage camels with lots of tread left."

"Save us a couple. How's the family? Ruth? Mom?"

"Of course, it's night here in Bozrah, and Mom has turned in. Ruth is out at the hospital. Ought to be here shortly. Been a busy, hard day, but everyone's healthy. People just keep showing up. The pronouncements by Moses and Elijah are having their effect. More and more are believing."

"People in bad shape?"

"Yeah," Jimmy drawled with his Texas accent. "The world's falling apart and so are the people. Ruth and I work from sunup to sundown, but we love every minute of it. Wouldn't have missed the trip for the world."

"Ready for the earthquake?"

"We think so, but we're not sure what God's special protection will mean. We can only go by the quake earlier in the summer. We expect to feel effects but not suffer damage. We are far more worried about you. Southern California is not a great place for a really big shake."

"I know, I know," Ben sighed. "The whole group will be out here with us when it comes. At least we'll be away from LA where the big catastrophes will happen. We think we're prepared."

"We'll be praying for you."

"Better sign off," Ben concluded. "Don't want to stay on too long in case we've got any eavesdroppers. So long until the next visit."

"Peace!" Static filled the speaker.

Ben switched the set off. Everyone applauded.

"It worked!" Isaiah shouted. "We're beating the system!" Someone clapped. "More lemonade for a toast," George demanded. The entourage rushed for the door and stampeded down the stairs.

"Cindy . . . ," Jennifer stopped at the door. "Could I ask you for a favor?"

"Of course."

"We can't bring the children out here." Jennifer's face suddenly looked drawn and sober. "We would only endanger the whole mission. We will have to stay behind with them."

"Oh, no!" Cindy protested.

"No. Joe and I have already discussed the matter. They could easily betray us because of their flippant attitude. We will try to take them to another safe place. But I was hoping that you might at least witness to Erica before next Tuesday. It's almost our last hope."

Cindy's brow furrowed. "You know that I would do anything in the world for you and certainly to help the children. But . . . it . . . seems only the people that Michael directs us to or that seek our help respond. And he warned when we go beyond those boundaries we could be in serious jeopardy. I just wouldn't want to raise any false hopes."

"Sure, I understand. I guess Joe and I are getting desperate."

Cindy hugged her friend. "I'll see her tomorrow if you'll set it up. Don't give it another thought."

"Well," Jennifer hedged, "maybe we ought not . . ."

"Tomorrow," Cindy insisted. "I'll pray and do my best."

☐   ☐   ☐

"Ruth!" Jimmy pushed the microphone to the back of the table. "You just missed Ben. Things are going great with them."

"Oh, rats!" Ruth plopped down in a chair. "I've not talked to them in two weeks. Are they ready for the other shoe to drop next week?"

"Sounds like they are. I tried to be optimistic, but I'm not sure that we are. I don't think anyone can really get ready for what's coming."

Larry abruptly walked into the room with exposed studs and rafters. There were no windows; only holes in the siding let the breeze blow through the single room. "Couldn't help overhearing you outside. Sorry that I missed Ben."

"He's moved into the new house. The transmitter worked fine."

"Good." Larry sat down in a simple wooden chair. "I just don't know how we're going to care for this multitude. So many are suicidal. They've lived with stories of the World War II Holocaust all of their lives, and now history is repeating itself. Obviously, Gianardo acts like Hitler reincarnated. It's too much for many of them to bear."

"Is it true that another psychiatrist has come in?" Ruth asked. "I heard people talking at the hospital."

"Yes. Frank Kohl is a Christian who escaped from Germany. Amazing man. I'm sending him to Petra to work with the people camped down there. He's going to help lift the load by treating the psychotic ones."

Jimmy stood up and stretched his legs. "We didn't build the hospital big enough. We're going to need a lot more space. But then again the whole thing may collapse next week."

Larry laughed. "What a gem you are, Son. You've done an outstanding job supervising the men and working with the Arabs. No, I've got a hunch that the hand of God is going to be good to those walls you've put up. Just maybe we'll see the story of Jericho repeated in reverse form."

"I pray so." Jimmy looked at the blisters on his hands. "I'd hate to start over again."

Larry put the chair against the wall. "I think I'll turn in. Dawn comes mighty early around here. You two take care of yourselves and turn out the lights when you leave."

"Sure, Dad." Ruth called after him.

Ruth and Jimmy shut the door behind them and walked out into the brisk night air. The dry heat of the summer day had given way to the cool of the desert night. The sky was filled with stars.

"Great night." Jimmy looked at the silhouette of the black mountains against the dark sky.

Ruth put her arm around his shoulder. "We've come a long way since that summer afternoon two years ago when you made your little declaration of moral principles to my parents. Who would ever have believed it would lead to this place?"

"Seems like a million years ago on another planet."

"It was another time. An age that is gone. Disappeared. Vanished in the twinkling of an eye."

Jimmy looked at the camp fires dotting the hillside. "Sometimes I feel so set adrift. Everything I once held to is gone. Of course, my faith sustains me, but if I didn't have you, Ruth, I think I'd come unglued."

"You make me so very happy." Ruth's eyes filled with tears. "I didn't dream I could find a man who would be so thoughtful and considerate. So loving."

"You're crying?"

"I'm just overcome. I'm so happy. Here I am in the midst of this unmitigated chaos with the world exploding, and I am deliriously happy with you. That's why I'm crying."

"Just don't ever leave me." Jimmy suddenly hugged Ruth. "You are my life."

The young lovers walked toward their little wooden house on the edge of the tent city. People noticed them and nodded respectfully as they passed by.

The next afternoon Jennifer drove Cindy to the McCoys' house. As she led Cindy up the walk, Jennifer explained, "Erica and a group of girls are working on cheerleading yells. They should be going home shortly. I'll let you know when I think Erica's friends are gone. There's quite a bunch of them."

"Why have your children been so resistant?"

"Painful question." Jennifer opened the front door. "I anguish over that issue, and I'm not sure that I fully understand the answer yet. Joe and I were good parents even though we were gone a great deal of the time when Joe, Jr., and Erica were small. We couldn't support a southern California life-style on one salary. I guess today you'd label our children as affluent latchkey kids. Perhaps the lack of contact developed their tendency to give more credence to their friends. That's sure the way they are now."

Cindy felt for a chair. "Just pray that I can get through to her today." Sam lay down at her feet.

"I'm going to take you outside to the backyard and let you sit by the gate. A couple of comfortable chairs are there. When the squad leaves, I'll send Erica out with a glass of lemonade."

Noise echoed from fence to fence as the girls yelled, danced, and waved pompoms. Cindy sat in her obscure corner listening. Sam watched the scene intently. In about twenty minutes the rehearsal ended, and the laughing voices drifted away.

"Mother said to bring you this drink," Erica's familiar voice jolted Cindy out of her prayer.

"Erica!" Cindy turned toward the sound. "Sit down. I haven't talked to you in weeks."

"Well," Erica was hesitant and distant, "I have to leave with my friends. We're meeting some guys for pizza. I really can't stay."

Cindy felt the cold glass touch her hand. "Erica, we might never have the opportunity to speak together again. I've got to say several things to you. The hand of God is moving very quickly."

"Please," Erica begged, "we shouldn't be talking about religious stuff. I know you're sincere, but you and my parents are playing with fire."

Cindy set the glass down and took the teenager's hand. "In a few days the earth is going to be nearly shaken out of orbit. We're all going to slosh around like terrified fish in a goldfish bowl. Nothing of this magnitude has ever happened. Most of what you see around you will collapse."

"Look," Erica's voice was hushed, "I'm sure you believe these things, but some of these kids would turn us in to the authorities just for laughs. I have enough trouble making sure my parents' Bibles are well hidden when the girls are over here."

"I understand . . ." Cindy looked down. "I really *do* understand, but your eternal destiny is at stake. Even if something terrible happened to me, I would do everything I could to tell you about Jesus."

"You're a very good person, Cindy. Kind. Giving. I've watched you when you've been here with Ben. But the world doesn't have a place for people like you anymore, and I have to go on living with some of these creeps who call themselves my friends. I must leave religion alone for the good of everybody."

"Erica, no one has much time left. The days are numbered. In a very short while your friends and their opinions won't matter. They *will not* be here. But God has a plan for your life for today and for all of your tomorrows."

"Look." Erica chewed her lip. "After next week, I'll listen. I've got to catch up with the gang now. But I'll talk if you'll just wait until then."

"I'm going to be praying for you. I'll ask God to keep you through what's coming Tuesday. There is no power on earth greater than the Lord Jesus."

Suddenly, the backyard gate swung open. Mary Higbie stepped in and stared at both of them. "I wondered where the God talk was coming from."

"M . . . Mary! You . . . you've been listening!" Erica stammered.

"I came back to find you. The girls are waiting. I just happened to come in the back way."

"Mary?" Cindy asked uncomprehendingly.

"You Christian freaks!" Mary sneered at Cindy.

"I don't understand," Cindy answered vaguely. "Who are you?"

"Really weird conversation, Erica." Mary smirked. "I thought your family was straight. Next thing we know you'll be leading cheers for Jesus." The girl spun on her heels and ran toward the car waiting in the driveway.

"Mary!" Erica darted after her. "Mary! Stop it!" Her voice trailed away as she chased her old nemesis. "Please. Don't make something out of nothing."

Cindy heard the door slam and the car drive away. The backyard seemed intensely silent. "Michael warned me," she said to herself. "He cautioned me about just such a danger."

20

Gianardo quickly looked around the Oval Office in the White House and glanced at his watch. He glared at the adviser standing in front of his desk next to Prime Minister Rathmarker. "Monday's a busy day," he snapped. "It's almost five o'clock, and I have things to do this evening. I think this whole idea is nonsense and you are being reactionary."

"Mr. Emperor," the prime minister cleared his throat, "I think we need to consider carefully some hard data in this report."

"Take seriously the prediction by those two Israeli impostors?" Gianardo raised his eyebrows and rolled his eyes. "Been listening to the prime-time show put on by those actors calling themselves Moses and Elijah? I consider their warnings of an impending earthquake to be in a class with Elvis sightings."

"Sir." The adviser handed a stapled report to both Gianardo and the prime minister. "We are not reacting to the press speculations or popular fascination with those men sitting by the Western Wall."

"Then why the sudden investigation of possible earthquakes?" Gianardo snarled. "I'm not about to let the world think that I am even slightly affected by those two freaks. I remain the primary religious authority as well as the political authority. Do you understand?"

"Absolutely." The aide smiled nervously. "We will release nothing but your insights and personal warnings."

"Forget that." Gianardo opened the file. "No matter what you've found, we are not going to appear preempted by those two frauds." The emperor scanned the page. "What's your reading, Jacob?"

Jacob Rathmarker puckered his lips and hesitated. "All the indicators point to the immediate possibility of a massive shift of the Eurasian Plate down to a depth of sixty miles below the surface. Hard facts here suggest the Scotia Plate below South America and the Caribbean Plate would also move. Several scientists including our major adviser, Terbor L. Esiw, are convinced that a corresponding shift would result in the Philippine Plate as well as the Somali Plate off the coast of Africa. A big danger to ignore!"

"Sir." The aide flipped through the pages. "Look at the bottom of page eight. The diagram clearly indicates what could happen in this country. The Juan de Fuca Plate near Mount Saint Helens is likely to move. Of course, the San Andreas Fault would shift. No one can possibly calculate the extent of the chain reaction that would follow."

"But you want me to warn people that something *could* happen in a couple of hours because it coincides with the sunrise in Israel ushering in the ninth of Av!" Gianardo charged. "Impossible. Every religious nut on both sides of the ocean would claim that I'm about to abdicate my position of religious preeminence and have a conversion experience. Anyway, there's nothing here that says exactly when such a shift of the Eurasian Plate might occur. Who knows? Maybe it will happen in thirty minutes or in a hundred years. At best I'll wait until Av 9 is over."

"Our fears are that the recent atomic exchange has created immediate pressure," the aide argued.

"Well . . . ," the prime minister paused. "I'm obviously not going to be seen as reacting to the warnings

of Moses and Elijah or whoever they are. We haven't
been able to kill the two freaks so they obviously have
some sort of supernatural powers. But I'm going to
make sure that I'm protected during the next twenty-
four hours."

"Like where?" Gianardo shrugged. "If such a big
shake comes, there are no guarantees of safety anywhere. Even a cave might fall in."

"We were thinking of calling for a military alert at
least," the aide ventured.

"No chance." Gianardo tossed the report aside. "I've
got more pressing matters. Come back tomorrow after
those two clowns by the Western Wall have been dis-
credited, and I'll talk about future precautions. Let's
not forget who is running the world these days." Gianardo pounded the table. "Me!"

☐　　☐　　☐

The entire UCLA Bible study group worked frantically, making their last-minute arrangements at Ben's
farmhouse. Jugs of water were being lined up outside
and furniture stacked out of the way.

"What time is it?" George asked.

"It's 7:30 P.M. West Coast time," Mary answered.
"We've only got about fifteen minutes left. We need to
hurry."

"Put the metal box with the electronic equipment out
in the open," Ben pointed to a space in front of the
house. "Sure don't want anything to fall on that precious commodity."

Cindy felt her way along the walls. "Is all the food
secure?" she called out.

"Got enough for two weeks." Ben passed her, carrying a large sack of cans. "We should be able to wait out
whatever comes. I sure hope Michael shows up. A little
insight would be really appreciated."

"Since the ninth of Av is almost here, I'm sure he'll
visit soon," Cindy added.

"Everybody outside," Ben called. "I want us to sit in a circle out here in the open where we're completely away from anything that could fall. The cars are scattered far enough away from the house that they won't be touched unless the earth opens up."

The students spread blankets on the ground well in front of the farmhouse. Each had a Bible. Even though it was nearly 7:45 P.M., the summer sun was well above the horizon line. Sam began to pace nervously. He sniffed the air and began a low growl.

"I sure wish that the McCoys were with us," Cindy told Ben. "I'm very concerned about them."

"Joe said they were taking their kids out if they had to tie them in the back seat. Maybe the trip will shake some sense into their little heads. I think they were going to drive toward the Sultan Sea and sit out the shake in a flat area."

"I hope they took plenty of food." Cindy sat down on the blanket. "They may have a hard time getting back into the Newport Beach area."

The students huddled around Ben. "In just moments the sun will rise over Jerusalem, and the Lord Yeshua will break the Sixth Seal. When He opens the scroll, He will proclaim judgment on those who have unrepentant hearts. Each of the signs that we have witnessed is a warning to the world to turn from wickedness. Tragically, the sinful are blinded by their own perversity and will not read the warnings that the earth itself is giving us. Even Emperor Gianardo must be using gross denial."

Ben felt unsteady and looked down. The ground moved slightly. Students looked at each other in wonder. "I think it's really happening," someone exclaimed.

"Remember He is with us." Ben looked nervously around the group. "No matter what happens, the Lord Yeshua will not abandon us." Suddenly, he fell backward.

A deafening rumble seemed to be rising out of the earth and from the hills as the ground shifted back and forth. Ben rolled to one side as he reached for Cindy's hand. Sam began to bark and howl. The blankets began to move up and down, and the entire field shifted and turned like a giant carpet being readjusted. The roar increased.

"Look!" George pointed beyond the end of the fence line toward the base of a distant hill. The ground had risen up like a ten-foot wave coming in on a beach. The tidal wave of soil and grass was moving straight toward them in an ever rolling crescendo of motion. The students watched in horror as the grassy field buckled up before their eyes. The blankets and students were picked up as if they were little floating air mattresses in the ocean and thrown behind the incoming surf. Ben clung to Cindy, realizing that she was tumbling over him as they were slung backward off the blanket. Sam's barking turned into a terrified whine.

Ben tried to get to his feet but fell down. He looked up and saw that the swirling motion of the earth was surging. The house, the large oak tree, the cars, and the students had been picked up and dropped in the swift sweeping movement. Kids and blankets were scattered in every direction, but the house was still standing in what looked like relatively good shape.

Cindy clung to Ben's leg. "Help me!" she choked. Sam tried to crawl under her.

"Hold on! Another shock is bound to follow."

The rumbling was ominous and terrifying as the ground continued to shake violently. Cracks split the soil along the road, but none were big enough to be dangerous.

"Look!" Deborah pointed upward. "The sky is exploding."

Gigantic luminous flashes exploded overhead. Fireballs streaked across the sky, and meteorites plunged and disappeared. The darkening sky looked like a gigantic fireworks display. Huge clouds of black smoke began to fill the sunset.

"Electrical inductions," Mary shouted. "I studied the

phenomenon at UCLA." She pushed herself up on her hands and knees. "They're coming from the sources of the earthquakes. The whole atmosphere around the earth is rolling up like a scroll."

The ground was still trembling, but the violent upheaval was slackening. Ben was able to sit upright. "I'm sure volcanoes have erupted by now. Michael said many would parallel the ocean trenches around the Pacific Ocean. The tidal waves have started."

Mary shielded her eyes but kept looking up. "Some of the tsunamis will be a hundred feet high and come in around 250 miles per hour. Thank God, we're on the back side."

"People on every continent must be terrified." Cindy clung to Ben. "Oh, I pray my parents are OK. I tried so hard to get them to come with me."

"Look!" Mary pointed to the west. "The smoky atmosphere is making the sun appear to be black. But look at the moon that's coming up! It's blood red!"

☐ ☐ ☐

"Emperor Gianardo! Emperor Gianardo! Are you hurt badly?" an aide pulled a big piece of plaster board off Damian Gianardo. "Are you all right, Sir?"

For a few moments the emperor of the New Roman Empire groggily shook his head. The aide pushed another piece of plaster board aside, and Gianardo struggled to his feet. Blood ran over the old scar from his previous head wound. Dust filled his nostrils and he coughed.

"Sir!" The aide panicked. "Can you talk?"

Finally, the emperor cleared his throat. "What happened?" He was barely audible. A few sounds of shifting timber and falling boards came from behind them. There were no voices.

"The complete front of the White House collapsed. Guards are lying under the pillars. You have amazingly escaped alive!"

Gianardo staggered past the bewildered man and then stopped abruptly. What had been the front wall and a window was gone. Up and down Pennsylvania Avenue, trees were toppled, and buildings were in shambles. Cars were scattered as if the hand of a giant had casually tossed them around the landscape. "Ohhh!" the emperor pointed at the sky. "The moon has turned red."

The aide limped beside him, realizing for the first time that a large gash ran down the side of his leg. The arm of his coat was torn, and his face was covered with dust. "Gone." He stared out toward the Mall. "The Washington Monument has broken into pieces."

An errie silence was punctuated by occasional explosions and the noise of water gushing from broken fire hydrants. People were still lying stupefied on the sidewalks and grass. A few sounds of movement came from deep within the White House.

"They were right," the aide muttered. "Totally right. The quake came just as they predicted."

"I wonder how those two Jews set this up?" Gianardo held the side of his head. "How did they figure out the timing?"

The assistant stared angrily at the emperor.

"Got to get to our communications system." Gianardo hobbled back into the crumpled building. "We've got to get to the National Security Building next door."

"Too late now," the aide snapped. "Don't go back in there. The rest of the building may collapse."

"I'm sure the elevator won't work." The emperor rubbed his head again. "Electricity must be off everywhere."

The whole building began to tremble as an aftershock rumbled through the city. "I'm getting out of here!" the aide panicked. "I knew from the first time we were in Israel this was all a mistake. We were warned! . . . We were warned!" His voice trailed away as he ran for the street.

□ □ □

Sam Eisenberg scampered up the mountainside with Larry Feinberg right behind him. The sun was just coming completely up over the hills and mountains around Bozrah, spreading a glorious burst of golden glow over the desert.

"I can't believe how well we came out of the earthquake," Larry puffed. "Jimmy's hospital is still standing. You'd think we'd just been through a leisurely Sunday afternoon shake in southern California."

"Yeah," Sam agreed, picking his way carefully along the rocks, "it was like we were on a plate of the earth that just gently floated while everything around it crunched together."

"I heard the soldiers moving last night." Larry pulled out a pair of binoculars. "Sounded like the whole Jordanian army was trying to surround us for a morning attack."

"I'm glad we knew that the surprise was going to be one big surprise on them." Sam reached the top of the rock pile. "I think we can survey the entire area from here."

"Look!" Larry brought the binoculars to his eyes. "Troop carriers littered all over the thirty-mile safety zone." He stopped and looked carefully. "The vehicles are upside down and turned over."

"There are huge cracks in the ground!" Sam pointed to a winding crevasse that split the desert floor. "Soldiers have fallen inside."

"They're trying to retreat!" Larry studied the scene with the glasses. "It looks to me like the entire army is wrecked."

"A rock slide got many of them." Sam pointed to the base of a large mountain across the plain. "Looks like the entire top and side of that bluff slid down."

"Wow!" Larry exclaimed as he lowered the binoculars. "God's really given them something to think about today up in Amman. The Jordanians won't be coming out here for a good while."

The two men sat down on boulders and watched the soldiers crawling around the desert floor. Just then an aftershock rumbled across the valley, and the soldiers fled in every direction. After ten seconds, the movement stopped, and dust started to settle once more.

"Can you believe that we have lived through the greatest earthquake in human history as easily as a robin sitting on her nest in a spring shower?" Sam beamed. "Thank God, His hand has been on us."

"Indeed!" Larry stretched his legs out. "I calculate 1,260 days equaling 180 weeks of Tribulation. We've come through the first 16 weeks in amazing condition."

"We've got a fer bit to go." Sam imitated a Texas accent. "Still, 90 percent of trouble lies down the trail, but I think we'll make it fine."

"Sure thing, partner." Larry laughed as they started back down the hill toward the Bozrah camp. "Thank God, we're the good guys!"

□   □   □

I watched the students gather up their blankets and slowly collect themselves. I knew the major aftershocks had passed, and there would be little disruption in the area around Lancaster for the next several hours. The time was right to appear and speak to the entire group. Once more I stepped into human history at a point about ten feet from the front porch of the farmhouse.

"Peace be unto you!"

"Michael!" Ben spun around. "We knew you'd be here!"

"I can see him!" Deborah exclaimed. "I'm actually seeing an angel!"

"It's really him," George pointed. "I can't believe my eyes."

"Today I come to all of you as a sign of favor. Behold, you have found a special place in the sight of God. Rejoice! For as this world passes away, you chose the better portion that is eternal."

"Michael, tell us what has happened." Ben took Cindy by the hand and led her forward. Sam strained on the leash behind her. "Bozrah . . . is everyone OK?"

"God's hand has more than protected. Your family and friends have endured very well, even as their enemies were being swallowed by the earth."

"Praise the Lord!" Ben shouted.

"What about the rest of the globe?" Mary walked forward cautiously.

"Do not fear. Come close and listen."

The students huddled around the farmhouse steps.

"Many people will be ready to receive your witness now. I will send each of you to those who are hungry for hope. Yet be prepared for danger to increase! The times are becoming more desperate with every judgment. People are increasingly treacherous."

"What's happened to California?" a student ventured.

"Judgment has engulfed San Francisco. Their wickedness has been called into accountability. The city is no more."

"LA?" George held up his hand.

"The city is in flames, and many sections have been leveled. Yet other portions in Orange County stand. Railways, overpasses, and bridges have buckled before the glance of the Lord."

"And our people?" Cindy asked. "The Christians? And my parents who are not Christians?"

"Your own parents are alive and well, my child. When you see them next, you will find new receptiveness to your message. But the last sixteen weeks have taken a great toll. Over seventy thousand witnesses have become martyrs. Hundreds of thousands of Israelis who embraced Yeshua as Messiah have paid with their lives. Those who have fled the persecutions of

Gianardo compose a new diaspora. Bozrah has become a haven for these people of the truth."

"What are we to do now?" Ben asked.

"I will talk with each one of you separately. I have many assignments for you to fulfill in the coming months. You will find that the time flies as you complete your mission. Yet for the world, each day will seem an eternity of agony. As the end of this period approaches, you will know what to expect next. Watch the skies, for the next great judgment will come from above. Now come and receive your divine appointments."

21

Jimmy looked out over the large audience listening in rapt attention to his teaching. The warm sun made sitting outside very pleasant, casting lengthening shadows over the group. Many of the students looked oriental, some were black, while others were fair and European. Some of his class were patients who lived in the large building he had helped construct.

"Now you can see the significance of the lineage of Yeshua in Matthew's Gospel and how the name adds meaning to today's special celebration called Christmas. He was and is the fulfillment of every prophetic expectation for the Messiah." Jimmy picked up an eraser from his portable chalkboard. "Any questions?"

At least two hundred people were scattered across the sand in front of the hospital. The older people were sitting in chairs; many of the young couples sat on blankets on the ground. Many men stood around the back.

An older man held up his hand and waited for Jimmy to recognize him. "I lived around the Christians during my life in Egypt." His clothes looked at least ten years old, worn and dusty. "I don't remember anyone ever explaining that His coming fulfilled Torah prophecy. Your words are wonderful."

"Nor I," a young man called out. "In America, Christmas was a merchant's dream and little more." Others agreed immediately.

"We were all victims of many misconceptions," Jimmy acknowledged. "That's why we are holding these classes. It's important that we get the facts straight. We want your newfound faith to be anchored in Scripture. I think that's enough for today. Everybody back to work."

The group applauded and then dispersed. Jimmy folded up the chalkboard stand and carried it back inside the hospital.

"You're getting quite a reputation as a teacher," Larry called out from across the examination room when Jimmy put the stand down. "People from Petra want to start coming up to hear your Bible studies. Your skill must be hereditary."

Ruth and her mother came in from a corridor of the hospital. "Merry Christmas, everybody," she rushed over and hugged her father. "I'm so glad everybody's here."

Sharon kissed her son-in-law on the cheek. "Must be strange to celebrate the nativity out here in this desert. The whole Christmas experience is new to us since we didn't really recognize Christian customs. Just Hanukkah."

"Sit down." Larry waved to his family. The bare walls smelled of pine. Overhead, rafters ran from one end to the other, making a spartan contrast with the home left behind in Newport Beach. "Gather around the table and let's enjoy ourselves today. Each of you certainly works hard enough." The only furniture was Larry's desk, a table, and six chairs. He opened the refrigerator door. "I have a little gift for each of you. Been hiding this for weeks." He set four cold cans on the table.

"Cokes!" Jimmy clapped his hands. "Wow! How did you ever find these?"

"Believe it or not, they were in the bottom of a box of canned goods Sam Eisenberg brought in several months ago. I hid them for a special occasion."

Ruth popped the metal tab and took a long drink. "I didn't think any of these were left in the whole world. Wonderful!"

"Best Christmas present I've had in years." Jimmy reached for his Coke. "It's amazing how special the common things have become. We certainly took a lot for granted in the old days."

"Not many luxuries left." Sharon laughed. "Hot water's about it. I think I've lost at least thirty pounds."

"Since you mentioned water," Larry observed, "you're the one who keeps up on the logistics, Sharon. How is the water supply holding out?"

"No signs of atomic contamination in the water we desalinate from the Dead Sea, and the water wells are certainly producing at more than acceptable levels. Our irrigation is so efficient that we'll still be harvesting crops after the Tribulation passes. I don't know about the rest of the world, but we won't starve here."

"Simon Assed's factory is turning out dried food like crazy," Ruth added. "How's everything in your department, Dad?"

Larry turned away. "I wish I hadn't brought the subject up." He paused for a few moments. "We're starting to run low on insulin. I'm afraid our diabetics are going to be in trouble soon. I can also see that we could eventually run out of antibiotics. We've got over two years to go, and I don't think our supplies will stretch that far."

"We're going to have trouble with the psychotics," Ruth observed. "The antipsychotic drugs will probably run short too."

Larry ran his hands nervously through his hair. "I just pray we don't find too many AIDS problems. We surely can't cover them, but we can comfort them and give them love and support."

The group silently drank the cold Cokes. Outside they could hear the sounds of people talking and walking down the wooden corridors. Finally, Larry broke the somber mood. "Hey, it's Christmas! This is the day to celebrate the birth of hope. We're sitting in the only protected space on earth. Let's be joyful."

"Absolutely." Ruth set her Coke can firmly on the table. "I almost forgot to tell you why I called this meeting in the first place. In all this gloom and doom, I got sidetracked from the Christmas present I have for all of you today. Are you ready for glad tidings?"

"Of course," Sharon brightened. "This is the season of cheer. What do you have for us?"

"Really, the gift is for Jimmy, but each of you will be blessed in your own special way so I chose a moment to tell you at the same time. I have my own angelic annunciation. Are you ready?"

Everyone applauded.

"I'm going to have a baby."

"What?" Jimmy dropped his empty can. "What did you say?"

"I'm one month pregnant," Ruth said quietly.

"Wonderful! Wonderful!" Sharon clapped.

"Sit . . . sit down." Jimmy rushed to her side.

"I am sitting, silly."

"My first grandchild!" Larry exclaimed.

"Merry Christmas to each of you." Ruth smiled broadly.

"Like Moses," Larry exploded, "a child born in exile. How very appropriate."

Jimmy looked at his watch. "Ben ought to be getting up about this time. Let's call him and spread the good news around the world."

The family darted down the hall to the little office where the radio transmitter was kept. Jimmy threw the switch and carefully set the dials. "Woman in the Desert calling the End Times Prophet. Calling the Prophet. Calling the man."

"Oh, I hope he left the transmitter on last night," Ruth fretted. "We told him that we would call him Christmas Day. I bet he's still asleep."

"Calling the Prophet," Jimmy repeated.

The static popped and the pitch of the humming changed. "Hello . . . hello," a groggy voice answered.

"Ben, are you awake?" Jimmy asked.

"I am now . . . had to get up to answer the radio."

"Merry Christmas!" the whole family shouted in the microphone.

"Sounds like everyone's there," Ben's voice reverberated with a distant roar. "Merry Christmas to you."

"You must have stayed up late partying," Jimmy chided.

"Actually . . . ," the words faded in and out, "went to bed . . . very late . . . police chased us . . . most of yesterday . . . had to hide . . ."

"What?" Sharon grabbed the microphone. "We can't hear you well. You all right?"

The static eased. "Yes," Ben was louder. "No one got caught, but they ran us across the UCLA campus. Only the hand of God saved us. We escaped through some old sewer tunnels."

"Good grief!" Sharon handed the microphone to Larry.

"The McCoys," Larry asked, "how are they surviving?"

"Been tough. But the big earthquake had a decided effect on their children. I think they are beginning to come around. Cindy's made headway with Erica."

"Good. Good," Larry answered. "Tell them to be careful."

"I have a special Christmas card for you," Ruth broke in. "You're going to be an uncle in about eight months."

"REALLY? NO KIDDIN'?"

"Thought that announcement would put a little something in your Christmas stocking this morning, Ben. Wanted you to be among the first to know."

The radio popped and faded, ". . . very happy for . . . Cindy will be very . . . McCoys . . . be here today and I'll . . ." The sound faded away.

Jimmy tried to fine-tune the radio. "We're getting atmospheric interference. Maybe we better sign off."

He spoke loudly in the microphone. "Hope you can hear us. We're signing off. Everyone wishing the End Times Prophet a happy holiday. May God bless you, Ben."

"I do hope he is eating well." Sharon frowned.

"I'd be terrified if I didn't know that Ben had an angel looking over his shoulder." Larry shook his head. "But if anyone is the chess master of escapes, it's my son."

"Find anything else in the bottom of that box?" Jimmy asked his father-in-law. "Like a candy bar?"

"Well, let's go back and see if Santa Claus stashed anything else in the back of that refrigerator."

Everyone stood as the emperor walked briskly into the national security strategy room. The large assembly area was lined with huge maps running up the walls to the top of the high ceiling. Extra telephones and electronic equipment had been placed around the amphitheater-style room. Banks of desks sloped toward a central podium in a horseshoe shape. Damian Gianardo stepped to the walnut speaker's stand and laid a file on the roster. The generals and their aides snapped stiffly to attention.

"At ease." Gianardo motioned for the generals to be seated. "On this January 2, 1998, we face a new year with many severe challenges. We must think together about a common approach to the serious issues that must be resolved. As we all know, recent atomic and natural disasters have destroyed our economic reserves. We are not able to rebuild in many sectors. Even the White House still lies in shambles. The worsening atmospheric situation poses a serious threat to our health. I am here to receive your counsel and guidance. I will begin by asking the chief of staff for his assessment of our military posture."

A large white-haired army general on the second row

slowly rose to his feet. Across his chest were numerous rows of medals. "Mr. President . . . ," General Crose paused. His refusal to say "Emperor" was obvious. "As I warned on many occasions, we have enemies who still have the capacity to strike with nuclear warheads. Another confrontation is certainly possible. Frankly, I don't know if the world could survive another exchange, but our enemies do have the capacity to strike."

"Crose, you've never agreed with any components of my foreign policy," Gianardo interrupted. "But I have prevailed in the face of this lack of support. *Nothing* should have penetrated the Star Wars Strategic Defense System!" The emperor pounded the table. "A major blunder."

"We no longer have the resources or equipment to either repair or improve the system." The general slumped back down in his chair. "We do well to remember these limitations."

"Sir?" A general on the second row raised his hand. "I have been reviewing data on our health care needs and am greatly alarmed."

"Please stand." Gianardo beckoned.

The general thumbed through a thick file. "We are on the verge of collapse. The continuing increase in AIDS and cancer patients was straining our limits *before* the great earthquake. Now we have the additional pressure of fewer functioning hospital units around the country. We must siphon money from the European countries that are part of our federation."

"No! No!" An aide popped up on the front row. "I have the latest polls from Europe. They will not tolerate any further drain on their economies. The empire is increasingly unpopular. We have already gained far too much at their expense."

"Sit down!" The emperor's voice was cold and threatening. "Europe will do what we tell Europe to do. Understand?"

"No." General Crose answered without standing. "Those days are past. The world is in too much chaos.

We cannot command and expect immediate compliance. Face it, these are the new facts of life."

Damian Gianardo's eyes shifted around the room, quickly assessing the cold stares he saw everywhere. The general's obvious defiant attitude made him very nervous. Gianardo bit his lip, fighting back the angry outburst that usually followed such a confrontation. The emperor knew that he could not afford to appear weak in this meeting, but neither could he depose the general in front of his military colleagues. Anarchy might follow.

"Our leadership has cost the world greatly," Crose continued. "Moreover, your obsession with concentrating all religious power in your office has cost us the support of the Muslim world. They still sell us their oil, but Babylon is certainly gouging us with exorbitant prices."

"*Our* leadership?" The emperor forced a smile. "Really? Am *I* the one who directs our missiles toward our aggressors, general? Please don't blame the failures of your planners on me. *You*, not I, designed the Star Wars System."

The room took on a stony silence, and the general's face became crimson. Gianardo walked around in front of the podium, smiling condescendingly. Once the emperor sensed that he was again firmly in control, he continued. "I want to hear the report of the National Aeronautics and Space Administration people. Samuel Goldstein, your report please."

A distinguished-looking man in his forties stood up. Goldstein was wearing an expensive business suit and horn-rim glasses. "Please turn on the overhead projector." The lights dimmed and the large maps lit up. The scientist began projecting a series of slides on the screen behind the emperor.

"For a number of years there has been serious speculation about some comets that appeared to be moving dangerously close to the earth." The scientist clicked the slide machine rapidly. Displays of the solar system filled the screen. "Within the last month we have come to conclusions that we have no qualms about presenting to this group and to the public. We are deeply concerned about the path that the so-called Doran and Whiton Asteroids have now taken. There is no question that they are on a collision course with the world. Both are quite large . . . over a half mile in diameter." A picture of a fiery star came on. "We calculate that one will hit the world around April 11 and the other on Saturday, July 11. A smaller comet we have labeled Comet Wormwood is probably going to hit about August 1. Gentlemen, we are facing another considerable natural disaster."

"Exactly what do you mean?" General Crose's deep voice rumbled.

Goldstein took off his glasses and rubbed his eyes. "Thousands of large asteroids cross Earth's orbit every few years. Any one of them could wipe out a civilization. Smaller ones that have the capacity to destroy entire cities also streak past. Fortunately, we get hit by a large one only every million years or so. A small one may hit every hundred years. A direct hit from a lesser asteroid would be the equivalent of ten Hiroshima bombs."

"But a big one?" The general bore down. "What's the possible effect of this Doran or Whiton Asteroid?"

"Asteroids come in at a speed of about fifty thousand miles per hour," Goldstein continued. "The power of such a collision would be more like a million Hiroshima bombs creating an abyss several miles across. On the opposite side of the world, the earth would actually bubble out and crack. Earthquakes would follow. Dust and debris could clutter the atmosphere so badly that they might even block out the sun and moonlight for a period of time. Just the tail of a comet passing by can create galactic tidal waves."

"But can we do anything?" General Crose threw up his hands. "What's even possible?"

"I suggest that we begin preparing immediately to

shoot nuclear-equipped rockets at these asteroids in hopes of breaking them up before they can penetrate the atmosphere."

"That can't be done," the general barked. "First, we need to be ready for possible future attacks from our enemies. We can't chance a lack of preparedness for retaliation. Second, we both know that trying to hit a foreign object coming in at fifty thousand miles per hour would be like throwing a baseball from a moving car at another car coming from the opposite direction. Wouldn't ever work."

Goldstein looked nervously at the emperor and then at the assembly of military leaders. "Certainly, the task would not be easy. But we must do something. We must try."

"Last time we *did have* warnings about the big earthquake, but we didn't pay any attention." The general looked menacingly at his colleagues, but his remarks were obviously directed at Gianardo. "I suggest that we immediately start work on this problem. This time we don't want any cover-ups."

Damian Gianardo's eyes narrowed, and the muscles tightened around his jaw. He appeared in control, but his hands gripped the speaker's stand with such intensity that his fingernails turned white and his knuckles looked as if they would pop through his skin. He listened silently as the military experts bantered over the possibility of hitting a traveling object in space, but his eyes never left General Crose. Gianardo's face was hard and set.

□   □   □

Three days later, Joe McCoy called Ben at the farmhouse. "Calling from a pay phone, Ben. Don't want to chance being tapped."

"Where are you now, Joe?"

"I just dropped Erica and Joe, Jr., off at school. I went around the block and came back to see what was happening. I was shocked to see security police in front of the high-school building talking to the kids on the steps. I'm not sure what to make of it, but I wanted you to be alert. The whole matter may be routine, or we could be in big trouble."

"But I thought Erica had accepted Yeshua and Joe was coming around?"

"Both Jennifer and I believe that we were seeing a change of heart. That's what's really got me scared. I don't think that my own children could deceive us that completely. I'm not sure what to make of any of it."

"Want to come out here?" Ben asked.

"Not yet. After all, nothing's predictable anymore. Did you see the paper this morning?"

"No."

"Another big explosion in Washington, D.C. Chief of Staff Army General Crose's car was blown to pieces. Killed Crose and several other generals. No one can understand how such a thing could have slipped past the vast security network of Gianardo's secret police."

"You're right. Nothing can be taken for granted. We'll be praying for your family. Let us know if we need to meet you somewhere or you need to hide out here."

"Thanks, Ben. You don't know how much it means to know that you are standing with us."

During the following months, the secret police interrogated the McCoys' children several times. Joe and Jennifer suspected there was a leak in their parents' Bible study group, but no one could be sure. The McCoy children were making significant spiritual breakthroughs, but Joe, Jr., had not yet trusted Jesus and was terrified whenever the police cornered him. Each time the police were professional and polite. Their questions were vague and their demeanor non-threatening. Mostly, the investigators asked about the possibility of Joe and Jennifer pushing religious ideas on the kids. They also asked questions about Cindy Wong. Joe, Jr., and Erica answered well enough and tried not to leave openings for further probes.

Although I remained invisible most of the time, I did not cease to watch over Ben and Cindy, and on several occasions I had to intervene. One evening I foresaw the police setting up radar detection to follow the movement of Ben's car. A signal transmitter was attached under a fender. After the police left, I put the bug on the car next to Ben's. Three secret agents nearly lost their jobs for being so incompetent in selecting the wrong car. The officers were totally bewildered by their "error."

In late March the secret police nearly cornered Ben

and George in one of the UCLA dorms that survived the great earthquake. I saw that the police were preparing to surround the building. Ben and George were in a sophomore's room sharing the gospel. We did not have much time to spare so I materialized in the hallway when the rest of the students were in their rooms and I knocked on the young man's door.

"Can I help you?" the puzzled student said as he opened the door. "You're not the one that I thought was coming."

"I believe there is a Mr. Ben Feinberg here."

"Yeah, sure." The sophomore answered uncomprehendingly.

"Michael?" Ben asked from across the room. "Sounds like Michael."

"Yes. Some urgent business has just come up."

"What?" Ben bounded across the room. "What in the world are you doing here?"

"We *must* run. Time is short, *very* short."

Ben stared for a moment and blinked uncomprehendingly. Suddenly, he understood. He grabbed George's arm. "Hey, we'll try to be back tomorrow." He jerked George past the startled student. "See you then." Ben pulled George into the hall and shut the door behind them.

"Michael! What are you doing here?"

"Police are closing in on the building. The student you have been talking to is a plant. The secret security people will be in here any minute."

"What can we do?" George looked panic-stricken.

"We're on the second floor!" Ben looked desperately up and down the hall.

The student's door flew open, and the sophomore ran down the hall toward the stairs at the opposite end.

"Quick! Ben . . . George . . . into the student's room. Lock the door and turn out the light. Get on the ledge outside his window. Give the police time to get in and then drop into the bushes and run for it. I will be your decoy inside the dorm."

Ben and George slammed the door behind them, and I opened a janitor's closet and grabbed a broom. In less than thirty seconds the police were charging up the stairs and pouring onto the floor.

"Stop!" the lead cop shouted. "Who are you?"

"Just one of the janitors. Cleaning up."

"Three men were here. Where did they go?"

"Three men?"

"Two college students and a big guy! About your size, I'd guess."

"Oh, they left. Might have gone up the stairs at the other end."

The first wave of police disappeared, running up the exit stairs to the third floor.

"I'd recognize the other guy." The sophomore's voice was loud and nervous as he bounded up the stairs with the second detachment of police. "Sort of a strange-looking man."

I stepped into the little janitor's closet and back into eternity as the secret police ran up and down the halls.

"Where'd the janitor go?" The leader of the first group came back downstairs.

"What janitor?" one of the second group asked.

"The man sweeping the floor."

"The janitors aren't here at night," the sophomore interjected.

The security officer glared at the college student. "Don't mess with me. I'm not blind. I want to know where the janitor we talked to went." The man swung the closet door open and looked inside. "If this is a college prank . . ." He jerked the sophomore forward by the shirt.

"Hey, I don't know what you guys are talking about. I'm on your side, remember?"

"There's just no one here," a policeman who returned from the top floor reported. "This thing smells like a little joke pulled on us by the boys' dorm."

"Where's the janitor?" the policeman growled in the

sophomore's face. "We'll teach you to trifle with national security personnel."

"No . . . no . . . no." The student flattened against the wall. "Really there were people here pushing religion on me. Honest. HONEST . . ."

"Try this room." One of the policemen reached for the door. "It's locked."

"Can't be." The student fumbled for his keys. He swung the door open. Curtains were blowing gently in the evening breeze.

The policeman ran to the window. "There they go!" He pointed across the campus. "Two guys are running into those trees."

I left the student and the secret police to their discussion and followed Ben to make sure he returned to the farm without any interruptions. The next night I knew that I must remind the group of the instructions that I had given them much earlier.

The group gathered around me in the farmhouse living room. "Let us review our procedures. On what basis do you contact people?"

"You put us in touch with the people whose hearts are open," Cindy answered.

"What went wrong last night?"

Ben and George looked knowingly at each other.

"We've got the message, Michael." Ben looked discouraged. "No one sent us. We thought the guy was open because he was talking about his religious concerns in the cafeteria when we were witnessing to a student you assigned to us. We just jumped the gun."

"Right. You must be wise as serpents and gentle as doves. Assume nothing."

"We won't make that mistake again," George apologized. "Thanks for saving our hides."

"Michael?" Deborah held up a newspaper. "We've not seen you for quite a while. The papers are filled with speculation about the three comets speeding toward the earth. I've figured out that the Doran Asteroid is scheduled to hit on April 11, which is also the day of Passover. Obviously, something big is afoot, and Passover is just days away. The papers are censored and don't report the predictions of Moses and Elijah. What's ahead? Level with us."

"I have not previously revealed anything so that you would study and learn to read the signs of the times for yourselves. You have done well. Yes. On Passover the Seventh Seal will be broken, and God's First Trumpet Judgment will blow. You will remember from the book of Revelation that there are seven "seal" judgments, which have already passed. Now there remain seven "trumpet" judgments and seven "bowl" judgments— the last bowls of God's wrath."

"The meteor is going to smack us?" George asked fearfully.

"No, not directly. But the consequences will still be severe. Even as we speak the National Aeronautics and Space Administration has fired a nuclear missile at the asteroid. Our heavenly Father will allow a direct hit in order to give one more warning to the world."

Mary held up her hand. "Can one bomb really stop something as large as the Doran Asteroid?"

"No, but the atomic explosion will fragment the asteroid. A very large portion will strike one of the isolated Aleutian Islands off the coast of Alaska, causing a large but regional earthquake."

"And the rest of the exploded asteroid?" Ben asked.

"Millions of particles will streak across the sky as they enter the atmosphere. You will see the greatest fireworks show in human history. Thirty minutes prior to the impact in Alaska all wind on the earth will cease. Suddenly, the particles will fall, looking like great drops of blood."

"Earth can't avoid being hit by large chunks of the meteor," Mary probed. "I know damage must result in many places."

"Censorship will prevent a full public accounting, but one-third of all the trees and grasslands on planet earth will burn. Yes, the judgment will be significant."

"What about the other two?" one of the younger students asked. "Will the Whiton Asteroid and Comet Wormwood be a problem for us?"

"The Whiton Asteroid will fall on July 11, and the Second Trumpet will sound. Be ready for the asteroid's impact in the Mediterranean Sea. Ben, you must warn the people in Bozrah and Petra to send out the word for people to stay far above the coastline. A tidal wave will sweep in. Surely, the hand of God shall move and strike until every idol is broken and the world has seen the glory of the Lord. Comet Wormwood will fall on August 1."

"July 11?" Ben snapped his fingers. "That's the seventeenth of Tammuz. The Fast of Tammuz! And August 1, 1998, falls on Av 9."

☐   ☐   ☐

In the predawn skies across the world the Doran Asteroid flashed its bright red tail, scattering millions of burning rock particles over earth's stratosphere. Alaska shook as the remaining central chunk burned its way into a small coastal island. If it had not been for sudden and prolonged rain, the burning forests and grasslands might never have stopped burning. More smoke billowed up into the already polluted atmosphere. In the following days, the night skies were a constant display of showers of exploding and falling stars, but their frequency lessened.

By June most of the unusual night displays had subsided and people were back indoors. The sun was setting much later, and the public's fear and fascination were passing. Erica McCoy took the bold step of inviting her closest friends to listen to her parents explain what was happening in the world. The group of five girls gathered outside around the McCoys' swimming pool.

Joe pointed to the sky. "I'm not trying to frighten you, but these strange occurrences are warnings God is giving the world. We still have another asteroid and a comet headed toward the earth. Unless we repent, a great price will be paid."

Erica's best friend, Melissa, interrupted. "My science teacher says the odds have just caught up with the earth. Sooner or later we were bound to get hit by something big anyway."

"Sure." Joe walked back and forth in front of the group, holding his Bible. "But the real issue is timing. Think. How many things are happening right now that fit the Bible's timetable for the final days of history? And why are so many happening on Jewish holy days? Is it really a coincidence? How can Moses and Elijah predict the precise times and dates so far in advance if God isn't telling them?"

"My parents don't want us to speak about the possibilities at home," another classmate named Paula declared. "But I hear them talking when Mom and Dad think we are asleep. They went to church when they were children and know what you are teaching us is the truth."

"None of us would be here," Melissa added, "if Erica hadn't sworn us to secrecy. I know we're in danger, but I want to know the truth."

Joe, Jr., spoke up. "My sister and I really rebelled against our parents for a long time, but the earthquake changed our minds. My parents told us for weeks that it was coming. When I saw everything falling in, I knew they were right. It's taken me a while to say it out loud, but I know now that what the Bible says about Jesus is the truth."

"We have a special Bible study group for parents," Jennifer said. "We help people like Paula's parents. I think your mothers and fathers would be more open than you think. The police system works by fear. Once you refuse to be intimidated, they've lost their hold over you.

"Girls, that's our story." Jennifer joined her husband and son in front of the group. "Our family has gone from being another southern California wreck to a real unit that stands together. Sure, it's scary, but I wouldn't give anything for the joy that has been restored to us. Even if we were hauled in tomorrow, we have the joy of knowing that we will face eternity together."

"You probably have questions you'd like to ask," Joe added. "Erica, Joe, Jennifer, and I will be here for any response you have. If you don't have any questions, then grab a cola and we'll break up in a bit."

While the girls talked with the McCoys, three cars were pulling up down the street. Plainclothes security officers quietly shut the car doors. A teenager got out of the last car and pointed to the McCoys' residence.

"How do you know they are there?" the policeman in charge asked.

"Because they didn't invite me," Mary Higbie answered indignantly.

"These are the people you told me about several months ago?"

The teenager smiled cynically. "I've overheard a number of conversations in the McCoys' backyard when the Chinese girl was pushing Christianity. I've seen Bibles lying around their house."

"And you'll testify to these facts?"

"Absolutely," Mary said defiantly.

"Got that on tape?" the leader turned to the man behind him.

"Every word of it."

"What?" Mary puzzled.

"We don't want you to back out," the man in charge grumbled. "We've been waiting quite a while to make a big bust, and we're going to hit these people hard. Your testimony is what makes it stick."

"Hit hard?" Mary retreated. "I just want them arrested. Humiliated like Erica treats me . . . but nothing more."

The police drew their weapons and began inserting

the bullet clips. "This isn't some kind of game, kid."
The officer began pointing in different directions and
his men moved quickly. "We're going to make a real example of these fanatics."

"Well, sure," Mary said nervously. "But I don't want
anyone to *really* get hurt."

"Hurt?" The policeman laughed. "Pain is our business. Let's get them, boys!"

Suddenly, the men dispersed into the trees and
shrubs. The first carload of agents charged the front
door. One lone agent held Mary tightly by the arm. "We
want you to identify the suspects."

For a couple of minutes Mary and the policeman
stood under a tree. They could hear distant shouts.
Then an agent came out the front door and motioned
for them to come in. They hurried through the house
and out into the backyard. The teenagers were huddled
together on the ground with police circling them and
pointing their guns. Joe and Jennifer and their children
stood together. Police were aiming guns at them too.

"Identify the traitors," the chief agent ordered Mary,
who stood at his side.

"Mary!" the girls echoed. "How could you?"

"Really," the terrified teen muttered, "I think I've
made a mistake. Yes. This is all a big mistake."

"Identify the McCoys!" the agent demanded. "We already have your accusations on tape."

"I didn't mean for this to happen." Mary tried to pull
away.

"IDENTIFY THEM!" the man exploded.

Mary pointed a trembling finger at the McCoys.

"Get the women first." A policeman grabbed Erica's
wrist while another man reached for Jennifer.

Joe suddenly pushed the first man backward so
forcefully that he fell in the shrubs. Pulling Erica and
Jennifer with him, Joe darted toward the side gate.
"Run!" he yelled to Joe, Jr.

A policeman charged out of the shadows and swung
the butt end of his Uzi into Joe's face, sending him

sprawling in the grass. Two other agents rushed Erica and her mother. One man wrapped his arm around Jennifer's neck in a stranglehold. The other man hit Erica in the stomach with his fist. She doubled up with an agonizing groan.

"Get 'em over here." The policeman pointed toward the edge of the swimming pool. "Line 'em up."

The secret police dragged Joe through the grass and dropped him on the swimming pool tile. Erica was pushed down by his side. A big man held Joe, Jr., by the edge of the water while another agent pushed Jennifer next to her family. The teenagers began screaming.

"Shut them up!" The man in charge motioned to the other police. "We don't need a bunch of crazy girls!"

"Please stop!" Mary pleaded. "I didn't want any of this."

"Stop it!" the policeman in charge yelled. "Or they'll get it right now!" Immediately, the girls became silent.

"The man assaulted us." The policeman with the Uzi kicked Joe's hand aside. "I should have shot him then. Let me finish them off now."

"We don't know about the status of the girls," another man interjected. "Are they witnesses or victims?"

The leader of the secret police walked over to the terrified teenagers. "Do you believe what these McCoys were preaching here tonight? Are their ideas representative of your convictions?"

"No! No!" the girls whimpered and pleaded. "No! Never!"

"OK," the leader snarled. "They're victims. Get their names, addresses, and parents' names, and then let them go. Photograph 'em as well as this backyard."

"And our criminals here?" The policeman pointed his Uzi at Joe's stirring figure on the ground. He tried to sit up but couldn't stabilize himself. Blood was running out of Joe's mouth, and his lips were already extremely swollen. "He tried to escape. So did the girl and her mother."

"You won't get away with this!" Joe, Jr., strained against the man holding him. "God will judge you for what you are doing to us."

"You know our orders," the agent in charge grumbled. "Get these teenagers out of here and then shoot the family."

Ben read the *Los Angeles Times* intently.

"Can you believe today is July 10, 1998?" Cindy interrupted him. "The Fast of Tammuz begins here tonight at sundown, which will be dawn of July 11 in Israel."

George pointed at the paper. "Look at the headlines. Everyone is terrified that the Whiton Asteroid is going to destroy the earth. Since the news is so heavily censored, who can believe anything you read in the papers?"

"Michael warned us that an asteroid would land in the Mediterranean." Cindy sat quietly in the living room of the farmhouse. "We know at least some sort of collision is ahead."

"Time is running out." George ran his hand nervously through his hair. "If the entire asteroid hits, the impact will be catastrophic." George returned to reading over Ben's shoulder.

"I'm very concerned about the McCoys," Cindy interrupted their reading again. "No one has heard from them in over a week. My father drove by their house once and didn't see a sign of anyone there."

Ben laid the newspaper down on an end table. "I've prayed continually about Joe and Jennifer. Strange. I just feel a deep emptiness, but I'm not disturbed. I don't know what else to do."

George added, "We certainly don't dare go around their house during the daytime, and making inquiries is dangerous. Since we kept our two groups apart for security reasons, there's no one we can call."

"They know all about Michael's message about the asteroid so we don't have to worry about them being caught by any surprises," Ben concluded. "But if we don't hear soon, I think we ought to make a night run to their house and see what we can find."

"I'm counting on Michael showing up tomorrow," Cindy interjected. "I know he can clear everything up for us."

"Let's see what the radio says." George pointed to the tuner on Ben's stereo set. "It's nearly noon. Maybe we'll get some sort of idea what's really happening."

"OK." Ben punched the power button. "Maybe the announcer is telling the truth today."

As a commercial faded, the radio voice spoke urgently and rapidly. "Ladies and gentlemen, we have just received the latest update from NASA. The Whiton Asteroid's collision course with earth is due completion at midnight East Coast time. The asteroid was over a mile wide with the potential to do overwhelming damage. However, two nuclear missiles have just intercepted the asteroid and successfully fractured its mass. Unfortunately, a portion of the asteroid is still going to collide with our planet. NASA is now anticipating a point of contact near the middle of the Mediterranean Sea."

"Michael was right on target." Ben laughed. "The Second Trumpet Judgment of Yeshua is about to blow!"

"The remaining piece of the asteroid appears to be the size of a small mountain," the announcer continued. "Such a mass could create tsunamis of immense proportions around the entire Mediterranean basin. In addition, similar property damage can be expected comparable to the catastrophe in Alaska. Unquestionably, there will be a great loss of sea life."

"The world is warned," Cindy said sternly. "I don't understand how people cannot see the truth. With blind eyes, even I would be able to recognize that the times are beyond the control of any emperor, president, or man."

"Must be quite a blow to Gianardo's ego," George smirked.

"Expect the night skies to be filled with millions of meteorites," the announcer added. "Be prepared for more fires. No one is sure what this strike will cause. Therefore, earthquakes are possible during the night."

"I'm glad the gang will be here tonight," George mused aloud. "We need to be together in case something unexpected happens. Fortunately, we already know an earthquake's not coming."

"Oh, Michael!" Ben cried out. "Wherever you are, please show up soon!"

The moment had come for me to appear. Once more I stepped into history at about the same place on the porch that I had materialized on my last visit. Everyone continued looking at the sky for several minutes, not realizing that I was present.

"I'm going to find out what the radio reports." George turned toward the house. "Look!" he pointed. "It's Michael!"

"Peace to you on this night of consternation."

"Michael!" Cindy turned toward the house. "I knew you'd be here soon. Tell us what is happening."

"Sit down and listen carefully."

The students quickly assembled around the porch steps.

"First, let me tell you about the condition of the world. The fires of the past months have seriously defoliated most of the forests. There are much less rain and ozone. Rising temperatures last spring hampered crops. Fresh water is diminishing. You must be aware that the decreasing food supply will result in increased violence. Soon guns will be worth more than gold. People will kill for water."

"What's happening to the population?" Cindy asked.

"AIDS and drought have decimated the continent of Africa. Zimbabwe is nearly deserted. In Kenya the soil is baked clay. Drought has spread from the Cape of South Africa to Cairo. Starvation has taken a great toll."

"And South America?" a dark complected student asked.

"El Niño winds have caused drought from South America to Australia. Except for Israel, the whole world is experiencing the full judgment for corrupting the atmosphere. Only Israel continues to enjoy normal production. The hand of God has been heavy while He waits patiently for the nations to turn to Yeshua as Messiah. However, in Israel the land is being prepared for His return and rule."

"What's happening here?" Ben asked. "What is going on in southern California?"

"Even you can feel the effects here tonight. Although air pollution has blocked one-third of the sun and moonlight, nothing is stopping the increase of ultraviolet radiation. Not only skin cancer but incidences of terrible cataracts are increasing. Respiratory illness is rampant. What is occurring in the skies is the Fourth Trumpet of Judgment. Each of you has been affected in ways that you do not feel but have begun to take their toll. It is important that I pray for you and relieve the effects. Even as our Lord did, I am going to lay hands on you that you may be healed of what has accumulated in your systems. Kneel and let me walk among you."

The students bowed on the ground. Some even lay prostrate on the grass with their faces in their hands. Slowly, I moved through them, touching them on their heads prayerfully as the power of the Holy Spirit cleansed and renewed their eyes, revitalized their respiratory systems, and healed their skin lesions. The darkness of the night continued to be broken by thousands of intermediate bursts of meteoric explosions of light.

"Now let me share with you the heavy words that I must bring for this hour." The students gathered once more around the steps. "In the days ahead, nuclear attacks will occur again, and the final woes will be visited on those who have rebelled and been disobedient. The Evil One prowls the earth; he knows that his final hour is at hand, but he is too obstinate to face the implications. You must understand that he is not alive and well but wounded and dying. His final weapon appears to be death, but it is not so. He can use only fear and anxiety to deceive you. Death will come, but you must not be dismayed. Dying is only an unredeemed part of the natural process that continues to work in this world. For the unbeliever, death is terror, but for you, it must be seen as the final means of transformation."

"Why are you giving us this instruction?" Ben interrupted. "Sounds rather ominous."

"You must remember that faithfulness does not exempt you from the consequences of life on this planet."

"Some of us are facing death?" George asked hesitantly.

"All of you have the potential to fall at any time, except Ben, who is one of the 144,000 and is absolutely protected."

"Michael, what are you suggesting?" Ben bore down. "What lies ahead?"

"Remember, martyrdom is the mark of ultimate victory . . . not defeat."

"The McCoys!" Cindy gasped. "You're trying to tell us that something has happened to our friends."

The group became deathly quiet. Ben blinked apprehensively and reached for Cindy's hand.

"Yes. The McCoys have entered into their reward. Let your loss be tempered by the knowledge that they went as a family and now stand together before the throne of God. The faith and patience of the parents ultimately resulted in both children trusting Yeshua."

Cindy's often stoic features froze in place. The absence of any appearance of emotion screamed at the night. Ben bit his lip and closed his eyes. Two of the students gathered around Ben and Cindy, putting their hands on their shoulders.

"They were faithful to the end . . ." Cindy's voice broke uncharacteristically, and she began to weep.

"Such good people," Ben muttered. "Was . . . was the end terrible?"

"Swift and without pain. The bullets came instantaneously, and the McCoy family left this troubled world together."

"We must at least hold some sort of memorial service for them and mark graves for them." Ben pointed beneath a large oak tree next to the house. "We should honor our friends."

"Yes," Deborah agreed. "Let's make crosses out of the old lumber behind the house. We can write their names on the crosses and stick them in the ground as grave markers."

Without anything more being said, the students started preparing a special site under the thick branches of the spreading oak. Some of the youths piled up rocks while others tied two-by-fours together with pieces of rope. Deborah wrote the McCoys' names with an indelible marker she found in her back pack. Soon the four crosses stuck out of the heap of rocks.

After the students gathered around the rocks, Ben began reading from the fourteenth chapter of John's Gospel. " 'Let not your heart be troubled; you believe in God, believe also in Me. In My Father's house are many mansions; if it were not so, I would have told you. I go to prepare a place for you.' " Ben stopped and looked at the little group circled around the four crosses. "Would anyone like to say something?"

Deborah spoke softly. "Without Cindy's testimony, Erica would have perished in her sin. We don't have a choice about living or dying, but we make a decision about where we go. Cindy made that difference in Erica's life."

Silence settled over the group. Finally, Ben read again, "'I am the way, the truth, and the life. No one comes to the Father except through Me.'" He closed the Bible and the group starting singing in hushed, broken tones, "Amazing grace! How sweet the sound that saved a wretch like me . . ."

Their strong young voices filled the night air as they sang louder with each succeeding verse. Their hymn faded, and they stood quietly beneath the great oak tree, watching the thousands of meteors explode in the black sky. Someone said, "And now the McCoys have joined the heavenly constellation."

24

In the summer of 1998, the hot, dry winds of August blew down from the hills and swept over the desert floor. The people in Bozrah and Petra tried to stay indoors during the hottest part of the day. Conditions were increasingly cramped as more Jews poured in after the collision of the last comet—Comet Wormwood—with the earth on August 1, the ninth of Av. Its long trail of gases poisoned a third of the fresh water supplies of planet Earth, resulting in millions of deaths. The environment became so polluted that the amount of light was decreased by a third, both by day and by night.

Larry shut the wooden door of his hospital office behind him and sat down at his desk. He scanned the charts that were left for review. After scribbling several prescriptions, he put the papers in a pile and flipped on the radio transmitter.

"Woman in the Desert calling the End Times Prophet. Woman in the Desert calling." There was no response. Slowly, the sound changed. "Come in," he tried once more.

"The Prophet's answering service," a woman's voice answered.

"Ben? Ben there?" Static became intense and then cleared.

"It's Cindy," the distant answer finally came.

"Cindy, how good to hear you. Is Ben there?"

"I'm not at the farm . . . got another transmitter . . . I'm talking from my room at UCLA."

"Really?" Larry put his ear closer to the receiver. "A new radio?"

"A student smuggled it out of an electronics lab. I can call Ben from here, and it allows us to save on travel time. I was tuning in tonight . . . with students at school. What can . . ." The call faded away.

Larry adjusted the dial. "Cindy? Cindy? Can you pick me up again?"

"Can't stay on long . . . too dangerous. But I hear you better now. How is Ruth?"

"That's why I called. This morning she began having pains. Looks like it could be any time now."

"Wonderful! Ben will be pleased . . . I'm hearing doors . . . slam in the parking lot. I must . . ."

"Cindy, what's happening? Can you hear me?"

"Trouble . . . big trouble . . . police cars are surrounding the dorm . . . I'll . . ." The radio went dead.

"Cindy!" Larry shouted into the microphone. "Cindy! Answer me!"

Larry could hear only empty humming. "God help us," he prayed as he turned the switch off. "I've got to call Ben some way." The doctor slumped back in his chair, frantically trying to think of some alternative to waiting for Ben to call.

The door burst open and Sharon rushed into the room. "Larry! Come quickly. Ruth really *is* in labor. Hurry! I think we have a serious problem."

"What?" Larry bolted out of his chair.

"Ruth started having strong regular contractions about an hour ago. I called for the new Egyptian doctor to check. Dr. Zachery's been delivering babies for thirty-five years. I knew he'd be best."

Larry was across the room and out the door. "What did he say?"

"Looks like the baby is breech."

"Oh, no!" Larry grabbed his temples as he trotted down the corridor. "We don't have equipment to handle such a problem."

Sharon tried to keep up. "Ruth is down the hall in a room by herself. All we have is a regular bed."

Larry shot through the door with Sharon running behind him. Dr. Zachery was bending over with his stethoscope on Ruth's bulging stomach as she writhed in agony. The Egyptian looked gravely concerned. A young Arab woman was sponging Ruth's forehead. The expectant mother's eyes were closed and her jaw tightly clenched.

"What do you think?" Larry crowded at the doctor's elbow.

The doctor beckoned the parents to follow him outside. "We're in trouble," he talked rapidly. "Ruth dilated well and quickly for a first baby, but the baby is in breech position. You understand the seriousness of our problem unless we can get it turned."

Color left Larry's face and he nodded mechanically.

"I cannot find any of the basic medical equipment that we need," the Egyptian doctor wrung his hands. "The contractions are increasing in intensity and rapidity, but without forceps I don't think that I can manipulate the child."

"You've got to try!" Sharon clung to Dr. Zachery's arm. "Please do whatever is necessary."

"Where's her husband?" the doctor asked Larry.

"He's teaching outside."

"He must be informed at once and be here. Sharon, go find him. Dr. Feinberg, you and I will work together. I see no other hope."

Sharon ran for the door. "I'll be back with Jimmy," she called over her shoulder. "I'm going to call for the people to pray."

The two doctors returned to Ruth. An Arab nurse hovered over her, mopping large drops of sweat from her forehead. Ruth moaned softly as another contraction locked in. As the pain increased, Ruth's knees drew up and she cried out.

"We don't have much time, Dr. Feinberg. Talk to her while I get these gloves and gown on."

"I'm here with you, Ruth." Larry held his daughter's hand tightly. "Don't worry. We're praying. The people are praying. Hang in there. Jimmy will be here shortly."

Ruth opened her eyes and tried to smile. She squeezed her father's hand.

"Hold her tightly." Dr. Zachery moved into place at the end of the bed. "I'm going to start applying pressure."

After a few minutes, Jimmy burst through the door and rushed to the opposite side of the bed. "I'm here, dear." He placed his cheek against hers. "Don't worry. We'll get through this together. Even if it takes all night."

Sometime during the next two hours Larry remembered his radio conversation with Cindy and started to tell someone to attempt contact with Ben. At that moment, Ruth began to hemorrhage again, and the recollection was swept from his mind. Sharon returned and alternated between holding her daughter's hand and running reports out to the gathering community. By the end of three hours, everyone in Bozrah was aware of the situation and praying. The Arab nurse was assisted by two Jewish nurses.

But each sweep of the minute hand on Jimmy's wristwatch seemed to take longer and longer as hope slowly faded. Jimmy kept his mouth close to Ruth's ear, quoting from the Psalms and praying. He fought recognizing the red flush of her cheeks and the pale whiteness of her neck. With the deepest reluctance he turned his head toward the end of the bed. Dr. Zachery's gown was soaked in blood as were the sheets and mattress. His father-in-law was listlessly staring at the floor. His eyes were empty and his face marked with despair. Sharon was slumped on the floor against the bed, clutching Ruth's limp arm.

Dr. Zachery straightened up and once again put his stetheocope against the swollen stomach that had become perfectly still. He listened a moment before taking Ruth's hand from her mother. The doctor searched for a pulse for several minutes, then placed Ruth's arm on her chest. The hand slid down to the side of the bed. Mechanically, he placed the stethoscope on Ruth's chest. The Egyptian kept shaking his head until he finally covered his eyes and walked out of the room.

"We can make it, darling," Jimmy insisted. "Together, we can make anything . . ." Only then did Jimmy notice that Ruth's eyes weren't really closed. Her glassy lifeless stare was fixed on some eternal point far above the ceiling.

"No," Jimmy barely gasped. "No." Each negation was more a cry than a word. "It can't be." He slowly stood. Tears were so profuse he could no longer see clearly. "Oh, God," he pleaded, "it can't be! Please, don't let it be."

Larry looked up at his son-in-law but couldn't speak.

"No!" Jimmy screamed at the top of his lungs. "Not Ruth! Not my wife and child!"

Sharon slumped into a heap on the floor with her face buried in her hands.

Jimmy's final cry rang through the thin walls of the room and echoed down the corridors. The door stayed wide open as he ran down the hall and through the crowd that had gathered around the entrance to the hospital. People stood reverently when he rushed past them. He ran without any sense of direction toward the desert sands.

Several times Jimmy fell and staggered to his feet again before he was outside the limits of the city. He clawed his way up the rocks and through the hot sand, running toward the top of some nameless plateau. Only when he reached the top did he stop. The burning sand stung his face as he lay face down. Time lost all meaning. Eventually, his eyes seemed to run dry, and his voice was replaced by a dry hoarseness that no longer made speech possible. His clothes were wringing wet, and his head throbbed with dull, unending pain.

Finally, Jimmy crawled beneath the shadow of a large boulder and stared down on the tent city in the valley. He could see a multitude gathered around the hospital. Many people were on their knees. The entire scene seemed strangely surrealistic, detached, remote.

Unexpectedly, he seemed displaced. Once more he felt like a little boy in Dallas, Texas. For the first time in years, he wanted to talk to his father. The loss of his parents bore in upon him as he thought of his mother.

The desert landscape became a mural he seemed to be observing, a scene from a movie about desert warriors he remembered watching at the corner theater when he was a boy. Everything felt achingly strange and foreign.

A great loneliness engulfed him. Jimmy wanted to die. To be gone. Dispatched. Anywhere in eternity. Never again in this lifeless land. Dissolved. Departed. Dead.

From somewhere down below, Jimmy heard men calling his name. Before long they would find him. He tried to stand, but his legs ached and his hands hurt. Only then did he realize that the knees had been torn from his pants, and his legs were lacerated. His palms were scratched and raw. Feeling was gradually returning. Jimmy took a few steps toward the edge. The men were not far away and kept calling.

One of the searchers saw him and began to wave. Jimmy raised his hand slowly and then let it drop. With no alternative, he started the descent by himself, hoping the group would not catch up with him. When Jimmy arrived at the edge of the camp, he tried not to look at anyone. Hands reached for him, but he walked stoically onward.

The crowd in front of the hospital parted. Jimmy stepped in Dr. Feinberg's office. Larry was bent over his desk, and Sharon sat in a chair next to the wall. Sam and Angie Eisenberg were trying to comfort them. No one said anything when Jimmy shut the door behind him.

"Jewish custom demands a quick burial," Larry said without looking up. "The climate leaves no choice."

"The time of separation will be short," Sam consoled. "The Tribulation won't last many more months, and then we will all be reunited."

The words seemed to fall at Jimmy's feet. He said nothing.

Sharon stood up and looked at Jimmy with deep longing. Suddenly, she rushed forward and threw her arms around his neck, sobbing incoherently. If Angie had not offered physical support, the two would have collapsed on the floor.

"You were the best thing that ever happened to my daughter," Sharon cried. "Thank you for giving my daughter such profound happiness."

The dry wells filled again and Jimmy cried quietly. He did not hear the women walk past the door and down the hall to begin preparing the body, nor did he realize that men were carrying a plain wooden casket down the hall.

"When?" Jimmy eventually asked. "When do we finish it?"

"Tomorrow I think." Sam answered. "Perhaps at noontime."

The long line of mourners followed the family as they walked toward the ancient cemetery of Bozrah. The merciless sun blazed straight down. The plain wooden box was carried on the shoulders of six men. Sam Eisenberg led the way. Carefully, the coffin was lowered into the gaping hole in the ground. As far as anyone could see, a surging mass of people crowded the cemetery and spilled over into the surrounding wilderness.

Jimmy was barely aware of what was happening around him. As the Mourner's Kaddish was recited, the strange sounds of Hebrew made the moment feel even more unreal and detached.

"*Yit-gadal ve-yit-kadash shmei raba,*" the crowd chanted. "*B'alma divra khir'utei ve-yamlikh mal-khutei*" arose toward heaven.

Sam Eisenberg read in English, "Hallowed and enhanced may He be throughout the work of His own creation. May He cause His sovereignty soon to be accepted, during our life and the life of all Israel. And let us say: Amen."

People answered, "Amen," and continued to pray until Sam ended the moment. "He who brings peace to His universe will bring peace to us and to all the people of Israel. And let us say: Amen."

The "Amen" roared across the desert.

Larry stepped forward and threw the first handful of dirt on the casket. Sharon followed the ancient custom. Others dropped in handfuls of dirt and sand, but Jimmy couldn't move. Sharon slipped by his side and filled his palm with sand.

"It is our way," she said simply.

Jimmy stepped to the edge of the grave. The sand trickled between his fingers until it was gone. He wanted to jump in and throw his body over the box, letting them cover him as well. He felt the gentle tug of Sharon's hand pulling him back into the crowd.

Larry locked his arm in Jimmy's, and Sharon supported him from the other side as they started back. A bent little woman stepped in front of him.

Her wrinkled features and sagging eyes made her look ancient. She wore a faded black scarf and a heavy black dress. Most of her teeth were gone. The woman reached for Jimmy's hand. Her fingers bent beneath large, distorted arthritic knuckles. She looked up in his eyes; tears stained her face.

"Fifty-four years ago," the woman said in broken English, "I lost my daughter at Auschwitz. I was pregnant, but the baby was stillborn. I do not know why I lived." Tears again ran down her face. "I still ask the Holy One why He did not take me. I would have preferred to have taken the place of the many who died. Sometimes it is so much harder to stay with the living."

The old woman reached up and kissed Jimmy on the cheek. "Now I know that I was not left alone. The Holy One was always there. Believe in life! *Chaim!*" She shuffled back into the crowd and was gone.

For the first time Jimmy was strangely comforted.

25

Ben Feinberg stood in the shadows of the UCLA building, watching people come and go from the girls' dorm. George reported his findings.

"Deborah is inside talking to some of the girls on Cindy's floor to see if anyone will tell us anything." George talked rapidly. "No one has seen anything of Cindy for at least the last two days. It just doesn't look good."

"I don't understand it." Ben shook his head. "She was going to take radio calls from Israel and stay in her room. No one could have followed her anywhere. I expected to hear from her around ten last night, but I got nothing."

"Deborah has an 'in' with one of the student resident supervisors on Cindy's floor. I think she can get a pass-key to Cindy's room. Look!" George pointed to the side door of the dorm. "Deborah's coming out."

Deborah walked toward the two young men hiding near the large building. She abruptly turned and started down the walkway in the opposite direction.

"Hey!" George scratched his head. "She knows we're over here. Where's she going?"

"Something is very wrong." Ben watched Deborah walk away. "She's making a detour to warn us. Deborah must fear that she's being watched or followed. I think she must be heading for the parking lot. Let's circle around behind this building and see if we can head her off."

Both students ran for the back side of the building and then cut diagonally across the campus. They reached the parking area just as Deborah arrived.

"What's happening?" Ben called out.

Deborah waved casually almost as if she didn't recognize her friends. With a fixed smile, she answered softly, "Get out of here. Meet me at the Pizza Hut down the street, but watch yourselves. The police may be anywhere right now."

Ben and George sauntered away as if they had just said hello to an acquaintance. As Deborah sped away in her Honda, the two friends kept looking in every possible direction. When they reached the end of the lot, they jumped into the thick foliage. They ran down the thick row of trees and shrubs until they came out near a busy boulevard. Immediately, they ran into the traffic and through the cars. On the other side they trotted toward the familiar Pizza Hut. Deborah was already sitting at a table.

"OK," Ben puffed, "what's up?"

"No one knows all of the details for sure, but here's the composite I've put together. The girls are terrified and won't talk about anything, but yesterday the security police suddenly showed up and surrounded the building. Cindy's blindness made her a very easy catch. After they ransacked her room, they took her away in one of the cars."

Ben turned pale and could only shake his head.

"I got into her room. The place was torn apart, and one thing was clear. The police got the radio. It's gone." She paused. "I found Sam in the corner." Deborah shook her head. "He was dead."

Ben bit his lip, swallowed hard, and looked up to the sky. "God, please help us!"

"We're in this together." George put his arm around his friend. "Don't panic. God hasn't abandoned us."

"Either she was watched for some time, or she was talking on the radio," Deborah concluded. "The secret police apparently hit like lightning. They clubbed the poor dog to death. No one heard him make a sound."

"They must have known about the radio." Ben's hand began to shake. "I'm sure that's what triggered the raid. I shouldn't have let Cindy keep the thing in her room. It's my fault."

"No, no, Ben." Deborah squeezed his hand. "We've all known that anything could cause one of these attacks. The radio has actually offered security to Cindy. You were able to warn her and keep in contact."

"What am I going to do?" Ben wrung his hands.

"Listen carefully." George took charge. "First, don't make any more calls to Israel for some time. We can't chance that they will find a way to get an instant fix on you. The radio must be silenced. Next, I'm getting the students together. The most important thing that we can do right now is pray.

"Ben, if there's anything that we have learned during these days, it is that God's sovereignty is being vindicated through all of this chaos. The world may be falling apart, but He stands supreme above the flood. The Lord Yeshua is preparing to return as Lord of lords. You've taught us to trust Him for everything."

"Yes . . . yes, that's true." Ben's eyes were misty. "But Cindy is so little . . . and frail. What can she do if they decide to torture her?"

"Ben, you must not return to the farmhouse until we know what's really happened." George was resolute. "Stay with me until we know the police haven't uncovered our base of operation."

"I don't think that I have any choice." Ben's voice was weak and shaky. "I feel like a ship that was just torpedoed."

"Deborah, can you get the word out to the girls to be at my apartment by seven tonight?"

"Sure, George."

"I'll work on getting the word out to the guys. We'll pray this thing through, Ben. You'll see."

"I don't think I'd better go back around the girls' dorm," Ben barely whispered. "They may already know who I am. I feel so helpless. I just don't know what to do. Our only hope is to find somebody who can get inside information on the secret police."

"Fat chance." George shook his head.

☐   ☐   ☐

Cindy sat quietly in the interrogating room of the LA Police Department. Jack Wilson stood across from her, smoking a cigarette and studying a piece of paper. On the table in front of him was a thick file filled with pictures and papers.

"We've been watching you for a long time." His oily voice was condescending. "We know everything about everyone so you can save us and yourself a great deal of trouble by simply answering the questions."

"If you know all about me," Cindy smiled pleasantly, "then there is nothing for me to tell. You already know."

The plainclothes policeman's eyes narrowed, and he licked his lips. "Don't be cute! We will wring out of you what we want to know one way or the other. Do you understand?" Jack Wilson growled.

Cindy nodded her head. "I am a very small and in many ways helpless young woman. You killed my guide dog; you can kill me. But I know who is in control of my life. Whatever you do will happen because in some way it will lead to the glory of God in the end."

"Oh, how I hate you fanatics!" The man blew smoke in Cindy's face. "You're such fools. Don't act like my ripping out your fingernails will be a picnic for you. I'll yet see you on the floor begging for mercy from *me* . . . not your God!"

"Do you prove how strong you are by hurting a blind girl and killing her dog?"

"Don't try to play on my sympathies." The security

agent eased down on the table in front of Cindy. "I've shot kids younger than you and never blinked an eye. I hate you innocent-looking types most of all."

"How could I possibly harm you? Hurt anyone?"

"You're a pawn. An insignificant blip. But we can't let you or your kind run free or you multiply. If we don't keep a lid on unpatriotic subversives, you'll spread like rats. Don't look for mercy from me. I don't even understand the word."

"But what have I done?"

"I'd show you the pictures, but you couldn't see them." Wilson spread a handful of photos across the table. "Here's one of you with a teenager. Another with the same teen and several of her friends. Then I have several of you with other students who are known enemies of the state. Here's a picture of you and some Jewish-looking guy."

"What do the pictures prove?"

Wilson flipped on a cassette player on the credenza behind him and shoved in a tape. "Listen," he demanded as Cindy's voice filled the room. "We've got miles of these conversations between you and the people in the pictures. We had special listening devices trained on you."

"It must be very disconcerting to be so afraid of what a little Chinese girl might say."

Instinctively, Wilson doubled up his fist and drew back but something seemed to hold his arm in the air. No matter how hard he pushed forward, his fist stayed locked in place. Only as he relaxed his grip could he slowly lower his arm. He quit talking for a moment and stepped backward. Several times Wilson tried opening and closing his fist. As the strange sensation passed, so did much of his impulsive anger.

"As I was saying," Wilson started again, "we know everything about you. Now tell us about the boy. The guy who leads you around."

"You mean Alexander?" A sly smile crossed Cindy's face.

"Alexander?" The policeman puzzled.

"Alexander Bradshaw? He's just a friend."

"Don't give me the friend business. You fanatics only run around with your own kind. There's no such thing as casual acquaintances. We want the man's address."

"I'm not sure what Alexander Bradshaw's address is." Wilson made notations on a pad. "Come on. What town does he live in?"

"Possibly Anaheim."

The agent reached out with his thumb and forefinger to get a hunk of Cindy's cheek. He squeezed but couldn't seem to close his fingers. Wilson stepped back in astonishment and stared at his hand. "If you're lying to us, we'll soon know. I guarantee you that I will spare no pain in pulling the truth out of you. Do you understand?"

Cindy nodded her head mechanically.

"If you've deceived me, next time I'll hook up electrodes to places on your body that you didn't dream were possible!" The secret police officer pressed an intercom button. "I want a full-scale dragnet on one Alexander Bradshaw from the Anaheim area. Check UCLA records as well. Now take this woman back to her cell."

□   □   □

For the next three days the students met in a house near the campus, fasting and praying. Cindy spent most of the time alone in her cell. Three times different policemen interrogated her about her friends. Each time they bore down on the name of Alexander Bradshaw, threatening her with harm if their search continued to be unfruitful. They had not yet identified any of the pictures of Ben Feinberg.

Cindy knew that time was running out. Although she had not lied, her clever deflection of the secret police's question would soon be exposed. She had simply pulled a name out of the air. By now Wilson would know her identification was only a ploy.

In the small barren cell Cindy knew that there were

no windows and that a single light bulb was never turned out. Her hands had explored every square inch of the cubicle. In one corner was a toilet and opposite were a bunk and uncovered mattress. Strangely, she had not felt afraid or alone during the past four days. And yet Cindy knew escape was completely impossible. Her best guess was, she had been taken to the bottom of the county jail in an old unused section reserved for people the police wanted to keep in seclusion. Cindy sensed from the echoing sounds that there must be other empty cells in the area. She reached up and felt the cold steel bars.

"Heavenly Father," she prayed quietly, "I count it a great privilege to be imprisoned as were Peter and Paul. Should I be called to suffer for the sake of the Cross, I would rejoice in the opportunity to walk in His steps." She stopped and wiped a tear from her eye. "And yet I am weak. How can I stand up against these terrible men? I fear I will break and betray my friends. Please! Should I become too frail, take my life before I say anything that could hurt Ben."

Cindy's prayer was interrupted by an unexpected sound. Her keen ears would have heard footsteps long before anyone reached the cell door. Yet she clearly could tell that the old lock in the door was turning. It was followed by the noise of the heavy metal hinges grinding together as the door opened. Cindy listened intently but heard nothing else.

A man's tight grip clamped around Cindy's arm, and she felt herself being lifted to her feet. "Who's there?" she cried out. "What are you doing?" Instantly, she reasoned they had padded their feet and were preparing to use some form of psychological torture. "I'm not afraid of you," she tried to sound brave. "You're not going to frighten me with some gimmick."

Without a word the man pushed her toward the cell door. His firm grip was not painful, but she couldn't elude the stealthy guard. He led her in the opposite direction from the usual route taken by Wilson. She nearly stumbled going up the steps. The man began walking so fast that Cindy reached out, fearing that she would bump into something, but he forced her hand back to her side.

"Why are you doing this to me?"

The relentless hand only forced her onward. Another door opened, and Cindy could hear people talking in the hall in front of her. Policemen were discussing a car wreck and didn't make any response as she walked past. At the end of a long corridor, Cindy heard an electronic door buzz and then open. A few steps away, the man opened another door. On the other side she could hear many people buzzing and talking. The place sounded like a large waiting room.

"What's happening to me?" Cindy protested again. "Where am I?"

The man said nothing but forcefully moved her right through the middle of the crowd. Cindy felt a very large door open and a sweep of fresh air rushed at her face. The slightly burning, polluted sensation smelled like the usual LA atmosphere. "Are we outside?" Cindy puzzled.

Nothing was said as the man guided her down a number of steps and toward the street. They waited for a moment before Cindy heard a bus pull to the curb. Her captor pushed her toward the bus steps. Cindy gingerly climbed up the three steps and took a couple of cautious steps forward before the guard pulled her down on a seat.

"I demand to know where we are going!" Cindy exclaimed in exasperation.

Abruptly, the talking around her stopped. "We're on the 405," a kindly older woman's voice explained. "You're on the bus that goes by the coliseum. Do you want me to tell you when we're near the campus?"

Cindy's mouth dropped. All she could say was yes.

For a long time she sat bewildered as the bus jostled and lurched down the street and over the freeway. Eventually, her guide pulled her to her feet and shuffled her toward the back exit.

"You're just about there," the woman called after her.

Cindy reached for the safety bars to direct her way but by now was confident that her abductor would not let her stumble. The bus slowed down and the door opened. Immediately, the unseen arm led her down the steps to the street and back up on the curb. Nothing was said as he moved her inside a shelter for bus passengers.

"You did quite well," the deep bass voice boomed.

"Michael!" Cindy nearly shouted. "You've been there all the time."

"For the last four days to be exact."

"You've sprung me from the jail!"

"We walked right past every one of them!"

"I can't believe it!"

"Oh, I have been releasing Christians for nearly two thousand years now. I even helped set Paul and Silas free once."

"I can't believe it! I'm actually out of that terrible place."

"I have materialized now and am going to walk beside you. Follow me and we will catch up with your friends. Ben and the gang are not far from here."

"I just can't believe it! And I feel so good! They didn't feed me much, but I feel so energized."

"Ben and the students have been fasting and praying. You have been receiving the benefits of their intercessions on your behalf."

They hurried down the boulevard and cut down a residential side street, walking as quickly as Cindy could go. Just before they reached the front door of a small, plain stucco house, Michael stopped. "I want you to tell the group several important things. Ben is not to use the radio until I tell him to do so. At the right time, I will explain and tell him how to proceed. The police are now ready to cue in on the frequency you have been using with Israel. Understand?"

"Most certainly!"

"At some time you will wonder why you have been rescued when the McCoys . . . and others . . . have not survived. All these matters have an explanation, but the issues are so complex that you could never fully grasp their significance. God's plan for each and every individual is so vast, interwoven with so many lives, all that is past and present, and with so many options and alternatives, that no computer in the universe could track the eternal dimensions of what happens in time.

"When people tragically lose their lives because of evil or the fallen nature of this world, their family and friends have the choice of succumbing to bitterness or growing in grace. Ultimately, the issue is not what you can understand and explain even to yourself, but your capacity to believe in the sovereignty of our heavenly Father. Remember not to measure events by your standards of justice, but leave the consequences to be tried by grace. Give this teaching to your friends. I am going to leave you now. Just take two steps forward and knock. The group is inside in prayer."

"Oh, Michael! This is the most terrifying, wonderful adventure of my life. I can't wait to tell Ben that I have my own Seeing Eye angel!"

"I cannot wait to watch that little Nazi Wilson explain to his superiors how a blind girl unlocked maximum security and walked right out of the building through the traffic court!"

Damian Gianardo sat hunched over his desk in the National Security Building. The emperor grumbled as he read the report Prime Minister Rathmarker handed him.

"Sir," the military chief of staff sitting across the desk sounded professionally distant, "there is no question that the Chinese are still producing nuclear weapons."

"I have threatened them!" The emperor shook his fist. "It is nearly the first of October, and they haven't complied."

The general kept his military posture and avoided eye contact with the emperor. "We estimate that they still have a billion citizens and an army of two hundred million, including reservists. Earthquakes, pollution, and fires have certainly taken a toll but not to the degree we have been damaged. The Chinese don't like paying our high tariffs and have rebellion on their minds."

"I'd burn them like a paper dragon." Gianardo shook his finger at the general.

"The United Muslim States are equally belligerent," the general observed stoically. "Should the Chinese and the Arabs work out a treaty, we would be forced to the wall. We have been able to stomp around the world as

if we were wearing steel boots. An alliance in the East
would expose our clay feet."

"Don't ever talk like that again in my presence!" The
emperor rose to his feet. "I expect optimism. Don't
come in here with this nonsense about vulnerability. I
am invincible! Now get out!"

The general snapped to attention, bowed his head in
respect, and turned on his heels to march out of the
room. Gianardo picked up the report and slung it
against the far wall of his office. "Send in the next
bunch," he barked to his prime minister. "Give me the
secret police people."

Rathmarker hurriedly opened the door and three
men in suits and ties entered.

"Sit down, gentlemen." The emperor pointed to the
chairs in front of his desk. "I want an update."

The men looked back and forth at each other until
Sloan, the largest of the three, asked bluntly, "Do you
want the truth? Or shall we just make you happy?"

"Level with me," Gianardo said sourly.

"The size of our payroll is dragging us to the bottom.
We now have more public employees working for us
than any other profession in this empire."

"You should be pleased," the emperor sneered. "I've
gotten you everything you want, haven't I?"

"Our reign of terror is the only thing keeping the lid
on the country," the second man interjected. "People
hate us and don't want to pay the taxes to fund their
own surveillance. We've become the target for every
form of hate imaginable. The whole operation is becoming counterproductive."

"What about the religious fanatics?" Gianardo
pointed at the third man. "Collins? Have you stamped
them out?"

"We've tried everything and continue to do so." The
security chief pulled at his collar. "Again, the persecution has backfired. In the beginning citizens were glad
to turn in the religionists, but now they've become he-
roes. These believers go to their deaths with a smile on

their lips and joy in their eyes. The more we persecute them, the more the Christians reproduce. Right now we're trying to combat a new outbreak of fanaticism in Los Angeles. College kids are turning to Christianity at an incredible rate. Sheer madness has broken out on some of the college campuses. It's their way to rebel against authority."

Sloan added, "Messages keep getting smuggled in from Moses and Elijah in Jerusalem. Unfortunately, their predictions have an uncanny 100 percent accuracy. People are desperate for direction. Those two crazies sitting by that ancient wall are creating a lot of problems for all of us. Can't you do something about them?"

"I think I can solve our mutual problem." Gianardo flipped on his intercom once more. "Call the press," he shouted into the microphone. "I've just fired Sloan, Davies, and Collins as department division heads of national security. New competent appointments will be forthcoming."

"But Mr. Emperor!" Davies jumped up. "You wanted the truth."

"I wanted results," the emperor screamed in the security officer's face. "Now get out of here while you can still walk!"

The three men stumbled backward out of the room as quickly as they could leave.

"Fools!" the emperor ranted. "I am surrounded by nothing but fools and idiots." Gianardo slammed his fist onto his desk. "I'll get rid of those two Israeli actors if I have to kill them myself!"

In the main hospital office Sam and Angie Eisenberg held the hands of Larry and Sharon as they prayed for their friends. "And please comfort Jimmy. Nothing that we say seems to be able to reach him," Sam concluded.

"Each of us needs Your blessing in a personal way. Amen."

"Amen," the three responded.

"Do you know where Jimmy is?" Angie asked.

"He should be back by now," Larry answered. "He goes out to Ruth's grave this time each day. Sometimes he's back earlier." Larry gestured aimlessly. "Sometimes much later."

"No one can comfort Jimmy." Sharon wiped her eyes. "We've talked about the reunion God promises at the end of this terrible time, but nothing helps."

"Facts don't do much for pain," Larry sighed. "Every psychiatrist knows the limits of knowledge to heal the soul. I once read the work of Victor Frankl, the Viennese psychiatrist who survived the Auschwitz death camp. He wrote about the importance of finding meaning in our suffering. I think this is what has made everything so confusing to Jimmy."

The door opened. Jimmy walked in, nodding to each person but not speaking. He walked over to the table and laid a flashlight down, turned, and started out again.

"Mind sitting down with us?" Sam asked.

"I don't think so," Jimmy looked straight ahead. "I have things to do."

"The people really miss your teaching," Angie added. "Every day the immigrants ask when you'll be back."

"Not for a long time," Jimmy's voice was barely audible.

"You have so much to offer," Sam joined in. "You are a truly gifted teacher."

"I'm not sure I believe any of it," Jimmy suddenly turned on the group. "I don't think anything that I told those people is true. In fact, if it wouldn't get me killed to leave, I would be out of here right now."

Angie said, "I know how you feel—"

Jimmy cut her off. "No. You don't know how I feel. You can't possibly know how I feel. You mean well, but you'll leave here with your husband in a few minutes and go home to your kids. Look!" He pointed out toward the camp. "What's so great about being chosen? Most of those so-called chosen people have spent their entire lives on the run because God picked them out to be His special project in history. Big deal! I'd just as well be a happy little nobody who never got any of that divine attention."

"It's hard." Sharon bit her lip.

"Oh, you bet it's hard. I was a happy little man selling cars and making money in LA on my way to the top before I got into this mess. Now I'm out in the desert as isolated as one of those ugly lizards that runs every time a human shows up. If God is in all of this terror and misery doing us some big favor, then please let me out. I'd just as well skip Christmas this year!" He bolted for the door and slammed it, but the wooden door only bounced open again. No one got up to shut it.

"Jimmy doesn't even ask about Ben anymore," Larry lamented. "He's trying to shut the world out."

"How long since we've heard from Ben?" Sam asked.

"Over two months . . ." Sharon clasped her hands together so tightly that her knuckles were white. "Not since the night we heard from Cindy and the radio went *dead.*"

The word sailed through the room like a boomerang. Each person stiffened.

"What if they've got Ben?" Sharon burst into tears. "I don't think I could stand to lose both of my children." She doubled up with her face in her hands.

Larry dropped to his knees in front of his wife, hugging her and crying. Sam and Angie stood helplessly weeping with their friends. The couples silently grieved as time lost all meaning.

At the sound of footsteps, Larry looked up. "Jimmy!"

"I'm sorry." Jimmy stood limply in front of them. "I didn't even get five feet down the hall. I've been so lost in my pain that I didn't even want to hear about Ben and Cindy." He paused and ran his hands through his hair. "He's your son. How could I possibly speak of what this additional loss could mean to you?" Jimmy began silently weeping. "I'm sorry . . ."

Larry struggled to his feet and threw his arms around his son-in-law. "We will always have two sons," he tried to say clearly. "And we will be eternally proud of both of them."

"We can make it." Sharon put her arms around both men. "Yes. Together we can make it. He who is the bright morning star will yet come and shine upon us."

Larry, Sharon, and Jimmy walked together out of the room and down the corridor toward the outside. Sam and Angie watched from the window as the family stood under the stars looking into the night sky.

During 1999, the year that followed Ruth's death, the world's food supply continued to dwindle. Economic pressure on the large population centers made life increasingly treacherous in the Los Angeles area. As the price of gasoline also escalated, more desperate people were forced to their limits. Violence was common and unpredictable. Ben found his farmhouse to be a haven in the midst of an unstable world.

On Friday, May 21, the Feast of Pentecost or Shavuot, the next woe fell on the world. Gianardo was in his office in the National Security Building dictating to a secretary when he noticed strange insects creeping under his door. The large ugly bugs looked like locusts with scorpion tails.

"What's that?" the emperor pointed to the floor.

"I don't know." The secretary stared, horrified, as more and more insects scurried across the floor.

"Doesn't anybody pay attention to sanitation around here?" The emperor stood up and peered over his desk.

"I've never seen anything like this!" The woman stood up and then tried to stomp one of the pests. The insect made a cracking sound. A putrid smell arose from the floor.

"How is it that I can control the world but can't keep swarming insects from invading my office?" Gianardo threw the switch on his intercom. "Get security in here on the double," he demanded."

"Owww!" the secretary screamed. "They bite! Ohhh!" She began hopping about the room. "No! They sting!"

Gianardo suddenly slapped his pants leg. "Ouch!" he bellowed. "These things are poisonous!"

Two policemen rushed into the room. "What's the problem?" The first man prepared to draw his gun.

"We're being attacked!" The secretary pointed to the floor.

The second man spun around looking in every direction. His feet nearly went out from under him as the scorpionlike bugs squished into a slippery goo under his shoes.

Gianardo plopped down on the top of his desk, slapping at his legs. "I'm on fire," he gasped. "Look!" He pulled up his pants, exposing large red welts up and down his leg.

The first policeman began dancing around the room trying to get the insects off his shoes.

"I demand you stop them!" Gianardo screamed. "I'm the emperor! I run the police! I demand that this stops!"

But it didn't stop. In the following weeks the people of the world, like Pharaoh's subjects in ancient Egypt, found a plague consuming them. No repellent could deter the mysterious bugs that came out of nowhere, leaving infection and unbearable skin irritation in their wake. From coast to coast the infestation became an all-consuming concern. And unlike the temporary severe pain of a normal scorpion sting, the pain from these insects lingered on and on.

The plague did not keep the secret security police in Los Angeles from being relentless, but the growing Christian movement among college students made their job much more difficult. The young leaders Ben had trained during the preceding months began taking new responsibility for meeting the growing requests for spiritual help. Most students had been raised in the wide open permissiveness of the early nineties and naturally rebelled in the opposite direction. The intellectually critical world of the college campus had been the first place to perceive clearly what was ahead for the environment and world politics. Initial hopes that Gianardo had raised for national superiority and economic prosperity were turning into complete disillusionment. The secret police were equally troubled, discerning what was intellectual dissent from religious sedition.

In late summer, mistaken identification resulted in several UCLA professors being shot and a number of politically oriented student leaders being arrested. Government pressure was no longer able to suppress the story, and the scandal rocked Gianardo's administration. For a period of weeks, the police were forced to retreat, but the public embarrassment only spurred on Ben and Cindy's group.

During this time, Ben felt it was safe to attempt radio contact with Israel. Unfortunately, the Feinbergs no longer maintained constant surveillance of their radio. A week passed before contact was established. Ben was overwhelmed when he learned of his sister's death and the loss of the baby. Weeks dragged by as Cindy and the group prayed, counseled, and encouraged their leader.

In Bozrah and Petra the crops flourished. The crosswinds blew polluted air out to sea. Refugees were well fed and healthy. Fortunately, life in Bozrah left little time for private reflection. Jimmy eventually returned to his teaching. Classes grew as the desert population swelled. He plunged into his work with a vengeance, trying to bury his loneliness in the demands the new students made on him.

The scorpion locusts also invaded Israel and inflicted great pain, but nowhere in the world were any believers stung by these pests. When Moses and Elijah warned of other coming woes, the word spread through the country. The heavenly Father stopped the invasion of the painful pests at the edge of the protected zone. As a result, more people poured into the Bozrah-Petra area. Many paid with their lives because the troops stationed around the mountain heights shot them.

On Wednesday, October 27, 1999, the seventeenth of Heshvan, the plague ended, just as Moses had predicted. God chose this date because of its great significance. On this day God spared Noah and his family once the rains began to fall, giving humankind a new beginning. This same day in the Jewish calendar on November 2, 1917, the Balfour Declaration gave Jews a national homeland in Palestine for the first time in nearly two thousand years, another new beginning. The locusts shriveled up, cracked, and died as if their life expectancy was spent. The stench of billions of dead insects around the globe was overwhelming.

Two months later, the next warning of Moses, the Sixth Trumpet Judgment, began to unfold when the military chief of staff and the generals of the New Roman Empire met with Gianardo and Rathmarker in the National Security Strategy Planning Center. It was New Year's Day, 2000.

General Smith stared coldly at the emperor as the reports were given by other military officers. Gianardo listened without any visible emotion as the briefing covered every area that Smith had warned of months earlier. Once the historic context of the problem with China was established, another general switched on the illuminated maps.

"We have carefully pinpointed the new areas of military attack along China's borders. Each of these assaults came last night as part of a coordinated attack on all New Roman Empire forces stationed within China's official boundaries. As best we can tell, the Chinese have obliterated all of our men there. At least fifty thousand soldiers have died, and there is no indication that anyone was taken prisoner. Our current estimate is that

Premier Lei has stationed two hundred million troops along these same border areas. There is no question that they are prepared to attack."

"We must conclude that the Chinese are contemplating hostile action," Prime Minister Rathmarker stated. "I suggest that we plan a preemptive strike at once."

General Smith stood up abruptly. "Just before our meeting began, an aide handed me the following communiqué, which was received from one of our agents placed within the Lei regime. The premier will declare his independence of the empire within the next few hours and then strike against us."

Smith watched the emperor carefully. He could tell Gianardo was avoiding eye contact to keep from acknowledging the fact that he had ignored Smith's warnings, but Gianardo's hands betrayed him. Smith watched as the supreme leader slowly clawed a piece of paper into a tight ball, squeezing it so tightly that the tips of his fingers lost their color. He threw the paper on the floor and stood up.

"Get that worthless little Chink on the phone. Set up the translation so that every word is immediately typed on the television screens overhead. By the time he digests what I have to say, he'll be begging us for mercy!"

Gianardo continued his tirade of threats until the aide returned with the special translator who could type in the responses as he received them. The emperor was delighted with the immediate response from China, assuming that haste signaled respect and fear.

"Lei," Gianardo began without pleasantries or formal recognition of the premier's position, "we will not tolerate any form of resistance to our authority. If the reports of casualties among our troops are correct, we will expect complete and total reparations. Do you understand?"

For a few moments there was total silence in the vast hall. Then the television screen began to fill with words.

"Mr. Gianardo, your arrogance and imperialism are no longer tolerable, nor do we recognize your authority. All ties with the New Roman Empire have ended. In the future all trade agreements will be renegotiated. Your failure to recognize our sovereignty and independence will result only in damage to you and your government."

The emperor blinked uncomprehendingly at the TV screen. "You must have misunderstood him," he murmured to the translator. The man shook his head.

"You tell that worthless yellow-skinned fool that unless he comes into immediate compliance, I am prepared to blow Beijing off the map."

"No!" General Smith bolted from his chair. "You don't dare make such a threat!"

"What?" Gianardo turned around slowly. His intense black eyes squinted into narrow slits. His teeth clenched. "Have you forgotten yourself, General? Do you know who you're talking to?"

"Don't push them!" Smith stammered. "They have the capacity to retaliate. We can't lose our heads and do something rash."

"Unlock the box!" The emperor pointed to the sealed mechanism for sounding a nuclear alert. "I am the supreme power in the world, and I expect complete compliance with every word I utter."

"No, no," the general begged. "Intelligence reports indicate that Lei is unpredictable. Don't push him into a corner."

"Sit him down!" The emperor signaled to a guard standing by the door. "Keep the general in his chair until I indicate otherwise." Gianardo continued giving instructions in shrill tones. "Activate our Star Wars System. I want a missile ready to fire at the moment that I signal."

"We can't take another nuclear exchange," the general begged his colleagues around the room. "The environment can't stand it. The empire will collapse!"

"If the general makes another comment," Gianardo

instructed the soldier, "shoot him. Lack of support in a national emergency is treason."

Across the room men froze at their stations. No one looked at the other.

"Now that we have things under control, I will continue." Gianardo breathed heavily as he spoke. "Tell Premier Lei that he has one minute to signal his acceptance of our authority, or I will wipe out his capital city. NOW!"

The translator talked rapidly into the mouthpiece of his headset as he typed the emperor's message across the screen. No one moved. After ninety seconds the translator began typing again. "We have the satellite capacity to instantly register the firing of any missiles from anywhere in the world. Thirty seconds after any firing, we will detonate a hydrogen bomb that has been smuggled into New York City. For every missile fired, a corresponding bomb will be detonated in another major city of the New Roman Empire."

"Do they have that kind of satellite capacity?" Gianardo turned to the military panel. General Smith nodded his head.

"They couldn't hide a bomb in one of our cities!"

Again the general signaled yes.

"It's a lie," the emperor snarled.

"One last time," the general broke his silence. "We have detected suspicious activity among Chinese agents for some time. Now I understand the full meaning of those intelligence reports. They were assembling nuclear devices."

The soldier guarding the general did not remove his gun. Ignoring the general, Gianardo walked over to the nuclear detonation box. He picked up the receiver and punched in his top secret personal code. "Fire the nuclear warhead programmed for Beijing." The emperor slowly put the phone down and turned toward the TV screen.

Two minutes passed before the translator began typing. "Initial reports indicate that you have fired a missile. We will determine in two minutes if that trajectory is aimed at our country. If the missile continues and is not destroyed within three minutes, we will release an underground hydrogen explosion on Manhattan Island. We will proceed to respond to every missile fired with corresponding destruction of one of your cities. We are prepared to totally destroy what was formerly the United States of America."

"Bluffing!" Gianardo scoffed. "When this is over, each of you will be relieved that your country is in the hands of a man of steel nerves. During this crisis, I want every Chinese citizen rounded up and brought in. No telling who's been collaborating with Lei. Now get to your battle stations!"

Men instantly moved to their emergency positions. Electronic maps flashed on screens around the room. On the two center area overheads, maps of Beijing and Manhattan came up. In the flurry of activity the chief of staff's and the emperor's eyes met. Smith sat emotionless, watching Gianardo's lip curl and his eyes flash disgust at him. This time the general did not flinch or look away. He did not even blink until the emperor finally turned his back on him.

Suddenly, the electronic maps of New York City and Beijing began pulsating simultaneously with concentric circles of radiating light. For a few moments the rings of expanding brilliance moved out across the entire expanse of the cities and then began to fade and with them any indication of population. Everyone stared at the maps.

Smith spoke in somber tones. "They're gone. At least six million people are gone forever from each of the two cities."

By the time the two leaders agreed to a cease-fire, one-sixth of the existing world population was wiped out. In the weeks to come, another sixth would eventually die from the nuclear and environmental fallout. One-third of humankind would be destroyed by two egomaniacs in a matter of weeks.

28

Cindy Wong sat on a stool in the back of the family restaurant and listened to her father read the newspaper aloud. Her mother continued to stir a boiling kettle on the stove, preparing for their evening customers.

"Say here that emperor make peace with Premier Ching Lei three days after long nuclear disaster. Now that one week pass, it clear that in addition to many millions who die, millions more injured." Frank put the paper down and shook his head. "Craziness. Idiocy. Gianardo is mad man."

"The emperor's losing his grip," Cindy added. "We would never have seen such a story one year ago. He can't censor the press any longer."

"Empire is collapsing!" Jessica shook her finger in the air. "The evil man not stand forever."

The kitchen's swinging doors flew open, and a large man barged in. "Please follow me without saying a word," he commanded.

"Who are you?" Cindy's father dropped his paper.

"We must move quickly. Go out the back door now. Do not make a sound."

Jessica reached for a large chopping knife. "You not rob us tonight!"

"We only have minutes to leave before the security police arrest you."

Before Cindy could speak, the man pulled her off the stool and headed for the rear door. "Follow us," he commanded. "Secret police are coming in the front door this very minute."

The Wongs ran silently behind their daughter. The trio ran down the alley behind the shopping center, following the strange man. Near the back fence line, the large man pushed a piece of the broken fence apart and the Wongs slipped through.

"What happening?" Frank puffed.

"Get across the street!" The stranger took Cindy's hand and waded into the traffic, winding his way among the cars waiting for the stoplight to change. Only after they turned into the first street that ran into a tract house area did he stop.

"Michael!" Cindy exploded. "What in the world are you doing? I recognized your voice in the restaurant."

"Michael?" the parents echoed.

"Listen carefully. The government is rounding up all Chinese citizens tonight. You must hide for several days. Within forty-eight hours confusion and chaos will be so great that the emperor's decision will have to be rescinded and the government will be forced to release all prisoners. However, the police will be double-checking to find any Christians who might have been caught in the sweep. Cindy, they have your picture on file."

"Oh, Michael! You have saved me again."

"We have little time to talk. Listen to what I want you to tell the students that you are discipling. We have less than a year left. The Antichrist will become more desperate as his empire disintegrates. His inability to hold China will result in other nations such as Russia, the Ukraine, and the United Muslim States defying his authority. He will be even more reckless and dangerous. If the police had taken you tonight, you would have been dead before morning."

"Ahhh!" Jessica grabbed her daughter. "Help us!"

"Quiet! Just listen to me. After the next couple of days pass, there will be a period of relative quiet. Governmental leaders will be so involved in trying to handle the disasters in the various nuked cities of the empire that they will leave the Christians and the Chinese alone."

"Cindy tell us about you, Mr. Angel," Frank's voice quivered. "It difficult to believe . . . but we have heard your name often. We are old . . . foolish. But must believe in your Jesus now . . . tonight . . . this moment."

The shrill whining of sirens split the brisk night air. Police cars could be heard closing in from opposite directions.

"They are arresting your Chinese employees right now but do not worry. In three days they will be back to work. Catching Cindy would have been the death blow to all of you."

Frank began bowing up and down in the oriental polite manner. "Mr. Michael, when workers come back, I tell them to believe in Jesus. I tell them His angels never stop their work. Yes, we tell them we believe."

Cindy hugged her parents. "Mom. Dad. I am so relieved. Tonight my prayers have been answered. I thank God for your decision."

"Cindy, even though it is some distance away, you must walk to the McCoys' house. No one has been there for months. The police will not be expecting people to hide in that place because of its reputation for harboring disloyal citizens. I have already unlocked the back door, and there are still canned goods in the pantry."

"Ben will be terrified," she pleaded. "I must let him know that we are OK."

"I will appear at the farmhouse after I leave you. Do not worry. Tonight I must give special assignments to the students for the final months. I will put his mind at peace. Now go!"

"We believe. We believe," Frank kept saying over his

shoulder as the family scurried down the street and disappeared into one of the dark side streets.

As time passed, my prediction proved to be correct, and Gianardo backed down on his oppression of Chinese citizens of the New Roman Empire. By early spring of 2000, the Wong family closed the restaurant and moved into Ben's ministry headquarters away from the gangs that had become a significantly greater threat than Gianardo's secret police had ever been.

In Bozrah, Jimmy sat close to his father-in-law as the doctor made hasty notations on a pad. Both men listened intently as Dr. Zachery translated the radio broadcast coming out of Babylon in early spring.

"At least forty million Christians have been killed throughout the New Roman Empire," the Egyptian doctor dictated as he pressed the headset against his ear. "The reporter says that approximately seven million were Jewish believers. Also two million more Jews were killed. Another twenty million citizens of the New Roman Empire were executed because Gianardo's men determined they were unpatriotic in their allegiance to him."

Jimmy ran his hands through his hair in despair. "No one in the history of the world has murdered so many people simply because of their religious and political beliefs. The man is completely mad."

Dr. Zachery pulled the headset away. "The Muslims are saying that they have no love for the Christians or Jews, but no leader so treacherous can be trusted or tolerated. The announcer says that the time has come to join with China in a new alliance that will be more mutually advantageous."

"An announcer wouldn't make such an assertion unless it is the party line. No question but the Muslims are pulling out," Larry concluded.

"I'm sure that there are no Christians or Jews left in

Babylon," Jimmy added. "The stage is set for the final showdown in the next few months."

"What do you mean?" Dr. Zachery asked.

"Jeremiah 50 and 51 and Revelation 17 and 18 spell it all out." Jimmy pushed his Bible toward the doctor. "The city has both symbolically and literally been the place where God's people have been killed for over twenty-five hundred years. The Bible says that in one hour the hand of God will wipe the place out, never to be built again. We are going to see the destruction happen very soon."

The doctor put the headphones back to his ear. "Now the announcer is saying that it is time for the United Muslim States to renegotiate their oil prices. If the New Roman Empire doesn't accept their terms, then the Arabs are prepared to cut off all oil supplies."

"That's all it will take," Larry stated. "The final battle will be on. The Muslims are cutting their own throats."

Gianardo shut the door behind him. Five young generals sat around a small table in the center of the maximum security chamber. The soundproof room was totally secured against any form of electronic eavesdropping. Detection devices prevented anyone from wearing or carrying any form of recording or transmitting apparatus. No other room in the National Security Building was so totally sequestered. Gianardo sat down at the head of the table with Rathmarker at his right hand.

"Everything said in this room is of maximum secrecy." The emperor looked at each person. "Do you understand? Nothing is communicated to anyone about any detail of these consultations."

The generals nodded their total compliance.

"I am now surrounded by old fools and reactionary idiots. My New World Order is being assaulted by the last vestiges of resistance to my complete control. We must now be ready to crush the enemy without fear of disobedience or resistance from within our own government."

Each officer indicated understanding and agreement.

"Your time of opportunity has come. General Smith thinks that I am not aware of his attempts to thwart me. We must be ready to stop his men at a moment's notice. When the final strike against the Chinese and the United Muslim States comes, each of you must be prepared to assassinate anyone who stands in our way. You may have only one shot. You must not miss."

"You can count on us," one of the young men saluted.

"When this period is past," Gianardo spoke with complete confidence, "you will not only be commanders in this empire but the first military leaders of the entire globe. I congratulate you on a very intelligent decision to stand by me."

Gianardo pushed a file toward each person. "I have already appointed each of you to a new position that will take effect at the moment we strike. Askins will head security. Browning, your command will be the nuclear strike command. Jackson, I have selected you to coordinate all ground and attack forces. I want Imler to oversee domestic coordination of all legislative activities. Salino will handle the final details of surrender after we have humiliated our international enemies."

General Jackson smiled broadly. "We are your servants as together we write the history of the third millennium. What can I do at this time?"

"I want you to create a system that will circumvent the nuclear detonation device in this building. It must be portable since we will be taking it to Rome with us in a few months. We will reassemble our command post there. No one must be aware of what you have done except an expert that I will assign to you. Terbor Esiw will know what to do. He is the secret creator behind this effort."

"Who else is aware of this plan?" Browning asked.

"No one. You will note that my instructions are in my own handwriting. When we meet, you will tell your staff personnel that I have appointed you to an ad hoc task force preparing plans for the rebuilding of this country. Any other questions?"

"Can the world survive another war?" Imler probed. "I'm sure that you have completely covered this option."

"A world with less population will be much easier to manage." Gianardo smiled. "Yes, long ago I recognized the need to reduce population to a level that would be more controllable. In the future we will not have to worry with negative public response or the failure of any form of compliance. I will have completely united religion, politics, and all forms of philosophical thought. Gentlemen! We will be gods."

On April 5, 2000, Sam Eisenberg pulled his van into the parking lot across the street from the Dung Gate, which led to the plaza beneath the Western Wall. The afternoon sun was covered by storm clouds promising rain. He and Jimmy got out and locked the doors to the van.

"We have only a limited amount of time." Sam talked as they crossed the street. "We must assume security agents have our pictures and names on their computers. If we push our luck, we could be identified."

"Sam, do you really think I could pass for an Israeli?"

"You're concerned?"

"Sneaking out of the protected zone is no small matter, Sam. I just pray that we weren't followed."

"If we had been, the troops would have already caught us. No, Jimmy, we can breathe easy while we listen to Moses and Elijah. They always protect believers in their area. Just walk straight ahead like we're locals."

Jimmy spoke quietly. "Since our contact with Ben has been limited, we haven't received many of the special insights that the angel gives him. We need any new information we can learn from these two giants."

"Time is short. We shouldn't have many months left. I just pray our timetable is correct."

Jimmy looked pained but didn't answer.

The two men hurried past the armed patrol outside the massive ancient stone gate. Metal detectors were along each side of the entrance. Ahead of them they could see a long line of people. The huge throng made it impossible to see what was ahead. Sam edged his way to the railing that kept sightseers out of the excavations along the wall and the Temple Mount. Sam hopped up on a corner post of the railing.

"Good grief! The place is packed. The rumors were true. Jews are flocking in here to listen to Elijah and Moses. The reports of a revival really are right."

"How can we ever get through this crowd?" Jimmy called up to him. "People are packed in here like sardines!" He pointed to the apartment buildings behind them. "People are even hanging out of windows blocks away."

"The loudspeakers will let us hear what's being said," Sam concluded. "We won't have to actually get near to hear it all."

"Listen," Jimmy said firmly, "I risked my life to come in today. I want to get my money's worth. I don't care what it takes, I want to get as close as possible. What about the police and the soldiers?"

"Amazing. They don't even have their guns out. I can see them sitting on the sand bags ready to listen. Things sure have changed since the last time we were here."

"I've got an idea." Jimmy looked over the edge at the archaeological dig. "If the police aren't paying attention, let's drop over the side and work our way up to the other end. We'll just pop up by the wall."

"Here goes nothing." Sam vaulted over the side of the wire fence and dropped five feet into the grass beneath him. Jimmy followed and landed next to his friend.

"Make it fast." Sam started winding through the

stone foundations. "We could still get thrown out if we're seen down here."

"Just think!" Jimmy rolled his eyes. "We are actually walking on the same pavement that Jesus and the disciples traveled going up to the temple. What more appropriate path could we take to talk to two of the greatest men of the Old Testament?"

Sam pointed to the incline ahead. "When we get to the end, we'll have to make a mad dash up the side and over the fence. We'll try to drop down on the women's side of the wall and work our way out of there."

In their mad dash, Sam and Jimmy got separated, but each man worked his way to the next fence that protected the women's division in front of the Great Western Wall. Jimmy vaulted over first, but Sam was close behind. Only after they had waded into the crowd of women did the consequences of their actions become clear.

"What are you doing here?" A woman with her head covered pushed Sam backward.

"You crazy or something?" A small heavyset older woman beat on Jimmy's chest. "Get out of here!"

The women shoved and protested, pushing the two men backward toward the metal rails separating the two sides. Before Jimmy and Sam could completely recover, the irate women pressed them against the partitions. The two men quickly rolled over the railings, falling about ten feet from where Moses and Elijah were sitting.

Jimmy stared. Since their last visit, a wooden platform had been erected so everyone in the area could see the two imposing figures. Their simple chairs had been replaced by heavy wooden thrones. In the immediate vicinity, men were sitting on the ground to allow the people at the back to see even better. A wondrous light hovered about the awesome figures.

Moses turned his head and looked straight at Jimmy. The ancient lawgiver smiled knowingly like a regal head of state conveying recognition to an old friend standing in the midst of an adoring crowd.

Elijah stood up and looked over the assembly. The masses surged forward as Elijah held up his arms. Sam and Jimmy stood in awe.

"Passover is at hand," Elijah said with great solemnity. "This year we celebrate for the last time the meaning of our release from bondage. Never again will we eat the Pasch in anticipation, for within six months our deepest longings will be fulfilled. The Messiah is ready to enter through the Golden Gate to the east."

A great shout arose from the people. Clapping and shouting filled the air.

Elijah again held up his arm for calm. "Yet as the final moment approaches, the man of evil continues his work. The Antichrist's appetite for death is not yet satisfied. You must be ready for more terrible things that are yet to come. As the New Roman Empire crumbles, on the evening of the Passover Supper on the fourteenth of Nisan, the United Muslim States will announce their separation from the evil state. Stand ready! Within twenty-four hours, on the Feast of Unleavened Bread, Babylon the harlot will be severely wounded, then destroyed. In an hour the capital of evil will be silenced for eternity."

"That's April 20," Jimmy whispered to Sam. "In a couple of weeks Gianardo must be going to nuke the Arabs."

"We've got to get the word to Ben," Sam answered. "No telling what kind of chain reaction could be set off. Ben needs to make sure they have enough food stockpiled to last the next six months."

Moses pointed toward Egypt. "The day after the Passover supper, called the Feast of Unleavened Bread, is always on the fifteenth of Nisan because our exodus from Pharaoh began on this day after 430 years of bondage. After the fall of the temple and Jerusalem in A.D. 70, the last brave defenders of the state retreated to Masada. On the fifteenth of Nisan they gave up their lives rather than submit to the forces of tyranny."

Elijah pointed across the plaza toward the Church of the Holy Sepulchre. "On this same day, Yeshua our Messiah laid down His life on a cross for the sins of the world. Therefore, Adonai has chosen this day in the year 2000 for vengeance on the past and present Babylon. So shall the justice of the Lord come on the earth."

"Hear us, O Israel!" Moses shook his staff at the sky. "You have been told these things that you might believe. When the smoke has cleared over Babylon, you will have less than six months left before the final days come. Use them well, for the final chapters of history are being written. Now let us bless the Lord."

Both Moses and Elijah dropped to their knees, and the multitude followed suit. At first, the prophets placed their hands on their faces and wept before the Lord. Then they straightened up and began singing the ancient affirmation of faith: *"Shema O, Ysrael Adonai elohenu Adonai echad."* The multitude echoed the chant. From somewhere in the middle of the crowd an elderly cantor sang out, *"Baruch ata Adonai Elohenu Melech holam."* Once more the people picked up the familiar hymn and sang mournfully.

As the melody faded away, Moses stood up and began reciting the second psalm. "Why do the nations rage, and the people plot a vain thing?" he quoted to the skies. " 'The kings of the earth set themselves, and the rulers take counsel together, against the LORD and against His anointed.' "

Rabbis in the crowd began to quote the psalm in Hebrew with the lawgiver: " 'Now therefore, be wise, O kings; be instructed, you judges of the earth. Serve the LORD with fear, and rejoice with trembling. Kiss the Son, lest He be angry, and you perish in the way, when His wrath is kindled but a little.' " People began shouting, "AMEN! AMEN!"

Elijah answered with the last line. His voice thundered from the address system, " 'Blessed are all those who put their trust in Him.' "

A great wind swept down from the Temple Mount, blowing hats and scarves in every direction. The mighty gale whistled down the side streets and over the tops of the apartment buildings at the very back of the whole area. People began weeping and crying out. Songs of praise arose with the mournful laments of people pleading before the Lord. The men closest to the wall pressed against the enormous stones while others reached with their hands to touch the rocks.

"Repent!" Moses preached. "The Day of the Lord is at hand. Repent and believe lest you perish as the people of Babylon are soon to do." Moses then pointed directly at Jimmy and motioned for him to come close. He whispered some brief warnings and instructions for the citizens of Bozrah and Petra into Jimmy's ear, explaining the seven bowl judgments that remained before Yeshua would return.

"I'm sorry, but we better get out of here." Sam pulled Jimmy toward the back of the plaza. "Television cameras have been panning the audience. They could be running a security check right now. Time is running out."

"Maybe." Jimmy gave a final wave to his new friend. "But today time has also been fulfilled."

Four days later Damian Gianardo's jet circled above the Rome airport. *The White Horse* slowly cruised, waiting for all runways to be cleared for the emperor's landing. The five young generals sat nervously facing their leader with Rathmarker at their side.

"Where did this report come from?" The emperor shook the teletype paper in the air. "The newspapers in Babylon are warning of an immediate attack on the city. Only one of you could have known that such a plan was in motion for a possible assault."

Salino raised his hand cautiously. "They're just guessing. Since our negotiations on oil prices collapsed, they are assuming that our threats might take the shape of an attack, even though the Chinese pledged to stand behind them with nuclear support. Lucky guess."

"Guess? On the very day that the attack is planned!" Gianardo exploded. "The report says that we will bomb the city on April 20! There's a leak!"

"In my new capacity as head of security, I have already checked the matter out," General Askins answered smugly. "An extensive investigation began immediately after this headline appeared."

Gianardo turned slowly toward his young lackey. "Well, he said, "Askins scores again. You managed to put a bullet in the back of General Smith's head at precisely the right moment. You had the other resisters arrested in minutes. Now you tell me that you have the inside on our leak?"

"No leak." Askins smiled broadly. "The source of this story comes from Israel."

"Israel?" Gianardo started.

"Yes. Apparently, Israeli intelligence has found some correlation between our statements and our actions."

"What does that mean?" The emperor frowned.

"Well . . ." Askins paused momentarily.

"Tell me!" Gianardo demanded.

"The only official reports I've received say that Moses and Elijah announced our intentions to the nation at exactly the same moment that we were discussing how a missile attack on Babylon would be conducted and how we would move government control to Rome should China retaliate."

"Moses and Elijah!" Gianardo screamed at the top of his lungs. The generals fell back in shock. The emperor was on his feet, waving the report in the air. "They've done it again! I hate them. They must be wiped out at once. If you can't silence those two impostors, I will kill them myself!"

"I don't understand," Askins fumbled. "All attempts to kill them have failed."

"How dare they undermine my position! The Jews have threatened some of the mightiest rulers of the world from Pharaoh down to Saddam Hussein. Now I have to contend with these freaks from a time warp! I will not allow them to make a fool out of me."

"I don't think we ought to harm them." Askins reached into his briefcase for another file. "Reports indicate an amazing nationwide turning to faith in Jesus as the Jewish Messiah. They call Him Yeshua. We don't understand how, but there's no question that these two figures have effected a major revival in the country."

"How dare you retreat!" Veins on the emperor's neck bulged and his face turned crimson. "How dare you insinuate that we should fear anyone—much less them! How dare you suggest that I retreat from those two apparitions!"

"I'm sorry." Askins's eyes widened as he frantically looked from one general to the other. "I did not mean to imply weakness."

"Where's the code box, Jackson?" Gianardo demanded.

"It's in this special case that Terbor Esiw built. All the controls are there. I have it stored in the back."

"Good. I don't care what the Chinese say. We'll use this story to put additional pressure on them. Tell the United Muslim States they have one final chance. Negotiate or else."

Browning added timidly, "There is the matter of the massive buildup of Chinese troops that might strike if . . ."

"Are you with me or not?" Gianardo screamed at the shocked generals.

The young men's heads bobbed up and down like little boats on a stormy sea. As the men scurried to the back of the airplane, Gianardo stared out the window. He ripped up the teletype report and dropped the pieces on the floor.

April 20, 2000, was a significant day in more ways than one. For believers in Yeshua, it was the Feast of Unleavened Bread and Passover with all the symbolic meaning involved. For Gianardo and Rathmarker, it was the day they broke off negotiations with the United Muslim States. For Babylon, it was the day one of Gianardo's nuclear bombs wiped out half the city, and the surviving half fled for fear of radiation poisoning. And for the United Muslim States, it was the day they changed their minds and agreed to lower oil prices for Gianardo's empire. But they determined that it was only a temporary lull before the storm.

30

The depleted ozone layer made it a blazing hot and dirty day in late summer in LA. Ash was visible on this dark afternoon.

Ben raced the car engine, waiting impatiently for the light to change. Isaiah watched out the back window while George looked down the side street. A group of eight men eyed them from the other side of the intersection. The motley crew wore battered clothing, they were unshaven, and their uncut hair was stringy and dirty. The pack studied Ben's car like wolves following a deer in the winter.

"We've got scavengers on our flank." Ben nervously shifted into low. "If they charge, we're going through the intersection regardless."

"The light's changed!" George pointed overhead. "Here they come!"

Ben's car whizzed past the first man swinging a baseball bat. One young man clutched at the door handle, but the car flew by so fast that he was hurled out of the way. The rest of the gang didn't get close.

"Wow!" Ben shifted into second. "I thought the police were bad, but now I wish they were back. It was easier to elude the security people than these gangs that roam the streets everywhere since food has become scarce. There's just no law and order left."

"The nuclear exchange back in January finished everything off," Isaiah said as he watched the men shake their fists in the air. "The bomb that went off in the Van Nuys area finished off the local police. Do you really think that Chicago was completely wiped out too?"

"With censored newspapers and television, it's hard to know anything for sure," Ben answered. "But the few ham operators I've been able to contact are saying that most of Chicago is gone. San Francisco's been fairly well gone since the last earthquake. I get the clear feeling that there's no one left running the country."

"I really appreciate you guys making the dash to pick me up." Isaiah settled back against the seat. "I was able to make all the contacts that Michael assigned me. Either people are turning to Yeshua, or they are turning into animals."

"We need to get out of the Costa Mesa area as soon as we can," George added. "The longer we are here, the more radiation we are exposed to . . . not to mention the danger of attack."

Ben turned the corner and pulled into the parking lot of a store that still accepted cash. "Got to get close to the building so we'll be protected. I'm not going into the grocery store unless the coast is clear." He pulled along the curb in front of a store with dirty windows and faded signs still advertising old specials. The stained posters hung at odd angles from yellowing tape. Beside the entrance men were crouched behind sand bags, training guns on their car.

"We're customers," Isaiah called out. "Don't shoot."

"Leave the car there." A man yelled back. "Walk in with your hands empty. We don't take any chances."

Ben turned the car off and walked slowly toward the door with his palms exposed. Isaiah and George did the same. Inside there were only a few customers, and most of the shelves were depleted. There were no fresh vegetables or meat.

"We don't barter or trade," a rough-looking employee

confronted them. "If you don't have money, don't trouble us."

Ben nodded and kept walking. "Look at those prices!" He stopped and stared at the few cans of beans left on a long shelf. "Ten dollars a can!"

"It's a good thing we stocked up before they nuked Babylon." George picked up some cans of tomatoes. Across the top in black marking ink was the price— eight dollars. "I thank God that we were able to plan ahead."

"We'll just get enough to trade out for gasoline." Ben gathered whatever he could find that they might need for the last two months. "Too bad we couldn't store a little fuel. I figure it will be gone before long. Get some canned meat for us. We aren't likely to see any until the Lord's return."

Shots of gunfire ended their conversation. They hit the floor and crawled toward the cash register. Near the end of the aisle they inched up to look through the large windows. Outside they could see a band of men running toward the store. The guards kept shooting. Two wounded men fell on the pavement; the rest turned back and dispersed. Ben hurried toward the counter.

"Don't worry," the dirty little man waved them forward. "We get these skirmishes every day. Have to shoot one now and then to keep law and order. You got real money?"

Ben nodded.

"Have to scratch out an existence." The checker began adding up the cost on a piece of brown paper. "Not much is left. Without supplies coming through, we have to charge what the traffic will bear. If the trucks run again, we'll drop prices."

Ben studied the man's face. An ugly eczema covered his neck, betraying an outbreak of skin cancer. His eyes were red and matter filled the corners. He looked as if he hadn't shaved in a week.

"Walk all the time now," the cashier rattled on. "Too dangerous to drive. Can't afford the gasoline anyway."

He stopped and looked at the three young men. "I don't think any of us will survive long. If we don't starve, the radiation will get us. It's all over for us and the empire."

"We have a great hope," Isaiah said urgently. "Could we share our faith with you?"

The man looked whimsical for a moment and then turned away. "No. I don't want to hear any religious talk. Don't believe in any of it. Living in this world is like living in hell, and when I die, I imagine that's where I'll end up. I'm consigned to it. Life's nothing but a disappointment anyway."

Ben laid the money out on the counter. "Nine hundred and twenty dollars covers it. Right?"

The man grunted and stuffed the money into his pocket. "Good luck," he grumbled after them. "Luck will get you farther than religion."

The young men walked out with two grocery carts full of supplies. For a moment they stood behind the barrier, looking across the empty shopping center.

"Get moving while you can." The guard lowered his gun. The top of his head looked as if large wads of hair had fallen out, leaving red blotches. On the back of his hand a dark lesion ran up his arm. "You never know when some of those scavengers will turn up. Starvation makes them unpredictable, and desperation turns them into madmen. Hurry up and get on with it."

Ben quickly unlocked the car and loaded his trunk. Even in the short time they had been inside, a thin layer of ash had settled on Ben's old BMW. "We're not going to stop until we get near the edge of town. Watch for a gas station that's away from any houses. We don't want to be ambushed when we stop."

The trio sped on, staying as close to the center of the street as possible. The usual afternoon sun looked dim and very distant behind the layers of ugly brownish haze. Dark smoke-filled clouds drifted overhead, and the air burned their noses. Here and there houses were burning, but no one was responding. Few businesses were left open, and many of the stores had been looted.

Finally, the young men found a station that looked relatively secure. After bargaining for several minutes, a deal was struck and the attendant unlocked a pump. Once the gas tank was filled, Ben started the engine and turned toward the freeway.

"What's that?" George sat up abruptly. "What's out there in the street?"

"Looks like a tanker truck had a wreck." Ben slowed down.

"That's no wreck!" Isaiah pointed to the side of the street. "One of the gangs has deliberately turned that vehicle over to jam the street. They've probably drained the tanks and then set up a road block to raid cars. Watch out! Men will be hiding behind the truck."

"Hang on." Ben shifted into second. "We don't have any choice but to run it."

"Can you see anything coming in the opposite direction?" George braced his feet.

"Yeah." Ben grimaced. "Two cars are coming down the other side. We don't have an alternative. We're going over the curb and around on the right."

When Ben hit the curb, the car bounced up in the air and landed ten feet ahead on the sidewalk, only inches away from a large tree. On his left he saw a blur of faces running toward the car. An awesome thump thundered overhead and the ceiling sagged. Ben abruptly jerked the wheel to the left, sending the car back toward the street. Once again they bounced over the curb and flew out toward the traffic. At that moment a man went sailing off the top of the car, smashing into the street. He rolled wildly toward the tanker, finally landing motionless on his back.

"He dropped out of the tree!" Isaiah stared at the caved-in car roof. "They had a real trap set for anybody who stopped or slowed down!"

Ben shifted into high and hit the gas pedal. "We're not stopping for stop signs until we get out of LA! We don't have any kind of weapon to defend ourselves."

"I hope that angel of yours is paying attention."

George looked quickly up and down the streets. "We're no match for these modern cavemen. Civilization's completely gone. There's nothing left but marauding tribes."

After Ben drove out of the populated area, he began winding up the hillside. The grass was brown and dead. Most of the vegetation was shriveled and blackened. The open space made it easier to detect any movement so the young men settled back in their seats.

Thirty minutes later the winding dirt road to the farmhouse opened before them. Students were carrying wood down from the top of the hill while two fellows stacked the sticks and chunks against the back of the house and next to the great oak tree. Some of the group were hanging wash on the clothesline out back. Ben pulled alongside the house. He could see Cindy's parents busily working away in the kitchen.

Every inch of the living room was taken. Bedrolls and pillows were pushed against the wall. The old farmhouse had become a full-scale dormitory, and the Wongs were the houseparents.

During supper, Ben explained, "We won't be making many more runs into the city. The area's entirely too dangerous now. If someone were hurt in there, we probably couldn't find medical care. We don't need anymore needless pain. Unless Michael appears and gives us assignments, we had best settle in here for the duration."

"Are you sure this will be over by October?" a student asked. "Can our food hold out that long?"

"Only if we stay on our self-imposed ration program," Ben said. "We certainly won't get fat. In fact, some of the time we may feel hungry, but we can make it. With the Wongs' cooking we will be able to use every scrap of food. How do you like their cuisine?"

The room exploded in applause. Frank and Jessica beamed.

"After today's narrow escape, I believe we need barricades around the house and across the road." Isaiah stood up. "If the scavenger gangs find out we have such a large stash of food, they'll attack. I volunteer to oversee the project."

"Here! Here!" rang around the room.

"We must live now as we shall in eternity," Ben instructed. "Tension builds when people live in close proximity. We must use these days to discipline ourselves to be ready for the kingdom of God to break forth. We face a great challenge."

Cindy held up her hand assertively. "Here's your first chance to show your sincerity. I have a chart my mother wrote out for who will be washing the dishes each day."

The students booed and laughed as they continued eating and talking together. Once they were through, the table was cleared for evening worship. Many sat in a big circle on the floor while others sat behind them. A few students sprawled on the steps going upstairs.

Cindy quoted from Psalm 83: "'Do not keep silent, O God! Do not hold Your peace, and do not be still, O God! For behold, Your enemies make a tumult; and those who hate You have lifted up their head.'" She turned around. "Anyone doubt this is the word of the Lord?"

Several students nodded no.

"Is it really true Gianardo has moved the seat of power to Rome?" Deborah asked.

Isaiah answered, "We didn't get much information in LA, but it's clear that no one is in control of anything. The rumor is that not much is left on the Eastern seaboard. They say that the remaining soldiers are being shipped out for a final showdown with the Muslims and Chinese. We heard that the emperor is in Rome to avoid the truth about how bad things are in this country, but they say lots of European cities were wiped out too."

Cindy began quoting again: "'They have taken crafty counsel against Your people, and consulted together against Your sheltered ones. They have said, "Come, and let us cut them off from being a nation, that the name of Israel may be remembered no more."' Once again we are living in a time of fulfillment of these very words. I would be totally terrified if it were not for the comfort that God's Word gives me."

"We must pray for our comrades who are still in the city," Isaiah added. "Many people are struggling to survive against terrible odds. The revival that we saw on the UCLA campus will dissipate since the school is now closed, but the word is still getting out. We must pray that our friends are able to hold their own."

Cindy stated the concluding lines of the psalm: "'Let them be confounded and dismayed forever; yes, let them be put to shame and perish. That men may know that You, whose name is the LORD, are the Most High over all the earth.'" She paused for a few moments to allow the words to sink in. "The psalmist prayed for the demise of the enemies of God, and we should do the same. The difference is that we not only know that their days are numbered, we know the number of their days. Let us pray for the victory of our God."

Across the room students bowed their heads. Some knelt with their faces in their hands. Ben watched quietly, feeling a deep sense of satisfaction in knowing that he had played a part in bringing so many of his friends to the faith that was now their literal salvation.

Ben looked at the Wongs who sat with bowed heads. Cindy held her mother's hand as they prayed together. God had blessed the little man and woman with new faith. The students loved the Wongs and encouraged them. In turn, Frank and Jessica had found great gratification in cooking for the kids.

Ben felt overwhelmed, realizing how the hand of God had molded this unlikely company into a community of faith, each now praying fervently for the other. At that moment he thought of Joe and Jennifer McCoy. The faces of Erica and Joe, Jr., drifted before his eyes. He remembered the New Year's celebrations and his family's times together.

And then Ben thought of Ruth. Memories of her and their family rituals swept across his mind. The football games, the teasing, and the family's special New Year's breakfasts. A great loneliness clutched at his heart. Ben looked around the crowded room. Every eye was closed except his, but he felt completely isolated.

Tears rolled down his cheeks, and Ben found it difficult to swallow. For the first time he allowed himself to face the blow Ruth's death was to his mother. He let himself feel the terrible pain that had cut through his Jewish mother's dreams of a grandchild. With great difficulty he prayed aloud, "Let them know that Your name is most holy and high over all the earth."

31

The concluding weeks of the summer of 2000 were unusually hot and dry across most of the world. August in southern California was nearly as scorching as the desert heat in Bozrah. Radiation and AIDS continued taking their deadly toll. Old diseases like cholera and bubonic plague reappeared. Animals and crazed dogs ran wild, attacking people, while gangs of thugs and criminals ran in packs far more vicious than anything found in the wild. Many decided erroneously that suicide was the best alternative to a life that was no longer tolerable.

Television and radio were out much of the time. For long periods of time there was no electricity. Blackouts became a way of life. Because refrigeration was unpredictable, lengthy storage of food became impossible.

Ben's crew found their ministry radically changed. Exciting forays into dangerous dormitories were replaced by quiet evenings in the farmhouse. No longer were secret rendezvous possible. The thrill of the chase was replaced by the solitude of nights on an isolated farm. Witnessing was replaced by prayer.

Intercession became a new way of life. The students organized themselves into a continuous chain of prayer, running twenty-four hours a day. A small bedroom was turned into a chapel where each student could take a turn praying for the families in Bozrah and acquaintances in the Los Angeles area. During the afternoons and evenings, the entire group gathered to sing, share, and encourage each other.

As the days dragged by, a slow metamorphosis occurred. The usual collegiate bravado and frivolity were replaced by quiet reflective maturity. No longer was it necessary to be cute or turn everything into a joke. Each person knew a sacred trust had been given and accepted. Every prayer was a moment of standing in the gap for someone who might be on the edge of the abyss at that very moment.

In the Bozrah-Petra compounds, people looked toward September with eager anticipation. Jimmy was teaching every day of the week, helping the new immigrants grasp the significance of what was immediately ahead.

Jimmy looked out over the crowd, which had swelled to a size that strained the range of his voice. Only the intense silence of the immigrants made it possible for him to be heard. "Originally, God intended Israel to divide history into fifty-year Jubilee segments. Every five decades on the Day of Atonement, Jews were to blow horns signifying the cancellation of all debts by the owners. Do you understand?"

The crowd nodded that they had grasped his meaning, even though Jimmy taught in English with a Hebrew translator.

"For financial reasons, the Jews did not keep the plan, but God still honored His timetable. I want you to recognize the wonderful truth that is about to be fulfilled. The year 2000 is a Jubilee year . . . a perfect symbol of Yeshua's atoning love for the sin of the world."

Throughout the gathering, people clapped and applauded.

Jimmy nodded his head enthusiastically. "The whole world gets a special Jubilee new start this year."

Earlier during May and June, Jimmy trained evangelists to leave the protected area and travel throughout the small towns of Israel, sharing their message. More than once the teams were attacked and casualties resulted. Nevertheless, each death only spurred on the new converts in their efforts to share their faith.

In July and August, Jimmy taught the new residents the basic facts of life in Yeshua during the cooler hours of the morning. He held his sessions on prophecy late in the afternoon; most of the people napped during the heat of the day. At night he discussed the meaning of suffering and how to face pain.

Larry and Sharon worked tirelessly, helping the distraught and terrified to bring their emotions under control. They counseled, listened, and often prayed with people who could barely speak English.

☐   ☐   ☐

There was no relief from fear in Rome. The ancient city had become a place of poverty as the fortunes of Europe fell with the demise of the empire. Radioactive fallout had taken a toll in the Eternal City as it had elsewhere. Food was scarce, and people lived in fear of what might next fall on them from the skies. The cheerful, emotional attitude of the Italians of the past had been replaced by apprehension and despair. Heavy smog clouded the normally bright summer sky.

Late summer had always been suffocating in Rome. Now the condition was unbearable. The old papal palace Gianardo had commandeered for a residence was not equipped with air conditioning. His arrogance was repaid with constant discomfort.

The new pope fled the country and was rumored to be hiding in France. Gianardo stopped all worship in Saint Peter's Basilica. Instead he periodically strolled across the chancel and sat on the high altar, proclaiming to any observers his absolute power.

As the United States disintegrated and other countries began pulling away from the empire, Gianardo became even more obsessed with his role as the supreme religious leader of the world. He commissioned bizarre religious inquiries into how religious dignitaries and leaders had designated their positions. Robes were designed and vestments constructed that would blend the symbols of political power and religious authority. Occasionally, Gianardo made public appearances wearing the papal miter. Many of his aides fought to keep from snickering at the strange sight of the emperor walking about in a modern business suit carrying the crosier and wearing the pointed hat of the pope.

In late August, 2000, the emperor summoned the five young generals who now controlled all military operations to the Sistine Chapel. Full-scale maps, drawings, and plans were laid out on long tables beneath the ceiling that was Michelangelo's greatest accomplishment. Each man stood at full attention, making his report of the state of affairs. Gianardo sat against the wall in the golden chair normally reserved for the pope.

"Therefore," Imler concluded, "no longer is there a necessity for any legislative activity. The United States is a country without a center of power. People are not out of control as much as they have been reduced to a meager quest for survival. The entire nation must be rebuilt."

"Good," Gianardo smiled as he talked, "exactly where I want things to be. When the last conflict is over, we will rebuild the old U.S. according to our design. No resistance will be possible because people will be grateful simply to have a means of surviving. I will be unquestioned. In the end, the citizens will recognize me as their source of life. Is this not clever?"

General Imler cleared his throat and smiled weakly. He sat down quickly.

"And the state of the movement of all troops?" Gianardo turned to General Jackson. "Are the troop carriers in motion?"

"Even as we speak, the army and the entire fleet await your direction. You are the only person in the world who knows what we are doing." Jackson looked nervously at his comrades. "Time is running out. We must quickly tell our men where to land. There is a great sense of disarray among the military."

"Excellent!" Gianardo stood up and walked to the table with the maps. "I have personally planned every detail of what lies ahead." He unfolded a map of Israel and began motioning with a pointer. "We are going to land on the beaches near the ancient city of Megiddo. I want to prepare for a drive down the Valley of Jezreel, called by some Armageddon. We will cut the country into two sections."

Browning leaned over and stared at the map. "Armageddon? Why there? In fact, why in the world are we going to Israel of all places?"

"Two reasons," the emperor snapped. "For some unexplainable cause, the Israelis are the only people who have escaped the ecological damage visited on the world by my enemies. They have the only real estate left where we can hope to escape the effects of pollution and radiation. We will govern from Jerusalem until the rest of the world cools off. In addition, their capital has religious significance. In the future, Jerusalem will be a more suitable place for my throne."

"But why is the entire military converging on their shores?" Browning gestured aimlessly. "I mean . . . all our troops?"

"The Muslims have been bargaining with Russia and China. We know the Chinese are moving their hordes toward the Middle East. We are going to meet them in one great showdown that will finally secure the empire."

"This valley is a strange place," the general protested. "Moreover, we are no match for the Chinese army, particularly since the Japanese have joined them. We will be totally overwhelmed."

"Lots of secret military hangars that once housed the Israeli air force are located in this valley. We are going to use them to house the last of our tactical nuclear weapons. Our remaining portable warheads will equalize the numbers quickly."

"But then even Israel will no longer be safe from radiation—"

"I want all forces to be prepared to land by September 1," the emperor cut the general off. "Since they are already at sea, it will only be a matter of telling them where to land. We must be ready to hit the ground running. I suspect the Chinese will be converging on the area quickly. I will personally be on the scene to supervise the final assault when our armies lock in battle."

Browning blinked. His mouth was slightly ajar.

"Some problem with the plan, General?"

Every eye in the room was trained on the general whose face had become rather pale. Browning slowly slid into his chair at the table.

"Jackson, begin immediately to prepare detailed maps of the Megiddo and Armageddon areas," the emperor continued. "I want full-scale reports on all troop movements to our north. In addition, I want television coverage of my personal arrival in Jerusalem. Every radio and TV station is to carry every step of my journey throughout the city. Even though we will work out of the Knesset, I am going to set up a symbolic headquarters in the Holy of Holies in the rebuilt gold-covered temple of Solomon. At that particular place, I will consolidate my position. When I periodically step out of their temple, wearing the vestments of the Christian faith while directing the most powerful army in history, the world will know once and for all that their master has come. Can you not see what a statement we will make for all time to remember?"

No one had time to answer. The emperor stepped back and held his arms up to the painted figures high above him on frescoes across the ceiling. "Behold, ye prophets and saints of the past! I have come! The fullness of time is here!"

On Sunday, September 2, 2000, a helicopter lifted off the ground from the Ben Gurion International Airport in Tel Aviv. Every television camera in the country followed the emperor of the New Roman Empire as he flew across the countryside toward Jerusalem. His helicopter made an enormous sweep of the city before it swooped down over the Old City. Dirt flew in every direction as the chopper settled on top of the Temple Mount.

Soldiers with drawn guns hustled to surround the vehicle as the blades slowed. Damian Gianardo jumped from the open door and immediately was encompassed by troops. The emperor walked briskly toward the gate and steps that led down to the plaza in front of the Western Wall. Generals Askins and Imler trotted behind him.

Even before the entourage had started their descent, the crowd began to disperse. Many Israelis pushed toward the Dung Gate to escape. Other citizens rushed for various passageways into the Old City. By the time Gianardo reached the square, the area had been cleared, except for the soldiers standing behind the sand bag barricades.

Gianardo's men fanned out over the area, forming a protective shield for the emperor. Gianardo did not slow his pace until he was standing directly in front of the two ancient figures who sat passively on their wooden thrones, watching his arrival.

Gianardo turned and faced the prophets. For a minute he studied them as television cameras zoomed in on his face. He seemed more intrigued than dismayed. Finally, Gianardo began edging forward. When he was only ten feet in front of the two giants, he stopped again.

"Why are you here?" the emperor asked sharply.

There was no response.

"The ruler of this world is speaking to you!" Gianardo barked. "Do you not understand the precarious nature of your position?

Again neither Moses nor Elijah spoke, but both men smiled condescendingly.

"I have the power of life and death in my hands." The emperor's voice was menacing. "You nuisances have been allowed to stay only because of my choosing. Do you understand that in a moment I can dispatch you back into the mist from which you came?"

Moses suddenly laughed. Elijah looked sternly for a few moments and then began to smile. Finally, he, too, roared. As the ancients laughed, Gianardo's face turned red. Their laughter turned into an echo, resounding against the plaza. Like no other sound, the laughter rumbled less with frivolity and more with judgment.

Suddenly, Gianardo turned to a soldier behind him and jerked the man's pistol from his holster. The emperor cocked the gun and ran directly in front of the prophets. "Now let the world see who laughs last!" he screamed. "Let every eye see who has the power!"

The emperor swung the gun up and fired two shots directly at Moses' chest. Before the lawgiver had even toppled from his chair, the emperor fired at Elijah. The prophet bolted backward, and Gianardo shot again. The great white head dropped backward. The prophet collapsed and slid from the chair onto the platform.

Gianardo turned around to the stunned multitude behind him. No one moved. Complete silence descended on the holy sight. The emperor's gaze darted back and forth. There was no look of awe or exaltation; only dumbfounded disbelief and dismay covered people's faces.

"I am the most powerful force in the world!" the emperor screamed. "Do you understand? I have exposed these frauds. I have done what even Pharaoh of Egypt could not accomplish." His voice split the silence. No one moved.

"The world thought some abstract idea called God was the power of life and death. I alone am this power. I am the supreme one! Throw away your superstitions! I decree these bodies be left in the city that the world may watch. No one touch them! Watch and see them rot!"

When no one moved, Gianardo threw the gun down and stomped back toward the steps. Soldiers fell in around him. A lone detachment of troops formed a line in front of the thrones. Even before the emperor reached the top of the Temple Mount, the square was empty except for the guards.

Gianardo crawled into the helicopter. The two generals slipped in beside him and buckled their seat belts. "Let's go," the emperor commanded the pilot. "I showed them," he said.

But again no one answered.

CHAPTER

32

The sun broke over the mountaintops, bathing the far corners of the plaza in front of the Western Wall in arid sunlight. Only a stray dog broke the stillness surrounding the sleeping soldiers. Thursday, September 6, 2000, offered no more promise than the other dog days of that late summer. But then a finger moved. The hand opened and closed and opened again. Slowly, Moses stirred.

For three days the great leader had lain face down on the platform next to the throne. Two jagged holes were ripped open in the back of Moses's robe where the bullets came out. No one had dared to touch his body, but now the man himself pulled his legs together and stood up. The entire front of his robe was covered with dried blood. He rubbed his eyes before he picked up his staff.

Elijah was slumped against the front of his throne. During the previous days, his legs jutted out at grotesque angles. The front of his robe was also stained with ugly brown blotches of dried blood. At first he slowly moved his head from side to side. Once more life surged through his body. Elijah reached for the arm of the chair and pulled himself up. After standing for a moment, he dropped down in the large wooden chair.

The two prophets silently surveyed the strange scene before them; a ring of fully armed troops slept on the stone pavement. Most soldiers rested their heads against wadded-up coats and backpacks. About a hundred feet away other combatants slept in front of piled-up sand bags.

After a few moments of reflection, Moses thumped his staff on the wooden platform. The hollow sound echoed menacingly across the square. One soldier raised his head, blinked, and then lay back against the makeshift pillow. A second later the terrified man was on his feet.

"They're alive!" the soldier scrambled for his gun. "Look!"

Some men grabbed weapons while others could only stare at the two imposing figures looking down on them. "Call the CO!" a soldier yelled from the back.

Moses stepped down to the pavement, paused, turned, and kissed the wall before walking toward the retreating soldiers. Elijah followed. The front row of soldiers dropped their guns and ran toward the rear.

"Do not fear us." Moses waved them back. "Rather fear him who would steal your soul. The time is short. Repent now, for the era draws to a close."

The prophets walked through the parting soldiers and out the gate. Just as they had entered the city months earlier, they now retraced their steps up the Kidron Valley toward the Mount of Olives. As they walked, teams of TV journalists sped toward the ancient hillside but they were too late. The best the reporters could do was photograph the awesome scene from a distance.

Clouds began boiling in the sky, just as they had on the day of the appearing. Once Moses and Elijah reached the site of Jesus' ascension, they held up their arms toward the heavens. Suddenly, the ground began shaking, and a great roaring noise filled the valley. Several television crewmen thought they heard the words, "Come here." Others attributed the sounds to the earth shifting.

Cameras hummed as Moses and Elijah lifted slowly

from the earth. For a few moments they seemed to hover, and then the clouds closed in again. The crew caught the last moments as a swirl of cloud covering wrapped around Moses and Elijah like a billowy quilt of cotton. And then the prophets were gone.

The ground began to shake. Within seconds every building in Jerusalem rumbled. Light fixtures swung back and forth and walls cracked apart. The earthquake split the ground; on the southern outskirts of the city, where Gianardo's soldiers were camped, a huge crevasse opened up through a main street. Whole buildings fell in, and seven thousand of Gianardo's men disappeared as the earth kept shifting, swallowing them alive.

Throughout the rest of the day, aftershocks rocked the city. Cracks in the street closed public access to the Mount of Olives, and rock slides obliterated other roads. Footage of the final moments of the ascent filled the TV screens on an hourly basis. The entire city was in a state of uproar, watching the alternating stories of the earthquake damage and the amazing resurrection of Moses and Elijah. Reporters interviewed the soldiers guarding the Western Wall, but no one could explain how they could possibly have come alive.

The next morning Damian Gianardo sat slumped behind his desk in the makeshift military headquarters set up in the Knesset Building. He stared hollow-eyed at an Israeli commander, who was explaining his soldiers' behavior.

"Our men are good soldiers," the lieutenant in battle fatigues complained. "You are not fair to accuse them of incompetence and irresponsibility. They had no reason not to be asleep. They were ordered to keep anyone from burying two dead men . . . not keep them from walking away."

"Don't be impertinent," Gianardo sneered. "I'm not superstitious. I don't believe in ghosts."

"Perhaps you would recognize that our country has

the highest resurrection rate in the world," the soldier answered coldly.

"Don't push your luck with me." The emperor stood up. "I still want a detachment of troops set up on the site of the ascension. If anything else comes down, I want your men to shoot first and ask questions later."

The soldier saluted and turned on his heels. As he opened the door, General Browning entered.

"I have an update on how the troop landing is progressing." He brushed past the Israeli without acknowledging his presence. "We believe that our units are moving at top speed to secure the entire area near the entrance of the Jezreel Valley." The general stopped and looked out the window. Although there had been no signs of a storm, a bolt of lightning flashed across the sky. A great flash of light filled the room, followed by an explosive roar.

Gianardo and Browning rushed to the window. A large tree across the street was now a smoldering splintered stump. As they watched, an electrical storm broke across the entire sky. Streaks of lightning flew through the air. Terrible popping and crackling sounds bewildered people on the street. They ran for shelter in the closest buildings.

"The earth is coming apart," Browning sputtered. The building shook again. Across the street large rocks began hopping as another earthquake began. "I'm losing it." The general's eyes widened. "Everything is coming unglued."

"Get a grip on yourself, Browning! The environment's messed up from the pollution and A-bomb attacks. Don't go nuts on me."

A file cabinet toppled over, and Gianardo's desk began sliding toward the opposite wall. The general lost his footing and nearly fell. Staggering like a drunk, he tried to reach the door. "I'll try to get some kind of a report for you." Browning ran, not even trying to close the door behind him.

☐   ☐   ☐

Throughout the rest of the day the Seventh Trumpet of the Lord continued to blow the world apart. It was a warning that God would send, in rapid sequence, the final seven bowls of His wrath on those who refused to repent of their sins against their fellow human beings and against Him. Eventually, a 9.3-rated earthquake in the middle of the Atlantic Ocean sent great tidal waves crashing across the Mediterranean. Many of the empire's ships anchored off the coast of Israel were picked up like children's toys and slung helpless into the rocks and beaches. On the opposite side of the world, the shores of North America were again smashed by corresponding walls of water. Near dusk, polluted hail the size of basketballs fell on many areas of the world. By night the world had once more been warned. Sadly, few understood that the call had come from the Most High.

One week later, the emperor moved his command post north to be closer to the scene of the impending battle. As troops marched, the Bowls of Wrath began to be poured. The First Bowl was terrible sores and boils that appeared on all who were true followers of Gianardo and Rathmarker. They gnawed their tongues from the pain.

On Sunday, September 16, a sailor was the first to recognize the next consequence of global disobedience, the Second Bowl. At first a red coagulation began to cover the surface of the oceans. The seas took on the cast of pinkish blood serum, and all sea animals died. Dead fish and animals bloated and floated on the surface. By the time the seaman's report was registered, other coastal residents noticed the Third Bowl—streams running into the oceans started backing up with the same blood-red covering. As more and more dead sea animals rotted, along with most freshwater animals, the stench was staggering. Within two days, most of the drinking water was in danger of contamination. However, Damian Gianardo wrote off the phenomenon as another result of environmental pollution.

On that Thursday, the Fourth Bowl of Wrath was poured over the atmosphere. The clouds evaporated. Nothing stood between the sun's rays and the ozone-depleted covering around the globe. In a short time the average temperature across the globe rose to 115 degrees at night and 135 degrees during the day. The generals watched as thousands of their finest soldiers dropped from the heat and dehydration.

On Saturday, the terrible sores from the First Bowl recurred, but this time only on Gianardo's inner circle of power players. It was the Fifth Bowl.

Five days later, the latest military reports arrived on each commander's desk. The combination of manipulation of a Turkish dam and the oppressive heat had dried up the Euphrates River. The coagulated blood-red waters left the soil a baked hard red clay. The demise of the environment caused Premier Ching Lei to move his troops prematurely. Lei pressed the remnant of the Muslim world into his conglomerate of Japanese, Russian, and Chinese troops, and the march was on. The massive horde of advancing soldiers rumbled toward the valley known to the ancients as Armageddon. The gathering of the kings of the East down the dry Euphrates River bed to oppose the New Roman Empire of the West was the Sixth Bowl in preparation for the final Bowl: the Battle of Armageddon.

Each of Gianardo's young generals read with increasing alarm the identical report: "At least two hundred million men and women have crossed the dried-up Euphrates River bed. Japanese air and ground forces have joined the drive as well as some contingents of troops from other Asian nations including Korea. We have also been able to identify soldiers from the following countries: Syria, Iran, Libya, Ethiopia, Egypt, Lebanon, Jordan, and Iraq."

General Browning had barely completed reading the top secret dispatch when an aide appeared and handed him another sheet of teletype. Browning scanned the latest data, put the report down, and summoned Imler and Jackson to a conference. Within thirty minutes the three men gathered in the open air just down the hill from the excavations of the ancient city of Megiddo.

"No one should be able to monitor us here," Browning said quietly. "Does each of you understand the significance of the report you received this morning?"

Each man nodded his head gravely.

"We are preparing to enter the greatest bloodbath in history. The numbers of the enemy alone will overwhelm us!"

Jackson agreed. "Even if we nuke a good percentage of their ground troops, I don't think we can stop the air force."

"Atomic response?" Browning's shoulders sagged and he wrung his hands. "If we win such an exchange, I believe the result will truly be the end of the world. What we have seen in the last month is nothing short of the world falling apart."

Browning pulled the latest communiqué from his pocket. "In a few hours you will receive this update. The report you read earlier turned out to be dated. We now have confirmed that Lei's march has passed the Syrian portion of the Golan Heights and is infiltrating the eastern half of the Jezreel Valley. By nightfall I believe they will have established initial outposts from the top of Mount Tabor to Mount Gilboa. The Israeli army is so small now that its numbers are relatively meaningless, but we assume the soldiers will continue to remain under our command out of fear alone. The army has retreated to avoid an initial confrontation, but it is poised to protect its homeland."

Imler looked hard into Browning's eyes. "We're on the western side, and we'll soon be coming across this great valley. At any moment the great battle could start."

Jackson cupped his hand over his eyes and looked out over the rich, fertile valley and the plain at the bottom. Vehicles were moving everywhere. Overhead, the sky was filled with planes. "Could make the Normandy invasion look like child's play," he said cynically. "Bodies will be stacked up out there until the valley is level."

"No question," Browning snapped. "The war will begin tomorrow."

An hour later each man returned to his post and began monitoring his portion of military preparation. As dusk fell, the ground rumbled with the movement of vehicles; the sounds of a mighty army filled the valley. At 8 P.M. Gianardo summoned his military staff.

"Just at the break of sunrise I want our air force to hit them with everything short of nuclear strike weapons. The remaining battleships will lob shells from the ocean. I want the biggest weapons we've got firing point-blank into their positions. After the initial assault, we will unleash the Israelis in a vicious counterattack designed to kill as many of the enemy as possible. We won't win the day immediately, but we will greatly reduce the odds against us."

Gianardo sneered at his generals. "Before this week is over, I will have rewritten the military textbooks. Now implement what I've said."

The generals hurried out to prepare for the dawn assault.

33

Well before dawn, the eastern side of the Jezreel Valley exploded with terrific bursts of fire. Phosphoric pieces of smoldering debris hurled through the night. Tracers and flares signaled locations, and shelling immediately followed. The once beautiful hillside was pitted, burned, and torn. At the break of day, bombers dumped their bombs, and the sky filled with fighter jets locked in mortal combat. The earliest light of day was obscured by the smoke that hid the hillside and mountaintops. By ten o'clock, the fallout and dust were so thick that it was even difficult to breathe several miles away along the coastline.

Only after the thick cloud cover of smoke was established did the emperor release his own ground forces. Tanks and armored vehicles sped across the plain to support the assault troops that stung with the force of a million hornets. By noontime, the Chinese made their counterattack. The premier's strategy was relatively simple. He was willing to buy victory at the price of sacrificing any number of troops necessary. By late afternoon, the eastern slopes and the terrain down and out into the valley were filled with dead bodies of Chinese and their allies.

The generals of the empire were sequestered in a bunker deep underneath Megiddo. In a separate room, the emperor had a personal command post where he monitored all decisions and carefully controlled every aspect of the attack.

"What's happening overhead?" Browning called to Imler across the room.

"Stalemate. Looks like we've about neutralized each other's air power. Not much left of either air force."

"Bad news!" Browning hit the table with his fist. "Means the balance of power will shift to their ground forces. They greatly outnumber us."

An allied general hurried into the strategy room. He was covered with dirt and smelled of smoke. The man's face was blackened, and his battle fatigues were torn and grimy. "We're slaughtering them like pigs!" he talked rapidly. "But for every one that falls, two take his place. We're fighting behind piles of bodies, but they won't stop coming. I think we'll run out of bullets before they run out of personnel." The general went to the emperor's quarters to make a personal report.

The afternoon wore on with many identical reports coming in. Near sundown the battle settled into a lull. Heavy artillery fire became more erratic. The sound of airplanes faded; the roaring of the big guns was replaced by the steady fire of infantry rifles and machine guns. Several hours passed before Gianardo summoned the five generals to his quarters.

"What do you think?" Gianardo asked the grim-faced assembly. "Where are we on this Friday night, September 28? If memory serves me right, tomorrow's the big Jewish Feast of Trumpets. Anyone requesting leave for the holidays?"

No one smiled. Finally, Browning answered, "I have always prided myself on being a soldier, not a butcher. Never have I witnessed what has happened out there today. Surely, the carnage exceeds the worst ever seen by the human race."

The emperor dismissed the general's comments by not even acknowledging them. "I'm sure you are wondering where we go next," Gianardo spoke in a monotone. "My plans have gone exactly according to schedule. I have before me a communiqué so secret that not one of you even knew of its arrival. I established contact with Premier Lei without your knowledge. Surprised?" He grinned cunningly at the shocked generals.

The weary group only stared in response.

"Premier Lei has responded to an overture that I made earlier this evening. I lied to him and told him that we were both out of nuclear weaponry, but I told the truth about losing great numbers of our people. I suggested that we cease hostilities and begin negotiations at dawn. He has heartily accepted. Let me share a line or two." Gianardo looked around the room with obvious great pleasure.

" 'The smell of death arises from every continent, and so it will soon be in this place,' " the emperor read aloud. " 'What do we gain? We both have already paid a great price in past wars. I am pleased that you offer peace. We can come to terms. I will expect your next response by morning.' " Gianardo laid the paper down. "Am I not also a man of peace?" He smiled at his leaders.

"What . . . what will you propose?" Browning sputtered. "What will you tell Lei?"

"Listen to some of what I have written." The emperor picked up a scratch pad. " 'I am a mighty man of war, but I am also the prince of peace. In the morning I will bring peace to the globe.' " He laid the sheet down. A smirk crossed his lips and his eyes narrowed. "But this plan I will follow as surely as I live. I will propose that we stop all fighting before dawn and that we both meet on the plain of the battlefield at 9:00 A.M. to settle all differences. But at precisely 8:50 we will hit them with every last nuclear weapon that we *do* have. Because Lei will be in the valley, we'll get close enough to his location to annihilate him and most of his people with the first bombs. When the smoke clears, we will have completely won!"

"You offer peace while planning to totally destroy him

and his allies!" Rathmarker declared proudly. "This will be the war that ends all wars. World dominion with no opposition will finally be ours. Let's go for it!"

"Brilliant, is it not?" Gianardo smirked. "This is not the time to back off."

"You are quite right." General Browning slowly rose to his feet. "This is not the time to back off."

The late evening hours of Friday, September 28, 2000, seemed blacker than any night in history. The moon and stars were completely obliterated by the smoke. One great cloud appeared to envelope the entire globe. Months of environmental deterioration were taking a final toll. Life was being systematically snuffed out. As dawn approached, an awesome stillness hovered over Jerusalem.

Just before dawn, a few citizens arose to begin their preparations for the Feast of Trumpets. Smoke from the great catastrophe in the Valley of Jezreel rolled in like a gray mist from the north. From one end of the Plain of Armageddon to the other, men dug in for a final assault. The armies of the empire and Ching Lei were poised to resume attack. Neither side was sure of the intentions of the other. Fumes and soot were so thick they could no longer be sure where the battle lines were drawn. The emperor and prime minister huddled together, ready to decide what response could be made to any surprise moves by Lei and his allies. Vultures hovered overhead, ready for the feast of their lives.

At the exact moment that the sun started to rise, the clouds over the Holy City broke, and a great shaft of light shot through the sky like a beacon light in a stormy night. The spear of illumination cut through the murky smog and shot out toward the ends of the globe.

The citizens of Jerusalem awoke to wonderful morning light streaming into their windows. They rubbed their eyes in amazement at the shimmering daybreak no one had seen for several years. Out in the streets, people looked awestruck toward the sky. The glorious aurora did not blind their eyes but felt soothing and healing. To their astonishment, the continuing glow seemed to swallow the smoke and pollution, imparting a renewed brilliant clarity to the sky beyond what anyone remembered.

The center of the expanding illumination lingered above the Mount of Olives. Suddenly, the Source of the light broke through the clouds on a great white horse. Wearing a golden crown and holding a sharp sickle, the risen and exalted Yeshua once more rode into human history, this time as Lord of the Third Millennium. The magnificent stallion snorted and threw its head back in proud defiance. Across the dazzling white robe of the Messiah was emblazoned in Hebrew "King of kings and Lord of lords." As the Lord Jesus rode, He and the horse radiated the glowing resplendent luster.

On the opposite side of the world, pitch-black night had promised southern California some relief from the heat and ultraviolet rays scorching the earth. Ben and his friends huddled together in a late night prayer meeting in the dim living room of the farmhouse. A few candles placed on end tables were slowly burning down. The unexpected, unprecedented rise in temperatures had pushed the group's water reserves to the limit. The students were praying for water when the sudden worldwide burst of light split the night and shot into the open windows.

In contrast to the day, the night light was not hot but cooling. Immediate relief followed as the glow surged through the house. Brightness filled the room as if it were noon. The moment each student was bathed in the light, the sallow color of the skin turned to a new pink, healthy glow.

"For goodness' sake," Frank Wong looked around the room in bewilderment. "What happen?"

"He's returned," Ben's dry raspy voice was barely audible. "The Lord has returned! Today is a Feast of Trumpet's Day we will all remember for eternity."

"We're saved," Isaiah gasped. "We're going to survive."

"Praise Him!" Deborah raised her hands toward the ceiling. "Praise God! Praise Yeshua, His Son!"

The night had turned into a glorious sunrise. The usual murky gray sky was changing to a brilliant blue. Even the trees and plants were visibly energized and revitalized.

"Oh, thank You, Lord!" Ben ran to the window. "The whole of creation is coming into its own!"

"So *that's* you, Ben!" a small delicate voice said from behind him.

Ben turned. "What? Cindy?"

"You do have a beautiful face!"

"What are you saying?"

"I can see you, Ben. For the first time in my life, I can see."

At that moment angels and archangels broke forth out of the stream of light covering Jerusalem. The heavenly hosts processed into the world, passing on both sides of the Messiah on His white horse. The vast multitude flew forth over the face of the earth as the exalted Yeshua sat suspended in the air. The mighty chorus proclaimed together, "The kingdoms of this world have become the kingdoms of the Lord and of His Christ. And He shall reign forever and ever!"

When the Messiah's horse touched the place of His original ascension nearly two thousand years before, the Mount of Olives broke apart. A great quake split the earth to its center, and the shock wave reverberated to every fault line across the globe, opening a path from the Dead Sea through the Mount of Olives to the Mediterranean. Lightning began flashing across the world, and the skies were filled with a staggering aerial display of color and explosions of energy.

Anticipating the Return at sunrise, well before dawn Jimmy and the Feinbergs had climbed to the top of the highest mountain in the area. Below them in the valley, thousands of Jimmy's students knelt in silent prayer even before the all-encompassing beam of light first shot across the sky. Once the procession of angels began passing overhead, the new believers covered their faces. They knew from Scripture that whenever the Battle of Armageddon was won by Yeshua, He would personally come to Bozrah to gather His brothers and sisters and lead them through the East Gate of Jerusalem to begin the forty-five-day transition into the third millennium A.D.

Jimmy fell with his face to the ground. Larry and Sharon huddled together with their heads bowed. A great chorus of overpowering singing and heavenly praise encouraged them to look again to the sky. They watched, awestruck, as millions of angels appeared in the clouds. An ever-increasing army of martyrs and saints followed, spreading out in all directions. Many in the cavalcade paraded above them, sweeping closer and closer to the ground as they passed by. The group appeared to be coming to Bozrah and Petra now.

White-robed saints waved to the citizens of Bozrah as if they knew them and were reunited with old friends they had been observing for a long time. In turn, the people began waving back. The Jews stood, clapped, held their hands to heaven, shouted, and prayed. They danced and waved to the hosts overhead. They wept for joy.

Jimmy stood mesmerized by the sound. He closed his eyes as his ears drank in the blissful music that exceeded any strain he had ever heard.

"Jimmy." Sharon shook his arm. "Two people are waving at *you*. They are trying to get your attention."

Jimmy opened his eyes. "Oh, thank God! My goodness!" He grabbed the sides of his face. "Look . . . look . . . I can't believe my eyes. There are my father and mother!"

"Jimmy! Jimmy!" Sharon began sobbing uncontrollably. "To your left. Look! In the white robe . . . it's Ruth!"

Open-mouthed, crying, Jimmy reached up on his tiptoes for the sky. The dark-haired beauty in the white robe extended her hand as she slowly descended.

"Ruth! Ruth!" Jimmy called. "It's really you!"

The Harrisons and Ruth steadily moved toward the trio standing on the mountaintop with their hands lifted as high as they could reach.

"A young man is holding on to Ruth's hand." Larry pointed to his daughter. "Jimmy! He must be one of your ancestors. He looks so much like you."

Jimmy found it nearly impossible to see through his tears. He danced from one foot to the other, waving, holding his arms outstretched. "Ruth . . . Mom . . . Dad . . . we're here . . . waiting . . . we've waited so long."

As they moved very close, Reverend Harrison opened his arms. His voice was loud and clear. "Oh, Son, we've been so proud of you. How pleased we are with what you've done!" Jimmy's father took the other hand of the young man standing with Ruth. "We are bringing a very special person with us. Meet my grandson . . . your son."

We are about to take a journey into the third millennium since the birth of Yeshūa (Jesus). What kind of journey will it be? Is there really an invisible, supernatural world out there somewhere that must affect our speculation about this journey, or are our ponderings a "universal neurosis of mankind" as Sigmund Freud suspected?

I am a psychiatrist, physician, scientist, and author—not a prophet. Throughout graduate school, medical school, and psychiatric training, I have been steeped in the scientific method and programmed to be a skeptic. But I have come to a few conclusions, after much personal inquiry, about this "journey" and would like to share them with you.

It was in medical school that we learned that the human body is made up of thirty trillion cells and that each cell has thousands of enzymes and other components. We also learned that each of those tiny components is made up of electrons, protons, neutrons, invisible force fields. Did this all bounce together out of nothing?

This skeptic says the only logical conclusion is that a design as complex as the human body requires a Supernatural Designer. To deny this would be the equivalent of claiming that *Webster's Dictionary* came about as the result of an explosion in a printing factory!

If there is a Supernatural Designer of the human body and human spirit, then it seems logical to think that this Supernatural Being probably left us some information—at least some hints about whether it loves us, hates us, or is indifferent to us. Hints about what this being plans to do with us—if anything—in the future. And hints about what type of relationship, if one is even possible, we can have with our Supernatural Designer.

If this Being did give us a form of communication—a

Bible, so to speak—which Bible is His? Which one—if any—
is correct? And if we determine which one is correct, how
do we know how to interpret it?

When we die, do we just die? Or is there life after death?
Just because I hope there is an afterlife doesn't necessarily
make it so! Are we really more than just an amazingly complex body? Are we really spiritual beings who will live forever in modified bodies?

I have obsessed about these questions since childhood.
And in my journey through life, I have come to the skeptical
and scientific conclusions that the God of the Bible is the
Supernatural Being for whom we are searching, and that the
best way to understand His communication to us is to read
the Bible as if we were reading a newspaper article—that is,
take it literally unless the symbolism is obvious.

Because of my compulsive desire to understand the answers to my obsessive spiritual questions, I didn't stop my
education when I finished my psychiatry residency at Duke
University. I continued my studies in theology at two different seminaries until I obtained a seminary degree just before
my 40th birthday.

When it comes to eschatology—the study of potential "end
time" events—I have grown to respect good and sincere
scholars who have a wide variety of views on the end times.
I hope people of all eschatalogical backgrounds have their
lives enhanced in some ways by reading this political/psychi-
atric/eschatological novel.

The Essenes, over 2,000 years ago, waited for the Jewish
Messiah and wrote their thoughts and their scriptures down
in the form of the Dead Sea Scrolls. I believe their Messiah—
Yeshūa—came, but did not conquer the world and make Jerusalem its capital as expected. He was a major disappointment to many people of many faiths.

What most "future-watchers" failed to recognize in the
Old Testament was that it repeatedly predicted *two separate*
visitations of planet Earth by the Creator-God in human
flesh—Yeshūa (Jesus) the Messiah. There would be a *First
Coming* and a *Second Coming,* a *Former Reign* and a *Latter
Reign* of blessings on the Jews and on the world.

The Old Testament had 48 predictions about Jesus' *Former Reign—His First Coming*—including His birth in Bethle-
hem (Mic. 5:2), His betrayal for 30 pieces of silver (Zech.
11:12), His crucifixion on a cross (Ps. 22:16), and His trium-

phal entry into Jerusalem on a humble foal of a donkey (Zech. 9:9).

The most remarkable prediction about the Messiah's Former Reign was written by Daniel the prophet, more than 600 years before Jesus was born, in Daniel 9:24–27. The Essenes had more copies of Daniel than any other Old Testament book—*eight* copies of Daniel compared to only four of the Torah. And yet Jews today are usually discouraged from reading Daniel. It is seldom read in any synagogues. Why is it withheld?

In Daniel 9:24–27, Daniel says that someday a decree will be made to rebuild the walls of Jerusalem. Sixty-nine prophetic "weeks" after that decree, the Messiah would make His *First Coming*. A prophetic week has always meant seven Hebrew years of 360 days per year. Then He would be *"cut off."* Thus, 69 "weeks" equals $69 \times 7 = 483$ years $\times$ 360 days = 173,880 days. The only major decree to rebuild the walls of Jerusalem recorded in history is the decree of Artaxerxes Longimanus (Neh. 2:1), on May 14, 445 B.C. Add 173,880 days to that date and it comes out to April 6, A.D. 32, the day Yeshūa made His triumphal entry into Jerusalem on a foal. Needless to say, Daniel's prediction over 600 years earlier was fulfilled to the exact day. Messiah was cut off—crucified, resurrected, and ascended from the Mount of Olives. As He ascended into heaven, He promised to *descend* on that same mountain when He returned to Earth for His Second Coming—His Latter Reign—at which time He would conquer planet Earth and make Jerusalem His world capital. The Essenes expected Him to do this the first time.

If we had lived through the Roman oppression, you and I would have hoped as the Essenes did. Even Yeshūa's disciples didn't understand the separation in time between His *Former Reign* and *Latter Reign* until Jesus explained it to them *after* His resurrection.

The timing of Yeshūa the Messiah's Former Reign was specific and clear. Any scientist or common person could have added up the days and gone to Jerusalem's Eastern Gate (which must remain closed until His Latter Reign entry) on April 6, A.D. 32 and waited for Messiah to show up.

But can we predict from the Bible the date of the Rapture of the Church and the Second Coming of Messiah Yeshūa (Jesus)? I believe we can, to some extent, because of what the Bible says, but in a less specific way. The Bible tells us no

one knows the *day* or the *hour* of the rapture, but it doesn't
say we won't, as that day approaches, know the era.

Allow me to show you another remarkable prediction.

In the Torah, Moses wrote (Lev. 26:18 *and* elsewhere) that
in the future, whenever Israel sins greatly as a nation God
will allow calamity to come their way. He will however, give
them time to repent. If they, as a nation, do not repent after
their warning period, then the remainder of their punishment will be multiplied by *seven*.

Over 600 years before the birth of Jesus, God used Ezekiel,
a contemporary of Daniel, to show Israel her sin. In Ezekiel
4:3–6, God told the prophet to lie on his side for 430 days to
signify the *430 years* Israel would spend in exile for her sins.
Another contemporary of Daniel's and Ezekiel's, the prophet
Jeremiah, predicted that the first 70 years of that 430 years
would be a Babylonian exile (Jer. 25:11). That was Israel's
warning period.

Sure enough, as predicted, Nebuchadnezzar came along
and transported the Jews from Jerusalem to Babylon in 606
B.C. Then 70 years later, Cyrus the Great of Persia conquered
Babylon in 536 B.C. and said he would pay for the millions
of Jews to go back to Jerusalem. But the Jews refused. Only
50,000 devout Jews went back. The rest didn't want to interrupt their businesses in Babylon (now Iraq).

This obviously made God angry, so take 430 years of exile,
subtract 70 years of warning, and multiply the remaining
360 years times 7, as Moses instructed in the Torah. You will
get 2,520 *prophetic* years of 360 days each = 907,200 days
from the day Cyrus made his decree to return to Jerusalem,
which comes out *(are you ready for a shock?)* to May 14, 1948,
the day Israel became a nation.

Read Matthew 24 now, and you will see that Jesus Himself
described the terrible events of the Great Tribulation, a 1,260
day, future terrible period in human history that would end
when Jesus returned for His Latter Reign (Second Coming).
His disciples asked Him when all these things would happen
in the future. When people see that a "fig tree" (which com-
monly refers to Israel in the Bible) buds forth its branches,
Jesus said, the generation alive at that time will not all die
before these things are fulfilled.

I am still a scientist so I can't be dogmatic. I don't know
for sure what "buds forth its branches" means—maybe May
14, 1948. Maybe getting its borders extended in the 1967 war.

Maybe some future Israeli event. I would guess May 14, 1948. I think Messiah Yeshūa will return within 70 or 80 years of that date.

We know that when a world leader goes into a rebuilt Jewish temple in Jerusalem and desecrates it by declaring himself to be a god, our Messiah will return precisely 1,260 days (3½ prophetic days) later. We know that the world ruler (the Bible calls him the antichrist) won't be that until after the Holy Spirit is temporarily taken out of the world. Logic dictates that will most likely occur at the Rapture of all true believers, spoken of in 1 Thessalonians 4. The Bible strongly hints that true believers in the pre-Rapture church age will not go through the great Tribulation, although there are good Bible scholars who disagree and think we will endure the Tribulation.

When Daniel prophesied 69 weeks until the Messiah's First Coming, he also predicted a 70th week—a seven-year period preceding Messiah's Second Coming. Contrary to popular opinion, the Bible *nowhere* predicts that the Rapture will occur seven years prior to Messiah's Second Coming, although it very well could. I believe in a pre-Tribulation Rapture, but the great Tribulation will only last 3½ years, so I believe the Rapture could occur 3½ years *or more* prior to the Second Coming, even 100 years prior to the Second Coming if God so desires.

When the antichrist desecrates the temple, the Second Coming date becomes predictable—1,260 days later. It is only the Rapture that is relatively unpredictable, though many religious personalities may try to convince you otherwise.

Daniel says at the very end of his prophetic book that the Messiah will return 1,260 days after the desecration of the temple by the antichrist, and 1,290 days after some mystery event. (I take the ending of sacrifices and the appearance of Moses and Elijah on Earth literally—but these are my guesses.)

Daniel says in 9:24–27 that the final seven-year countdown before the Second Coming (7 years × 360 days = 2,520 days) will begin with the signing of a peace treaty with Israel by the antichrist. The antichrist, according to Daniel, would be a descendent of the people who would someday destroy Jerusalem and the temple, Titus and the Roman legions in A.D 70. The antichrist will be a future world leader of a new, revived Roman Empire.

Lots of believers think the Rapture *has* to happen seven or more years before the Second Coming because the Bible says that no one will know for sure which world ruler *is* the antichrist until after the Holy Spirit is temporarily taken out of the world and everyone will know who he is when he signs that peace treaty with Israel. I thought that too, until I realized that Israel has signed several peace treaties and will sign more of them—and may have signed a secret one in November of 1993, when the Prime Minister of Israel met with American leaders here in the U.S., 2,520 days before Feast of Trumpets of the year 2000. Several world rulers sign each of those treaties with Israel. I don't think anyone will know for sure who the antichrist is until he desecrates the temple. It is highly unlikely that more than one world ruler will do that.

The first 3½ years of that final seven-year countdown will probably be no worse than our world is right now. One or two of the seal judgments—maybe even three—could happen just prior to the Great Tribulation of 1,260 days (the Seal Judgments are listed in Revelation 6). I believe the Rapture will probably occur anytime from right now until Seal Judgment #1 occurs.

In this novel, I have the Rapture occurring about five years before the Second Coming, but only so my readers will keep their minds open to the fact that good Bible scholars disagree on when it will occur. I taught for 12 years at Dallas Theological Seminary and studied under John Walvoord, whom I consider the world's leading scholar on eschatology. I remember the day Russia invaded Afghanistan—a real shocker to the rest of the world. Dr. Walvoord walked rapidly into the faculty lounge and—with a wink in his eye—said, "I sure hope we're right about this pre-Tribulation Rapture!"

I want to close with a few remarks about why I think the year 2000 will probably be a significant time and the Third Millennium A.D. will bring the Second Coming. Remember that I am a scientist and psychiatrist, not a prophet, so I am *not* saying the Rapture or the Second Coming will occur in the year 2000. My research has turned up some very interesting observations, though, which make me think *something* significant will likely occur then.

1) Hosea 6 is one of those many passages in the Old Testament that contrasts the Former Reign from the Latter Reign. It predicts Messiah's Former Reign, His public ministry which began in A.D 28. He was "raining" His healing, and

His blessings, His teaching, and the gospel on the Jews and on the world—a blessing indeed.

Then Hosea mentions the Latter Reign and discusses what will happen in between the Former and Latter Reigns. Hosea states (Hos. 6:1–3):

> "Come, and let us return to the LORD;
> For He has torn us, but He will heal us;
> He has stricken, but He will bind us up.
> After two days, He will revive us,
> On the third day He will raise us up,
> That we may live in His sight."

The word *day* in the Bible is a vague term. Sometimes it means a literal 24-hour day. Sometimes it means a 1,000-year period (the Old and New Testaments both say 1,000 years is but a day to the Lord). Usually, it means a 360-day prophetic year, but it can't mean that here because nearly 2,000 prophetic years have already passed.

If it means 1,000-year periods, which seems logical here, the 2,000 prophetic years after the Former Reign (A.D 28.) will end in the fall of the year A.D. 2000. That's why I think the year 2000 could be a significant year, and I will be carefully studying the events surrounding every Jewish holiday that year if I am alive and ticking! Many Old and New Testament passages say masses of Jews will realize Yeshūa is their Messiah before His Latter Reign (Second Coming). The year 2000 would be a great choice for the Second Coming or the Rapture, but there can be no dogmatism there. The Second Coming *will not* happen in the year 2000, remember, unless Israel signs a peace treaty in 1993 and the eventual antichrist is one of the signators. It also *will not* happen in the year 2000 unless the antichrist desecrates a rebuilt temple of Solomon in Israel in 1997, 3½ prophetic years after the signing of the peace treaty. And remember that even if Israel signs *a* peace treaty in 1993 or 1994, we won't know for awhile whether or not it was the one spoken of by Daniel.

2) A second reason I think the year 2000 may be a significant year is because of another set of astounding predictions by Daniel. Over 600 years before Yeshūa, Daniel predicted that Babylon would be overthrown by a man named Cyrus leading the Persians. Then he said the tiny nation of Greece would eventually defeat Persia. Daniel predicted that when the Greek leader died (Alexander the Great), his kingdom

would be divided into four parts—which is exactly what happened. The Greek Empire would eventually fall to a Roman Empire, then someday the Roman Empire would be revived with ten loosely-held-together nations. The antichrist would come from a "little horn" which could mean a small nation like Belgium, but more likely refers to a *young* nation that descended from Europe, like the United States of America. The United States is currently the greatest military and nuclear superpower, and Daniel and the book of Revelation both predict the antichrist will have such great military powers that he will take over three nations, then seven more without going to war, forming the ten-nation revived Roman Empire.

The prophet Ezekiel spent chapters 40–48 of his book describing the Millennial Temple in Jerusalem when Messiah returns. It also describes some reinstitution of some animal sacrifices, possibly because people will be so loving and good during the Millennial Kingdom that they will need to be reminded that Yeshūa had to die for their sins.

In Daniel's astonishing predictions of future world empires, he makes an astounding prediction. He says one of the four Greek divisions (after Alexander the Great) will be ruled by a leader who will be a "type" of the future antichrist by actually desecrating the temple of Solomon. This prediction was fulflled by Antiochus Epiphanes on December 16, 168 B.C. In Daniel 8:14, Daniel says that leader would stop animal sacrifices (which he did) and that animal sacrifices would be restored in Jerusalem 2,200 days later. (Some versions say 2,300 days; a few say 2,400 days. Jerome, the church father who translated the Latin Vulgate Bible, preferred the 2,200 days. We don't have the original book of Daniel, only copies of it, so we don't know whether 2,200, 2,300 or 2,400 is what Daniel actually wrote.)

The eight copies of the book of Daniel found in the Dead Sea Scrolls are the oldest copies we have, so probably the most accurate. *In all eight copies,* the number is torn out and missing, which seems like an extreme coincidence or an act of deception. Did that number really wear out of all eight copies? I doubt it. Did the Essenes tear it out of all eight copies for some reason? I doubt it. Did the Dead Sea scholars who have been hiding the Dead Sea Scrolls for nearly 50 years tear it out? I don't know. Why would they?

I *do know* that if 2,200 prophetic "days" (or 360 day years) is accurate, then Daniel implied that 2,200 years after Antiochus Epiphanes desecrated the temple and stopped sacrifices, the Messiah would come and restore sacrifices. That 2,200 years (360 day years, remember) will have been completed in fall of the year 2000. Be reminded that "2,200 days" could have a host of other possible meanings. What seems logical to me may seem foolish to another eschatological researcher.

3) A third reason I think the year 2000 may be a very significant year for God to show us some supernatural signs or events is because Jubilee Years were very important to the / Lord. Moses told the Jews to make every fiftieth year a special Year of Jubilee to cancel all debts and set all slaves or workers free of their contracts. It's not difficult to figure out why the Jews never once obeyed this Jubilee Year celebration. It was economically unpopular with the wealthy. God even punished the nation of Israel from time to time for ignoring His Jubilee Year commands.

Significant events in God's timetable occurred on Jubilee Years. For example, the Bible says that Israel crossed the Jordan River and entered the Promised Land on a Jubilee Year (probably 1451 B.C. but this date could be off by a year or two). If 1451 BC. is correct, then Yeshūa also began His "Former Reign" public ministry on a Jubilee Year (28 A.D.). And the year A.D. 2000 would be the fortieth Jubilee Year after the Former Reign and the seventieth Jubilee Year after Israel entered her Promised Land. The numbers 40 and 70 are repeated often in Jewish history and prophecy. Jubilee years were to be declared on Yom Kippur of each Jubilee Year. In the year 2000, because of *two* leap days in February of that year, it will fall on October 8.

If you still have any lingering doubts about whether a *sovereign* Supernatural Being is intimately involved with our world and with the Jews in particular, think about this: Moses declared the 17th of Tammuz and the 9th of Av (21 days apart) as special Fast Days of Mourning annually. Zechariah said that in the Millennial Kingdom, however, these Fast Days would become Feast Days of celebration.

Moses broke the Tablets of the Law on a 17th of Tammuz. The 12 spies were sent out and 10 returned with a bad report on a 9th of Av, resulting in 40 years of wandering around in the wilderness.

In 587 B.C., the Babylonians broke through the walls of Jerusalem after a two-year siege and stopped sacrifices for the first time in over 400 years—on the 17th of Tammuz.

Twenty-one days later—on the 9th of Av—they destroyed Solomon's Temple.

In A.D. 70, Titus and the Roman legions besieged Jerusalem and catapulted large stones onto the rebuilt Temple, killing many priests and stopping sacrifices. The historian Josephus records that this occurred on the 17th of Tammuz. Twenty-one days later—on the 9th of Av—they destroyed the Temple and burned it, removing every stone to find the melted gold. One year later, the Romans plowed Jerusalem to make it into a secular city, fulfilling a prediction the prophet Micah wrote hundreds of years earlier in Micah 3:12. The date this occurred? The 9th of Av, A.D. 71.

In A.D. 135, Simeon Bar Kochba led a Jewish uprising against Rome. His army was totally wiped out—which, by the way, was on the 9th of Av that year.

The Crusades began and Jews were killed on Av 9, 1096 A.D., and the Jews were finally expelled from England in A.D 1290. I'm quite sure the British did not know they were declaring this on the 9th of Av that year. France also expelled the Jews on the 9th of Av, but in 1306.

The Jews were expelled from Spain March through August 2, 1492—their final day to get out. It was the 9th of Av. It was also the same day that God manipulated Spain to foot the bill for Christopher Columbus, an Italian of probable Jewish ancestry who kept it a secret, to discover America, where Jews and others would find religious freedom for more than 500 years. A coincidence or a paradox? By the way, America gained her independence on July 4, 1776—the 17th of Tammuz. Polish Jews were massacred on Av 9, 1648. The pograms against Russian Jews began on Av 9, 1882.

World War I broke out in 1914 and the Jews were immediately persecuted in Russia—on the 9th of Av. Hitler and his henchmen met at Wannsee, Germany on Av 9, 1942 to produce their final plans for the destruction of Jews worldwide.

Ezekiel predicted a future war between Russia and Israel in Ezekiel 38 and 39. Remember that he predicted it 2,600 years ago. He also predicted Russia's allies in that war would be Syria (Persia), Libya ("Put") and Ethiopia, among others. Five-sixths of the Russian army would be killed, quite possibly with nuclear weapons. Israel will be surprised because it will come during a time when they have a peace treaty. Israel will spend seven months picking up dead Russian soldiers.

If the Second Coming occurs in the Feast of Trumpets/Yom Kippur/Feast of Tabernacles season—and I'm quite sure it will some year—then the antichrist would have to desecrate a rebuilt Temple at Passover, 3½ years earlier. Sacrifices would probably cease at Purim, one month before Passover. Seven months prior to Purim will be about the 9th of Av—a good but not necessarily accurate guess for the date of the future Russian-Israeli war.

Russia will also be there again at the Battle of Armageddon, along with 200 million soldiers from China (this number was predicted in the Bible when the whole world population was only a few million). The antichrist, his false prophet, and the revived Roman Empire soldiers will also be there. So will Yeshūa, and He will win the battle. Zechariah (chapter 14) says that peoples' skin and eyes will melt and fall off of their skeletons before their skeletons would have time to fall to the ground. Written under the inspiration of our loving but just, sovereign, communicative Creator-God more than 2,500 years before nuclear weapons were invented, this can *only* be describing the intense heat of nuclear warfare.

How long will humans use gross denial to avoid seeing the obvious? The odds against all of these things being mere coincidence is beyond calculation. Tell Yeshūa this very moment that you are depending on His death and resurrection at His Former Reign to pay for all your past, present, and future sins. He promises He will. He keeps all His promises.

Then tell Yeshūa (Jesus) that you will serve Him the rest of your life, the best you can, while you wait with great excitement for the Rapture and eventually for His Latter Reign—His Second Coming—to set up the *Third Millennium A.D.*

Paul **Meier, M.D.,** co-founder of the Minirth-Meier Clinics, has an M.A. from Dallas Theological Seminary and has taught pastoral counseling in seminary. He received an M.S. degree in cardiovascular physiology at Michigan State University and his M.D. from the University of Arkansas College of Medicine. He completed his psychiatric residency at Duke University. Dr. Meier has written or co-authored over thirty books, including *Love is a Choice, Don't Let Jerks Get the Best of You, Happiness is a Choice, Worry-Free Living, Love Hunger,* and *Beyond Burnout.* This is his first novel.